"I was immediately absorbed by the story, characters, and vivid writing. I absolutely love Chrysalis!"

Diane Hartman—A former editor for The Denver Post and book reviewer for 25 years.

"Jacques Voorhees' time-travel novel is a richly-woven adventure that will entertain readers. Unique and fun!"

David M. Salkin—Author of *The Team* series, and other great thrillers.

"I look forward to reading Jacques Voorhees' new novel. He is devoted to good writing."

Nancy Price—Author of *Sleeping With The Enemy*, now a major motion picture.

Chrysalis

Jacques Voorhees

Rex Imperator
New York

CHRYSALIS

Published by Rex Imperator, New York

Rex-Imperator.com

ISBN: 978-0-9835572-6-5 Paperback

ISBN: 978-1-7344041-0-4 eBook

Printed in the United States of America

PROLOGUE

THE WIND THREW Avelyn's auburn hair into disarray as she stared east over the Irish Sea. Two hundred feet below, waves pounded furiously against limestone cliffs. Clouds drifted across the sun, creating a chill which forced the young woman to clutch her wool brat tightly. It was late, and a storm was near. Avelyn knew she must return to Ballycastle—the village where she lived but somehow did not belong.

Where did she belong? Not there.

The wind increased, the sky darkened, and raindrops blew against exposed skin. Avelyn tarried, ignoring the weather, and gazed over the waves almost desperately.

Something was out there, coming for her. Or was she expected to go find it? Or was it all just imagination and her future was as bleak as this cold wall of rain?

Finally, defeated by the elements and with a cry of frustration, Avelyn raced down the stony path towards the village gates—still open and awaiting her inevitable return.

1

Istanbul, Turkey

"SEASICK CHICKENS WEREN'T in the job description," growled the sailor, spitting over the leeward rail.

"Just wish they'd quit their damn squawking," added the cargo officer, eyeing the several hundred wooden crates lashed to the deck and crammed with hens.

"What we need's a shotgun. Whichever bird's squawking the loudest—kaplooey!"

"Sure," agreed the cargo officer. "That'd calm 'em down. Couple of shotgun blasts and they'd all go to sleep. Can't believe we didn't think of that earlier."

Captain Thomas Milo looked down from his station on the bridge with squinted eyes. He was more concerned with the barometer than the chickens.

"Full left rudder, all engines back one third!"

"Full left, and all back a third. Aye, Captain," came the voice from inside the wheelhouse.

The small coastal freighter, its steel deck plates

vibrating from the furious backwash of the propellers, eased into its assigned berth on the European side of the Bosporus waterway.

"All stop. Rudder amidships."

The swirling, murky water settled quickly and was soon lapping gently against wooden pilings. From the bow and stern of the freighter, light heaving-lines soared across to waiting dockhands just as the first rays of the morning sun hit the ship's forecastle. Thick cables followed, emerging from the oily water like captured sea snakes, and were quickly secured around massive bollards on the wharf.

"Granby!" yelled Milo to the foredeck with a gnarled voice that could still make itself heard through typhoons. "Keep your eye on those lines. Storm may be coming and I don't want 'em to chafe!"

Barometer readings, in Milo's opinion, rarely received the attention they deserved, with so much reliance these days on fancy electronics and GPS navigation. *Who needed seamanship, when you had technology?* That's what the younger ones seemed to think.

The steamer up the wharf blew its whistle in a long, tired note, signaling to a tug its readiness to get underway.

Milo looked past his ship's bow and over the soaring minarets of downtown Istanbul. Just visible was the dome of *Hagia Sophia*—a Greek Orthodox church built in the sixth century.

His concentration ebbed briefly, and he allowed his imagination to peel back the layers of history. Before the Ottomans. Before even the Crusaders. In an earlier time, a graceful *bireme* had rowed past, powered by 100 oars, and bearing Emperor Constantine to the new capital of the Eastern Empire, Byzantium; or as it would soon become known, Constantinople.

Milo forced his head to clear. Glorious past be damned. Today, Istanbul was merely another polluted, corrupt city—one of the armpits of the Mediterranean—as disappointing as most other places his career in the merchant marine had taken him.

Milo veered away from those thoughts. His career was too depressing. At his age, he should be retired.

A sudden commotion on the bridge ladder returned him to the present. Cargo Officer O'Donnell—shirttail out and cap askew—hurried up the steps and rushed over, breathlessly.

"Excuse me, sir. It's about the chickens."

"Calm down, Pete. I know they're seasick but we're tied to the wharf now and—"

"They ain't seasick no more. They're dead."

"Dead?"

"Granby thinks he knows what happened. Says he lived on a farm and knows chickens."

Milo walked over to the starboard rail, leaned against it, and looked over the harbor. The cargo officer hurried after him.

"Granby says the chickens was stressed from being seasick but when that whistle blew they up and died o' fright."

"Died of fright," Milo repeated, addressing the horizon.

"And the shipping agent arrives in one hour and I don't think he's going to sign for dead chickens."

"Would you?"

"'Probably not, sir."

"Well, there you are."

"And in this weather, they're gonna rot and the harbormaster will freak, 'cause I'm told he's a mean-ass. You know these Arabs, sir."

"Actually, they're Turks," said Milo, indifferently. "Until World War One this was the seat of the Ottoman Empire, which at one time ruled half of Europe."

"Right. And when those carcasses start to rot, that harbormaster's going to shit a brick, so Granby says let's toss 'em overboard and let the tide take 'em, and I said 'Hell, this here's the Bosporus and it's a goddamned river and just because the tide's flowing one way right now, in another few hours the current's going to be going the other way and all them chickens are gonna come right back to this ship. You may know chickens but you sure as hell don't know the Bosporus.' So that shut up Granby pretty good."

"You know that there aren't any tides in the Mediterranean?"

"There aren't?"

"No, but the Bosporus is complicated, because of the Black Sea, and you have almost half a foot of tidal drop here."

"You're saying Granby was right?"

"We'd have to check the tide tables. Look, you're new on board and the cargo officer isn't responsible for navigation, but I can loan you a book on seamanship in the Levant if you're interested."

"Sure, OK."

Milo didn't think the youngster looked very interested.

"So—what do you want me to do about the chickens?"

Thomas Milo, sixty-eight-year-old merchant sailor and would-be historian, looked despondently at the crates of now worthless carcasses and wondered—not for the first time—why God had bothered to put him on the planet.

2

Riverside, Long Island

"SO THAT'S WHY electromagnetic waves move towards the red scale, which we call redshift, but when a celestial body is *approaching*—"

A ball of chewing gum soared gracefully over three desks and landed in a nest of honey-blonde hair belonging to the school's most popular cheerleader.

He was losing the class. They were less interested in the approach of celestial bodies than in the approach of prom night this weekend.

Michael Kittery, a guest lecturer for the twelfth-grade physics class, glanced at the clock. Another thing approaching was the end of the school day, which meant he could return to his own studies.

At twenty-five, his thin face framed light-blue eyes which sometimes appeared grey when he was in deep thought. The unkempt brown hair, and two-day-old beard were less a fashion statement than a symptom of occasionally forgetting to use a comb—or even shave. When he smiled, dimples appeared which gave him a boyish, almost impish look. But the young man's smiles often sprang from a sudden insight into a vexing scientific problem or the grasping of a mathematical equation.

Technically a student himself, Kittery was working on his dissertation for the Yale University, Ph.D. program in particle physics. Right now, as a volunteer lecturer, he was trying to explain the concept of redshift to a class of teenagers whose minds were elsewhere.

So was his.

Kittery was pondering a *Physical Review* article about the Stanford experiment with mutrinos. Unexpected measurements had been observed and it was now a scientific free-for-all to explain them.

Little was known of mutrinos—a recently-discovered, sub-atomic particle—and the Stanford experiment didn't help, for the results stumped everyone. Mutrinos vanished at breathtaking speed, and their counterpart—anti-mutrinos—vanished almost fifty times faster. Why?

A girl near the back began to giggle—surreptitiously pointing out the object still stuck in the cheerleader's hair. It forced Kittery to quit daydreaming about mutrino mysteries and at least try to regain the kids' attention.

"OK, show of hands. Who's ever been stopped for speeding? Anyone?"

A dozen hands went up.

"Did the cops nail you with a radar gun?"

"Bet your ass," one of them said loudly. Everyone laughed.

"Any of you watch baseball? Did you know they measure the speed of the pitches the same way?"

"No kidding?" someone said.

"Unless it's the Mets—then there is no speed," noted another, to more laughter.

"Wanna know how those machines work?"

That got their attention.

Kittery briefly explained how Doppler radar—measuring a shift in the frequency of electromagnetic waves bouncing off an object—could deduce speed based on the relative movement of a car or a baseball, versus an observer with a radar gun. He saw a few heads nod in understanding. They could relate to this.

"Speaking of cars," he continued, "redshift is a bit like how other cars pass you on the highway. If one is coming towards you, from the opposite direction, it approaches very fast, and disappears fast, right?

"Especially if Shawn's driving it," said one girl, lightly kicking the guy next to her. More laughter.

"Exactly! But what if Shawn's car is approaching you from behind—in the passing lane. He's driving the same speed as before, but he won't pass you nearly as fast, right? Because your *relative* speeds are maybe only a few miles per hour apart. So your *perception* of his speed is different if you're moving in the same direction. And our *perception* of the light from a star is different, depending on how the star's moving compared to the Earth. That's redshift.

"Goddammit!" exclaimed the cheerleader, leaping to her feet and spilling her notebook. "OK, who the hell threw gum in my hair!"

She peered around the room malevolently.

"Someone is just such a total *asshole*!" she declared, before gathering up her supplies and sitting back down.

The class waited for the teacher to continue. But Kittery was staring at the back wall, apparently frozen in thought.

Redshift. Relative movement. Cars passing on highways. Could it be that simple?

The class became restless and one student coughed noisily.

"Let's quit here," Kittery said abruptly and fled the room.

Running down the corridor and up the flight of steps to his temporary office, ignoring the disapproving stares, the physics teacher was desperately frightened.

He finally understood why the mutrinos were disappearing—and why the anti-mutrinos vanished so quickly.

The implications were staggering.

3

Northern Ireland

THE FIRST RAYS of the morning sun spread gently over the meadow, dissolving the mist and warming the lush, dew-scented grass. One portion of the sunbeam slipped between the hinge of a shutter and fell mercilessly on the face of a young woman lying on the straw pallet just inside.

Avelyn woke up.

Little could be gained trying to fight the sunbeam, especially today when a pile of robes waited broodingly for attention. That was the basket containing vestments for the monks which needed mending. Yielding to the inevitable, she rose swiftly and prepared to face the day.

The floor of the hut was clean if bare earth can ever be, and the carpet of sheepskin was soft to her feet. A single bucket of water, brought from the well last night, waited on a small wooden table. The bucket was heavy and she gasped in her struggle to avoid spills, as she poured carefully into a large earthenware bowl. Every drop was spoken for: the amount needed to bathe her face, produce hot water for drinking, and provide for other morning rituals.

She turned her attention to the remains of last night's fire. The hearth was barely sufficient for heating the one-room cottage, but being small it was better for cooking. Avelyn uncovered the embers, then used a bellows to bring the fire back to life. A small pile of kindling burst into flames but kindling was valuable. She pulled several bricks of dried peat from a sheepskin bag and set these over the kindling, to serve as less expensive fuel.

The water, the peat, and the wood were all valuable commodities. Even the peat allowance was only sufficient to heat the water for the infusion of scented leaves she drank each morning. Breakfast consisted of dried fish and two coarse black rolls, baked yesterday.

An accomplished seamstress who worked mostly on the churchmen's simple clothing, she'd created for herself several everyday dresses and outerwear. They were of linen and wool but were patterned after designs she'd seen in the monastery—from paintings of faraway places that fascinated her.

She donned one of the dresses. Olive green and brown, its subdued earth tones contrasted with the garment's high-neck, form-fitting shape, gracefully-draping sleeves, and lace-up bodice. She knew most of the women in the village, who typically wore simple woolen tunics over linen undergarments, thought her attire mildly outlandish, but she didn't care. The clothes made her feel both elegant and in harmony with the Earth and Sea spirits. And when she wore them, it helped her dream of faraway places, where she imagined everyone dressed like this.

Avelyn slipped on sandals, grabbed a basket, and left her wattle-and-daub hut for Ballycastle's market.

The springtime rains had abated and the young seamstress was able to navigate around the remaining bogs and puddles. A week earlier, she'd have simply walked through them.

An hour after sunrise, the streets were busy with women of all ages—the men being mostly in the fields. Harskins the blacksmith was in his forge, plumes of smoke billowing from his stone hut down Castleridge Lane. As might be expected, this road led to the castle, that dark malignant presence visible from almost everywhere in town.

In Avelyn's opinion, Baron O'Ruairc, lord of Ballycastle, was evil. Perhaps this was from Father Conardy's stories in which everything was good or evil. Faeries, for example, were typically evil. The abbot had less difficulty with faeries if he could cast them as an underclass to Satan. The Church was liberal in terms of possible forms satanic messengers might take. Avelyn appreciated this about Father: he explained the beliefs of the Druids—the more traditional religion—as a misinterpretation of truth, not something entirely false. His treatment of faeries was an example.

From those stories, Avelyn learned that mankind was pulled between good and evil and, with the intervention of Jesus Christ, became one with the good. Baron O'Ruairc had become one with the bad.

He never murdered outright. But last year during the famine he'd confiscated much of the grain and many had starved. Once when a farmer refused to work his share of the fields, on the grounds he was not permitted to keep enough yield, his entire family was killed—by outlaws who somehow were never caught.

But it was his plundering of the village girls that made Avelyn shudder.

O'Ruairc would tour Ballycastle on horseback. A dewy face, or the curve of a breast, or even a bared ankle would catch his fancy. Servants would arrive, politely bearing an invitation for the girl to dine at the castle. Such invitations must be accepted. The last time one was refused, the family's house had—a week later—mysteriously caught fire and burned to the ground.

The servants would escort the girl away, and she might not be returned for a week. Often it would be days before the victim even spoke again, going through her chores as if asleep, unmindful of surroundings, shame branded on her face.

In Ballycastle, ugliness was a blessing, but Avelyn was not ugly. She knew that from the looks she received each day. She read envy from the women, which was bad enough. But in the men, she saw lust. She wasn't sure how she felt about that. It was frightening, and sometimes she felt it in herself which was dangerous. The priests, or as some were now calling themselves, monks, had—with embarrassment—provided instruction about her role as a woman, considering it their duty to the young orphan. And while she had not understood everything, she guessed those feelings of lust ended up producing children. The girls who returned from the castle often gave birth months later and Avelyn knew lust had been involved.

So far she'd been spared the horror of Baron O'Ruairc but only because of the priests' protection. And would they offer that protection if they knew she kept to the old ways and was secretly a heretic? How long could a Druidess pretend to be a Christian?

A morning cloud hovered over the castle, casting a shadow even while sunshine warmed the valley. Its moss-covered stone walls and heavy wooden gate looked like the mouth of hell. Avelyn shivered at the thought of being dragged in there. She would die first.

Shrugging off these thoughts, Avelyn glanced around, recognizing most of the other women converging on the market. They were dressed in typical fashion: woolen smock, leather sandals, and a knit brat to keep out the chill. Briana, the constable's wife, led a mule with two wicker panniers slung across its back. The constable did much of the dirty work for the baron and the mule was a reward. Avelyn noticed several of the women engaging with Briana, hoping to gain favor, although what good that might do was unclear.

No one smiled at Avelyn. She was not much liked. She knew they resented her situation, protected by the priests and free to do as she wished. They considered her a threat, although what threat she could be was as much a mystery as what favors Briana could dispense. Regardless, the women of the village treated her coldly. By contrast, there was nothing cool about the men's attention. But most were in the field and that kind of interest could not be reciprocated anyway, as the priests had explained.

So Avelyn was without friends. It was why she spent

so much time alone outside the village gates, roaming the fields of heather and looking over the sea from the cliffs. She handled the monks' knitting on market day because that was when she could most readily buy the yarn and wools needed for the job.

Most of the merchants had their wares on display when she arrived. There were no booths or tables set up in Ballycastle's market as Avelyn once heard was the case in larger towns. Instead, simple felt or sheepskin blankets were draped over the ground.

Avelyn recognized one woman as the wife of a peasant blessed with two healthy cows who produced more milk than her childless family needed. Nearby was Jaren, a boy of twelve, sitting cross-legged on the ground surrounded by his mother's pottery. Jaren's father had been killed in one of the *Ard Ri's* wars against Connaught. There was Triesty Wexner, the carpenter's daughter, helping her mother sell their family's only production, hewn chairs. The carpenter was lame from a fall last winter but he made a handsome chair and that kept the family from starving. Buyers from all over Antrim fief came to Ballycastle to acquire Wexner chairs, although why a person even needed a chair was more than Avelyn could understand. Even so, she owned one.

If there hadn't been so much work back at the hut Avelyn might have strolled around the market. Instead, she walked to the middle of the square and stopped beside a woman sitting comfortably in a Wexner chair, goods surrounding her like petitioners at a court.

Mrs. Mulcody was not Avelyn's favorite person but

she was the only one who sold yarn. Hopefully, a quick business could be made of it.

"Well, if it isn't pretty little Avelyn." Mrs. Mulcody's smile was more a sneer. "You've come to join us. How sweet."

"Thank you, ma'am. All I need are two skeins of your gray yarn and if you still have some—three arms of the black felt."

"Well, of course, dearie. Always happy to sell to you, Avelyn. You always have real coins. The rest of us must make do with a crock of cheese or a bushel of onions, but you always pay in coins—though how you come by them I'm sure I don't know."

"I work for the monks, ma'am. They pay me in coins."

The woman knew everything about her, of course. But why rise to the bait?

"Oh, yes, the monks. They do pay you well, Avelyn. Feed you and clothe you and pay with silver coins. I hear they come from Angland. Angle coins they are. You must do a lot for the monks for them to give you all that."

Avelyn felt herself blush but ignored the taunt. It had been made often enough. "Please ma'am, could I just have the yarn?"

"Of course, dearie. Here it is. Take all you want. Take everything I have. I'm happy to take your Angle coins. At least I will have earned them as an honest woman..."

A group had formed, enjoying the ridicule.

"Not so fast, Fiona. Who says Avelyn's not honest? She's never denied what we all know is true. Can't call her dishonest now, not with all the other names that would fit."

If so much as a single monk were to appear, these

women would be prostrate with terror, Avelyn knew, begging forgiveness and kissing robe and sandals. But absent Church authority they were free to torment. Tears moved into position, but Avelyn would not let them out. She tried to avoid confrontation yet these days never seemed able to, not realizing the animosity was triggered by her growing beauty.

In any case, she'd had enough. The supplies could wait. She had spares. This time, just this once, she would fight back.

"I don't need your cloth," Avelyn said coldly. "And as for my coins, I guess you won't be seeing any of them today!"

An unexpected cloud suddenly blotted the sun, and an icy wind shot down the hillside.

Avelyn turned her head with a snap and left the market. The predictable jeering that followed wasn't as enthusiastic as she'd expected. Silver coins were very rare on the north coast of Ireland in the year 792.

4

North Atlantic

A THOUSAND FEET under the waves lurked a fearsome creature: cold, black and powerful. It could sense most everything, though it had no eyes or ears. It could destroy whatever it met, though it had no teeth or claws.

It was U.S.S. *Chrysalis,* the most advanced attack submarine ever launched.

"Bearing two-five-eight, Captain. Twelve kilometers. It's not moving, sir. I think it's Beta."

The nineteen-year-old sailor, only recently out of sonar school in Pensacola, kept his eyes locked on the holographic imager and his hands tight on the controls, a bead of sweat trickling down his nose.

"That's fine, sonarman. Holler if you think she's up to something."

"Aye aye, sir."

Captain Perry Hamilton was nervous himself, although he'd been on sub duty fifteen years. The chief liked to tell rookies "If a man's got any screw-up in him, you can bet your ass it'll come out on a submarine."

Hamilton knew he had a lot of screw-up in him but so far had contained it. Because of that, he was now commander by rank and captain of the world's most sophisticated submarine.

But that just made him more nervous. Hamilton knew he'd have made a better accountant than ship commander. But you didn't get promoted in the military by being an accountant and by God if you were one of Blair Hamilton's boys you went into the Navy, you stayed in the Navy, and you got promoted in the Navy. Perry Hamilton was a naval officer by breeding.

Fortunately, in another year—with no surprises—he'd make captain by rank. And in the submarine business that probably meant a desk and cushy shore position. If you screwed up at a desk some supplies would get sent to the wrong base, or a ship would head out to sea with too many cans of peas and not enough carrots. Hamilton could handle the peas and carrots duty, no problem. If he could get through one more year at sea he had a reasonable chance of living up to his old man's expectations.

But anything could happen in that year. Like with Carter, his pal from Annapolis, who'd made a mistake in navigation and ended up 600 yards off the Syrian coast; then made a second mistake by surfacing and nearly getting sunk by a wooden gunboat with a brand new Russian ship-to-ship missile launcher which—thank God—the jihadists hadn't figured out how to aim. Then he made his third mistake by firing the ship's five-inch cannon into the gunboat, which exploded into kindling. Finally, Carter did something right which was pull the plug and get out. His pal was now *out* of the Navy.

He thought of Hank, shipmate on *Boston*, who'd taken command of *Sacramento*, only to have an admiral dumped on him. And the admiral saw enough screw-up to hand his friend a desk even before he made captain. Which meant he never would.

"Please, God, don't let me surface accidentally off the Syrian coast," Hamilton said in silent prayer. "And don't send me an admiral. Let's make the next twelve months as routine as they can be, and I'll never complain of boredom. Promise."

So far, God was granting the captain's request.

Chrysalis was first in a new class of attack, or "hunter-killer," submarines. The unusual name was a departure from the tradition of submarines being named after American cities or states. The Chairman of the House Appropriations Committee—in an attempt to secure funding for the expensive new weapons system—insisted on a national contest to name the first one. The competition went viral, the whole country got excited, and public support for the program soared. *Chrysalis* was the winning name.

Hamilton had googled it and learned that a chrysalis was the hard-shelled pupa of a butterfly. The ship was hard-shelled, of course, and roughly cylindrical and rounded at each end like an insect's chrysalis. But the name might refer to what a chrysalis did, which was to provide a structure for miraculous change. How that could apply to a submarine was unclear.

Whatever its name, the ship was impressive. With twin screws and reactor power, she could cruise at thirty-two knots and break forty in a pinch, submerged. Forty knots! *Chrysalis* could dive to 1800 feet, officially. But over dinner with the ship's design team they'd boasted she wouldn't leak at 2,000, and could probably survive three.

And the new class hadn't been shortchanged on firepower. *Chrysalis* carried 75 Mark 48 torpedoes, six cruise missiles, and the usual complement of small arms: fully-automatic M-16 rifles, .45 ACP handguns, grenade launchers, anti-tank weapons, and even flamethrowers. Hamilton had once joked with his XO, Mitch Simpson, that someone at the Pentagon must have foreseen a sub battle in the future with both boats on the surface, fish shot away, and carrying on the fight with flamethrowers at fifty yards.

Take that! Ouch! Take that! Ouch!

They'd laughed so hard Simpson had fallen off his chair.

Another attribute of *Chrysalis* was her automation. The captain felt like he was playing video games when he sat behind the consoles, and was pleased his latest recruits looked more like Grand Master "StarCraft" players than traditional seamen.

"Beta's screws are turning, Captain," the sonarman reported, breaking in on Hamilton's thoughts. "Computer says she's making turns for eighteen point five knots. Speed six point five knots and increasing.

"Computer says her rudder's turned 10 degrees left. No course change apparent yet. No, there it is now. Computer says she's turning left through two-zero-five degrees heading."

"Sonarman, please just give me the information. You don't need to keep saying 'computer says.'"

"Aye aye, sir. Sorry, sir. Now bearing one-nine-six."

"OK. Flank speed, close on Beta," ordered Hamilton.

The Officer of the Deck entered some commands into his terminal and the ship came to life. There was no increase in noise this far forward of the engine room, but the slight acceleration and turning could be felt by everyone. *Chrysalis* was on the move again after two and a half hours sitting dead in the water.

"Range twelve kilometers and closing fast, sir. We have a solution."

"Fire One. Fire Two."

More commands were entered on another keyboard and two very slight tremors could be felt in the ship. The Mark 48 torpedoes broke loose from their starting gates at the bow of the giant submarine, one chasing the other in silent, deadly pursuit of an unseen enemy.

"Torpedoes closing and on target, sir."

The captain was silent, more interested in the reactions and performance of those around him than in the progress of the torpedoes.

"She's hit! She's hit!" a young voice screeched. "Oh my God, there's the second one! Two hits!"

"Give me a proper report, please, sonarman."

"Oh, aye aye, sir. Two hits on Beta," he said, calmly. "Target destroyed, sir. Sonar confirms it, sir."

"Very well."

Hamilton paused briefly. He wanted the sonarman's

mild reprimand to have the floor for a moment. But the moment was up.

"Secure torpedo doors. Make turns for ten knots. Course two-seven-eight. Five degrees up bubble. Level off at antenna depth."

The captain waited while his orders were barked to subordinates, and entered into the computer.

"Raise number one antenna."

"Number one antenna up, sir."

Hamilton walked over to his console, logged-in by thumb-print reading, and began typing.

CHRYSALIS TO COMSUBLANT.
THIRD PRACTICE DRONE
DESTROYED. MISSION COMPLETED.
RETURNING TO JOSEPHINE.

So far, this shakedown sortie had gone smoothly. Hamilton knew his boat. The crew was learning its duties. Soon, *Chrysalis* would be sent out on actual patrol, most likely to some distant part of the world.

She would probably stay submerged for three months. They would conduct drills, follow orders, burn up a few kilograms of uranium 235, and then return to port.

It would be routine, predictable, and most likely very safe. On his return, there'd be a fourth stripe and a comfortable desk where he could count peas and carrots while awaiting his eventual promotion to admiral.

As long as nothing unusual happened.

5

New England

LAUREN KITTERY FINISHED her vodka tonic, stood up, and considered throwing the cocktail glass against the stone fireplace in the living room of her 12,000 square-foot mansion in Darien, Connecticut. It was tempting, but the servants were off on Sunday. Instead, she threw the pages of the report she'd just read. The stack of sheets made it halfway to the fireplace before exploding into twenty-seven pieces and floating down to the plush Berber carpet.

"Damn him to hell!" Lauren swore as she stood up and began pacing. "Damn them *both* to hell!" she added, realizing it might be unclear to which man she was referring—her husband, or the private detective she'd hired to tail him.

Michael Kittery, a physicist working at Brookhaven Lab on Long Island, was currently volunteering as a guest lecturer for a week at Riverside High School. Such a selfless gesture was incomprehensible, so she credited it with a hidden motive—probably one directed against her.

Lauren had married three months after graduating from Mount Holyoke College when Michael was starting work on his doctorate. That had been two years ago and what seemed a perfect match at the time had become a nightmare.

Lauren's family wasn't crazy-rich like the Kitterys but had at least been comfortable. Her father had driven a BMW, her mother a Mercedes. Lauren had received an Audi A4 convertible the day she graduated high school. In a society where status was measured heavily by a family's stable of automobiles, the Brownings appeared well-off. But that was changing, which was part of the nightmare.

To Lauren, always a pampered child, life was about social climbing. It just made sense to follow one's skill set.

The next step after graduation was to marry well. That summer she attended every charity ball, yacht-club soiree, and A-list private party in Fairfield County, whether invited or not.

She was always welcome. The Browning's only child had that cover-girl look about her: platinum blonde hair which fell loosely on slender shoulders, pouty red lips that shaped a mouth seemingly eager to tell secrets, and high-cheekbones punctuated with deep green eyes that could hypnotize prey. Combined with a fashion sense worthy of a debutante, Lauren not only turned heads when she entered a room; she broke hearts when she left.

Female classmates at Holyoke admitted defeat

whenever Lauren arrived at a party. Not only was the bitch gorgeous; she flirted like a pro.

Perhaps because Lauren believed she could attract any man she wanted, she never really fell in love with any of them. There was always another party and another interested man to toy with. She was in love with the game, not the players.

So when Lauren set out to find a husband, a formidable talent was unleashed on Fairfield County society. Three months later she was engaged to Michael J. Kittery, oldest son and heir apparent to the Kittery fortune, and probably the most eligible bachelor in New England. Good-looking, athletic, and rich, he was a triple-crown.

After the wedding—Lauren's victory celebration—she wasn't sure what social ladder was left to climb. Worse, Michael proved serious about continuing his work as a physicist. Really? His passion for physics was not hidden during their courtship, but Lauren had assumed that was like a five-year-old declaring they would become a fireman or astronaut. With the Kittery-family fortune surpassing twelve billion dollars, why work at all? She'd hoped he'd pursue something more dignified, perhaps in politics.

She remembered the day Michael came home waving a letter, ecstatic he was being offered a postdoc position as a research scientist at Brookhaven, as soon as he finished his Yale Ph.D.

"Wait. You mean you honestly thought they'd turn you down?" asked Lauren. "Your family donates a hundred thousand dollars to Yale each year, and I'm sure some phone calls were made. Of course you got in."

That had been the catalyst for their first fight and Lauren knew that was the moment Michael began to fall out of love. She'd never experienced a man losing interest and had no coping skills for handling rejection. She tried getting his attention back using old tricks but it didn't work.

He saw through her now and wanted out, even though they should have still been in the honeymoon phase. His tactics were transparent—provide enough rope she'd hang herself in divorce court. Otherwise, thanks to no prenups, it would cost him millions. He turned cold but agreed to most anything she asked for, from cars to second homes, to vacations (for her), and to anything she cared to do with her time. But his own was dedicated to physics and the pursuit of a Ph.D. No one could accuse him of ignoring his wife, exactly. He often slept at home, but now in a separate bedroom. And they were occasionally seen together at social events—though mostly to thwart rumors of marital trouble. But they both knew the marriage was dead.

He was hoping her lack of patience would cause Lauren herself to request the divorce, on more reasonable terms.

It was a good strategy but it wasn't going to work. There was no longer a vacuum of objective in her life. Her goal now was vengeance. Or rather, vengeance and wealth.

The latter was important. A malpractice suit against her father's law firm had left the Brownings facing ruin. The cars and a lot of other property had been sold. As a Kittery, Lauren could help them financially but without that lifeline, the Brownings would go Chapter 7.

Lauren would always be able to marry money, but

family bankruptcy would be socially unbearable. Gossip columnists were already circling. Thus Lauren needed to come out of the marriage a rich woman, and the easiest way to do that was to discover incontestable grounds for divorce.

All she needed was infidelity on Michael's part. Hence the private detective and the twenty-seven-page report. *But the fool of a detective couldn't find so much as unpaid parking tickets on the guy*. Lauren was furious at both of them and paced the room in frustration.

So Michael was also competing to win. Fine.

Lauren gazed past the scattered sheets of paper and planned her next move.

6

MICHAEL KITTERY LOOKED resentfully at the clock on the wall, knowing it would contain bad news. He'd been sitting in his temporary high school office for twelve hours, and it was three in the morning.

While the cheerleader was jumping up and spilling her notebook, Kittery's brain—one of the brightest ever to come through Yale—had solved the riddle of the mutrino experiment. The concepts of redshift, relative perception of movement, and cars overtaking each other on highways provided the clue.

He now understood both the results of the Stanford experiment and the frightening implications. He'd raced to his office, opened a new Word document on his laptop, leaned back, and stared at the ceiling.

The mutrinos were moving in time.

He repeated the sentence to himself, shocked by the power of the words.

Had ancient astronomers felt this way when they realized the Earth was a globe? Or that planets orbited the

Sun? Or that shooting stars weren't stars? Once grasped, it was obvious.

Mutrinos were the subject of Kittery's dissertation. He knew the results of every experiment performed, but until now no one had understood them. Juxtaposing those results against his new insight, everything made sense.

The mutrinos were moving in time. That's why they passed through our universe so quickly. But why would anti-matter mutrinos ("anti-mutrinos"), carrying a negative electrical charge, disappear more quickly than did regular mutrinos with a positive charge? Because they were moving from the future into the past—like a car approaching from ahead and passing quickly into the distance behind. The positive mutrinos were moving from the past to the future. They were going the same time direction as our universe, just faster. So we could perceive them longer—like a car traveling beside us but going more quickly in the passing lane.

Once the initial shock abated, he spent several hours typing out the theory. His hands trembled as they moved over the keyboard. With some polishing and the addition of mathematical models, those pages could be submitted to any scientific journal in the world, which would be thrilled to publish them. He'd have a finished dissertation, his Ph.D., and probably the Nobel Prize for physics. He should have been elated.

He was terrified. The implication of particles moving in time was almost too staggering to grasp. There was danger here; danger beyond anything faced even by those who had split the atom. He'd written down the theory only as a mechanical process—almost a duty to the scientific community. Now he had to decide what to do with it.

He'd spilled out his thoughts in a disorganized, flow-of-consciousness format knowing he could clean up the writing later. He also knew the words, phrases, and concepts would make anyone but a physicist's eyes glaze over. He glanced through some of the key paragraphs, starting at the top.

Mutrinos As Time-Travelling Particles

A Theory By Michael J. Kittery

Mutrinos are always produced in pairs: mutrino and anti-mutrino. We now know they are emitted continuously by neutrons…

And further down…

Mutrinos have no effect on the neutrons they are emitted from, and only a very subtle effect on their surroundings..

Nearly all that is known of mutrinos is that each particle and anti-particle have a mass only slightly greater than an electron, and they have opposite electrical charges.

Later…

The Stanford researchers used their linear accelerator (SLAC) to create beams of mutrinos focused on targets of hydrogen (mostly protons) or lead (protons and neutrons). In an experiment at CERN—the European research facility—they sent beams of mutrinos running one direction around the accelerator ring so they would collide with an electron beam going the opposite direction. The goal was to study the debris from the collisions. Only there was no debris and there were no collisions.

Researchers claimed they couldn't get anything to collide with a mutrino because it ceased to exist before impact. The mutrinos themselves could only be sensed for approximately 100 femtoseconds. The anti-mutrinos disappeared almost fifty times faster, in roughly 2.14 femtoseconds.

...

This theory postulates that both the positive and negative versions of mutrinos are traveling in time. They can be perceived from our time universe only as they pass through it. They are perceived longer if they are traveling forward in time, relative to our universe. They are perceived far more briefly if they are traveling backward in time. Mutrinos are analogous to a car passing us from behind, in the fast lane, and anti-mutrinos are analogous to a car approaching us from the opposite direction and disappearing quickly.

There was a light knock on the door and Kittery forced himself out of his near trance-like, analytic state. He looked up. The door opened hesitantly, and an elderly face peered in.

"Scuse me, sir, but I'm the janitor here, and I'm cleanin' the rooms. Was 'bout to clean this one but then saw through the glass you're in here."

"Oh, uh, no problem. Look, you don't need to clean this one tonight. We're good."

"Sure?"

"Yes, have a good evening."

"You too, sir."

It took only a moment for Kittery's brain to resume its journey. He skipped through several pages and focused on one of the most important paragraphs.

> *Upon closer examination of the data, there was something else unexplainable. In the SLAC experiment, the concentration of hydrogen atoms decreased in the presence of the mutrino beam. Some of the protons were disappearing. Similarly, in the CERN experiment, the number of electrons decreased when an electron beam passed through a mutrino beam. Some of the electrons were disappearing*
>
> ...
>
> *This theory postulates that the "missing particles" are being picked up and carried off by the time-traveling mutrinos—either forwards or backward compared to our time-vector. Mutrinos (both positive*

and negative) appear to have the ability to not merely themselves move in time, but to essentially attract a sub-atomic particle of matter from our universe, and carry it with them. Negatively-charged anti-mutrinos, not surprisingly, carry off positively-charged protons. Positively-charged mutrinos, equally not surprisingly, carry off negatively-charged electrons.

. . .

We do not yet understand why mutrinos are emitted continuously by neutrons, but we may theorize that the neutron is the portal between time dimensions; the "gateway particle," we might say.

Mutrinos, representatives of that alternate universe, somehow enter our universe through neutrons and then immediately pass on, perhaps out through another particle not yet discovered, or in some other way. It is all happening in the quantum realm, so measurements of particle location and momentum will be difficult and in some cases may be impossible. (Heisenberg's principle)

While the precise mathematics will need to be resolved through further observation, this basic theory of mutrinos as time-traveling particles—able to capture sub-atomic particles from our own universe and carry them off to a different time universe—explains fully the observations and measurements that have come out of the SLAC, CERN, and other experiments.

[END]

Kittery stopped reading, stood up, and paced back and forth in front of his desk. What he'd written was the exciting, Nobel-prize-winning part. What came next was horrifying—and for that reason, he hadn't written it down at all. It was too dangerous. But he reviewed the concepts in his head, building to the inescapable conclusion.

Creating mutrinos was easy if you had neutrons. And for those brief units of time in which the particles could be sensed, they were easy to control with magnetic fields. An experiment that physicists could replicate easily was the encapsulating of multiple particles inside a plasma of mutrinos. In every case, as soon as the mutrinos vanished, the collection of other particles disappeared as well. A slight amount of energy was given off in the process, so the assumption—until now—had been that the missing particles had converted to energy, perhaps by annihilating with the mutrinos.

Kittery realized this wasn't happening at all.

He glanced out the window and noticed a full moon rising in the East. He briefly imagined the yellow orb as a gigantic threatening mutrino and shivered slightly. He firmly shut the blinds and turned away from the window, continuing his thoughts.

While a beam of mutrinos might carry off a single subatomic particle here or there, a plasma of mutrinos carried away everything inside it—positive or negative.

The energy given off was a by-product of changing the time-vector of the encapsulated matter.

If you thought of the matter as being reversed—or

accelerated—in normal three-dimensional space, based on the amount of energy given off and the mass of the particles affected, you could determine their relative speed in a new time vector—either going backward or forwards from our own.

Kittery glanced at his notes. It came to about twelve hours per second.

The physicist sat down again and stared at the ceiling. Given that the mutrinos could be controlled by magnets via their electrical charge, and given the fact that any regular matter encapsulated by them would be carried off in a different time-vector, it was obvious that he had the theoretical knowledge and perhaps even the technical ability to build, well—

If he could move particles of matter in time, then he could move a larger mass in time. And if he could do that—he hesitated—then he could…

"Travel in time," he said softly, to an empty room.

7

AVELYN'S PLANS FOR the day vanished with the incident at the market. She was in no mood to return to her hut and mend robes. It was a beautiful summer day although the priests would call it Spring. For Druids, it was summer because, past equinox, days were now longer than nights. Whatever the season, it was hardly weather for working on a basket of robes in a stuffy hut.

In such mind, Avelyn might have left the village, passing through the rock arch and down the main road southwards. A mile along, she would have veered to the left and taken a secret path that led to the high cliffs and the unsettling view of the Irish Sea.

But she was not walking in that direction.

Ballycastle was built on a hillside that sloped to a long, thin bay, containing a harbor for the fishing boats. Only the poorest of the village's residents were forced into such a grubbing and dangerous living. No one liked eating water animals, but for some, it was necessary to stave off hunger. During the famine, some had no choice but to eat the horrid insect-like things which crawled along the bottom of the sea. *Lobsters*, she'd heard them called, shivering at the memory.

The Irish living on the northern coast knew how to fish but preferred their fields of wheat, oats, and barley. Those few who chose the ocean had, over centuries, developed a small craft known as a *curragh*. Designed for coastal work and with no enclosed cabin, it was suitable as a fishing boat for day trips. Despite its modest size the curragh was exceptionally seaworthy and could handle the rough waters of the North Atlantic.

The boats were made of stringers bent protestingly across stocky oak frames; the whole covered in tough, sewn goat hide, made waterproof with grease and fish-oil. As long as the hide was kept oiled, the boats would not leak. But they did smell.

Avelyn found herself at Ballycastle's harbor, where the curraghs were built and mended. The fishermen had left before dawn.

Shelby Balfour was there. He was too old to fish. The stiffness in his joints was not helped by the wet cold, and he would not be a useful addition to the fishing crews.

To most villagers, Shelby was a simple-minded fool who roamed the waterfront and patched up the curraghs, yet Avelyn enjoyed his company. Like her, he was an outcast, left behind every day, and often the object of taunts and jeers from the young boys.

Only the *shanachies*, the village storytellers, recalled that Shelby's grandfather, Eoin, had been a Druidic priest. They claimed he possessed ancient powers derived from the Earth and the Sea and before he died had passed on the arcane knowledge to his son Brian, Shelby's father. But Brian became a farmer and no one believed any of the old priest's power had filtered down to Shelby. Nonetheless, some maintained that his cloak—which he rarely took off—had once belonged to old Eoin himself and that it was the cloak which held the magic.

But that was just superstition.

Shelby always had a smile for Avelyn, and usually a kind word.

"Why, good morning, lass!" he said, looking up suddenly. "Didn't expect to find someone pretty as you down here by the water among all these smelly boats and old men."

"Good morning, Shelby. And don't try to scare me away. The rest of the village chased me out, and the smelly boats and old men are my only refuge. Mind if I stay?"

Avelyn had meant to adopt a cheerful, carefree tone but it hadn't come out that way. Shelby glanced up at her sharply.

"You've been crying, haven't you? Come over here, lass. 'Tis too fine and rare a morning for sadness."

A seagull screeched in triumph, overhead, as it spotted something worth eating, collapsed its wings and dove into the water. Avelyn watched a moment, then walked over to a stack of recently-delivered oak logs, finding a place to sit among them.

"I'm fine, Shelby, don't worry about me. What are these logs for? Building a boat?"

"Well, now, thought I might. You know, the last dozen

years I've done nothing but repair curraghs, and repairing curraghs makes me think of decay and death."

Avelyn sat quietly, content to let Shelby ramble.

"Yes indeed, a curragh is like a person. Starts frail and worthless, like a baby. Then it grows into something strong and useful as the goat hide is laid across and soaked with oil. But soon enough, the fabric starts to rip or the stringers give out or the oil dries. You can fix any of these things, but once they start happening it seems to get worse until in the end the kindest thing you can do is just fill an old boat with stones and let it sink.

"Now I'm not trying to sound melancholy, but that's about the stage I'm at myself. Pretty soon someone's going to come along and decide the kindest thing they can do with old Shelby is fill him with stones and let him sink."

Avelyn giggled. "Don't be ridiculous! No one's going to fill you up with stones."

"Well, I'm not so sure. Fact is, the other morning when we had that frost I woke up and knew for sure someone filled me up with stones 'cause that's what I felt like—a bag of stones. I got out of bed and I could hear them crunching and rolling around inside me. You can bet I stayed away from the water that day 'cause I knew for sure if I'd been pushed in, I would've sunk like an old curragh, and that's a fact."

"Is that why you're building a new boat, so you and your silly stones will have something to float in?" asked Avelyn, laughing out loud.

Shelby's eyes twinkled and he winked at her. "That's better, lass! Now, I may be old, but I can still make a pretty girl smile. When I've lost *that* skill, best just drop me in the sea, because life won't be worth living."

The old man paused and looked around as if he had lost something. Finally, he shrugged and kept talking.

"But since you ask, truth is I don't know why I'm building a boat. No one's asked me to, that's for certain. The planting's gone well I hear and there aren't as many fishermen now. Seamus Orson just sold his curragh to one of the Constead boys, and that family didn't need it. So about the silliest thing a man could do is build a curragh, but that's what I'm doing."

"But why?" asked Avelyn, enjoying his soothing voice, and wanting it to continue.

"Why? Well, you see, trying to repair all those old dying boats was making me feel like one of them myself. So I says '*Shelby, it's been too long since you did anything but repair torn goat hide and at this rate, you're going to turn into a piece of torn goat hide yourself if you don't get off your arse*'.

"So you can call me crazy if you want, Avelyn, and if you do you'll be right. But you can't call me a piece of goat hide anymore, and you can't call me a bag of stones. So I figure I've made some progress even if I don't know what I'll do with this damned thing once it's finished."

Avelyn was enjoying the story, content to lie back and watch the seagulls dive at the water, while the sun warmed her face. Yes, others had challenges too. That had been Shelby's message, and she loved him for it.

But it didn't solve her problem. The women of the village still hated her. And what was she to do about that? This was where she lived. The high cliffs provided only a temporary retreat. No matter how strongly she felt or prayed that something was coming to save her, it never did. She now doubted it ever would. What she needed was a secret hideaway; a place to escape from everyone and everything—her very own sanctuary.

"Shelby, where would you go to get away from all this?" She gestured toward the village." You've lived a long life and explored just about all of Antrim. I bet there's a cave or something you know about."

"Ah lass, you're not going to solve your problems living in a cave. I know something about caves. Lived in one for years. Had to fight off the bear that got there first."

"Hey, stop kidding around. I'm serious."

"So am I. Let's see now. That was back during the wars with the High King at Tara. Old Baron O'Ruairc. Not that waste of human life up there now, but let's see, would be his granddaddy. Of course, grandad wasn't much better. Old Baron O'Ruairc was refusing to pay tribute and forced all the peasants around these parts to fight against the Ard Ri's army, but that was plain stupid because everyone knew the High King would win and you'd just get killed in the process.

"So I up and moved into a cave. Fished for my living and snuck into town at night every few weeks and traded for bread. When the war was over, 'bout half the men from the town were dead and the Ard Ri'd won just like we all knew he would, and the baron had to pay twice what he'd been asked for originally. But he just took it out of the peasants' mouths. It was rough times but I was happy in my cave. Leastways happy as a man can be living in a cave. And that's my point, Avelyn. T'ain't no place for a pretty young lass."

Avelyn sighed and noticed a light wind had picked up from the west.

"I know I'm not going to solve my problems living in a cave. I suppose the only real solution is to get married," she continued, speaking as much to herself as to Shelby. "But I'm not ready to lose my freedom. So, for now, I just need a place to get away from everything occasionally. Is that so wrong?"

The old man walked over and squinted at the pile of logs. Finding one that met his standards, he used his feet to roll it into position against two large boulders. Then he attacked it with an adz and a sledge, driving the spikes in at proper intervals and striking them deep. When he was finished he had the beginnings of a rough stringer—one of the longitudinal pieces for the new boat. Grunting in reluctant satisfaction, he took it over to his workbench—a log-and-plank affair under a small tent—and began shaping the stringer into a thing of smooth, slender beauty.

"Guess there's no harm in a young girl wanting a place to get away for a while," he conceded, wiping sweat from his brow with a shirtsleeve. "I know how cruel those hens in the village can be. They just envy the hell out of you. Can't stand it that you're so young and beautiful and independent. Drives 'em crazy. Drives the men crazy, too, but in a different way. And that's part of the women's problem. Probably do *everyone* a speck of good for you to be able to get out of town when you needed to."

Shelby paused a moment and stared out to sea.

"Problem with that cave is—and I'm not counting the bear, he might have come back—problem is that the only way to get to it is by sea. It's about two miles down from that headland you see out there, cut right into those granite cliffs you get to from that path just south of the gate."

"I didn't think anyone knew about that path but me!"

"Well, girl, who d'ya think made it?" Shelby said, with a hearty laugh. "It was me and my pappy back when we worked that field. That's how we brought the goats to market. One day, a pack of wild dogs came on those goats and just went crazy. So did the goats. Stampeded right over the cliff. That was the end of the goats and the end of our farm. Turned to fishing to keep our bellies full and that's why I'm here now, not up on those cliffs where I'd like to be."

"You love them too, then."

"'Course I do! Best time to do your thinking is when you're looking out over the sea."

"But what about the cave? How do I get there?"

"Well, you can't. Only way is by boat. That's why it's such a great hiding place. The fishermen never head down that direction 'cause the water's too deep; not good for the fish. So the village-folk who ain't fishermen *can't* get there, and the fishermen don't want to get there, so it's 'bout as private a place as you can find."

Avelyn stood up suddenly and put her hands on her hips, facing him.

"How'd the bear get there, Shelby? Did the bear have a boat?"

"Hmm. Hadn't thought about that," he muttered.

"Maybe they can swim." Stroking his beard he shrugged and went back to working on the stringer.

"Shelby, that's it!"

"Course it is. Bears can swim, I'm sure of it."

"No, no. I mean the boat. The only way to get to the cave is in a boat, and you're standing right in front of me building a boat. I'll buy your boat, Shelby. I'm perfect for it!"

"You? Sail a curragh? Avelyn, you're a fine lass and I enjoy talking to you and I'm not saying you're not capable, but a girl can't sail a curragh!"

"Why not?"

"No female's ever sailed a curragh in the history of Ireland, that's why not."

"Well, perhaps no female *needed* to, Shelby. Did you ever think of that? And I'm willing to pay for it, which makes me the only buyer."

Avelyn had more actual money—coins—than anyone in the village suspected. The priests paid her more than they should for their own reasons, and Avelyn had rarely found anything in Ballycastle worth buying. So she saved her coins in a clay pot underneath her bed, suspecting that if an opportunity—or whatever was going to rescue her—were to arrive, she might need money. And she'd been right. If only Shelby would agree to sell her the curragh!

The old boat-builder looked at her strangely for a moment, then walked down to the water's edge and gazed over the harbor. He squatted down and placed both hands in the water. Then he stood motionless and, as Avelyn watched, it seemed he was no longer a living man but had become part of the landscape—like a tree or a rock that had been fixed in that position for hundreds of years.

When he returned his expression was surprisingly serious, and if it hadn't been such a sunny day it might have frightened her.

"Very well, Avelyn," Shelby said. "I will build this curragh for you, and when it is ready I will teach you how to sail it. And if you wish I'll even show you the cave."

The young girl threw her arms around him and kissed his cheek.

"Thank you, Shelby. You've given me back my life!"

Avelyn was thrilled. She hadn't thought he'd agree. To own a curragh, to sail the ocean! This was something not even *her* dreams had encompassed.

"Now, lassie, all I'm giving you is a curragh. And I'm not giving it to you since you offered to pay."

"Anything. I'll pay anything you ask!"

He looked at her fondly. "Well, I reckon you've paid me quite a bit already," he said and gave her a wink.

8

"YOU WANT ME to *what*?"

"You heard me."

Lauren Kittery curled her pouty lips into a smile as she gazed directly and promisingly at Andy Henderson, the private detective she'd hired to trail her husband.

A former police officer now in his mid-forties, Henderson was thoroughly unimaginative, ploddingly competent, and physically unremarkable. It was doubtful he'd had much success with women and Lauren guessed he'd be easy to manipulate.

Andy stood up, flustered. "What you're suggesting is called framing," he explained. "I'm pretty sure it's illegal, and anything we gained could never be used in a divorce court."

"Please hear me out, Mr. Henderson," Lauren began. She stood up as well and placed a perfectly manicured hand on his shoulder for reassurance.

"Please, sit back down. I insist."

With her hand touching him, he became putty. The private detective sat down promptly.

"Look at it this way, Mr. Henderson. We know my husband's cheating. Or at least I know it, and I'm not exactly an uninformed bystander. No one blames you for the fact he's been able to hide the affair. Of course he's hiding it! My husband's not stupid. He's a Ph.D. candidate you know."

Lauren let that comment sink in, aware Andy Henderson had dropped out of his first year of college.

"In matters regarding infidelity, you should trust me. I know something about the subject."

This too would throw him off balance.

Lauren's voice softened, and she turned towards him, arching her body in a way that maximized the effect of her blouse's plunging neckline.

"It's very simple, Mr. Henderson. With the precautions my husband's taking to hide his mistresses, it could take *years* to find the evidence. I'm happy to pay for your time, it's just that I'm sure there are other—well—more enjoyable things we could be doing if I didn't have to review these endless written reports."

There was that direct gaze again. Lauren's breasts moved closer to the private detective, nipples straining against sheer fabric. Shifting her position, Lauren's right foot brushed his leg.

"And I need to clarify something. I don't want you to think I'm greedy. I know I could just walk away from this marriage, and ask for nothing. But you see, it's my parents. They're in financial trouble right now. I need a reasonable divorce settlement so I can help them monetarily—that's just the kind of daughter I am."

"That's reasonable. And your husband can certainly afford it."

Lauren didn't add that the divorce settlement she anticipated would not only include the pittance needed to help her parents, it would also leave her with tens of millions as well—enough to never have to work again, and live a life of luxury. The detective had no idea how wealthy the Kittery family was.

"We just need a bit of leverage over my husband, to get him to see reason. And I think a night with a prostitute—assuming you can get pictures—would make him suddenly very reasonable."

"Well, 'er, yes, I see your point," Andy stuttered "But like I said, it's against the law. I used to be a cop, you know."

Andy smiled as if assuming that would impress her.

"Even if we hired a prostitute, and she did succeed in arranging a liaison with Mr. Kittery, and even if I got pictures, you couldn't use them in court. Or if you tried to pressure him outside court, it would be extortion. You don't realize what you're asking!"

"Oh, but I do, Andy." It was time for first names. "It's just that—"

Lauren didn't finish her sentence. An outbreak of emotion suddenly overcame her and she fumbled awkwardly for a tissue.

"Sorry, where was I? Oh yes, it's just that ever since I became aware of, you know, his cheating, I haven't been able to think about anything else. It's just really been hard."

Lauren had taken acting classes in college and could summon tears. Despite the Kleenex, somehow the first tear rolled down her face and dropped to the floor. The second escaped the tissue as well. Lauren tried to recall some of the old movie scripts she'd read, and imitate their maudlin tone.

"My marriage is over, I have to be honest. But until the whole divorce thing is behind me, I can't get on with my life. Michael's away so much, and when he's home he's just ice to me. I'm completely alone. I have no one to turn to, no one to talk to. Sometimes I think I'd pay a million dollars just to have a shoulder to cry on, a shoulder to lean on. Does that sound so terrible, Andy? Am I such a bad person because I want to be cared for; because I—too—need to be held sometimes?"

Andy was about to protest, but Lauren raised a hand. She was determined to go on, despite the pain.

"But until the divorce is settled, it would be wrong to be seen with anyone in public. That's why I wanted you to come here, so we could meet privately. If we'd met at a restaurant people might think, well—

"And you know what?" Lauren continued, brightening slightly as if a pleasing thought had come to her. "I'd enjoy meeting you at a restaurant. I'd enjoy just being able to talk to you, about anything, anything at all. Lord knows this isn't my favorite subject. But, as I said, it could be years before Michael slips up. And I can't wait that long, Andy. I have my own needs. Can *you* wait that long?"

Lauren thought that question brilliant. It wasn't quite a proposition, but it almost was.

"Mrs. Kittery—" Andy began, unsure what to say.

"Please, call me 'Lauren'."

"Of course, Lauren," the private detective began again, and then smiled shyly and glanced at the floor.

"So as I was saying, Andy, if we can just get this thing over with, we can get on with our lives. I'd enjoy that."

She looked directly at him again, through lowered eyelids.

"And maybe it is against the law, I don't know. But if it is, it shouldn't be. I mean there he is, one of the richest men in the country. He's cheating on his wife, and I don't believe it's wrong to try to stop him. Maybe it's against the letter of the law, but can it be against the spirit of the law, is that the right expression?"

Andy nodded.

"So I don't know what's legal or not legal, but I know what's right and wrong, and what my husband is doing is wrong. And I'm going to try to stop it anyway I can. And if you help me I'll be…" She paused and looked at him meaningfully. "I'll be *extremely* grateful."

"Mrs. Kittery—Lauren—please, you know I'll do anything for you. OK, maybe you're right. Maybe just knowing we have the pictures will be the only motivation needed. Look, being a cop for eight years, I dealt with prostitutes, organized crime, that kind of thing. I still have some contacts. It will take some money."

Lauren started to speak, but Andy waved aside her protest.

"I know, money won't be a problem. I just want you to realize what these things involve. I'll need a cash advance.

Let's say $5,000. And it really should be in cash. We don't want a paper trail."

"Of course. And I'm so grateful you're handling all these details. Where would I be without you? I think I have that much upstairs in the safe. The one in my bedroom…"

Lauren allowed the last word to hover in the air, while she pretended to consider the matter.

"I guess you'd better wait here," she decided, rising languorously from the couch and straightening her blouse.

She made a point to look at the clock.

"You see, Andy? It's after ten and my husband is nowhere to be found. He's probably at some sleazy bar with a new tart. I just wish I could think of some way to pay him back."

She wafted sensuously up the stairs knowing his lustful eyes were following every step.

9

LAUREN'S HUSBAND WASN'T with a woman, or at a bar. The young physicist was holed up in his office at Riverside High School, his mind churning with the implications of the discovery.

He could build a time machine. He could travel in time. The mutrinos were doing it. All he had to do was harness them.

A time machine. The words had a surreal, fantasy-like quality.

But the fantasy always led to the inevitable question of whether the past could be changed. And if so, it created the time-traveler paradox. Could a man go back in time and kill his father before that father had a chance to produce a child? If so, who would have killed the father? There were several theories.

One held that because the scenario was impossible it must, therefore, be impossible to go back in time.

A second suggested that, because it was impossible, the

man would not have been able to kill the father—something would have prevented it.

Yet a third held that the man *could* kill the father, and thereby change all that he had left behind in his own time—in fact, that time would be "re-written."

The latest crazy theory was the "quilted multiverse," in which every combination of time, matter, people, places, events—everything—existed simultaneously. If you *changed* anything in a previous time you would move from one of these universes to another.

But what if someone did change the past? How would that affect the present universe? A time-machine might cause unimaginable destruction, conceivably wiping out friends, family, and some or all of the seven billion people on the planet. If one could travel back far enough they could conceivably wipe out the planets themselves, the galaxies, maybe everything. Of course, Kittery reasoned as he stared at the acoustic-tile ceiling, any such disruption or re-writing of time would generate an alternate universe, with different people, cultures, planets, etc.

Perhaps the new one would be an improvement if you were willing to take the risk.

And what about a terrorist angle?

"OK, I want ten million dollars, an airplane, and my three comrades released from jail or I step back in time and waste this universe!"

Kittery wasn't smiling. The danger of time-travel technology disrupting the current status of three-dimensional space/history was very real. It's why he'd left his classroom almost in a panic.

Scientists who invent a dangerous weapon often consider hiding it.

Kittery could destroy his notes, leave Yale, and forget everything he'd learned in the last few hours.

But, as others before him had reasoned, someone else would figure it out too. Best if the first experiments were done by a scientist who appreciated the danger, and had a social conscience.

He had no idea which, if any, of the theories on time travel was correct. Some cautious experimentation done in absolute secrecy would be necessary.

And he was the one to do it. Kittery had the necessary scientific knowledge and even technical ability. Equally important, he had resources.

The young scientist's wealth had never before been relevant to his academic work. Now it would be vital. Building a time machine would require a place to work, access to materials, tools, security, food, a place to sleep, and much more.

With funds, acquiring physical *things* would not be difficult. But what about people? He couldn't do it all himself, but he didn't want a large team. Visualizing the challenge ahead, Kittery decided he'd start with just one person, an assistant.

He didn't want a physicist or for that matter any scientist. Kittery had to be in control and couldn't risk someone who might abscond with the knowledge and pursue their own plans.

So if not a scientist, who? A technician? A mechanic? He had those skills himself. A well-muscled bodyguard? If he were to go back in time there might be situations where that could be useful. But he wanted something more than *The Hulk.*

He stared upwards with eyes closed, pondering this one detail that against everything else seemed minor, but which might prove vital. Finally, it came to him. He was going back in time. What kind of expert did he need?

Michael Kittery needed an historian.

10

THOMAS MILO, UNEMPLOYED merchant marine captain, nursed a double vodka at his favorite bar in Montauk, Long Island, and wondered what he'd done wrong with the dead chickens. The shipping agent had rejected delivery, as predicted.

The problem came with the harbormaster, who had given Milo twelve hours to dispose of 5,000 carcasses.

The obvious solution was to cast off and head back into the Marmara, or better yet the Black Sea, and dump them overboard. But the harbormaster, suspecting that plan, wouldn't grant a departure permit.

They'd called all over Istanbul trying to find a waste disposal team, but none were available on short notice.

They couldn't leave port without a departure permit, as that meant immediate confiscation of their vessel by the Turkish government.

Finally, with time running out, Milo opted for Granby's original suggestion and jettisoned the cargo—hoping the current, tide, or even the wind would carry them at least out of sight. But not only had the waterlogged fowl refused to go anywhere; they floated on the surface and swelled-up like beach balls, visible to anyone with a searchlight.

The harbormaster had thrown the crew and officers in jail, and it required the ship's owners (via the U.S. consulate and the payment of some heavy fines) to secure their release. The crew was sent back aboard, a new captain arrived to take command, and Milo was told his employment had ended.

After three days in a Turkish jail, he was happy to accept the offer of a plane ticket anywhere state-side in place of a court battle over severance pay.

Arriving at Kennedy Airport, Milo needed to re-think his career, breathe some sea air, and have a drink—but not necessarily in that order.

Ignoring the recently-completed AirTrain connection in favor of needed exercise, Milo walked three miles to the Long Island Rail stop at Jamaica and caught a train to Montauk. The stockbrokers on Wall Street hadn't left work yet and the cars were empty, giving Milo an unwelcome chance for serious contemplation as the landscape of fresh grass and newly-budding trees rolled past.

It wasn't springtime for him.

Arriving in the touristy seaport of Montauk, the unemployed sailor gratefully breathed the salt-laden air, enjoyed the wind off the sea, and then promptly headed to the nearby Old Lighthouse bar.

Now he was parked in a dark corner, enjoying a drink, and—despite no other customers—not even occupying the attention of the waitress more interested in the *All My Children* episode playing too loudly on the LCD screen.

Where was an aging, merchant-marine captain going to find a job without references? He could ship out as an able seaman. That would guarantee his next meal, but these days you had to have a union card, some seniority, and most likely a thousand bucks to bribe the crew agencies back in Jersey. Milo's assets consisted of twelve hundred fifty-nine dollars and thirty-six cents in cash, plus a couple of credit cards that were stretched pretty thin. It was more than enough for a second double vodka.

And this time, depressing or not, he thought back on his career.

It all began with a lie. At seventeen, the high-school drop-out had to add a year to his age when completing forms at the Navy recruiting office in Alameda and used his mother's Irish maiden name to further conceal identity. The military, in its wisdom, sent the newly-minted seaman to a filthy harbor tug operating out of Bainbridge Island, Washington—in hindsight probably the best vessel there was in which to learn raw seamanship. After three years he was a petty officer, and second in command of a much larger ocean-going vessel.

His learning was not confined to the Navy. Bored in traditional classrooms, Milo spent his time at sea reading avidly. History and ancient languages were a passion, and military history his specialty. Yet, the more he read, the more he realized how unimpressive was his own life.

Rescuing crippled ships on the high seas was important work. But it wasn't *war.* It wasn't the glory, sacrifice, and heroism Milo read about in books. So at twenty-one, he applied to the Navy SEALs and six months later was a fully-skilled, combat-ready, hard-as-nails, bastard-from-hell—ready to kick some ass. And some ass needed kicking: Viet Cong ass.

Finally, Milo got the war he wanted—sort of. Stationed on a recommissioned WWII submarine playing cat and mouse games with Soviet U-boats outside Haiphong harbor, and sometimes being inserted at night on secret missions via river patrol craft, Milo played commando for real. He performed so well that by 1975, he was wearing full lieutenant stripes and was considering applying for duty on a nuclear-powered boat.

But the fall of Saigon changed everything. Milo wanted no part of a military so mismanaged by Washington it had to flee from guerrilla armies. He resigned his commission in disgust.

Navy credentials were sufficient for a job as mate on the MV *Henry Todd*, a rusty freighter working the Texas coast. Milo didn't consider the foul-smelling, Intracoastal waterway *The Sea*, and shared this opinion with the captain one night over a bottle of tequila.

The skipper told Milo that if he didn't like the ship to get the hell off, and a second bottle provided the courage to do so. When the sun rose, Milo was lying in a cheap hotel in Galveston, his ship gone, and his discharge papers pinned to a shirtsleeve. The next decades were similar.

The merchant marine was ill-equipped to challenge the SEAL commando, and Milo retreated once again to history books and the study of languages which at least staved off boredom. While plying the Gulf coast at twelve knots, and later in the Mediterranean, Milo studied the battles of Trafalgar and Campordale, the Norman takeover of England, Celtic migrations, the Viking invasions, and even the Romans and their Latin language. There had been so many wars Milo felt cheated, and knew he'd been born in the wrong century.

At least the ports had bars, poker games, and women. But these distractions often left him feeling even more empty and useless.

Unfortunately, Milo's irreverence and defiance of authority did nothing to whisk him up the promotion ladder. His career advanced like…dead chickens floating in a stagnant harbor, he thought, ironically.

He turned fifty-five before earning command of his own ship. And now, in his late sixties, he was out of that job as well. And broke.

A smooth-talking stockbroker on Wall Street had vaporized Milo's savings just before the market crashed. Now all he had left was knowledge of history and half a dozen languages, mostly dead ones. With no academic credentials, what did those count for? What did his whole life count for?

Not much, Milo decided, starring at the ice cubes in his near-empty vodka glass. He could relate to those ice cubes: going nowhere, and dwindling.

He noticed a tall, serious-looking young fellow walk in, and uncertainly glance around. Milo guessed this guy hadn't spent a lot of time in bars, and would probably get carded. He damned sure looked young enough. But maybe not. A twenty-year-old would be nervous about that, and this youngster, whatever his age, had weightier concerns.

Looked as if life had come down hard on this poor bastard as well. You didn't ask a face like that for ID, you handed over a good stiff drink and thanked God it wasn't you wearing that face.

Milo forgot his own troubles for the moment, propped his legs on the far side of the corner booth he'd claimed, and watched the newcomer.

11

MICHAEL KITTERY HAD been to the Old Lighthouse before, as it was a hangout for Brookhaven physicists. When a magnet failed in the accelerator, or some other dysfunction occurred requiring hours to repair, someone would say "Screw it, let's head to Montauk for a drink."

Kittery was in that mood now.

But at 4:00 p.m., with bright sunshine illuminating the deck outside, a gloomy red-vinyl bar smelling of yesterday's beer probably wasn't going to help his spirits. Yet he'd driven three hours to get here and, with the difficulties of the last week, probably nothing would lift his spirits. So he might as well be in Montauk. Kittery sat at the counter and, during a commercial break in the *All My Children* episode, was able to coax a Heineken from the female bartender. He took a pretzel out of the basket, eyed the liquor bottles on the wall, and wondered if it was a mark of society's sophistication or decline that it could offer so many choices of alcohol.

From the moment the physicist had realized he needed

the aid of an historian, he'd been trying to find one. His volunteer job at the high school was a starting point. Of the two history teachers, one was a middle-aged woman who styled herself after 19th-century school-teachers, brandishing old-fashioned clothing and a solemn, uninviting demeanor. Kittery didn't think Ms. Evans was the right choice for embarking on voyages out of the known universe.

The other history teacher was a thirty-five-year-old playboy whose scholarly quest (according to rumor) was getting in the pants of comely female students. Statutory rape charges were probably just around the corner but for now, he wasn't looking for a career change.

Kittery turned next to Yale, and with no greater success. The prestigious university had history experts, but it seemed there was a correlation between expertise in history and incompetence in life. He could not imagine wanting any of those narrow, ivory-tower intellectuals along on a journey that might require resourcefulness and ingenuity. On the pretext of a research project on physics in the 17th century, he'd then visited Columbia, Pace, Rutgers, and half a dozen other "institutions of higher learning." The results were similar. Good historians apparently did not make good traveling companions, at least for the travel Kittery envisioned.

So while his scientific work had progressed well, the search for a history expert was stalled. What he was hoping to find was someone who not only knew history but also had common sense—and extra points if they could handle themselves in a bar fight. Apparently, people like that weren't common in faculty lounges at prestigious universities.

Kittery picked at the moist label of his Heineken bottle, scraping off little morsels of paper, and making a mess on the bar.

Compounding the problem, he sensed Lauren was up to something—now of all times.

Two days spent at home made him suspicious. Lauren was unusually friendly—the first time in months—which could only mean she thought things were going her way. And that meant she had a new plan for coming out of a divorce with lots of Kittery money. Lauren wouldn't be smiling otherwise.

But he wasn't in the mood for small talk with his scheming wife. He needed a place to think clearly. So he made up an excuse about needing to work at Brookhaven and explained he'd be spending the night in Montauk. Lauren had taken the news better than he'd expected, so he'd left immediately and driven out to the tip of Long Island. On the way, he'd reserved a suite at the Montauk Yacht Club, with a balcony overlooking the Atlantic Ocean. But the Yacht Club bar was a pricey watering hole, best suited for sipping chardonnay while your mahi-mahi was sautéed in lemon butter at the table. Kittery had spent his entire life in these kinds of places and had never felt comfortable in them.

Serious drinkers went to the Old Lighthouse where—went the saying—you ordered a beer or a shot of Wild Turkey, or you got the hell out. So he sat at the counter and sipped a Heineken and wondered how he was going to find the right historian.

This proved a mistake, for the soap opera was

distracting, and he began to focus on whether Nina, the pretty ingénue, should have married so quickly since her deceased husband's body had never actually been discovered. Was he really dead? The peroxide-blonde waitress had an opinion and was eager to share it.

Suddenly a new voice joined the conversation. "If Nina knew how to treat a man right, she could probably have any guy she wanted."

Kittery looked up. The woman beside him was exceptionally beautiful: dark-haired, heavily made-up, and—in a strapless red dress—apparently ready for a night on the town. The scientist was not experienced enough to think it odd such a woman would walk into a bar by herself, dressed like that, at four in the afternoon.

"Mind if I sit here?" she asked, her sultry voice making the words flow from her tongue like melted butter. She didn't wait for a response but merely slid onto the stool beside him. She gave Kittery a side glance that revealed devastatingly-long eyelashes.

The scientist's engineering background forced him to wonder how a natural human eyelash could have the necessary cantilever strength to reach out so far.

He quickly forgot about the waitress and the soap opera and—even though he was not the type to randomly strike up conversations with strange women at bars—managed to blurt out the right words.

"What will you have?" he said. "I'll buy the first round."

"I'll have what you're having," she said amicably, crossing her legs and revealing provocative thighs.

"My name's Michael," said the physicist with a nervous smile.

"I'm Danielle. Very happy to meet you. Do you come here often?"

"Maybe not often enough," said Kittery, pleased he'd thought up such a witty response.

"Perhaps I don't either," said Danielle, with a trace of shyness, as she glanced down at her drink.

The waitress made a gagging gesture at the end of the bar, but no one noticed.

"My boyfriend just walked out on me," continued Danielle. "I've been in tears but I couldn't stand just sitting at home any longer. I guess I'm here looking for a friend. What about you? What are *you* looking for?"

The question took Kittery by surprise.

"I'm looking for an historian," he blurted out.

"You're looking for an *historian?"*

The woman seemed momentarily confused.

"Yes. And I'm not having much luck."

"Maybe that's because you're in an empty bar," she said with a smile, teasingly. "Seems like an odd place to find an historian."

Kittery laughed, took a sip of his beer, then lifted his bottle to hers for a toast.

"You're sure right about that."

The woman adjusted her dress, exposing more skin.

"Well, ask me a history question. Maybe I'll get it right." She glanced at him demurely.

"That's OK", said Kittery. "I don't think I'm going to find the historian I need in Montauk."

"Maybe you'll find something even better in Montauk."

He laughed uncertainly, raised his eyebrows in acknowledgment, and took another sip of beer.

❧

Thomas Milo watched, bemusedly. If there was one thing he knew besides history and ships, it was whores. But the guy had just said he wanted an historian. Why would he want an historian?

He took another look at the girl's expression, and the guy's expression, and figured if he didn't intervene fast the woman was going to leave with a new customer and he'd never know why an historian was needed.

Milo pushed back his chair as noisily as he could and ambled conspicuously over to the counter. He leaned against it and set his glass down hard.

"Couldn't help overhearing," growled Milo. "I'm an historian. What can I do for you?"

❧

Kittery took his eyes off Danielle with reluctance but sobered quickly. If this unshaven, ornery, well-muscled old man really was an historian, his search might be over. He held out his hand.

"Michael Kittery," he said. "Pleased to meet you. Have a seat."

Sometime later Danielle shrugged, got down from the bar, picked up her purse, and walked out of the room. Her stiletto heels clicked against the floor in unconcealed annoyance.

12

"SO WHAT YOU'RE saying," Kittery summed up, "is that you're former Navy, a merchant marine officer by trade, and an historian only as a hobby. You're self-taught, in other words."

Milo bristled, about to respond that being self-taught sometimes meant you had the best teacher, but something about the guy's tone made him pause. The words had been spoken approvingly as if they vindicated some privately-held belief.

"Yeah, I guess so," Milo replied, neutrally.

They'd moved to a booth and Milo was now being asked very specific questions about his background and present situation. The kid was presumptuous, asking all these questions as if he were a prospective employer. It was the kind of thing one of his former bosses would do.

Milo allowed the interrogation. Something in his gut told him this guy was different. The man introduced as Michael Kittery seemed preoccupied not by his importance, but by the importance of something else. So Milo checked his pride and continued answering, knowing Kittery would reveal what he wanted to, eventually.

"I appreciate you answering my questions," said Kittery as if reading his thoughts, "when you don't know why I'm asking them. I hope you'll indulge me further. I promise I'll explain it all in a moment."

"Sure," said Milo. "I'm not exactly in a hurry." As if to prove his point, he held up the vodka glass, recently refilled on Kittery's tab.

"I don't know much about history myself," Kittery confessed. "So it's difficult for me to judge expertise."

Milo thought this a refreshingly-honest statement.

"But if you could humor me, let's put it on my terms. If we had with us the Professor of History from, let's say, Yale University, a Ph.D. of course, and I asked both of you a question, something like—I don't know—'Why did the Hundred Years' War take so long?' Would you be able to give as good an answer as he would?"

"Define 'good.'"

"I mean accurate. I'm assuming his answer would take longer to deliver." Kittery smiled.

Milo took another sip from his drink, stared at the ceiling, and set the glass gently back on the table.

"OK, why did the Hundred Years' war take so long? That's your question, right?"

Kittery nodded.

"Because it was several wars, not one. Historians later grouped them all and called it the Hundred Years' War. Kind of like if historians one day lumped together World War One and Two and called it the 20th Century War."

"Interesting," said Kittery. "Was there a common theme to those wars; a reason to lump them together?"

"Yeah, actually there was. The common theme was that certain Kings of England kept thinking they should also be Kings of France."

"Who won?"

"France. Otherwise, they'd probably all be one country now."

"OK. And what were the long term consequences of the war, beyond the fact that France stayed independent?"

"My theory?"

"Sure."

"When they finally gave up trying to take over France, the English eventually turned their attention to the sea—which makes sense given they're an island. When Queen Mary finally lost Calais—arguably the *true* end to the Hundred Years' War because it was England's last territory in France—it paved the way for Queen Elizabeth to turn her attention towards becoming a sea power. Which she did. Francis Drake and so forth. This new focus away from continental Europe and towards the sea was the true beginning of the British Empire, in my opinion."

"Wow," said Kittery. He paused, obviously thinking carefully. His fingers idly picked at what was left of the Heineken label. "OK, you're hired."

"Hired for what?" said Milo.

The young man took a long, deep sigh, as if not sure what his next words should be.

"Let's start at the beginning. As I told you, my name's

Michael Kittery. In a few months, I hope to receive my Ph.D. in physics from Yale University."

Milo wasn't impressed with labels, degrees, or fancy schools. But he refrained from rolling his eyes.

"Pleased to meet you again," he said, wondering where all this was heading.

"Let me ask you a question." Kittery leaned in, the way one does when sharing something of confidence with an old friend. "Do I appear insane?"

"Huh?"

"A simple question. Take a moment to think about it. Do I appear to you to be insane, crazy, off-my-rocker?"

"You seem OK to me." Milo squinted at the young man, wondering if he couldn't handle his alcohol or something. Although the guy wasn't slurring his words.

"You may change your mind in a moment. But if we can agree I'm not insane then if I tell you something, please don't look at me and say 'you're crazy!'"

"Why would I do that?"

"You'll know soon. Anyway, I'm what's called a particle physicist. As part of finishing my dissertation, I'm working with a group doing experiments at the National Research Lab in Brookhaven. That doesn't have to be taken on faith. It can be confirmed. The point is, you need to be convinced upfront that I'm not a lunatic."

"Look, son, I don't give a crap about Yale University, or Ph.D.'s, or some National Research place. But why would I think you're crazy or some kind of lunatic?"

"Because of what I'm about to tell you."

"So tell me, for Chrissake!"

Kittery paused, obviously wrestling with a decision. Then he looked up and spoke with quiet helplessness.

"I think I've invented a way to travel in time. In short, a time machine."

There was silence.

Milo grinned. "Are you serious?"

"Yes."

"Then you're batshit crazy!" Milo burst out laughing. He smacked his new friend on the shoulder. "Either that or you've thrown back one too many, kid. Maybe you should cool it on the drinks."

Kittery said nothing but merely looked at him steadily. Milo noticed the guy was only halfway through his first beer, so it wasn't the alcohol.

He glanced around the room. If this maniac started getting violent he wanted to be able to call for help.

"If you'd prefer to leave the table, go ahead," said Kittery.

Milo considered it. The good-looking whore was probably still hanging around Montauk. That possibility sounded more enticing than listening to a lunatic rave. Although this guy wasn't exactly raving.

"You gonna keep buying the drinks? Maybe a cheeseburger?"

"Anything you want."

"OK, I'm listening. Let's hear what you have to say. But I still think you're crazy."

"Fair enough. If you didn't, I'd probably think *you* were."

Milo was silent.

"So, here it is. I believe I've discovered a method for moving matter through time. It's based on experiments done recently by physicists working with sub-atomic particles. That's all I'm going to say about the science. I'm not sure it will work because I haven't tested it. But I'm pretty confident. I'm going to test the theory and then, based on those tests, decide on what to do next. I consider the whole matter extremely dangerous, and I'm scared."

"Scared?"

"Yes, scared."

He provided a summary of the time-travel theories, and the destruction a time-traveler could cause.

"I'm going to need an assistant, a helper. I don't want another scientist. I've decided an historian would be the best choice. I don't know enough about history, and I might—"

"Wait. How far back do you think you can go?" interrupted Milo.

"I don't want to go far at all, at least in the beginning. Maybe only a few minutes. A day, at most. But if I make a mistake I could end up anywhere. I might need to know what's going on fifty years ago, even a hundred, and what the implications might be of influencing events. I might arrive at a particular point in time and not even know where I was. That's why I need an historian. Until now, I haven't found the right person. Yet I trust my instinct. If you want the job, it's yours."

Milo sat back in his chair, sipped his vodka, and stared at the young man across the table. Like most historians, Milo fantasized about life in past eras, about how he would have managed in the nineteenth century, or the fifteenth century, or even in Roman times. Time travel was as common a fantasy to historians as making it on Broadway was to actresses.

Damn! The whole thing was too convenient. Here he was at the lowest ebb of his career and in walks Mr. Time Travel. Milo pinched himself on the thigh, not because he believed he was dreaming but because it was important to rule out the possibility.

If time travel *were* possible would it not be a bright young physicist who would invent it? His cargo officer, O'Donnell, would probably not invent it. That seaman who knew a lot about chickens wouldn't invent it. That damned harbor master in Istanbul sure as hell wouldn't invent it.

Of course it would be a physicist. They'd invented nuclear power. They'd developed The Bomb. They'd sent men to the moon. This was the kind of thing that physicists did. You never heard much about them until some city blew up, or lasers were invented. And Yale probably had some good physicists, so why the hell not?

And, kidding aside, Kittery didn't seem crazy. If he wasn't crazy, and if he was a physicist from Yale, and if he believed he'd invented time travel—well, maybe he had.

Milo weighed these questions while Kittery simply waited in silence. It was a difficult moment for the seaman. His recent actions had eclipsed any future he might have with the merchant marine. Throwing in his lot with a madman wouldn't help. But it couldn't hurt much either.

"OK," he said at last. "I don't think time travel is

possible. But let's assume I'm wrong, and let's assume you've invented it, and let's assume you need an assistant who knows some history, and I'm available. Now what?"

"I'm not sure," said Kittery.

Milo appreciated honesty.

"I guess the first thing we need to discuss are the terms of your employment," he ventured.

"Yeah, well, who's going to do the 'employing' exactly? I guess that physicists aren't paid as much as NFL linebackers. I'm out of a job and about a week from being hungry. I don't need a huge salary, but you don't look like Mr. Moneybags. So, how are we going to eat while we travel through time dimensions or whatever?"

Milo wasn't sure what he'd expected after this speech. He'd spent considerable time talking big adventures with shipmates. Most of their plans went on the rocks for lack of money. But the talk was fun. Milo figured the talk was about over here.

"I don't look like Mr. Moneybags?" asked Kittery. "I consider that a compliment."

"What the hell does that mean?"

"I've asked you to swallow some pretty heavy stuff, Mr. Milo. So here's some more. Because of the nature of the research, I receive an income of $18,000 per year from the Department of Energy. But, if the last letter from my accountant is correct, I'm also in control of 1.6 billion dollars of assets. So what salary would you like? I think I can afford it."

Milo spilled his vodka glass, and the thought flashed in his head: *maybe I handled the chickens correctly after all.*

Kittery walked over to the bar and ordered cheeseburgers.

"Food's on its way," said the scientist when he returned. "Let me ask, what was your salary at your last job?"

Milo grabbed at that question like a drowning man at a life ring, glad to be on solid ground.

"The company paid me $87,000 per year and paychecks were issued twice a month. On the ship, my expenses were paid for."

"Fine. Since I'm asking you to change careers precipitously, a raise is probably in order. Let's say we add fifty percent. That would be, well, let's round it off to $150,000. And expenses too, of course, during the project. Food, lodging, and so forth."

"A hundred fifty grand plus all expenses?" said Milo. "Seriously?"

"Sure. History professors earn far more than that at Yale. If it's convenient I'd like to begin work immediately. This afternoon. Right here at the table. Just so there's no misunderstanding, I'll draw up an agreement between us and I'll commit to employing you for a minimum of twenty-four months, starting today. If there's a falling out before then, I'll still pay the salary."

Milo just stared at him.

"The document will carry standard confidentiality clauses. Also, you'll need to agree not to accept employment or engage in any other commercial activities while you're working for me. Are those terms satisfactory?"

"Hell, Kittery. You know damn well those terms are extremely generous. An hour ago I was an out-of-work merchant marine officer. Now, if everything you say is true—and you can't take offense at that— "

"None taken."

"—then right now I'm a well-paid historian. But let me ask this. If I'm the only other guy on the project, you'll have me running errands, taking care of routine chores, that kind of thing? I'll be kind of a gopher in other words."

"I suppose so. Yeah, all that stuff. Whatever's needed. Are you willing to accept the job?"

"Sure. But it's kind of strange. For years my old bosses tried to turn me into a gopher, and I never let 'em. Now, I'm going to be one of my own free will." He made a mock salute. "Captain Thomas B. Milo, standing by for orders!"

The lines of care and strain on Kittery's face eased, and Milo thought he almost detected a smile.

13

THE DOWNTOWN IRT local screamed in protest as its wheels fought against the curved track. With a final shriek of brakes, the train came to a stop. The doors opened and passengers exiting were unleashed against those seeking entrance. Thomas Milo allowed himself to be carried by the in-flowing current and was soon deposited against the opposite door. The train began to move.

No stranger to New York City, he was finding this particular visit disorienting. He came to this area between jobs, looking for work. He did the rounds, checked in at the crew agencies, spent time at the bars frequented by seafarers, and hoped for a lead.

At no time did Milo feel so far down on the social ladder as when he was in Manhattan. Perhaps it was all the wealth concentrated on the island, or all those stockbrokers rushing around with a purpose, in Brooks Brothers suits.

But this time, Milo had a purpose.

If time travel worked, it was a discovery many times more important than all previous discoveries combined.

Milo was now part of a two-man team that might be on the verge of destroying the existing world.

Having a clear, printed record of what the existing world looked like—through history—seemed like a good idea. Kittery had agreed, so Milo was now assembling a library.

The self-taught historian had visited the obvious midtown stores such as Barnes & Noble, finding the trendy reference works he'd expected, and buying them since money was no object. Next stop was lower Manhattan, home to the antique book district. He'd been to this neighborhood before, killing time between jobs, glancing through obscure publications like *An Account of the Present War in Spain,* written by a British colonel in 1809.

This time his shopping pattern would be different. As he left the subway at 14th Street, he began walking quickly—much like the stockbrokers.

His search for the final bookstore led to a bewildering labyrinth of alleyways and crooked side streets in Greenwich Village. He paused in the dim light to re-read directions scribbled on someone's business card. And that's when they saw him.

The teenage thugs were not native to the area but found it lucrative, more so than the Bed-Stuy section of Brooklyn which was their home. They chose their marks swiftly, dealt mercilessly with the victims, and then fled back across the East River to the protection of their own neighborhood—safe from the Manhattan law.

The old man—not that old, but old enough—uncertainly pausing and checking street signs, was precisely the target they were seeking. Reasonably well dressed and likely a stranger to the Village, he would be alone, probably with cash, and easy to overcome. Vic-Roy, a moniker borrowed from his other life as a graffiti tagger, led the pack of three up behind him. At the last second, he pulled a small wooden bat from his overcoat and delivered a sharp blow directly behind the mark's left ear. The victim collapsed to the sidewalk.

Vic-Roy was indifferent whether he'd killed the man. It wouldn't be the first time and it wasn't what mattered. Their goal was to find enough cash or valuables to make the mugging worthwhile.

They dragged the inert form with surprising difficulty into a narrow alley and behind a dumpster. They needed to strip him and get out of the area fast, so they could search through the clothes at leisure. Often a mark had more cash in a belt or coat-lining than in his wallet.

Safely hidden behind the dumpster, Vic-Roy leaned over and began unbuttoning the man's trench coat. This was a mistake for it left the gang-leader's abdomen exposed.

The inert form suddenly came to life and thrust an eight-inch dagger upwards into Vic-Roy's chest cavity.

Vic-Roy's last thoughts, as his heart was pierced, were utter surprise mixed with unbearable pain. Neither lasted long. Vic-Roy was dead before he'd had a chance to scream.

A scream would not have helped him, but it might have warned the others. When the old man arose, throwing to the side their leader as if he were an inflatable mannequin, the younger one reacted first. He bolted in panic, running instinctively towards Brooklyn.

The older hoodlum took longer to appreciate the danger. In a few more seconds he would have worked it out and might have escaped, but those seconds were not granted.

Milo—who had only been feigning unconsciousness—retracted the knife, carefully waiting until he'd rolled the body on its side to avoid any cascade of blood, and jumped to his feet. Then he swiped the blade across the other punk's face.

It was a vicious weapon, won three years earlier in a Catania poker game. Two inches back from its tip, the knife had a small barb which produced an effect even Milo found gruesome. One of the hoodlum's eyes was yanked completely out of its socket, and his nose was sliced in half.

The face—what had been a face—was now a red mask and the hoodlum was screaming in shock and pain. Milo weighed his options, and also the options of a disfigured and partially-blind ex-mugger, and decided both their interests would be served by his next action.

The mugger was dead by the time Milo retracted the knife.

Using one of the corpse's shirt sleeves, he wiped the weapon clean, put it back in its sheath, and decided he'd been to enough bookstores that day. The two remaining volumes could be located better online from his hotel the next morning.

Milo hailed a cab on Sixth Avenue and was soon back in his room at the New York Palace. Sitting in the bar after dinner, enjoying the live music being played on a baroque harpsichord, he thought back on the day. In terms of the library mission, it had been successful. But it had certainly been unusual. Not because of the little incident in the Village. Knife fights had become routine for Milo in the Mediterranean. It was unusual because it was ending at a fashionable bar in a hotel where his room cost more than $700 a night.

That was very unusual indeed, the sea captain mused, as he swirled the ice cubes in his drink.

14

"YOU MAY BE the world's greatest physicist, Boss, but with all due respect, you don't know shit about running an operation like this. I do. It's that simple."

Milo took another coconut shrimp off the platter, dipped it in honey mustard, and chewed it whole. He'd never understood why others persisted in pulling the damn thing apart when it was the shell that gave it texture. Just like watermelon seeds.

"Well, the jury's still out on my ranking as a physicist, but I agree with the rest of what you said. And while we're on the subject, let's drop the 'Boss' crap. My friends call me Kitt."

"Kitt?" Milo took a swallow of beer as he considered the nickname. He leaned back as his gaze wandered over the Hudson River and the New York piers, 800 feet below their table at the Rainbow Room atop Rockefeller Center. In the distance, he could see the Statue of Liberty, all aglow. A few vessels were anchored out towards Verrazano, but they looked like pretty small stuff. In Milo's opinion, New

York was dead as a port. Bureaucrats and their regulations had made one of the best harbors on earth unusable.

A single-engine Cessna seaplane flew down the river, at their present altitude, ferrying the rich out to the Hamptons—for a weekend of whatever the rich did in the Hamptons. Then Milo remembered that one of the richest of them was sitting across the table. Milo looked back and grinned.

"OK, Kitt's a good name. My shipmates called me Milo or Captain. But you're still the boss, and you're still out of your depth when it comes to running this operation."

"I couldn't agree more. I'm supposed to use this meeting to tell you what to do next. But I don't know what to do next. The science is coming along fine, as I expected. The best breakthroughs are always simple. That's what makes them breakthroughs. I've even made progress with the engineering. But I'm out of my element when it comes to day-to-day plans. What *does* need to happen next?"

Milo took another shrimp.

"Two questions. How much time will be required, and what kind of laboratory or whatever will you need?"

"Well, we're probably looking at three to six weeks before we'll be able to 'test' anything. Based on what I've learned so far—and this is incredibly lucky—I'm not going to have to use anything at Brookhaven. That was my biggest concern. How do you carry out super-secret experiments with all of your colleagues looking over your shoulder asking what you're doing?

"What I need is some quiet place, with a lot of space, and with the ability to bring in supplies and special equipment—whatever it might be—without a lot of curious on-lookers."

"Can I make a suggestion?"

"Shoot."

"You stick to physics. I'll handle everything else. I'll give the day-to-day orders, and you're welcome to overrule me. Tell me what you need as far as the experiments are concerned. I'll figure out how to make it happen. Plus, I'll take care of some needs you haven't thought of."

"Such as?"

"Well, for one thing, you gotta quit being Mr. Michael-rich-son-of-a-bitch-Kittery. After we walk out of here tonight, you gotta start being plain old Kitt."

"I'm not sure what you mean, Captain." The scientist's tone had turned cool.

Milo held up his hand.

"Hey, don't get me wrong. I got nothing against being rich. And I got nothing against you whatever, I think I've made that clear. My point is, a billionaire maintains a high profile. Gossip columnists take an interest in you. You probably have business managers taking care of your money. My guess is you got half of Connecticut and half of Long Island kissing your ass—even if you're not aware of it. And knowing you, you're probably not. I mean that as a compliment by the way. Point is, we've gotta cut adrift from all that. As long as you're Michael Kittery, the billionaire, everything you do for the next six months is going to be under a microscope."

With the final shrimp left on the plate, Milo scraped

it over some cocktail sauce, popped the whole thing in his mouth, and chewed aggressively.

"Here's an example. This is the first time I've ever been to this Rainbow place. But it must be the classiest spot to have a drink in the Western Hemisphere. Have you checked out the restrooms? They've got a guy in there whose only job is handing out rose-scented towels.

"Anyway, how many tables are there? Maybe thirty? How many are by the windows? Seven? So you come in here at five p.m. on a Friday when the place is jammed and where do they put you? Right here at the best table in the house. If that's a coincidence, I'll eat my chair! They gave you this table because they know who you are, and the maître d' made sure the waiters know who you are, that's why they've been hovering over us like damned Egyptian water locusts."

"Yeah, you're probably right. I've lived with that for so long I don't even notice," admitted the physicist, sheepishly.

"Well, I notice and it scares me. When you walked into that bar at Montauk, you looked like we'd been invaded by Martians and they weren't taking prisoners. I understand that now. You're sitting on the most dangerous discovery in the history of mankind. Someone gets wind of what you're up to and it'll be front-page news. Most will laugh but the ones who won't are the ones to worry about.

"Every intelligence agency in the world will start tailing us, just on the off chance you know what you're talking about, even if you're not talking about it. You're going to have the FBI, Mossad, MI6, the Deuxieme, and Russia's FSB on our butts before we're even out of the starting gate."

"You're not making me feel any better, Captain. I hope you have a solution."

"Not a solution, just precautions. That's all we can do. For starters, I recommend that Michael Kittery disappear. I don't mean in some mysterious, sure-to-get-on-the-evening-news way. I mean drop out, go low profile, take on some boring out-of-the-country research project. Give the gossip columnists a reason to lose interest in you, and give your business associates and colleagues a logical reason for your absence. You'll have to fill in this part yourself, 'cause I don't know your world well enough. Is there some legitimate reason a rich scientist would go away for a while?"

Kitt thought for a moment.

"Did I ever mention my undergraduate degree included a minor in botany? Had a language requirement, so I chose Latin. I needed to understand all those plant names."

"Quam turpe est," said Milo quietly.

"You speak Latin too?"

"I speak a dozen languages. They come easily to me. Kind of a hobby, and part of what I liked to study on shipboard. Pairs well with history."

"I'm sure. Latin's the only other language I know. I joined the Latin Club on campus. We had our own floor in the dorm and always spoke it to each other."

"Let me guess—you had the best toga parties on campus?"

Kitt grinned. "Yep! But I learned to speak Latin fluently which made the plant names a cinch."

"So what does botany have to do with anything?"

"Oh, just—if I were a botanist, it'd be easy to disappear. I'd announce the need to do some field research in the rainforests of Brazil, and that's the last anyone would expect to see of me for months. It's quite the rage among botanists, you know. The rainforest sabbatical."

"OK, that's what we want. What's the physicist equivalent of the rainforest sabbatical?"

"There isn't one. At least not for particle physicists. I suppose an astrophysicist could spend time in the polar regions taking measurements of magnetic fields or something. Particle physicists need to stay close to the accelerators that produce the particles. A sabbatical would mean leaving one of the half dozen accelerators in the world and visiting another. That's not exactly dropping out though; it's more like dropping in."

"No good. We need you to get away."

Kittery was silent for a while, and his gaze shifted into the distance. One of the waiters misinterpreted and rushed over to be of service. Milo intervened, and with hand signals placed an order for another round of drinks and shrimp. The waiter scurried off.

"There's only one way to do it," Kittery said at last. "I could claim 'burnout'.

"What's it mean?"

"Burnout's a problem for physicists. It's happened to some of my friends at Brookhaven. They lose all interest in physics and find a new hobby. Like getting their private pilot's license or joining a reggae band. My best friend, Amit, dropped out and became a consultant to the Pentagon—and apparently built them a far more secure system of encryption algorithms—before returning to Yale."

"How does it work? Are you allowed to just drop out for a while and come back whenever you want?"

"Pretty much. The physics community has learned that if a burnout victim is given free rein for several months—even up to a year or more—the problem self-corrects and they return hat in hand, anxious to be allowed back. Often some of their most productive work comes right after these flings. So these days, the attitude is 'See you when you return and don't tell us where you're going.'"

"Nice work if you can get it," noted Milo, enviously.

"Of course, in my case, it would push back the Ph.D. for another year, but that's not important. And I already canceled this summer's lab experiment."

"Sounds like a perfect cover," said Milo. "But how about business associates, family?"

"Burnout is burnout. You know about Lauren."

Milo nodded, somewhat embarrassed. The day they'd met in Montauk, Kittery had opened up on the subject.

"My family has ties with an investment banking firm here in Manhattan, and one of their partners makes the decisions on handling our money. When I need funds, I just call and give him instructions for making deposits. What I can do is send him a letter or meet in person and explain my burnout situation. Give him the background, and tell him my plans."

"Which will be?"

"Oh, maybe that I'm buying a Porsche and heading west on Interstate 80."

"Pretty vague."

"Knowing George Lowry—that's his name—he'll probably say 'High time!' and slap me on the back with a leering grin. After that, George won't be surprised at any amount of money I ask for, nor will he be surprised at wherever I am when I ask for it."

"Perfect. OK, I want you to do all that. Talk to the investment banker guy. Do whatever you need with Lauren. Maybe send her an email saying you're in Pittsburgh and heading west, or something. And then the two of us will drop out of sight. The only question is…where do we go?"

Again they were silent, both lost in memories of places they had been, out of the way corners where questions weren't asked, yet resources were available. Kitt was first to break the silence.

"How do you feel about farming?"

"Huh?"

"I know the perfect place. I almost bought it a year ago, but couldn't think what to do with it. I was down at a symposium in Washington, some National Academy of Science thing. After three days it really was burnout, so I rented a car. Drove south out of Washington for a couple hours, stayed at a bed and breakfast in a town southeast of Richmond. I think it was called Three Forks.

"I got lost trying to find my way back to Interstate Five the next morning and happened to pass a 'For Sale' sign. I was curious and checked it out. It was an old tobacco farm overlooking the James River. 1,500 acres, a beautiful

18th century restored farmhouse, with a large barn. The funny thing is, someone tried to make a go of the place as a modern dairy farm. They'd paved 6,000 square feet of the barn, and put in fancy milking and pasteurizing equipment."

"A dairy farm?"

"The caretaker told me the syndicate making the attempt went bankrupt before the first cow was brought in, so the place is immaculate. Wired for industrial-level electricity, clean, well-ventilated, you could use it for anything. It's upriver from Norfolk so you're only barely in the sticks. Supplies would be no problem."

"I like the location. Is it still for sale?"

"Probably. The caretaker said after the bankruptcy the property went back to the original owner, who was an eighty-year-old D.A.R. lady living in Jacksonville. Some great-great-grandfather of hers had started the farm, and she didn't really want to sell it. The price was fifty percent more than the market would bear, but she wouldn't come down a penny. I could probably place a call tomorrow morning, agree to the asking price, and we'd own a dairy farm by tomorrow night."

"You know, Kitt, I just might learn to enjoy my association with you," said Milo. "I swear, lack of money has been the problem that's killed every idea anyone I knew ever had, including some of my own. But in this outfit, money's never a problem. It's more like a weapon."

Kitt smiled. "Well, maybe those hundreds of millions of dollars have a purpose after all. You know, other than merely procreating themselves generation after generation, and turning my wife into a greedy lunatic."

"Yeah," said Milo, distracted by the concept of hundreds of millions of dollars procreating themselves. He shook his head slightly.

"OK, here are the marching orders from your day-to-day commander. Buy the farm, talk to your broker, give your excuses to your scientific friends, send an email to your wife, and then drive to Virginia. This part is critical. I want you to take everything you need in the way of scientific equipment or computers or whatever with you. You won't be coming back until the project's completed."

Kitt began to take notes on his phone.

"Make sure you text me tomorrow at the hotel with the address of the farm. I'll drive there myself, separately. I'll take a cab to New Jersey and buy a used pick-up truck with an enclosed bed. That will give me some room to carry the shitload of history books I just bought.

"And one more thing. Let me see your billfold."

Kitt hesitated only a moment, then placed his pigskin Christian Dior wallet on the table. Milo examined the contents.

"Use one of these credit cards tonight. It won't hurt to place you in Manhattan on April 11th. That's normal. But after tonight, forget about these credit cards. Don't cancel them—that would be out of character. But don't use them. Get your broker friend to make a large supply of cash available to you. $100,000 for starters and I don't want it in travelers' checks. I want it in cash. Make up some story about the need to be a 'free spirit.' If he's concerned about the safety of the money, shrug it off with some comment like 'Who cares?' You want to appear slightly and benignly deranged after all."

Kitt nodded again, impressed with Milo's attention to detail.

"Then put 20k of it in a manila envelope and have it delivered to me at the New York Palace. I'll use that money to pay the bill and buy the truck. Let's make it twenty-five grand. I've been at the Palace a couple nights now.

Kitt was leaning forward, eagerly typing more notes. Finally, he leaned back and smiled.

"God, Milo, how did I ever get so lucky as to find you? You're just what I needed."

"Yeah, well, that cuts both ways, doesn't it? But I'm still concerned about one thing."

"Name it."

"We can make you disappear for six months, that's easy. But who knows how long this project will take? Our contract runs for two years. I can't imagine Connecticut society will let you disappear that long, or that your wife's divorce attorney will either. What are we going to do if this thing runs longer than six or seven months?"

Kittery leaned back in his chair, a new glass of beer making it halfway from the table to his mouth, and then retreating to the table. He giggled.

"Captain!" Kitt finally managed to blurt out, a bit loudly. Milo wondered if he'd had too much to drink.

"What will we do if it takes *longer than six months?* God, I don't believe it!" Kitt was now laughing uncontrollably, and Milo began to worry. Heads were already turning.

"My dear Captain. 'It', as you call it, will take no more and no less time than we wish. Have you forgotten what this project is all about? We will return whenever we want to return, perhaps even yesterday. Do you understand what I'm saying?"

Milo finally got it. While Kitt was on the verge of making a fool of himself, Milo raised his glass in a silent toast and smiled.

15

THE BOW CUT the water like a knife as the curragh healed to the freshening breeze. Avelyn laughed with excitement and held the tiller while Shelby eased the mainsheet on the lateen-rigged sail.

"When you're alone and a breeze like that hits you, lass, you'll have to head up. You won't have the ballast to run with it."

"I know, Shelby, I know. But I can't stand to slow down. Not on a day like this."

"So, is this the same girl who came to visit me two weeks ago, eyes red from crying?"

"No," said Avelyn, smiling. "This is a completely different girl."

"Well, whoever this new girl is, she's a natural sailor. She's learning faster than anyone I ever taught. Are you sure you're not a man?"

Avelyn stuck out her tongue at him and they laughed.

They'd decided to keep the project secret from the village. Avelyn's standing among the women would not be helped by revealing she sailed her own curragh. She would arrive at the dock before sunrise each morning, just after the fisherman had left, but before the village was sufficiently awake for roaming eyes and curious gossip. Making not a sound she would slip into the curragh, lie prone and out of sight beneath the thwarts, and place the food basket she always prepared between the oak frames.

Shelby would amble over, slide the craft into the water on the log rollers—hoist the sail himself while stepping deftly around her—and steer the boat out past the first headland.

Only then would Avelyn come out of hiding.

Today, having experienced the thrill of the wind's force against the sail from her unsavory position among the ballast, she was frantic to seize control of the craft. It was her fourth lesson.

"It's a perfectly splendid day and you've taught me how to sail already," Avelyn said. "Let's go see the cave."

A pained expression crossed Shelby's brow.

"Avelyn, lass, I'm sorry. There is no cave…at least not there. I made that story up, just like you suspected."

"Shelby!"

"Now, now. Listen to me. I understand what you're after. I've needed to get away a few times myself and I never had the whole village coming down on me as you do.

"So, if you need a place to escape to, a cave would be no good. They're damp and cold and hard to light a fire without smoking yourself out."

With one hand on the tiller and the other on the sheet, Avelyn regarded him curiously.

"Do you have somewhere else in mind?"

"I do, lass. You don't need a cave; you need an island."

"An *island?*"

"That's right. An island's far better than a cave. An island has its protection built-in because it's surrounded by water. And once you're on the island you don't have to stay hidden as you would in a cave. You're free to go about, build a fire, catch fish, explore. You need an island."

Avelyn considered this.

"You're right, Shelby. But where am I to find one? Or have you figured that out too?"

"There's Skellig's Rock, off to the west. It's more than a rock but not *much* more. There's Carnsore, as the fishermen call it. It'd be ideal, but that's the problem—the fishermen. Best fishing in the area and they'd never leave you alone out there. So that leaves Rathlin Island, due north of here—two hours sailing in a fair wind. But the fishermen have no use for it and it's too far for anyone else.

"Best of all, it's a large island. Took me nearly half a day to sail around it last I was there. There's even a cave on the island, but I'll tell you about that another time. Also, there's a pretty little cove on the south side—just what you need and no one to share it with."

"I think I've seen that island from the high cliffs," said Avelyn. "I used to think it was the land of the *Scotti* tribes, but finally realized it must just be an island. I'd love to sail there! Can we go now?"

"Head up as close to the wind as she'll bear, and hold that course."

Avelyn pushed the tiller to port as Shelby trimmed the sail.

"Nothing left to do now but lie back and enjoy the trip," he said. "Now lass, you didn't forget the food basket did you?"

Avelyn handed it to him with one hand, keeping the tiller secure with the other. The breeze was freshening and her long hair whipped across her face until finally she took a small length of twine and tied it back. The sea was developing a chop, but the curragh rose and fell gracefully with the waves.

Behind them, the mainland of Ireland faded in the morning mist.

16

"GAY? OF COURSE he's not gay!" Lauren was smiling beneath her exasperation.

"You're not saying he couldn't 'do it' with the prostitute are you?"

"No, Lauren," Andy began uncertainly. "It's just that the lady we hired couldn't figure out any other explanation," continued Andy, apologetically. "She was sitting at the bar flirting with your husband and then this old guy comes up—some kind of merchant marine officer apparently—sits down, and they started talking about history or something, and that was it. Michael lost suddenly all interest in her."

Lauren stood up and begin pacing.

"If I didn't know better I'd say there's a 'Michael Kittery Protection Society' out there trying to defeat us. Lord knows there are enough non-profits with the Kittery name in them."

"You're positive he's not gay?" pressed Andy. "That would sure make the divorce easy."

"Sorry, but I think I'd know if he was gay."

"Should we use another prostitute?" suggested Andy. "Maybe he'd gone to the bar specifically to meet that guy and the girl read it wrong."

"Perhaps," Lauren agreed. "But I'm tired of being in the dark on this thing. Something's going on with Michael. I can't figure it out, but something's different. He intended to work at Brookhaven through the summer and finish writing his dissertation. But when I called his office, explaining I'd been away and was trying to locate him, they told me the strangest thing. They said Michael had canceled all his plans for the summer term."

"Is that unusual?"

"It will delay his Ph.D. and he's never been willing to allow anything to do that. And this morning I got an email from him saying he had to take a long car trip and I might not hear from him for a few weeks—possibly longer. That's totally out of character. He travels occasionally, but usually just to a scientific conference or something over a weekend. Where could he be going for 'weeks or longer'?"

"OK, I think I should start routine surveillance again. That was my problem before, nothing ever changed. Mr. Kittery did nothing out of the ordinary."

"Yes," agreed Lauren, coming to a decision. "Start the surveillance again. You still have that micro-transmitter hidden in his car?"

"Yep. And remember I showed you how to access the location on-line? You pull up Google Earth and it's able to talk to the tracker program with an API."

"Of course. It's been fun watching him drive all over

Connecticut and Long Island, but now it sounds like he has a destination in mind."

"I won't try to tail him on a long car trip. We can just see where he goes, and make decisions accordingly. Maybe our luck's starting to turn."

Andy paused uncertainly.

"Lauren, there's one more thing I wanted to ask."

"Yes, Andy?" Lauren thought she knew.

"When this is over, and you get the divorce settlement, I'd like to invite you out for a bottle of champagne—on me!"

"Why, what a charming offer. I accept!"

Lauren's eyes twinkled and she smiled seductively at the detective. But she was thinking: *The moment I get my divorce settlement, I'm putting a thousand miles between myself and Andy Henderson.*

17

IT WAS DARK when Kitt turned down the long unpaved driveway to the Virginia farmhouse. He spotted a red Ford pickup with enclosed bed—just what Milo said he'd buy. Judging by the dents and rust spots visible even in the dim glare of the porch light, Kitt guessed most of the cash was still unused. Milo had obviously let himself in using the key which the real estate broker had left under the doormat.

They set to work the following morning, beginning with a tour of the property.

The farmhouse was in good repair. The renovated barn was a large, open room, with a floor of concrete.

"Whatever equipment we end up needing," said Kitt, "this place should hold it."

"For sure," agreed Milo. "I'll start building a workbench this afternoon."

Satisfied with the barn, they began a tour of the surrounding farmland. Heading south they crossed a small ridge and then had their breath taken away by the sudden appearance of the James River—nearly a half-mile wide—flowing right past the property.

"Some previous owner built this berm," said Milo. "I thought it looked a little unnatural. But you can bet your hip-waders that when the river floods this stretch of dirt's the only thing keeping water out of the living room."

A surprisingly-long jetty extended into the river and was apparently part of the property.

"Whoever built that setup knew the value of shipping by water," continued Milo. "Probably figured whatever was produced by the farm would be shipped downriver to Portsmouth rather than hauled out by truck. Smart idea too. Costs a hell of a lot less to ship by water."

"I'm sure," agreed Kitt.

"That dock looks solid enough to handle most any craft. Notice how it goes out fifty yards and then makes a T? That's so whatever ties up to it isn't broadside to the current."

"Why so sophisticated?" Kitt asked, squinting at the structure. "I'd think to get milk downstream wouldn't require much in the way of a dock."

"Not milk. Tobacco. This dock's been here awhile. I'll betcha it was put in by the old tobacco-grower himself. And let me tell you something, Kitt. This may look like just a river to you, but it's tidewater. They run river tows—barges—up the James all the way to Richmond. And when there's a need you could take a small freighter up this waterway. See those buoys out there?"

Milo pointed to a black can buoy floating 200 yards out from shore.

"That tells you it's a navigable waterway. They probably keep the channel dredged. My guess is at high tide you could dock anything with a draft less than thirty feet, and that's a good-sized vessel. The old man could probably load his tobacco right off that dock, and ship it anywhere in the world."

"So if we needed to bring in any heavy equipment that jetty could be useful."

"Made for it. I'm liking this place more and more."

Back in the house they sat down at the broad antique-pine dining table and planned their next move.

"Need any help hooking up that computer, or unloading your books?" Milo began.

"I could use a hand with the LCD monitor, but everything else is unloaded."

"Then here's the plan. We get to work immediately. Unpack, set up a place to study, and move in. I'm working on a list of provisions. Groceries, for starters. Plus I want to lay in a supply of miscellaneous stuff, lightbulbs, a tool chest, that kind of thing.

"Also, start making a list of what *you're* going to need. Maybe a slide rule or something?"

Kitt grinned.

"And when we've got our lists put together, I'll take on the job of procurement officer. That wide bed pickup may not look like much but it can haul cargo. I'll drive into Richmond and load up with whatever we need."

"Sounds good, Milo. I'll have a preliminary list by noon."

Milo stopped and looked at his business partner with a smile.

"So, Mr. Goddamned Smarty Pants Physicist, let's get this show on the road."

"Sure. But why the hurry?"

"Just this, Kitt. I'm fed up with the present. Lived here all my life. Now I'm ready for a vacation!"

18

LAUREN KITTERY SAT in her dining room and stared at the pulsing red dot on her laptop's screen. Her husband was now living in a farmhouse in Virginia—unfortunately not with a woman. Her detective was camped at a motel a few miles away, and keeping the farmhouse under observation several hours each day. From this, they'd learned that Michael's housemate was a guy who matched the description of the merchant marine officer who'd edged out the whore at Montauk.

Now the two of them were living in this secluded farmhouse, and working every day in the barn itself. And they'd brought in groceries, tools, materials and other supplies. The "road trip" that could have him gone for "weeks or longer" wasn't a road trip at all. It was a special project of some kind, happening in the Virginia countryside. But what? And how could Lauren use this information to her advantage?

She reviewed all the pieces of the puzzle, trying to understand how they fit together. A brilliant, and wealthy, young scientist suddenly abandons his research, walks away from his Ph.D. program, doesn't tell anyone what he's doing, and mysteriously and clandestinely sets up shop at a farmhouse hundreds of miles away. And works there secretly. With an elderly guy who runs all the errands.

What would make a young, independently-wealthy, scientist do something like that? She began pacing.

Not for the first time, Lauren found herself annoyed that her husband couldn't just be having an affair. It would make things so much simpler. Why did she have to marry a physicist, of all things? Everything in that world was so complicated! Why couldn't Michael be back in his lab, working with test tubes or particle beams, or lasers, or inventing some brilliant new—

She stopped pacing and gasped.

That was it. She'd guessed the secret. He *had* invented something. Something huge. Something so important it would justify walking away from his graduate program.

Yes, the pieces fit. It all made sense. Of *course* he had to go somewhere secret and isolated. He couldn't tell anyone. He had to test the invention, or build the prototype, or draw up a patent application, or any number of details. Her husband understood enough about the business world to know how to take these steps, and safeguard the value of whatever he'd invented.

Perhaps the older guy was a patent attorney, or mechanical engineer, or even a co-inventor. The hooker had mentioned something about Michael looking for an historian, but she'd probably misunderstood. *A patent attorney with some engineering expertise* was Lauren's guess.

So, all that was well and good, but how would it help with the divorce?

She returned to the dining room table and stared again at the flashing red dot. In a few moments, she had a plan.

19

MICHAEL KITTERY WAS ready for his first test. He'd built a miniature tokamak. He was using a small sample of Uranium 235, "borrowed" from Brookhaven as a source for neutrons. Using magnetic fields he grabbed the mutrinos being emitted and sent them into the tokamak. He had one chamber for collecting mutrinos and another for anti-mutrinos.

The point of the experiment was to see if he could send objects forward or backward in time. In either case, he theorized, the object should disappear visually. It should disappear just as certainly as all those particles disappeared for the Stanford and CERN researchers. That would be evidence it was moving in time.

In a moment of weakness at the grocery store, he'd picked up a bag of miniature Hershey chocolates, and— for lack of anything more appropriate—decided to use them

Wherever they ended up, they'd be appreciated, he reasoned.

He removed a Hershey bar from its wrapper and

inserted it into the anti-mutrino chamber. He flipped a switch.

Nothing happened.

That was disappointing. Was the device working? Kitt checked various instruments. Everything was working. The mutrinos weren't carrying off the Hershey bar. Maybe his whole theory was wrong. Or maybe only small collections of sub-atomic particles could be carried off—nothing with as much mass as a candy bar.

He tried it three more times, but the Hershey chocolate stubbornly refused to disappear. Then he tried the mutrino chamber—the one with forward-moving time particles. Same result. Nothing happened.

The young physicist was extremely frustrated. It wasn't working. The whole time-travel thing was a dud. The stupid Hershey bar had stayed in the present, and the only one who could enjoy the chocolate was himself. He pulled it out of the magnetic bottle and ate it.

He then unwrapped and ate three more, to compensate for his disappointment. He was about to unwrap a fourth, but instead—for no reason he could think of—he tossed it into the magnetic bottle containing the anti-mutrinos and hit the start switch.

The Hershey bar disappeared.

Most of it did.

Kitt gasped.

The Hershey bar and its foil wrapper were gone. The heavier paper wrapper on the outside was still there—now empty.

What the hell?

He unwrapped another one and put the naked chocolate into the tokamak. It went nowhere. Then he put in a fully-wrapped bar, hit the switch, and the same thing happened—the chocolate and foil wrapper disappeared. The outer paper wrapper was still there.

It was all about controlling for variables.

He took another bar, removed the paper wrapper, and put it in. It disappeared.

He put the paper wrapper in by itself. It went nowhere.

He removed the foil inner wrapper and—by itself—tried that. It disappeared.

The foil wrapper.

When the foil wrapper was included, the foil wrapper—*and anything inside it*—disappeared.

Foil? What was magic about foil? It was a sliver of aluminum—a very thin sheet of metal. Metal had special properties with respect to electromagnetic fields. But why would time-traveling mutrinos behave differently around metal?

Kitt started pacing, trying to concentrate his mind, which he already knew didn't concentrate well when it was forced to. It wandered, refusing to stay on topic. His eye glanced at the radio Milo had bought—for music and the occasional newscast while they worked. Kitt's mind was more interested in the radio than in the miniature time machine. He tried to force it back to unraveling the mutrino mystery, but it refused to budge.

He was becoming preoccupied with the damn radio. The more he tried to not think about the radio, the more he could only think about it. It was the lowest piece of low-tech imaginable—a stupid transistor radio that had been invented last century when they'd discovered transistors, and realized...

Kitt stopped in his tracks. He went over to the radio, reached out, and touched it, as if for reassurance. *Transistors.* Yes, that's what his mind was trying to tell him. That's where the secret lay: transistors—a type of semi-conductor. They only worked because of *quantum tunneling.*

And suddenly everything made sense. The time-traveling particles weren't staying around in this universe long enough to move the chocolate bar. They were only here for mere femtoseconds. And then—they were gone.

A few femtoseconds were enough time for a mutrino flux to surround sub-atomic particles. It was not enough time to surround a Hershey bar.

But if you introduced metal, everything changed. The mutrinos were dispersing throughout the metal using quantum tunneling, just as electrons did in semiconductors.

Kitt began pacing, letting the pieces of the discovery take shape in his mind.

You didn't need metal if you were merely trying to surround a sub-atomic particle—which is what they were doing at Stanford and CERN. But on larger scales, the mutrinos didn't have time to surround the object. On the other hand, if it was encased in metal, they *did* have time. Quantum tunneling—the same force which made that stupid radio (and a lot of other devices) work—was part of it. And the mutrinos likely had an affinity for metal. They were bonding with it—just enough to slow down their passage through our universe, and allowing them to encapsulate whatever was inside the metal.

So the metal itself disappeared, and anything it was surrounding—encapsulating—also disappeared. But the foil on the Hershey bar was not surrounding the outer paper wrapper. So the paper wrapper *got left behind.*

Armed with this knowledge, he walked back to the tokamak. He took a Hershey bar out of the paper wrapper but still within its aluminum foil sleeve, and placed it inside the magnetic bottle with forward-moving time particles. He hit the switch for an instant, it disappeared and then—and then…

It reappeared! He'd sent it a few seconds into the future, and then his time had caught up with it.

But the Hershey bars heading into history were gone forever. He'd never "catch up" to them because they were going the wrong direction.

His time machine worked. He could move significant amounts of mass forward or backward in time. All he had to do was *encase the mass in metal.*

And suddenly Michael Kittery knew how to build his time machine.

20

IT WAS AVELYN'S third trip to the island, and her first time sailing alone. Shelby's joints were acting up, and he'd urged her to go without him. The wind was moderate, out of the north. The sea was not rough. And the sense of freedom was limitless.

This is better than being up on the cliffs, she thought. *This is truly being alone; a place where I can relax completely.*

She was equidistant to both shores, a spot from which she could see the dark line of Rathlin on the far horizon, yet the Irish mainland had not vanished. Timing the moment carefully, she tacked the curragh, sweeping the tiller to starboard, pivoting the little craft's bow across the wind, easing the lateen sail and then hauling it in swiftly on the port side as it caught the breeze.

Avelyn's innate feel for the wind and the sea allowed her to nestle back against the transom, eyes closed, enjoying the warmth of the sun. She steered the curragh by sensing the air movement, and the action of the waves.

She loved reaching out with her senses, touching the elements around her.

As a Druid, at least as a follower of the old ways, touching the spirits of the Earth and Sea with her mind came naturally. It put her almost in a trance, this sublime awareness—this communion with—the life forces around her.

Yet it was so different from the Christian religion the abbot had raised her in. Jesus Christ and the Christian God were not something she could touch, or feel. They were—to her—abstract concepts. She'd dutifully learned all the trappings of being devout. She knew the prayers, the sacraments, and the liturgies. She could even read the Bible and found many of the passages hauntingly beautiful. She tried to be a good Christian—and she'd never admit she wasn't. Except maybe to herself, at moments such as this.

The day grew warm as the sun climbed out of the Irish mists, and soon she cast off her wool *brat*.

Avelyn's mind was relaxed, but it could not stay still. She let it drift to Shelby, and a smile appeared briefly, then to the women in the village which was not a pleasant thought. A chill seemed to come into the air, then. The visage of the old abbot—Father Conardy—took their place, and this calmed her.

Could she remember her real father? She tried, but it was too long ago. Yet she'd had a real father and mother once. They were gone and had been for years. She could not remember their faces, but she remembered a few images; tiny scraps of the past which had somehow survived—her mother's hugs, her father telling stories in front of the fire of the "worlds beyond," falling asleep in a warm and safe cottage. At the time she'd not realized how unbearably precious such moments were, and how quickly time stole them away.

By "worlds beyond," she now knew that he'd meant the land of the Scotti tribes across the Irish Sea. South of there was Angland itself, with the fabled kingdoms of Mercia and Wessex, ruled over by the tyrant Offa. And somewhere in Angland was the magnificent city of Londinium. Some said it was larger than a hundred Ballycastles, but of course, that was an exaggeration. No city could be that large—they'd never be able to feed themselves. But from her father's stories, initially, and later from what she learned at the monastery, she'd developed a desperate longing to visit such places. How could one learn of these things, and not wish to explore them?

She owed so much to the abbot and the monastery. She would have starved or died of the cough as had so many if they hadn't taken her in. For years she'd wondered why they'd done so, yet had been too afraid to ask—fearing that raising the question might force the issue and cause them to reconsider. If they ever abandoned her, she would join the many homeless that furtively prowled the streets of Ballycastle in search of food scraps thrown into the gutter. As if there would be food scraps in these times!

Yet after eight years of living under both the tutelage and protection of the priests, she could not keep the question inside any longer, even if asking would mean her downfall. Curiosity finally overpowered fear.

"Why did you take me in, Father?" she'd asked one

evening, over two years ago now. "I've never understood. And what do you want from me?"

Surprisingly, Father Conardy had not reacted as she'd expected. He had not wrinkled up his eyebrows and sucked in his cheeks as he did when a difficult question was posed. She had braced for that; braced for those wrinkled eyebrows as surely as a warrior braced for the fall of a broadsword. Yet none had fallen.

Father Conardy looked at her warmly and smiled softly.

"Why did we take you in? What do we want from you?" he repeated, his stern expression defeated by the grin that so often rested beneath the surface. "We wondered when you'd ask, and I suspect you've kept this inside for some time. I see in your eyes this is so.

"But it is the wrong question. You might better say 'What do you want with us?' For were it in our power to give, we surely would."

Avelyn could make nothing of this, except it did not seem to foretell her doom. Father Conardy had not been taken by surprise and it was almost as if his puzzling answer had been rehearsed.

"Your Grace," Avelyn replied softly, eyes downturned, "I beg of you to explain."

"Yes, it is time. Past time, perhaps. Very well." He slowly limped to the fireplace, turned the coals about with an iron, and sighed heavily.

He began his story still looking into the embers as if they helped him recall an ancient time.

"The first priest who came to Ballycastle was burned alive. It was over 200 years ago, and the good Lord Jesus had not yet come to these lands. The first priest arrived from the south, from the Kingdom of Munster, most likely, although those records are lost.

"We know only that he was hailed as an evil faerie, for he spoke against the pagan gods of your ancestors, and it was believed at that time only the faeries would be so foolish as to speak against a god.

"As was custom, the poor man was taken almost immediately after entering the town gates, for he stopped first and crossed himself in a way that made the townspeople suspicious. Food was in short supply then, much as it is now, and there was little tolerance for one who might offend the gods and cause the crops to fail yet again.

"All we know, Avelyn, was that he was burned the very day he entered the town, and it was many years before another priest followed his lead. But God was unwilling to see this land in darkness, and He caused others of our order to come hither and meet their fate as best they could. Six priests were burned in all."

Father Conardy looked away after reciting that grim statistic as if perhaps he too shared in the physical pain. Avelyn said not a word.

The old man sighed deeply, and the dimly-lit flames of the fire jumped and crackled as if in response.

"Anyway your father, Shanus, was first to raise a hand on behalf of the priests. 'Let him be!' he said after another priest had been seized and was being dragged towards the stake, calling on God to save him. Your father was not an important man; only a peasant like the others. The crowd that had gathered was stilled by his words not because he had authority, but because his statement was unexpected. 'Who would raise a hand for a priest?' they all wondered. And while they paused, uncertain, Shanus said something equally astounding. 'I do not believe this one is an evil faerie', he said. 'Let him stay here among us if he wishes. It would be wrong to burn him.'

"The people of Ballycastle were terrified of the evil faeries, at that time. You must understand that to realize what a great thing your father did."

The abbot paused and looked at Avelyn meaningfully.

"The fairies were blamed for sickness and death, and of course for the failure of the crops, or even for the actions of the baron in seizing young village girls. All these were caused by the faeries, as your people believed, and only the intercession the earth and sea spirits could protect them.

"But the Irish are not a vicious people, and your father used the right words in the few seconds granted. 'If he is not an evil faerie, it would be wrong to burn him,' and the townspeople couldn't disagree with this. For over a century it had lacked only one man to make this point.

"After that day the priests were left alone and soon more came, knowing the evil of Ballycastle was cleansed. That was how our order became established here. I arrived only seven years later but was treated with respect by the townspeople even then. Now, of course, it is us, the priests, whom they take care not to offend, and if the 'evil faeries,' as they persist in calling them, start to cause mischief, it is to our gate they come for succor. And of course in the Holy Jesus, they find it—whether their maladies be caused by the 'faeries' or by Satan, or most likely by themselves.

"But the point is that none of us would be here had it not been for your father's bravery, and that is something we will never forget. Surprisingly, he was cold to us afterward, and never even converted to Christianity, but that did not matter. God used him when it was needed. Shanus never asked for our gratitude, though it was always there, waiting to be given.

"So on the day both your parents died of the fever and you became an orphan there was little doubt what God required of us. We took you in—gladly—to discharge a debt so long owed. Yet it's little enough we have done."

Avelyn thought of that conversation now, as her curragh rolled gently to the waves and the sun shone on her face—eyes still closed in thought. That evening had been the awakening of her mind. No longer were priests the mysterious all-powerful entities who provided food, shelter, and—in repairing their vestments—an occupation of sorts.

Priests had once been vulnerable too. Yet if they could overcome their challenges, and rise to their present position of control over almost every aspect of Ballycastle life, then was there not hope for her as well? What might not she accomplish?

But so far, she'd accomplished little. She lived alone in a hut outside the abbey, a useful location for those increasingly-frequent times when too much ale had been drunk by one of the village youths, and unwelcome attentions resulted. Avelyn could flee swiftly to her small but safe home, knowing the sight of one or more strolling monks would quickly sober any pursuer.

Even the baron apparently knew of the special relationship between Avelyn and her benefactors at the monastery, for he had not sent for her. If he ever did, she would kill herself first, Avelyn vowed yet again. She was desperately grateful for these privileges, but instead of making her complacent they compounded her sense of destiny unfilled. Was all this protection merely to keep the priests' seamstress from harm, so she could patch their robes and bedding? What would her parents, dead now these nine years, think of her and the life she led?

What did she think?

Avelyn knew what the villagers thought: at seventeen, she should be married and having children and letting the priests look after their own sewing. And they were probably right. But that would mean an end to her freedom. No more walking up to the high cliffs overlooking the sea, carrying a picnic of bread and cheese, lying back in the heather and dreaming of the "worlds beyond." No more sailing her curragh. That would all come to an end with a husband and children, and the toil that dragged down young girls married at fourteen and fifteen to the point where they looked aged and bent when they were only slightly older than Avelyn. They did not seem happy, but was she happy?

Marriage could not be postponed forever. Even Father Conardy had been making suggestions that she should try to "meet more of the village folk," and Avelyn knew what he'd meant.

To be fair, not all of the young men were drunk when they approached her. Sometimes she'd be off on an errand,

and Larkin or Cary or one of the Flanagan boys would materialize, offering to carry her water bucket or bag of wools or just accompany her to wherever she might be heading. Admittedly, she enjoyed their attention.

There were even times she would lie on her straw pallet with the peat fire all but extinguished as the night advanced, and she would cry with loneliness. It was then she would think about Larkin or Cary and imagine one of them lying next to her. But in the morning she would shudder at the thought of becoming someone's possession and being forced to give up everything—even her studies in the monastery. Any contact with the priests outside a confessional would be gone if she were to marry.

But she had to marry. Ballycastle's traditions were too strict. Her freedom was temporary. And whatever was out there for her, across the sea, was probably just in her imagination.

Rathlin Island was close now, and the mainland had disappeared. Yet, she could feel its pull. It was calling her to return; calling her back from the island; calling her to abandon foolish dreams.

Worst of all, she didn't even know what those dreams were.

21

MILO WAS BUILDING a tool rack in the barn when Kitt poked his head in.

"Hey carpenter, let's take a walk! I need fresh air and advice, not necessarily in that order."

"I'm your man, Kitt. Those sub-atomic particles got you down again? Should I bring my slide rule?"

"Very funny."

"OK, I'll bring a six-pack from the fridge, instead."

"Yes, that will be more useful, given what I need to discuss."

Milo looked at him sharply and then went to retrieve the beer.

They walked underneath a blazing sun, soon arriving at the top of the berm that overlooked the James River. A loaded barge, pushed by a small tug, passed downstream.

"What'd I tell you, Boss? This river's navigable."

"Milo, I've reached an uncomfortable conclusion."

Milo popped open a beer and handed it to Kitt, taking another for himself. He kicked off his shoes, sat down in the grass, and gazed over the river, hoping to catch sight of another vessel.

"Let's hear it."

"The time machine we're building is based on mutrinos, as I explained. The key is to surround an object with enough mutrinos or anti-mutrinos so that it's essentially picked up and carried off by the particles."

"Like an army of ants carrying off a dead locust," suggested Milo.

Kitt grimaced. "Yeah, I guess. But in our case, the time machine has to be big enough to carry two people inside."

"So you called me out here to help decide the color of the upholstery?"

Kitt smiled. "Here's the thing. We're going to collect mutrinos inside a tokamak—that's a device that uses magnetic fields to contain particles."

"A taco-what?"

"Tokamak. They're machines used to—among other things—contain a fusion reaction."

"A hydrogen bomb!" Milo looked up, alarmed.

"No, a *contained, controlled* reaction. As in, a reactor based on fusion, not fission."

"Uh, OK," said Milo, hesitantly, trying to understand where this was going.

"Anyway, tokamaks—which some people call magnetic bottles—are built to contain protons. Those protons have mass. And in a tokamak, they are heated to very high temperatures, like in the sun. So you need strong magnetic fields to contain them. That means they have to be pretty big. We'll be containing mutrinos and anti-mutrinos which have far less mass than protons and can be at room temperature. So we can get by with much smaller magnetic fields. That's why our tokamak can be about the size of a steamer trunk, maybe."

"Is this something we buy or build?"

"Build. I've already built a very small one, for testing. That's what that weird thing is on the workbench. For our purposes, I'll build a bigger one. I'm pretty good at it. For my master's thesis, some grad students and I built one that's so compact it's still on display at the MIT Museum."

"Very impressive," acknowledged Milo. "So what's the problem?"

"The tokamak will hold the particles, but first we have to obtain them."

"Where do we obtain them?"

"Mutrinos are emitted continuously, by neutrons."

"Neutrons," said Milo, getting more confused by the minute.

"That was the big discovery a year ago. For some reason, neutrons emit mutrinos continuously. And they're emitted in pairs, a positively-charged mutrino, and a negatively-charged anti-mutrino."

"I'm with you, Boss, keep going," said Milo, having no idea what Kitt was talking about.

"So it's pretty obvious what we have to do here."

"You can see it a mile away."

Milo suspected his sarcasm was being lost.

"Our full-size tokamak will have two chambers, with opposite magnetic charges. As the quantity of neutrons increases, the mutrinos in each chamber will increase, becoming a plasma of charged particles. They won't stay around long enough to move us in time unless we can surround ourselves with metal. Do that and the mutrinos will flow over it instantly, using quantum tunneling, and *that* will allow us to move in time."

"It's so simple, Boss, I can't believe no one else thought of it."

"But you see the problem?"

"Yeah," said Milo, wondering what the problem was. "I totally do."

"The problem isn't where you get the mutrinos. It's where do you get the neutrons?"

"Where *do* you get neutrons," Milo asked, genuinely curious.

"You get neutrons from a fission reactor. When an atom of uranium in a fission reactor absorbs a slow-moving neutron it becomes unstable, splits apart into smaller atoms, releases energy, and produces two or three extra neutrons. If you get too many neutrons you have an atomic bomb. In fission reactors, there are control rods made of materials that absorb neutrons, so the whole thing doesn't blow up."

"Very glad someone figured that out," noted Milo.

Kitt continued, almost talking to himself. "If we can apply a magnetic field to one of those neutron-stuffed control rods, then the mutrinos and anti-mutrinos will peel off in opposite directions because they have opposite electrical charges. We can use two chains of electromagnets to direct the flow into our two magnetic bottles, inside the tokamak. But the key to the whole thing is a fission reactor."

"So is that the problem?"

"Yes, we're going to need one."

"OK, and I'm guessing they aren't small enough to fit in a suitcase. And obviously, it needs to travel with us in our vehicle. This means the vehicle's going to have to be bigger than a two-man Porsche, which means we'll need even more mutrinos to move it as well. Right?"

"The additional mutrinos are easy. Once we have a reactor, even a small one, we'll be able to generate as many mutrinos as we want. But let's leave that problem for a moment, 'cause there's another one."

"I see why you needed to take a walk. Have another beer, Kitt."

"Thanks. OK, let's assume we've figured out our first problem. We now have a vehicle with a reactor in it, and we've got enough mutrinos to start moving in time.

"Now my guess is that moving in time isn't much different than other kinds of movement. It's just a different dimension.

"So here's the problem. What if we climb into that Porsche you were just talking about, take it up to sixty miles an hour, and drive it into a brick wall? What would happen?"

"We'd have a smashed Porsche."

"Exactly. Now take that same Porsche. It's parked, but you move it in time—backwards to a point where there used to be a brick wall."

"Jesus!" said Milo. "I see the problem. But we can't know every physical object that's existed in a certain place back through history. That's impossible."

"Well," said Kitt, "maybe not impossible. What if we were out in deep space, like halfway between the Milky Way and the Andromeda galaxy. Seems I read once that in intergalactic space you're looking at about one hydrogen atom per thousand cubic miles. Our time machine could probably absorb the occasional hit from a hydrogen atom without too much trouble."

"Well, yeah, I guess that's a solution. What do you want me to do, hijack a space shuttle?"

"Not exactly."

Milo looked up sharply.

"No," said Kitt. "Nice as it would be, I think intergalactic space is out of the question. But what about water?"

"Water?"

"Yeah. Water's not like a brick wall. If you plunged into water at full speed, you'd suffer major damage. But if the Porsche were already immersed in water, and you started moving it slowly, accelerating up to maybe ten miles an hour, you'd probably lose your rearview mirror but probably that Porsche would be streamlined enough to take it.

"Now, why can the Porsche go through water but not through a brick wall? Because the water is malleable and displaceable. The water can go *around* the Porsche."

Kitt was talking so fast, he hadn't so much as touched his beer.

"Now let's apply that to our situation. We start our journey in time immersed in water. If water continues to surround that space back into history, then we're probably in good shape. We'd be displacing water in the dimension of time, not of space, but my guess is the laws of physics would work the same way."

"Well, Kitt, I don't see how that solves the problem. How do you know that where there is water in today's time, there will be water 100 years ago, or whatever?"

"Was the Atlantic Ocean where it is 100 years ago? Let me rephrase that. Obviously, there've been changes; banks collapsing, estuaries broadening, that kind of thing. I'm talking about the middle of the Atlantic. Was there water there 100 years ago?"

"Well, of course there was."

"OK, how 'bout 12,000 years ago?

"Yeah, you would have to go back over 100 million years before you need to worry about the middle of the Atlantic not being water. So is that the plan, float the time machine out in the ocean and let her rip?"

"Well, what would you think?"

"I see one big problem. Sure, there's been an Atlantic Ocean out there for a long time, but have you forgotten it's not been sitting still?"

"You mean storms?"

"No, I mean a few little things like the rotation of the earth. Where the Atlantic is right now, you're going to find the Gobi desert in about twelve hours. And if that weren't enough, the earth goes around the Sun, last time I checked. Isn't it true our solar system is part of a rotating galaxy? That's got to account for more movement yet. And how 'bout the big bang? All the galaxies are moving away from each other, aren't they?"

"Very good, Captain. Yes, there's all kinds of motion

going on out there, but it won't be a problem for time travel. You see, time is subject to the same laws of inertia and momentum as is mass. At least I believe it must be. Time dimensions are connected to the three physical dimensions we normally move in. That cloud overhead may have traveled a few miles west by the time the sun goes down, but it's not going to be over central Asia. Time dimensions are the same. They turn with the Earth, they revolve around the sun with the Earth, and they follow all those other motions, just the way our atmosphere stays with us."

"OK, you're the physicist, so I'll take that on faith." Milo dismissively waved the words away, like a pesky mosquito. "Then what you're saying is we start in the middle of the Atlantic, we go back a few years, and we're still in the middle of the Atlantic?"

"Yes. Maybe not in the identical position, because there may be some ebbs and flows I haven't accounted for. But I think it's a fair bet we'd be in water and not on land."

"OK, we need a nuclear reactor built into our time machine, so it's going to be a big mother. I don't know how we get the reactor, but maybe you've got some ideas. Then we put the whole thing on a raft or something and float it to the middle of the Atlantic, so we don't go bashing through some 19th-century brick wall. Is that about it?"

"That's about it."

"OK, so what do you need to build your tacomatic thing and the rest of it? What's our shopping list?"

Kitt gazed out over the river in silence.

"A few moments ago," he finally said, "you asked if I wanted a space shuttle hijacked."

"Yeah, I thought I was kidding. I *was* kidding, right?"

"I don't want a space shuttle. But there is something I'd like you to hijack for me."

"What?"

"A nuclear submarine."

22

MILO JUMPED UP from the grass.

"You want me to hijack a *what*?"

"A nuclear submarine. Is it possible?"

"Of course it's not possible. Is this a joke?"

"Not at all. I've given it a lot of thought. A nuclear submarine is what we need. It already has a reactor built-in, so there goes that problem. On a sub, we're inside a cocoon of metal, which is what we need for the time-flux to surround us. A sub lives in water. And it's self-contained and can operate independently of land. We need a submarine, Milo. You figure out how to get one."

"Jesus Christ, Boss, which end do you want me to begin at?"

"Which end of what?"

"The list of fifty reasons why this won't work."

"Start at the beginning," Kitt said, patiently, reaching at last for his beer. Between the two of us, we should be able to solve a mere fifty problems. And when we get to the end, we'll be time travelers. Everything else is done. Give me a nuclear submarine and we're on our way."

"'Give me a nuclear submarine and we're on our way,'" Milo mimicked in sing-song. "OK, let's warm up with this one. A U.S. Navy submarine carries a crew of 150, give or take. So how do you explain to them why you—a civilian—are driving their submarine?"

"I'm not going to be driving it. You are. Didn't you tell me you used to be an officer on a submarine?"

"So what? Being a junior officer on a World War II boat isn't quite the same as commanding a *Virginia*-class attack sub."

"Captain, you're not thinking creatively. The crew will know how to run it. You just have to tell the officers what to do. Like 'Let's go,' and 'Let's stop.'"

"Why would they obey me? Forty-five-year-old lieutenant stripes won't carry much weight."

"No, but an admiral's uniform will."

Milo stared at Kittery, speechless. Then he turned and walked towards the river, his beer forgotten. Reaching the shore he picked up a rock and threw it far out into the James. Then he threw another rock. After three rocks he came back and sat down.

"So what you're asking me to do," he said, "is impersonate an officer, get myself aboard a U.S. Navy submarine, give orders that will put me in command, and then steal her away so we can play our time games with a billion-dollar piece of hardware."

"Yes."

"Can I be blunt?"

"Have I ever stopped you?" Kitt was half smiling

"I'm probably the best man for the job."

"I figured that."

"Problem is, no sub captain will relinquish command to anyone, even an admiral, without receiving clearance from ComSubLant."

"What's ComSubLant?"

"Command, Submarine Forces, Atlantic. ComSubLant issues orders to subs via coded radio signal. Soon as I get aboard, the first thing the captain will do, unless he's already been notified, is send a dispatch to ComSubLant asking for verification that he's supposed to take orders from me."

"You mean a simple radio signal is all we need? It can't be that easy!"

"It's not a simple radio signal. It's a *coded* radio signal. If you don't have the code then you're out of luck. And that code is one of the best-kept secrets in the military. It has to be, to prevent maniacs like us from stealing submarines."

"So if you could somehow break into the military's communication system, you could send a message relaying orders to a sub."

"Sure, and if pigs had wings, they could fly."

"Remember back in New York? I was telling you about burnout, and how my best friend dropped out of Yale and re-designed the Pentagon's security system, using improved encryption algorithms?"

"Rings a bell."

"He's not just my best friend. He owes me."

"What's he owe you?"

"I met him when I was a freshman. It was our first semester, and he was going to have to drop out. His family back in India had some business setbacks, and they couldn't afford the tuition. I covered it for him—all the way through his Ph.D. which he'll complete next fall."

"How much did that cost?"

"Half a million, roughly. He's promised to pay it back but I've told him it doesn't matter. Every time I see him he says he's going to pay it back—lots of guilt, there, I think.

"Wait, are you saying the guy who created the Pentagon's communication codes owes you a huge favor? What are the chances of that?"

"Better than you'd expect. Most of those who go to Yale doctoral programs in math and science end up in high positions like that—you know, working for the Pentagon or military contractors or tech companies. I've done favors for a lot of them—monetary favors. It makes me feel less guilty about my inherited wealth if I can sort of run my own charity with some of the money."

"Kitt, if you can break into the Pentagon's communication systems, I've got your submarine."

23

BACK AT THE farmhouse, Kitt dialed Amit's number. The mathematician answered immediately.

"Hey, Kitt, what's up?"

"Quite a bit. Are you in New Haven?"

They chatted casually for a few moments and then Kitt popped the question.

"Hey, Amit, I'm hoping you can help me with something. Are you someplace you can talk privately?"

"Yeah, I'm in my apartment. Whatcha need? Got a math problem out there at Brookhaven you can't solve?"

"Not exactly. Look, Amit, this is a pretty big deal. I'm going to ask you for a huge favor, it's going to sound weird as hell, but I can't explain why I need it. It's just something I need you to trust me on."

"Oh, hell, Kitt." Amit paused a moment as if to get his words right. 'Dude, I'd trust you over any person on Earth, and I think you know why. And you can ask me any favors you want—as often as you want. At least until I've paid you back what I owe you. Ask away."

"This has to do with your work with the Pentagon, on those mutating-algorithm encryption systems."

"Sure, what about them?"

"You told me once that anytime you design a security system, you build a backdoor—so if the whole thing goes rogue—like SkyNet in the *Terminator* movies—and it won't let anyone in, you can still access it and fix the problem."

"Yep. I never mention it to clients, but I consider it *best practices* in my line of work. You just never know."

"Let me cut to the chase, here. I need to send a communication—a set of orders—to a US Navy submarine. It needs to come from ComSubLant, which is the—"

"I know what ComSubLant is."

"OK."

"Kitt, why the hell do you need to send orders from ComSubLant to a nuclear submarine?"

"Before I answer that, can you do it?"

"Sure. I can use my backdoor—which is hidden so well it's impossible to find—and generate any communications I want throughout the system. Once you're in at Command Authorization level—which I can get to, you can do it easily. Now can you answer the question? What the hell are you doing?"

"And this is where the favor comes in, Amit. I can't tell you. But I can tell you I'm not some lunatic trying to start WW3 or anything. What I'm involved in is a special project—nothing to do with warfare or weapons—and as part of it, I need to send orders to one of the Navy's submarines."

"You can't tell me why?"

"The secrecy on this is so high, I couldn't tell God why."

Kitt decided to play the professional-pride card.

"On the other hand, there's no way I want to cause trouble for you. If there's any way they could trace what you did…"

"*Trace it?* You've got to be kidding. No client has ever found one of my backdoors. They're impossible to find because I spread the code randomly—inserted at weird places over millions of lines. Then I comment-it out to make people think it does something else—which it also does."

"So you camouflaged the pieces in plain sight, by making them look like they do something else."

"Precisely."

"So there'd be no risk to you, personally or professionally or legally—since no one could find the backdoor and tie it to you."

"No risk at all."

"Amit, do this favor for me, and the half-million has been paid back."

There was a pause, and then Kitt heard a long whistle, as Amit internalized the offer.

"Did you just say I do this favor for you, and we're even?"

"Yep."

"Kitt, do I have your word of honor that what you're doing is OK? You know, on the level?"

"Here's what I can say. If I *could* tell you what I'm doing—which I can't—but if I *could*, you'd have no problem with it. I give you my word of honor on that. And I think you know me well enough to know that my word of honor is worth a hell of a lot more to me than half a million dollars."

"I do know that."

There was silence, and Kitt allowed him time to come to the inevitable conclusion.

"Oh, hell. Without you, I'd be back in Chennai waiting tables and we both know it. Sure, why not. And it'll be nice being debt-free. OK, I'm in. How do we handle it?

"Within a week, I'll send you the message that needs to be delivered, and who to deliver it to, within the communications system."

"And then?"

"Then next time I'm in New Haven, we'll go to that Chicago-style pizza place, and I'll buy the first pitcher of beer. You can buy the second."

"And you'll buy the third, right?"

They both laughed.

"Can he do it?" asked Milo after Kitt hung up the phone. "*Will* he do it?"

"Yes and yes. We just decide which sub we want—maybe you can use your contacts to figure that out—and then we write the orders and send them to Amit. Piece of cake."

"Care for a suggestion?"

"Shoot."

"Fifty miles downstream is the Navy base at Norfolk,

with one of the largest submarine pens on the Atlantic coast. In fact—" Milo's face lit up. "This is going to be too easy! I dress up as an admiral, and we send orders to one of the subs based in Norfolk that I'm coming aboard to take command. The first thing I do is conn her right up here to our pier! I'll check, but I'm pretty sure the James has enough depth in the channel. I'll figure out some excuse to give the captain. We can dock right here at the farm, haul the equipment aboard—and we're gone!"

"Perfect!"

"OK, Boss, this is looking pretty good. But there's still one more problem."

"What's that?"

"How do we explain to the officers and crew about moving in time? If we do explain it, there goes the secrecy. And if we don't, aren't they going to get spooked at what they might see?"

"They won't see a thing. The Atlantic Ocean is the Atlantic Ocean."

"Well, sure, as far as the water goes. But I assume we're going to be making landings—or at least using the periscope. Someone's going to see a clipper ship or something."

"Well, I doubt we'll go back that far, but one of your first orders will be to restrict the use of the periscope. And landings can be made on isolated coasts, where contact with people will be minimal. If anyone does see anything out of the ordinary, we'll just make up a reasonable explanation. The truth would never occur to them."

"Wait a minute, Boss. You think you can hijack a nuclear submarine, take command, move it back and forth in time, and then just walk away with no member of the crew being the wiser?"

"Yes, Captain," said Kitt smiling. "Or should I say, *Admiral?* With your help, that's exactly what I think we can do."

24

Sognefjord, Norway.

RISE—PULL—DIP. RISE—PULL—DIP.

Following a big meal, that rise—pull—dip motion was enough to put a person to sleep, thought Kren, watching the oars in their elliptical path. At least one person had already succumbed. Their commander, Kren's uncle Torsten, was lying on a sack of provisions near midships, eyes closed. Kren doubted he was asleep. It was more like his uncle to feign sleep, to impress the younger ones with his equanimity at the start of a sea voyage.

Kren glanced back towards shore. They were still there, waving their long poles side to side in a parting gesture to the fleet of eight longboats. He wondered where that tradition had come from. But there were at least a hundred of them, swaying back and forth like a woman's skirt in a dance. And the bonfire was roaring, to light the way of the warriors. Kren appreciated the thought, but when they rounded the first headland it would be the last they saw of the fire.

Their destination was a land only glimpsed from a distance by others. Those who'd fought the Scotti tribes claimed to the southwest was a large island-nation known as Ireland.

Torsten, chief of their village, owned a farm but found conquering new lands more rewarding than watching crops grow. So the ships were provisioned and crewed, the course was charted, the bonfire lit, and finally they were off. Kren could see Sigrid, Torsten's wife, standing apart from the rest. His uncle had asked her to stand motionless so she'd be easier to spot.

But not if his eyes were closed, Kren thought, bitterly.

There was small chance Kren could marry. A birth defect limited movement in his left arm, so he could never wield a sword or ax properly, or become a warrior.

"The Gods have spoken," Torsten pronounced. "You will never fight in battle. But the sea? Our ships are no less important than our swords. Wield a ship as your weapon, Kren. There is no dishonor in such a path."

Perhaps. But women preferred warriors to cripples. Even so, he took that path, and learned quickly he belonged at sea.

"You'd be happiest on a voyage that never ended," Torsten once remarked, and Kren knew it was true. Now he was a navigator, a full sailing master, and the youngest in anyone's memory.

He walked forward, not caring about those on shore. Kren rested one arm against the tall bow piece, its head carved in the shape of a laughing Valkyrie, and regarded it with distaste.

Its unusual height created windage too far forward. He'd have to move ballast so the longboat's keel would cut deeper at the bow.

*

Two days later, the fleet came to the mouth of the Sognefjord. The first gusts of wind smashed against the ships with a fury that frightened the young men who would call this voyage their first.

Towering ocean waves lifted the bow of *Freya's Song* and then as if reconsidering, dropped it carelessly into the waiting trough. But the craft was well designed, and exceptionally well built. Its fine bow cut the waves and softened the motion. Its long keel held their course. Kren gave an order to one of the crew and the large square sail opened, crackling and snapping until it was secured by the braided reindeer-hide sheets, and trimmed tightly against the wind.

Now the vessel heeled far to starboard and several of the younger men shouted with alarm until they were silenced by others. Kren ordered the oars brought inboard and lashed to the bulwarks. The shields (which had a similar function on land) were brought into position and set outboard of the oar scuppers, making it difficult for the waves to gain entrance.

Kren—as was his right—took the tiller from the steersman, and moved the helm hard to port. The craft fell off the wind several degrees. A large wave crashed broadside into the vessel, sending cold spray over those on the windward side. Kren tasted the salty residue and was exhilarated by the cold.

Torsten gave him a nod and then, perhaps to reassure the others, walked resolutely up to the bow and took hold of the Valkyrie's neck as if to draw strength from its spirit. He stared with deliberation out towards their destination.

Kren wondered what it would be like, this "Ireland." Some called it the Land of the Celts, whatever they were. Would it have high mountains, as did the place of his birth? Or fields of grain like the land of the Danes? Would the towns and settlements be wealthy or impoverished? Would their inhabitants fight his uncle's kind of battle, or capitulate and seek to ransom themselves as did so many in the land of the Franks? Many will die regardless, he knew, finding the thought depressing.

Torsten rejoined him by the tiller.

"This is more like it," said Kren, smiling "Being trapped in the fjord feels like being inside a crypt."

The Valkyrie smashed into the crest of the next wave, and the water dripped from its mouth, foretelling the blood that would soon be spilled.

"That girl's as eager as you, Kren!" said Torsten, chuckling.

The Valkyrie plunged again into the waves, drank deeply, and stared ever westward. But towards what, Kren did not know.

25

AMERICAN AIRLINES FLIGHT 228, from LaGuardia, landed harshly on runway 34 at Richmond International Airport. Lauren's head bounced against the window, forcing her out of a favorite daydream. She was sitting in a courtroom as the shriveled old judge read the verdict: *So the court finds in favor of the Plaintiff, Mrs. Kittery, and awards her the damages sought in the divorce pleading…*

She exited the fantasy reluctantly

The plane parked at the gate, the passengers rose up almost as one, and a middle-aged man in a business suit intercepted Lauren's attempt to wrestle her carry-on from the overhead.

"Why, thank you, sir!" Lauren smiled warmly.

"My pleasure, ma'am! First time in Richmond?"

"It's the first time I've met such friendly people here." Lauren gave him the benefit of her eyelashes.

"Oh, I find that hard to believe!"

"Just bad luck I guess,"

"Maybe your luck's changing."

"Maybe it is," said Lauren, with a teasing smile.

"Well, ma'am, friendly's my middle name! And Andy's my first name. Pleased to meet you!"

Lauren knew other men nearby were envious.

"Andy! Why that's my husband's name, and he's waiting for me just past security! Bye!"

Lauren enjoyed the stares as she walked towards the exit, never tiring of the game.

But the private detective was not waiting just past security. This was a surprise visit.

She rented a car and soon was following GPS directions to the Shenandoah Motor Lodge near Three Forks. She knew the address because his expense reports included copies of the receipts. And for what she had in mind, she wanted to show up unexpectedly, announce her plan, and start executing on it before the detective could think of reasons why it wouldn't work, or was illegal, or something.

She had her own room at the Shenandoah. She'd grimaced when making the reservation via *Expedia* the day before. It was a two-star dive with little kitchenettes, and knotty-pine décor that might have been fashionable in the fifties. But she could survive anything for one night.

Lauren pulled into the parking lot at nine p.m.—safely after dinner hour. She didn't need tedious conversation at some nearby greasy spoon. This place was out in the sticks; twenty minutes off Interstate 95. Did they even have restaurants around here? It didn't matter. She'd be back at the airport for a mid-morning return flight and could have breakfast there.

After checking into her room, she changed quickly

into a pair of Ralph Lauren jeans, Burberry sneakers, and a white, neatly-pressed button-down shirt. Her functional and spacious black purse with a shoulder strap had all the tools she required the evening: an iPhone with camera, and a flashlight. She left her room, walked three doors down to Unit #5, and knocked on the door. It opened.

"Well, hello there!" she gushed, warmly.

"Lauren, my God! Lauren, what the hell are you doing here?"

"Surprise visit!"

"Well, I couldn't be more surprised. Or pleased. Come in, c'mon in! Look, it's kind of a mess, I wasn't expecting…"

"It doesn't matter."

Lauren tried to convince herself it didn't, as she glanced around the little efficiency apartment that a single guy had been living in, and cooking in, for weeks.

"It's just, this was the closet place to the farmhouse. I know it's not much to look at, but…"

"But it saves tons on expense money, so you don't see me complaining, right?" Lauren grinned.

They sat together at the small dining table with two folding chairs.

"Yeah, to be honest, I'd feel guilty staying in anything more expensive, because I sure haven't produced much for you. I was just there today. No change. Michael works in the barn all day, and the old guy mostly does errands, small tasks, and so forth."

Lauren raised her hand to interrupt.

"Hold on. I've figured out what they're doing. And I've figured out how to use it to our advantage."

"Seriously? Well, that's the best news I've heard for a while."

"That's why I came down. Now, let me explain…"

Lauren reviewed her insight about an invention, and how it answered all the questions, like leaving the Ph.D. program and moving to some isolated location.

"I'm sure you're right, Lauren. It makes total sense. Wow. I can't believe I didn't think of it myself."

"Well, hey, we make a good team, right?"

Andy grinned. "Yeah, we sure do. So, what's the plan for how this helps us?"

"Just this. Look at the lengths to which my husband's gone, to hide everything. For some reason, the secrecy element is critical. He wouldn't have moved to a farmhouse hundreds of miles away if it weren't."

"Good point."

"So all we have to do is threaten to expose him. And to do that, we just need a little more evidence than we already have. We just need to get into that barn, take some pictures, maybe swipe some backup drives, grab paper schematics, anything we can easily put our hands on. Even if the backups are encrypted we can threaten to hire cyber experts who specialize in cracking that kind of thing. But I don't think we'll even need to. We just let him know we're on to him, we know he's working secretly on an extremely valuable new invention, and that we're going to turn over everything we have to CNN to spread to the world. The media loves stories of uber-rich people with secrets, so they can expose them."

"And Michael recognizes the threat and grants you

a divorce with the settlement money you need. It makes sense. This is probably even better leverage than pictures of him in bed with a hooker."

"I think so. This would threaten everything he's doing."

"Look, I've been in the barn. I was able to make a skeleton key to unlock the door. I've been going in at night, about once a week, but haven't learned much. They've been making some kind of machine, for sure. Now it's disassembled and they have packing crates which I think they're going to use to move it somewhere."

"So we only just got here in time, if they're about to move it."

"Exactly. So do you want me to go in tonight and take pictures and so forth?"

"No. Better if I do it. You can drive me there tonight, but keep the car hidden, and just take me far enough in where you can point out the barn. Give me the key."

"OK, but why do you want to do this alone?"

"It's not impossible we could be discovered. If he finds you, or the two of us, trespassing on his property and stealing secrets, the power balance changes. He might have a criminal case against us. He could call the police. It would just be messy as hell."

"But if it's you, alone?"

Lauren smiled innocently. "Show me the law that says it's illegal for a young wife, who's essentially been abandoned, to be trying to find her husband? How will that play with a jury?"

Andy grinned. "I see you've thought this through. So we go in tonight?"

"Yep, but I want to make sure everyone's asleep. Maybe around three or four in the morning."

"So in the meantime?"

I've got a room here, so let's both try to get a few hours of sleep. Let's be driving away at 2:30, so set your alarm accordingly. I'll knock on your door at that time.

"I'll be ready. Look, Lauren, I hope this isn't a wildly inappropriate thing to say, and I apologize if it is."

"Say whatever you wish."

"It's just that, well, I was thinking when all this is behind us, maybe the next time the two of us are at a motel we wouldn't have to be in separate rooms."

Lauren stared at him for a moment, letting his insecurities grow. Then she smiled.

"That certainly *was* an inappropriate thing to say. But the truth is, I was having the same thought. Good night, Andy."

She winked at him and slipped out the door quickly.

26

THE INTERCOM BUZZER sounded five minutes after Perry Hamilton fell asleep which, in his experience, was when it always sounded.

But it was unusual in port, with the sub tied to the dock. Hamilton was thankful he'd broken the habit of jumping out of bed and cracking his head on the ceiling. Some ship designer, damn his soul, had decided that a human being—captain or not—required little headroom while sleeping. So the captain had to bend forward eight inches before swinging his legs down and standing up. It was a minor thing, but it had taken months to learn, especially with the buzzer going nuts.

"Captain here!" he barked into the intercom, hoping his voice sounded like that of a serious officer mildly disturbed to be interrupted during a study of important ship's business.

"Sorry to wake you, Skipper."

Hamilton grimaced. His executive officer Mitch Simpson always knew when he'd been asleep.

"We just got a Priority One from ComSubLant. Your eyes only."

"On my way."

The captain sat on the edge of his bed for nearly ten seconds, which was a long time for a captain to sit on his bed with a Priority One message waiting. But Hamilton knew what it contained. When a boat was issued op orders for a patrol the message was always sent Priority One even when—as in this case—the boat was tied to the dock in Norfolk, the world was at peace, and the patrol itself little more than a glorified training exercise.

He slipped on trousers, tucked in his shirt, ran the requisite hand through his hair, and decided against wearing shoes.

Another tradition, important in its time, held that a submariner would never be criticized for not wearing shoes. Shoes made noise. Noise was both a submarine's greatest friend and greatest enemy, depending on who was making the noise.

Hamilton did not believe that wearing shoes in the control room would cause an enemy attack boat, sitting on the other side of Norfolk harbor, to pinpoint their position and fire a spread of torpedoes into *Chrysalis*. But the tradition spoke for itself and he would lose no respect by adhering to it, especially at one o'clock on a Sunday morning.

In fact, the captain realized that his choice of socks-only was a slap in the face to Mitch. If he couldn't fool the XO into thinking he'd been up working hard on classified matters, he could at least show he was indifferent to whether anyone knew he'd been called from his bed or not. Indifference was another attribute of senior officers and would serve equally well.

Hamilton stepped out of his cabin, walked ten yards to the control room, and decided to carry the ploy to its natural end by yawning conspicuously.

"Coffee, Captain?"

"Thanks, XO. Can't remember when I've been so sound asleep."

Hamilton caught a few smiles from the enlisted men on duty at their consoles. They were a fine team. Morale was excellent. And they knew the ship. The captain had no doubt they could take *Chrysalis* 10,000 miles to the Indian Ocean, drive her in circles for three months, and bring her home again.

That, Hamilton also knew, was exactly what the orders he was about to read would dictate. Maybe it wouldn't be the Indian Ocean. Maybe the North Atlantic, or even the Bering Strait. But it wouldn't matter because they'd be submerged for most if not all of the time.

With the satisfaction of a man who knows with certainty what the future is about to bring, and who is pleased by it, Hamilton took the coffee Mitch handed him, pulled up a chair in front of his personal console, and typed in his clearance codes. The following words appeared on the monitor.

PRIORITY ONE MESSAGE. CAPTAIN'S EYES ONLY

TO: CMDR PERRY R. HAMILTON, CAPTAIN, U.S.S. CHRYSALIS

FROM: COMSUBLANT

YOU ARE HEREBY NOTIFIED THAT CHRYSALIS IS RELIEVED OF ANTICIPATED PATROL DUTY UNTIL FURTHER ORDERS FROM THIS OFFICE. AT APPROXIMATELY 0500 HOURS LOCALTIME THIS MORNING YOU WILL RECEIVE ONBOARD REAR ADMIRAL MILO F. SANDUSKY, NAVAL INTELLIGENCE. EFFECTIVE IMMEDIATELY, CHRYSALIS IS DISPATCHED ON INDEPENDENT DUTY AND IS TO MANEUVER UNDER THE DIRECTION OF ADMIRAL SANDUSKY. CHRYSALIS SHOULD BE READY TO SAIL AS SOON AS POSSIBLE AFTER SANDUSKY'S ARRIVAL. DUE TO THE NATURE OF THIS MISSION, IT IS ESSENTIAL THAT UTMOST SECRECY BE MAINTAINED AND THAT ALL FURTHER COMMUNICATIONS ACTIVITY OF CHRYSALIS, OF ANY KIND INCLUDING COMMUNICATIONS TO THIS OFFICE, BE KEPT TO A MINIMUM. ACCORDINGLY, FOR THE DURATION OF THIS MISSION, ALL COMMUNICATIONS WILL BE CONDUCTED SOLELY BY ADMIRAL SANDUSKY. IN ALL OTHER RESPECTS, YOU WILL MAINTAIN FULL

AUTHORITY AS CAPTAIN. WHILE YOU WILL BE BRIEFED AS NECESSARY BY SANDUSKY ON ARRIVAL, YOU ARE HEREBY NOTIFIED THAT THE NATURE OF THE MISSION WILL BE LIKELY TO REQUIRE UNUSUAL AND PERHAPS TO THE CREW INEXPLICABLE OPERATIONS. YOU HAVE BEEN CHOSEN FOR THIS MISSION IN PART BECAUSE OF YOUR RECORD OF CONSISTENT AND CAPABLE EXECUTION OF ORDERS RECEIVED FROM SUPERIOR OFFICERS. THIS OFFICE HAS FULL CONFIDENCE THAT THIS RECORD WILL BE CONTINUED. ALL FURTHER QUESTIONS SHOULD BE ADDRESSED DIRECTLY TO ADMIRAL SANDUSKY. END OF MESSAGE.

Hamilton read through the Priority One without understanding a single word. Or rather, he did not see the words the message should have contained. This was gibberish.

By the third re-reading, and with his mug of black coffee long since drained, Captain Perry Hamilton knew his worst nightmare was about to begin.

27

AT 4:00 A.M. Michael Kittery gave up trying to sleep. He took a shower, got dressed, went to the kitchen, turned on the coffee maker, and admitted he was nervous. There were good reasons to be nervous. They were about to steal a billion-dollar piece of military hardware and not even the Kittery fortune would keep them out of prison if caught.

But that wasn't why he was nervous. Another reason might be that his invention was about to be tested and a certain amount of ego was involved.

The best reason of all to be nervous was the fact that by experimenting with time travel he might be on the verge of destroying the known universe.

That wasn't quite it either.

He was nervous because he felt someone was spying on him. The feeling had increased in the last few weeks.

It was impossible, of course. No one knew he was here. For that matter, no one cared. Yet he could not shake the belief that someone did.

To steady his nerves, he began preparing a large

breakfast of eggs, bacon, and toast. He'd already packed his duffel bag, now waiting by the front door. According to schedule, sometime this morning a nuclear submarine would arrive off the pier and become his new home.

They'd chosen U.S.S. *Chrysalis*. On the downside, this was the sub that had benefited from a national naming contest before construction, so it was one of the highest-profile ships in the Navy. But it was also the only submarine about to be sent out on patrol duty, yet based in Norfolk. That made it the perfect choice.

Of course, if their plan hadn't worked, Milo was probably in a military jail already and units of the FBI were en route to Three Forks. Best not think about that possibility.

The sizzle of cooking bacon brought him out of these thoughts. He pulled a plate from the cupboard and tried to eat. The only details remaining were what do to with the food leftover in the refrigerator. How long would they be gone? A year? A day? Did it matter, when they could reverse time and return before they'd left? If the two remaining eggs stayed in the refrigerator and became rotten, could they manipulate time to return in a mere twenty-four hours? And if so would the eggs still be fresh? What would have happened to the rotten eggs?

These kinds of thoughts had tormented Kitt for weeks, and it irked him now that he could not even enjoy breakfast without them returning. He needed a distraction.

A loud crash came from the barn and the scientist jumped up. This time it was not his imagination. *Someone was in that barn.*

❧

"Shit!" said Lauren in an urgent whisper.

She'd been in the barn almost ten minutes. Most of the crates were nailed shut, but on one the lid was ajar. She'd opened it partially and taken a few snapshots from different angles, of whatever was inside. Even better, pure gold was on the desk: a USB key labeled "Backup One." That was now safely in her pocket.

But now she'd backed into the tool bench and knocked a circular saw and boxes of nails onto the cement floor, creating a huge racket.

She'd be discovered! Sure enough, footsteps were crossing the gravel, approaching from the house. Those were probably Michael's footsteps.

Lauren panicked and completely forgot about Plan B—posing as a young neglected wife trying to find her husband.

With more time, she'd have remembered that strategy and prepared mentally to go on offense the moment Michael walked in. But she had no time. She couldn't be discovered. She had to hide.

Where? The barn was one large open space. The crates were the only things in it, and she couldn't hide behind them. If only—yes! The one she'd opened was long and low, like an oversized coffin, but there might be room.

Knowing she had only seconds, Lauren slipped awkwardly into the crate, scraping her arm on a nail but forcing herself not to cry out. There was enough space—barely. She was sharing the coffin with some long metal object, cold and oily to the touch. She forced herself to press against it but there was still not enough room. With a shudder, Lauren wrapped her left leg underneath and around the thing and squeezed in still farther. Her perfectly-coiffed hair was now sticking to the grease.

She was just able to reach up with one hand and move the lid back into place, turning an already dark world into complete blackness.

Michael Kittery noticed the door was unlocked, and couldn't remember if he'd left it that way or not. He opened it cautiously and flipped on the light switch. Everything looked normal. He walked around the room, expecting to find something or someone behind one of the crates, cowering. No one was there.

Walking over to the workbench, he identified the cause of the noise he'd heard. The circular saw and nails had been knocked over by the intruder. But where was the intruder? There might just possibly have been time for someone to have slipped out the door if they'd been near the door. But the workbench was on the other side of the barn and the intruder must have been at the workbench when the saw had crashed.

There simply hadn't been enough time for an escape. Whoever had knocked over the saw should still be in the room. But the only things in the room were the crates. Kitt let his eyes roam over the half-dozen large wooden boxes and decided there was no way a man could fit into one of them since they weren't empty.

The door creaked and Kitt spun around. Waldorf slinked in. Waldorf was the stray tomcat that had been hanging around the farm. Lately, they'd been leaving scraps for him on the back steps and the cat was now beginning to think the whole place his domain. Waldorf walked lithely over to Kitt and rubbed his leg, purring appreciatively.

"Waldorf you little tramp!" he exclaimed loudly, and mostly for the benefit of calming his nerves.

So the intruder was Waldorf. Probably he'd found a hole to get into the barn and had been diligently ridding the room of mice. With Waldorf roaming in the darkness, it was no surprise something got knocked over.

"Well, you old scavenger, I see you're up early as well."

Kitt was still on edge, from thinking someone had broken into the barn, and from the nagging sense that someone was following him. But since the intruder was merely the cat, maybe he was also wrong about being followed. He needed to quit being so paranoid and find a way to unwind.

Kitt walked back to the workbench and turned on the radio. At four-thirty in the morning, only the preachers down in Newport News were on the air, but he decided their monotonous droning might be soothing.

"And the Lord saith we are sinners!"

"Amen!" roared the audience.

"And the Lord saith we shall burn!"

"Amen!"

A pause.

"But I don't want to burn!"

"Amen."

The response was only at half strength, as if the congregation was unsure whether 'not wanting to burn' merited an "amen."

"Do you want to burn?"
"No!"
That was unanimous.
"Then do we need a savior?"
"Yes!"
Solid ground again.
"And is Jesus Christ that savior?"
"Yes!"
"Say Hallelujah!"
"Hallelujah!"
Say "Amen!"
"Amen!"

The cadence of the speaker and his audience was a salve to Michael's nerves, massaging and relaxing his brain as a vibrating machine would his muscles.

"...and this evil time has continued long enough! We are approaching Armageddon, my children! There shall come a time when the present days of lust and debauchery shall cease, and all shall be destroyed. There shall come a time when those before us, whom we thought dead, shall rise and live again! Soon now, my children, very soon! Are you ready to face those who have gone before, who shall wake from their slumber?"

Kitt reached over and turned off the radio. Was *he* ready to face those who would wake from their slumber? He sat back and stared at the far wall, wondering what madness possessed him to think he could manipulate time. And yet the madness continued. Like a car careening down a hill, better to stay at the wheel and control its course than jump out while in motion.

And everything was in motion now.

Waldorf lay beside him, occasionally flicking his tail, hoping for a response. Kittery reached down and began stroking the cat.

"God help us all," he whispered to the room.

28

NAVAL STATION NORFOLK—AMERICA'S largest naval base—contained an array of ships in aggregate capable of destroying any nation on Earth: three Nimitz-class nuclear-powered carriers, three guided-missile cruisers, seven frigates, a ballistic-missile submarine, and two nuclear-powered, attack boats. The carriers were at full fighter-complement, which meant nearly eighty planes apiece, mostly F/A-18 Hornets and EA-6 Prowlers. It was an incomprehensible amount of firepower.

Not surprisingly, the base was protected with state-of-the-art security. Radar and sonar maintained continuous coverage. The twenty-foot high, electrified fence that surrounded the base was constructed of high-tensile steel—impervious to wire or bolt cutters. Anyone trying to use an acetylene torch to break through would set off alarms as soon as they raised the temperature of any link as much as 100 degrees. Marines carrying automatic M-16 rifles patrolled the grounds continuously.

Access to the base could occur in only three ways: by

helicopter, by ship, or through the main gate. The gate was protected by steel and concrete barriers capable of stopping anything up to and including an M-1 tank. But the barriers themselves (at the moment) were guarded by only one man—a seaman first class, armed with a 9mm pistol.

At 0430 hours, car headlights appeared from the direction of the main road and momentarily blinded the seaman, who raised his hand over his eyes. Early morning arrivals were not uncommon. Often it was a supply truck benefiting from light traffic. But sometimes predawn arrivals took advantage of the darkness. On those occasions, it could be a new company of marines arriving from Parris Island. Or a cargo of nuclear warheads. Or an officer showing up to take command of a ship before the crew was expecting him.

This time, it was a taxi that stopped at the guardhouse gate. Officers usually arrived by taxi. The seaman tucked in his shirt, ran a hand through his hair, and walked over to the cab. The driver gestured towards the back seat.

The passenger window came down halfway and an arm emerged, holding a billfold with an identification card. Circling the sleeve was a broad band of gold and a single star. A rear admiral.

The guard took the proffered identification and held it up to the fluorescent lights.

"Sir, are you Admiral Milo F. Sandusky from Naval Intelligence?" asked the guard saluting, and following protocol.

"Yes."

"Sir, my log doesn't show you were expected. Is this an unscheduled visit?"

"Bet your ass it is, sailor." The dark face broke into a grin.

"Aye aye, sir! I'll mark the log accordingly."

The guard pulled a key from his belt and inserted it in a lock directly behind him. The anti-tank gate slowly opened.

"Welcome to Naval Station Norfolk, sir!" The guard snapped off another salute, and the admiral raised his hand halfway to his forehead before letting it drop back, as though already bored with the encounter.

As the cab passed, the gate closed. Naval Station Norfolk was secure.

29

ADMIRAL MILO F. Sandusky paid off the cab, straightened to his full five-foot, eight-inch height, and approached the solitary seaman guarding the gangway leading up to U.S.S. *Chrysalis*. Milo paused in wonder. She towered above him in the pre-dawn darkness, like a black wall of evil.

The conning tower alone soared twenty feet in the air. And the length—well the length was vague since much of it was submerged. But even above the waterline, *Chrysalis* stretched over 100 feet.

Milo reminded himself that, despite its intimidating mass, the vessel was controlled by human beings. His job was not to master the submarine but only the people who ran her. And that, he hoped, would not be too difficult.

The seaman occupying the one-man guardhouse leading to the boarding ramp stepped outside into the overhanging light cast by a single incandescent bulb.

"Please identify yourself, sir!"

"Admiral Sandusky," said Milo calmly. "Would you care to see my identification?"

"Not necessary, sir!" A smart salute punctuated the "sir," and Milo returned it crisply. The seaman stepped aside. No doubt he'd been warned to expect an admiral.

"Welcome aboard, sir!"

"At ease, sailor. Carry on."

Milo stepped lithely onto the gangplank, pausing momentarily as a wave of nostalgia enveloped him. How long had it been since he'd boarded a ship to the accompaniment of that "Welcome aboard, sir!" It was a dream.

But it was also a serious business. By impersonating an officer, Milo had just committed a felony. *No time to think about that now*, he told himself, shaking off the thought and continuing up the gangplank.

Several figures emerged at the opening of the sail and stood at attention. The sailor had called ahead. The whole ship would be on alert in anticipation of an admiral.

Before stepping physically on board, Milo stopped at the end of the gangplank, turned to face the illuminated American flag flying at the stern, and saluted it. Then, following Navy protocol, he turned to face the Officer of the Deck (identified by the sidearm on his belt) and saluted again.

"Request permission to come aboard."

"Permission granted, sir," said the OOD, returning both salutes. Another figure came forward as Milo stepped off the gangway and onto the steel plating of the submarine.

"Admiral, I'm Commander Hamilton. Welcome aboard, sir."

The mutual salute was followed by Hamilton's outstretched arm. Milo shook it intently and briefly, as was expected.

"May I present two of my officers, sir?"

"By all means, Captain."

Milo used the designation 'captain' as a courtesy. Although only a commander by rank, Hamilton was captain of his ship. These nuances of etiquette were like breathing for Milo.

"Executive Officer Lieutenant Commander Mitchell Simpson."

Another salute and a dark hand reached out. Milo shook it.

"Weapons Officer, and currently Officer of the Deck, Lieutenant Bob Makelvich."

"Delighted to be on board, Captain," said Milo after the introductions were complete. "Shall we go below?"

"Certainly, sir," said Hamilton.

The admiral was expected to enter first by virtue of rank, and did so without hesitation. Milo's eyes required only slight adjustment entering the passageway for at night it was lit with red incandescents.

Now that he was formally aboard, etiquette could give way to practicality.

"Captain, I'd be obliged if you'd lead me to your stateroom or anywhere we could talk privately."

"Certainly, sir." Turning to Simpson he said, "Carry on, Commander."

"Aye aye, sir."

Hamilton led the way past the control room where several sailors and a chief came quickly to attention, and then through the passageway to the left and into his cabin.

"Coffee, Admiral?"

"Love some. Black."

Hamilton pressed the intercom button and spoke a few words. He motioned the admiral to a miniature settee couch, and sat in the chair, opposite.

"Well, Captain?" said Milo, immediately taking the initiative.

This was both unfair, and effective at establishing authority. Hamilton was forced on the defensive.

"Admiral, a few hours ago I received a ComSubLant communication to the effect that you would be coming aboard. I am under orders to operate this vessel per your direction. Beyond that, I'm in the dark."

"I see. Sounds like ComSubLant was as terse and uncommunicative as their reputation holds. Unfortunately, I'm under my own orders to divulge no more about this mission than is required."

"Mission, sir?"

"Yes. I'd like to get underway as quickly as possible. Our first destination will be a small loading pier, about fifty miles upriver on the James."

"Fifty miles? Admiral, I don't think that river is more than forty or fifty feet deep in the middle of the channel. I need over a hundred just to submerge."

"No need to pull the plug. What's your draft on the surface?"

"Twenty-five feet, minimum. We could go upriver on the surface, but I doubt we're equipped with the proper charts. I guess we could download them."

"I brought the charts. Let me turn them over to you."

Milo reached into his small duffel bag and extracted some folded papers. Hamilton accepted them with reluctance.

"Admiral, may I ask a question?"

"Sure."

"Why are we taking a nuclear submarine up the James River?"

"To load supplies. My aide, Michael Kitt—he's a civilian—will be meeting us and will supervise the loading of certain classified equipment on board—"

A knock on the door signaled the arrival of coffee. The two were silent while a steward entered, served them both, and then excused himself. A steward intruding on a meeting of high-level officers was officially invisible and did not merit acknowledgment. He did merit an interruption in the conversation.

"Look here, Captain," said Milo, pretending to level with him. "Orders be damned. If we're going to work together you need at least an outline of what this is all about."

"I'd appreciate it, sir."

"Very well." Milo took a long drink from the cup and set it on the adjoining table.

"I'm from Naval Intelligence. I don't know if ComSubLant mentioned that."

"They did, sir."

"Then you can guess this whole business is sensitive."

"As you say, I expected it would be."

The admiral stared at his coffee as if deciding how much to reveal. He was enjoying the role-playing immensely.

"You've probably heard about the Donaldson case, even though they tried to clamp a lid on it."

"Sir, I don't believe I have."

Milo looked up suspiciously.

"Never heard about Donaldson? Well, I guess that's possible. I understand you've been at sea."

"Yes, sir."

"Well, the waitresses at the diners in Newport News know as much about it as us flag officers, from what I hear. So there's no harm in telling you. Donaldson was head of a spy ring, working for North Korea we think. I won't bother you with the details. Bottom line: Naval Station Norfolk is rotten. Moles everywhere. They got Donaldson himself, thank God, and he talked. So the sweep is beginning. But over in Intelligence, we have to assume the whole base has eyes. At least for the moment. I'm sure you understand."

"Absolutely, sir."

"So obviously we don't want to load classified, experimental equipment anywhere around the area."

"So is that why we're heading up the James River, sir?"

"Yes. Once we leave port the security leak is behind us. The loading facility is an old pier that sticks out into the river 100 yards or so. It will mean a little work for your men, but can't be helped. Loading that equipment on with a crane at Norfolk, or anywhere in the area, would be no better than sending an email to Pyongyang with an itemized list."

"I understand, sir. And what exactly is this equipment?"

"This is for your ears only, Captain. Do I make myself clear?"

"Sir, if you prefer, we never had this conversation."

"We didn't." The admiral wrestled with his conscience.

"Well, hell, you're the damned captain. You can't be kept in the dark." Milo leaned in closer. "It's like this. Some bright physicist figured out a way to make a submarine invisible."

"You mean exceptionally quiet?"

"I mean more than that."

"I don't understand."

"Well, neither do I. I don't think we're talking really invisible, just invisible to any form of scanner—sonar, radar, heat sensors, radiation field detectors, whatever. Something to do with bending electromagnetic waves. This device bends everything, makes it streamline past the hull in a way that creates invisibility."

"And we're supposed to test it?"

"Yes. Now I'm no physicist, but someone in the Pentagon got the idea that this was a serious business and a senior officer, from Intelligence, should be along to supervise and observe. So I'm supervising and observing. But I'll tell you behind this closed door, that I'd appreciate all the help I can get from you. I've spent most of the last twenty-three years studying the Kremlin, not our submarine fleet. Now, I'm supposed to manage both this submarine and a brainy civilian who's going to bring this device aboard and see if it works. I'm just hoping we can get this duty behind us and get back to our real jobs. How's that sound to you?"

The captain broke into a grin.

"Admiral, you can count on me completely. You tell me what you need. I'll run the boat, and we'll get this thing tested and out of here. No one will enjoy that more than I will, sir."

"Very well, I think we understand each other."

"We do, sir."

"But I need to warn you. During this voyage, I'll be making some very strange requests, and you may see some strange phenomena. I won't be able to explain everything. Just be prepared."

"ComSubLant warned me of that, and I understand."

"How we communicate all this to the crew, I leave in your hands. Just stay away from the truth. Now, are we ready to get underway?"

"We've been ready since 0300, Admiral. We had a few men out on liberty, but we got them back aboard. And since we were anticipating patrol orders, we've kept the boat on full ready alert. Supplies topped up. Everything."

"Then I'd be obliged if you'd set course immediately for this spot on the map."

Milo turned to the table where Hamilton had set the charts and pointed to a circle near the town of Three Forks. The captain studied it carefully, then reached for the intercom and barked some orders. Above him, they could hear the ship spring to life as preparations were made for casting off from the dock.

"Now, Captain, for the duration of this voyage I'll

need a place to bunk and it would be convenient if the civilian could share quarters with me. The less interaction with the crew the better."

Hamilton thought for a moment.

"Well, this settee can double as a berth. Why don't you take my cabin, sir? I don't think it will kill my XO to share quarters with another officer. I'll move into his room. Make yourself at home, Admiral."

At 0500 hours, Naval Station Norfolk was awash in shadow. Almost silently, with only the vaguest attention given to it by the few workers on duty, one of these shadows slipped away from the dock. At first *Chrysalis* steamed north, as the sky lightened with a hint of dawn. Then the shadow changed course and turned northwest. But already it had passed completely from the awareness of anyone onshore.

As was its intended military purpose, the submarine had vanished.

30

WHEN LAUREN REALIZED that Michael was planning to stay in the barn, her emotions exploded, touching on rage, fury, and despair before settling on resignation.

She knew Andy, watching from back near the road, would realize what had happened. He'd have seen Michael approach the barn. Eventually, the detective would put two and two together and realize she must have slipped into one of the crates and be in hiding. Surely Michael would leave the barn eventually. Why would he stay here at four in the morning? When her husband finally left, Andy would sneak in himself, and let her know she could come out. In the meantime, all she could do was wait. She'd been too keyed up to sleep back at the hotel, and her day had started almost twenty-four hours ago in Connecticut. She was tired. And when she finally closed her eyes, she slept deeply.

31

THE BLACK MONOLITH cut through the waters of the James River without any means of support to anyone who did not know it was the sail of a partially-submerged submarine. Standing in the bridge cockpit, Milo peered through a pair of binoculars seeking can buoy 26A that would give him a fix on the plantation pier. Captain Hamilton was at his elbow, looking apprehensively in every direction. With a springtime mist hovering faintly over the water, visibility was limited. Behind them, the sun was fully emerged which was fortunate. Navigating an unfamiliar channel in the dark would have been difficult.

"Admiral, what's going to happen if some fisherman or towboat skipper or even a farmer sees us? Won't we attract attention?"

"Is that why you're keeping the boat partially submerged?"

"Yes, sir. We're still tidewater even this far up the James, and I've got the depth, so why not use it? *Chrysalis* is a lot easier to spot when fully surfaced."

"Understood. But I'm not worried about someone seeing us. We're a U.S ship in U.S. territory so we don't exactly need to hide."

"Not if you put it that way, sir. But it does seem highly unusual."

"Captain, it *is* highly unusual. This whole assignment is highly unusual. But let's not pretend this is the first time either of us has been asked to do something unusual in the Navy. Now, where the hell is 26A?"

Milo continued scanning upriver.

Hamilton saw it first and pointed it out, while Milo put the binoculars again to his eye. With the river swollen from the springtime rains and rushing to the sea at twice normal speed, the buoy was pulled far over, the top of the can periodically dipping into the water as it tried endlessly to right itself.

26A was the buoy that had been visible from the banks of the farm and Milo shifted his gaze to the left, seeking the telltale sign of the pier. There it was just coming up now. Milo pointed it out to the captain.

Hamilton pressed the intercom switch.

"Two degrees to port."

Chrysalis changed course slightly and headed for the pier, still several hundred yards up-river.

"Bridge, I want continuous soundings."

"Aye aye, Captain." A few moments later another voice began calling the depths. "Twenty feet below the keel. Eighteen feet. Fifteen feet. Fifteen feet."

"Surface completely."

"Aye aye, sir."

The submarine rose smoothly, the sail now clearly attached to an underwater behemoth.

Thomas Milo allowed himself a moment of reflection. In his long and colorful career, nothing had come close to this. He was standing atop a nuclear submarine, far up the James River, giving orders to her captain, and about to tie up at a pier to load into her a time machine. If he ever got out of this alive, or even out of prison, he would surely have some stories to tell his old drinking buddies back on the Intracoastal. He surely would.

Captain Hamilton turned again to the intercom.

"Send the deck party topside."

Six seamen and a chief petty officer appeared from a door at the base of the sail, and proceeded onto the forward deck, still wet from immersion. Two of the men carried old-fashioned grappling hooks and line.

"Captain, do you think we'll have any trouble holding our position against that pier, with this river current so high?"

"I don't think so, sir. The pier looks sturdy, but of course we can't trust that. If we were going to be here long, I'd run a normal set of lines—forward and aft bow springs and quarter springs, plus a couple of long lines to shore. But since we'll be underway again soon, I think we'll just secure the bow onto the end of the pier and let the stern drift where she will. We'll have the engine room maintain turns sufficient to balance the river current, and we'll use just enough left rudder to keep the bow nudged against the pilings. As long as the OOD stays in phone contact with the engine room and the helmsman, we should be fine."

Milo nodded curtly and watched the approach to the pier with professional interest. Hamilton knew his seamanship.

"Come right one degree. Reduce speed to ten knots," ordered the captain. "That's about two knots relative to the shore, sir," Hamilton added.

"Do you think your engine room personnel are aware we're inland on a river?"

"Only if they bother to look at the depth gauge. They're below waterline already and probably assume we're submerged since the motion of the boat is much less than they're used to on the surface in open water."

Milo grinned. "Must be nice to lead such a carefree existence."

"Hardly that. As I recall, the engine room is due for inspection at eleven hundred hours. Chief Bryson's probably over them with a whip."

They both smiled. The pier was less than a hundred yards away. Milo let his eyes wander over the green unmowed lawns of Kittery's farm. Kitt was up there, probably trying to think of some last-minute things to take care of. No doubt he'd show himself any moment.

The gap was closing fast. Orders from the captain were continuous now, as he adjusted the speed of the twin screws to bring the sub both in line with the pier, and to bring their relative speed over the bottom to near zero.

"Mr. Bendel!" The captain shouted to the officer on the foredeck. "Proceed with your duty as soon as practical."

"Aye aye, sir," Bendel acknowledged and turned to confer with a chief who was eyeing the nearest bollard on the pier, while his other hand held a grappling hook at the ready. A coil of nylon line nestled below his feet, with the bitter end secured to a metal post.

Suddenly the hook sailed through the air, missed the bollard, but caught neatly around a two by four support. Milo instinctively realized the problem this would cause. But instead of trying to retract the first hook, the chief had a second one ready and this time the hook caught the bollard securely.

"Engine room, make turns for seven point five knots."

The submarine slowed further as they crept up to the end of the pier. Finally, it looked to Milo as if they might hit the dock.

"Engine room, seven knots."

Now she began to drift slowly backward. The current was only slightly more than seven knots close-in to the bank. Milo saw the line attached to the grappling hook tighten suddenly, the port bow of the submarine gently touched the dock and suddenly they were motionless. River current surged past but the submarine's relationship to the pier was fixed. The grappling party moved a boarding ramp into position and a sailor ran across it carrying another line, which was secured to a second bollard on the pier. The officer waved to Captain Hamilton, indicating the task had been completed.

"Officer of the Deck, post sentries. One, fifty meters upstream, the second, fifty meters downstream. One, fifty meters inland, and another at the gangplank."

"Aye aye, sir," said the officer, who began issuing his own orders.

The captain turned to Milo.

"I'll send for Chief of the Boat Pardey, sir. He and his men will retrieve the cargo."

In a few minutes, Pardey appeared. Milo was aghast at the man's size. The six-foot-three frame and 250-pound physique made Milo suspect he'd be a tough adversary in a bar fight. Pardey's hair was longer than what Milo had seen on most of the enlisted men, and was more unkempt. His uniform was sloppily arrayed and covered with grease stains. In Milo's experience, the competence of a chief was inversely proportional to the neatness of his uniform.

"Chief, you will accompany the admiral to a shore installation and supervise loading some stores on board. He'll take you up there now so you can look 'em over and decide the best way to do it."

"Aye aye, sir."

Milo led him across the plank and up to the farmhouse, noticing the sentries were already in place, guarding the submarine with M-16 rifles.

So far, Milo had to admit, things were going well. He'd estimated his arrival at the plantation at 9:30 a.m. and they were ahead of schedule by forty-five minutes. He was not surprised to find Kittery asleep in the barn, legs propped up on the workbench and his head leaning over at an unnatural angle. Probably he'd been there all night checking to make sure the crates didn't go anywhere.

"Wake up, Kitt, we're ready to move!" Milo said loudly but gently. The scientist moaned as he was pulled out of slumber. Coming fully awake, he looked around and scrambled quickly upright.

"Oh, sorry. Guess I dozed off."

"Best use of a man's time while he's waiting. Chief, meet Mr. Michael Kitt, civilian. Kitt, meet Chief Pardey.

Kitt smiled and held out his hand. Pardey had automatically begun a salute, stopping just in time to make it appear he was scratching his right ear. The chief changed course and shook the civilian's hand.

Milo was glad they'd decided to use slightly altered versions of their actual names. It would make it harder for anyone to trace them afterward, and yet they'd not have to worry about accidentally calling each other the wrong thing when they weren't alone. So it was Admiral Milo F. Sandusky and civilian Mr. Michael Kitt.

"Well, I'm ready at this end," said the young scientist. "'Er—Admiral, if there's a sub out there at the pier, I guess we just load the stuff up."

"Oh, *Chrysalis* is there all right, sir," said Pardey. "And the sooner we can load these stores aboard and get out of this damn river, the happier I'll be. Let's see now, how much ya reckon one of these critters weighs?"

The brawny chief went to the nearest crate and gave it a shove with both hands. It moved only a few inches.

"Rest of 'em 'bout the same, Mr. Kitt?"

"More or less."

"Well, I guess we're looking at a couple hundred pounds each." Pardey turned to the admiral.

"Sir, where are we going to want these stowed once we get 'em aboard if you don't mind my askin'?"

Milo nodded his head towards Kitt, deflecting the question.

"Near the reactor. I'm not familiar with the arrangement of the submarine, but I'll need complete access to the reactor, and this equipment will be installed around the reactor."

Pardey raised his eyebrows.

"Mechanical equipment for the reactor, huh? Well, there's a nice little storage room just for'ard of there, not much in it neither. Best thing is there's an outside hatch directly above. Guess someone figured a reactor needs spare parts 'ccasionally."

The chief was looking at the crates again and nodding.

"So what's the plan, Chief?" Milo wanted less talk and more action.

"Well, Admiral, you want the Navy solution or you want my solution?"

"I want your solution, Chief, because I want this job completed before the end of the year."

Milo knew how to flatter chiefs.

"Well, Admiral, guess you know the Navy solution would be to bring in a helo, lift the top off this barn, then lift the crates over to the sub, and drop 'em in. Once you got the helo here the job would be done in ten minutes, but you'd spend six months getting the authorizations.

"So my way—since you asked—would be to bring a dozen seaman up here from the boat. Six seamen could handle one of these crates, no problem. Twelve seamen, you're looking at four round-trips. Thirty minutes, tops."

"Very well. Report to the captain. Tell him what you need and make it happen. Mr. Kitt and I will wait here."

"Aye aye, sir."

Salutes were exchanged and then Kitt and the admiral were alone.

"It's working slicker than a seal's asshole, Boss." Milo grinned. "Who would have thought we could pull this off?"

"Remember this may be the easy part. And let's drop that 'Boss' stuff. From now on, I call you sir, or Admiral, or something respectful. And to you, I'm just Kitt. Otherwise, we're going to slip up when we think no one's listening. Right, Admiral?"

"OK, Kitt, you inconsequential civilian. Just hope I don't kick your butt too hard while I'm trying to be a good admiral."

Milo was in a giddy mood.

"Anything I should know about the submarine before those guys get back here?"

"No. You're not supposed to know anything about *Chrysalis*, so why pretend you do? I'll introduce you to the captain, and no doubt he'll want to introduce you to some of his officers. My question is, again, are you going to know how to hook up that taco thing to the ship's reactor when you've never been aboard the ship?"

"I think so. Reactors are a lot like gasoline engines. If you know what you're looking for you can identify the important parts. I'm sure they'll have schematics. Once I get those, I'm on home turf."

"Where's your duffel?"

"Oh, still in the house. I'll get it, lock up, and meet you outside."

A few minutes later Chief Pardey returned with his work party.

"Carry on, Chief," said Milo. "When you're done just turn off the lights and close and lock the door on your way out. The civilian and I'll wait on board."

"Aye aye, sir."

Pardey turned and began barking orders to his men.

As he headed for the door, Milo noticed the lid was ajar on one of the crates and walked over to it.

"Damn nails. Should have used screws, like my pappy always said."

Milo opened his hand, palm downwards, and gave the delinquent lid a blow. The plywood cover dropped neatly into position. A sleepy moan came from inside but no one heard it. The first crate was already on the shoulders of the seamen and heading for the river.

32

WITH THE EQUIPMENT aboard, and Kitt down in their cabin, Milo returned to the bridge cockpit atop the sail. He wanted to observe Hamilton's seamanship getting underway. With two screws, they could counter-rotate and produce opposite thrust, pivoting the boat into the main channel.

"Everything aboard, sir?" asked Hamilton.

"We're good, Captain. We can depart as soon as you're ready."

"Ready now, sir."

"Please proceed."

Hamilton bellowed with a voice that impressed even Milo.

"Cast off forward line!"

A seaman let slip one of the hawsers and Milo watched it snake around the bollard on the dock, fall into the water, and be hauled aboard.

Hamilton gave orders to the engine room, the propellers counter-rotated, and *Chrysalis* veered to starboard.

"Cast off the final line!"

The last hawser slipped free.

The submarine turned swiftly, moving against the current. As it veered perpendicular to the bank, *Chrysalis* began floating downstream, heading for the middle of the channel. Milo glanced back towards the farm, wondering when, or if, he'd ever see it again.

Surprisingly, there on the dock was someone waving their arms.

"Captain, could I borrow your binoculars again?"

"Of course, sir," said Hamilton, handing them over. Milo was glad the captain kept his own eyes downstream, attention focused on issuing rudder and engine orders.

Milo looked back at the dock with the binoculars. A gaunt, middle-aged man, was waving frantically with both arms above his head.

What the hell?

The man was wearing civilian clothes. He wasn't a sailor left behind. No one was expecting a visitor. The man was distraught and seemed to be yelling a single word—maybe a name—over and over again, his hands cupped around his mouth.

A neighbor out for a stroll might wave to the naval vessel, or just look on in awe. But this man was frantic.

Whatever the story, Milo could think of nothing to be gained, and much to lose, in turning the submarine back to find out who this person was and what they wanted. If the guy had business with someone on board, it wasn't going to happen. Milo handed the binoculars back to the captain and turned away from the crazy person on the dock.

"Where to now, sir?" asked Hamilton.

"Take us into the Atlantic. When you're past any nav markers, please follow a bearing of 090 to get some sea room. As soon as you're comfortable, take her down to normal cruising depth and speed. We're heading for a point northeast of Bermuda. I'll provide exact coordinates later."

"Aye aye, sir."

The springtime current swept the submarine downriver rapidly, and after the first bend, Milo knew they'd vanished to anyone watching from the dock.

Anyway, where *Chrysalis* was going, no one could follow.

33

THEY WERE A week out from land when Kren warned of a storm approaching.

"You see the petrel, Uncle? Notice how it flies close to the water. It's nervous, and foresees the storm also."

"Should we be worried?" asked Torsten.

"Only a fool is not worried by a storm, but I am ready for this one. I await it, and it knows."

"Baah! You speak as if this storm were a man. The wind blows. The waves build. We live or we die. Then it's over."

"I could say the same about one of your battles. You live or you die, then it's over."

"Yes, Nephew, but it's one thing to grapple with a man. Another to grapple with…"

"With the gods? Yes, it's very different to grapple with the gods, and we shall soon be doing so.

"Aksel! Another reef in the sail. Fritjof! Get those shields inboard!"

Fritjof ran over to where they stood at the bow.

"The shields protect us, Sailing Master. If a storm is approaching we would be fools to remove the shields!"

It was the young warrior's first voyage, and he had much to learn. The most important lesson was never to question orders.

Leaping to his feet, Torsten pulled out his broadsword, and swung the flat against Fritjof's side, bruising his ribs. The man collapsed on the deck, moaning.

"Jorg!" called Torsten harshly. "You take his place, up here on the bow."

"Yes, master."

Torsten nodded to his nephew. "Kren?"

Kren had watched the striking down of Fritjof with resignation. The moment his order had been questioned the event was unstoppable. Discipline required it.

"Jorg, bring the shields inboard and lash them down. I need to reduce windage on the vessel."

"'Er, yes, sir."

Jorg looked uneasy but didn't question the sailing master. He barked the orders and the shields were removed.

The waves would gain easier entrance but the handling of the longboat would be improved and that was far more important. Before the wind, the vessel was seaworthy no matter the size of the waves. However, once turned broadside it would capsize in a heavy sea.

The storm fell on them during the night. The first blow hit like a solid wall, and the longboat's mast snapped like a twig. Foreseeing this, Kren had rigged a small sail in the bow, stretching from the top of the Valkyrie to the stump of the mast. And he'd reinforced the bow piece with stays, so it could handle the extra force. The tiny foresail now kept the boat turned away from the wind, and its stern to the waves.

All night the wind blew. Those among them who had not been sick became so. Many would have been washed overboard if Kren had not insisted every man be lashed to his station.

Kren alone stayed active, maintaining his hold on the tiller and guiding the ship through the storm. As each monstrous sea came bearing down, their stern would lift and be pushed sideways, nearly broaching to. But Kren compensated with the tiller, and his diligence kept the ship under control. If the longboat rushed too swiftly down each wave she would bury her bow in the trough, flip end to end, and sink. Yet if he held her too far abeam she would be rolled.

Kren was master of this game and as long as he could stay awake the ship would not founder. Of greater concern were the other ships. Eight longboats were in this raiding party and each was piloted by a sailing master of Kren's choosing. But this was their first real test. Who would triumph and who would fail? Kren wrestled with this worry no less than with the storm.

In the morning the wind abated and the seas calmed. The flotilla had been scattered. But when the sun was overhead, seven of the longboats had re-grouped. The eighth was lost.

"It is the anger of Ireland," remarked Torsten, looking with disgust to the southwest. "She reached out and tore at my ships, sinking one of them and crippling the others."

"We shall not be crippled long, Uncle. You see, those which lost their masts have already jury-rigged new ones. The men are being fed now on venison jerky and bread. They will be strong again, as will the ships. When we arrive, we'll have reached full fighting strength."

"Except that we are seven longboats, not eight. And none of those brave warriors will ever reach Valhalla."

"Yes, now we are seven."

Kren knew his uncle did not blame him.

"Seven will be sufficient," continued Torsten. "We will have vengeance for this night. The Irish blood that will be spilled will do honor to our fallen companions."

"Yes, Uncle."

Kren thought it foolish to believe the storm had been sent by the Irish. If the Irish were capable of sending storms, they possessed power that could easily overcome their raiding party. The flotilla might as well turn back now. Kren knew the storm had been sent by the gods—to test their resolve and exact tribute. Their resolve had been proven, and tribute paid. These were good omens, but he grieved for the fallen warriors.

34

SEAMAN FIRST CLASS Gary Keldorf threw his cards on the table.

"A pair of twos. Do you believe it? I tell you this voyage is jinxed!"

"Not jinxed for me, pal," said Seaman Apprentice Tim Gabler. "These sevens are stronger than they looked a minute ago. And I'll be takin' the pot, thankee kindly."

"Twos! Not even threes, but *two's!* Woody, you're good at math. Isn't it true that a pair of twos is the mathematical worst hand you can get?"

Seaman Hank Woodruff looked up from his stack of old Playboys.

"Pair of twos? Had a pair of fours once—did the trick on a hundred dollar pot in Malta. Hey, now, look at this pair," he said, holding out the magazine. "Bet she knows some tricks."

"Pair of twos," said Keldorf again, shaking his head in disbelief. "With this kind of luck, I'll arrive back in port with less money than I started—even after the paycheck."

"That's the idea, pal, that's the idea." Gabler looked surprised.

"Play cards with yourself, Gabler, I'm going to check the reactor."

"Yeah, good idea, check the reactor. See if it's still there. Hey, there's a bet. Ten to one says the reactor's still on-board. Any takers?"

Keldorf couldn't help smiling, even as he left the crew's mess and walked aft. Arriving on engineering deck he came to a bulkhead door and turned the wheel fast three complete revolutions. It swung open.

The nuclear reactor was managed from the bridge, but back-up controls and instruments were in the auxiliary control room, adjacent to the reactor itself.

The critical instruments lined one wall, keeping the operators informed of core temperature, coolant pressure, boron-rod status, and others.

One of the fluorescent bulbs was flickering. Keldorf walked over to the light switch and flipped it off, then on. The flickering bulb stayed off.

Spare bulbs were in the supply cabinet, inside the adjacent storage room. He entered it and then froze. There was a noise coming from one of the wooden crates.

Thump, thump, thump.

"Hey, is someone in there?" Keldorf yelled at the crate.

"Let me out of here! Let me out!"

It was a muffled, female voice.

Thump. Thump.

"I can't breathe! Get me out of here! Goddammit! Open this thing up!"

Oh, geez, where's an officer when you need one, thought the sailor. He hesitated, worried he'd get in trouble no matter how he handled the situation.

Thump. Thump. Thump.

"Goddammit!" said the mystery voice. "Hurry up!"

Keldorf didn't want her to suffocate.

"OK, ma'am," said the seaman, loudly. "I'll get you out. Just sit tight."

"Are you trying to be funny, mister?"

"No, ma'am. Just hold on a sec."

Keldorf found a crowbar and removed the crate's lid. A woman's arm appeared, and then another.

"Help me, dammit!" she said, gasping. "Don't you understand I'm near death?"

Keldorf grabbed the arm and pulled her out. The woman's legs collapsed and she fell to the floor, pulling Keldorf down on top of her.

"Ohhh, my legs. Please, help me massage my legs."

The mystery woman was massaging her left leg, so Keldorf addressed the right. He kept massaging even after the woman had stopped.

"That's enough," said the woman suddenly, pushing Keldorf's hands to the side.

"Sorry, ma'am."

35

LAUREN TOOK STOCK of her rescuer, who was dressed as a sailor and looked about eighteen. He seemed confused and needing guidance, which could be fortunate. Lauren looked around, at what seemed a kind of storage room. Boxes and cartons lined the walls. At one end was a tool rack.

"Where am I?" Lauren asked.

"You're in number three storeroom, aft by the reactor," said the sailor.

"Aft? You make it sound like we're on some kind of ship."

"We are, ma'am. Don't you know where you are?"

"How could I!" she said angrily. "I've been locked in that crate for I don't know how long."

Lauren immediately regretted her tone.

"Sorry. I'm not myself yet. I apologize," she said, adding a touch of flirtation with her eyes, to see if it would have an effect.

The seaman stared. "Who *are* you?" he finally blurted out.

Should she use a false name or be honest? How honest? She needed more information.

"Well, before I introduce myself, I'd like to know where I am and who you are. That's reasonable isn't it?" she asked, smiling demurely.

"Yeah, that's reasonable," said Keldorf, continuing to stare.

"Well?" prompted Lauren.

"Oh, you mean—uh, well, you're in number three store room on board *Chrysalis*, ma'am. And I'm Seaman First Class Gary Keldorf, service number B986274. And if I can say so, you're the prettiest woman I've ever seen. Ever."

"Oh, you can't mean that. I'm a mess. There's oil all over my body—"

Lauren looked up suggestively.

Keldorf opened his mouth, wide-eyed.

"Are you for real!"

"Well, I'm no apparition, if that's what you're thinking." Lauren reached out and took his hand, placing it gently on her cheek. "Does this feel real?"

"Yes, ma'am! It sure does."

"Good, since that's settled, let me introduce myself. I'm Lauren. Now, when you say '*Chrysalis* 'is that the name of the ship?"

"Yes, ma'am. U.S.S. *Chrysalis*, out of Norfolk."

"Norfolk, Virginia? Is that where we are now?"

"Oh no, ma'am. We've been underway for hours."

"Underway? But that's not possible. There's no movement!"

Keldorf smiled.

"Well, there wouldn't be any. *Chrysalis* is a submarine. A nuclear submarine."

"What! You mean we're *underwater!*" The color drained out of Lauren's face.

"Yes, ma'am. About 500 feet under the Atlantic right now, making turns for about twenty knots, I'd guess, judging by reactor power."

"Oh my God!"

Lauren sat down, in shock. The last thing she remembered was falling asleep in the crate. How could she be on a submarine, underneath the Atlantic Ocean?

And how would she ever get off? She'd be stuck on board. Discovered. Unless— An idea began to take shape.

"Well, Gary, this is a surprise but perhaps it's for the best. My full name is Lauren Hawkins. Reporter. Washington Post."

"A reporter? A newspaper reporter?"

"I'm what's called an investigative journalist. For the past nine months, I've been investigating a matter that could be of the highest importance to the security of the United States. Gary, I have to ask, are you a patriot?"

"Sure I am, ma'am. That's why I enlisted. I love my country."

"Well, I'm going to give you a chance to do your country a bigger service than you ever thought possible. You see, I've been sent down from the Post to investigate the possibility that Arab terrorists have infiltrated the United States Navy."

"Arab terrorists!"

"I'm afraid so. This is a joint project between my paper

and three intelligence agencies within the government. I'm not at liberty to disclose which ones. I'm only a small part of the investigation, you understand."

"Uh-huh." Keldorf's eyes were bulging.

"You see, I was tailing one of the suspects. I had to hide in that crate to keep from being spotted and before I knew it someone slammed the lid shut. I couldn't yell for help because my cover would have been blown. But finally, I couldn't wait any longer. That's when I started banging on the crate."

She stopped suddenly, giving Keldorf her best doe-eyed expression. "Gary, you rescued me. I'm…I'm so grateful. And so is your country."

"Hey, I was just trying to help."

"You helped a lot. Now, the question is, am I going to keep tracking those terrorists who may be on board, or am I going to have to reveal myself and waste nine months of investigation?"

"If there are terrorists on board, I think we should let the captain know."

"You're right, Gary. But we're not going to know which ones are the terrorists until I've had a chance to do some more investigating—*undercover* of course. And for that, I'm going to need your help. Are you willing to help out America on this one, Gary?"

"You bet! Just tell me what you need."

"Well—," Lauren began. "Let's see. I need to use the toilet. And after that, could you bring me some food? And maybe a Diet Coke?"

36

GABLER WAS STILL playing poker, when Keldorf walked through the crew's mess, and into the galley. He explained to the cook he'd been ordered to work overtime in engineering and needed some grub for himself and his crewmates. The mess steward, resigned to every aberration in the schedule, handed over a bag containing half a dozen sandwiches and a six-pack of soda.

"Hey, what's with the grub?" said Gabler as Keldorf headed back. "Checking on the reactor must build up quite an appetite."

"It's not me. It's my new girlfriend."

"Dream on," Gabler said. "We don't have any women aboard on this cruise. Believe me, I checked!"

"Well, you missed one. And I'm keeping her to myself. But she said if I don't bring her food, she's breaking up with me. So, gotta go, guys."

Everyone laughed, not believing him for an instant.

37

LAUREN CONSUMED A ham and cheese sandwich while perched atop one of the crates in the storeroom. Keldorf sat on another and stared at her, mesmerized.

So far he'd proven a good accomplice, Lauren admitted. Keldorf had taught her not only the operation of the nearest head but had also provided fresh towels and shampoo for a hot shower. And he'd stood guard outside, prepared to stop anyone from entering because one of the seamen was inside getting sick. Fortunately, at least according to Gary, this storage area wasn't much frequented. But Lauren guessed it soon would be—with Michael's crates in here. She needed a hiding place.

In the hour since she'd been rescued, Lauren knew the seaman had fallen completely under her spell. Helping the Washington Post and three government intelligence agencies catch terrorist spies was only an excuse. At his age, all the training and discipline in the world could be overcome by a competent seductress.

Men are so easy to manipulate, Lauren thought. But

the bigger problem was how being on a submarine would affect her strategy.

Somehow the U.S. Navy was involved. Perhaps the invention had a military application. She didn't want to be shot as a spy. But the "abandoned wife seeking her husband" story would be hard to disprove—if she were caught.

But what if she stayed hidden? She guessed Michael was on board, and it seemed unlikely her husband would be on a submarine for long—no doubt they were testing something for a day or two. Then they'd be back in port, and she'd find a way off the ship. She had the USB key in her pocket—something she'd thought might help her find her husband if she had to go with that tale. Even if the invention involved sensitive military technology, that would increase her nuisance value for purposes of an attractive divorce settlement. Yes, it was worth trying to carry out the original plan.

"Gary, you've been great," she said. "But I think we have another problem."

"What's that, ma'am?"

"OK, first, please don't call me *ma'am*. It makes me feel like an old hag. Just call me Lauren. That's my name."

"Sure—Lauren." He smiled.

"I can't live in this storage room forever. Someone's going to find me."

"Well—"

"I need a place to hide, a place where I'm safe." Lauren pretended to think for a moment. "I've got it!"

"Where?" asked Gary.

"Your stateroom! Maybe I could move in with you for the time being?"

Keldorf was speechless.

"Well?" Lauren persisted.

"Ma'am—Lauren, I mean. Uh, I don't have a stateroom. I bunk in number six crews' quarters just forwards of here and up one deck."

"Oh."

This had not occurred to Lauren. She'd assumed everyone on a ship had a stateroom. She'd always had one. "Well, what am I to do then, Gary? We can't let the terrorists find me!"

"There's one place no one would find you," Gary blurted out.

"Where?"

"Right here. See that locker door, against the bulkhead?" Gary pointed to a small half-height doorway across the room.

"What's that?"

"The explosives locker."

"Explosives locker!"

"Yeah. But it's empty. That's where we put anything flammable or explosive that hasn't been stored properly yet. But there's nothing there now. I know, 'cause I'm in charge of that compartment. Me and Lieutenant Hoskins are the only ones who have a key, and the lieutenant don't give a shi— 'Er, I mean he won't care about an empty locker."

"What are you proposing, Gary? That I live in that hole?"

"It's not a hole. Just a tiny room. But I could bring a

mattress and give you the key and then you could come and go as you please. It's gotta be the best place to hide on the whole boat."

Lauren considered it. The head (as Gary called it) was nearby, and if there really weren't any staterooms on board, well, she could hardly share number six crews' quarters. She'd stay hidden for now. Worst case: if necessary she'd reveal herself to an officer along with a believable story—she could invent one—for how she came to be inside the crate.

"Very well, Gary. I accept your proposal. Let's find a mattress and get me 'checked in'."

"Checked in?"

"Where's your key, Gary?"

Keldorf handed it over and Lauren fitted it into the lock on the opposite wall. The handle pulled down easily and the door swung open. Inside was a cubicle—perhaps ten feet in each dimension and empty. It smelled vaguely of paint.

"Did you say we could bring a mattress in here?"

"Sure, there's a whole mess of 'em in storage just forward of here. I'll get one."

"Thank you, Gary. I really can't wait to...*get in bed.*"

Quit being so suggestive, Lauren reprimanded herself. Although she could never resist a good double-entendre, even in capricious circumstances.

Gary blushed, then rushed down the corridor.

38

KITT AND MILO sipped coffee and shared a tray of sandwiches from the mess steward. For two hours the young physicist had been studying the schematics of *Chrysalis'* nuclear engineering layout, provided by the captain, and Milo was getting bored.

"Well, Kitt, whatcha think?"

"What do I think about what?"

"Can you do it? Can you hook up your taco-maker to this ship and send us back in time?"

"Oh, that. Sure. The engineering is straightforward. I don't see any problems. No, it's the whole theory behind this that keeps getting to me. What's going to happen when we hit the switch? I can't get my mind off that."

"Uh, I thought you knew what was going to happen."

"I know what's supposed to happen. I know what my computer says will happen. But the whole purpose of this experiment is to find out what does happen."

"You say that watch just disappeared? Do you suppose we'll disappear?"

"To anyone observing, yes. I'm sure of it. But it probably won't seem so to us. I don't think the watch was aware it had disappeared."

"So all we can do is hit the switch and find out."

"Yep."

"Remind me again what the plan is. We're taking it slow, right?"

"Very slow. We'll start with a twenty-four-hour jump into the past—using the anti-mutrinos for two seconds according to calculations. Then we'll reverse and try to go forward using the mutrinos for the same amount of time. We need to make sure we can return to where we started."

"That'd be nice, yeah."

"If the jumps are successful, and nothing seems to be getting damaged, we'll try longer periods—a week, a month, maybe even a year."

"And then?"

"Then we see how brave we are."

"Assume we're brave. You're thinking maybe a decade, a century even?"

"At most. But we're getting ahead of ourselves. We'll want to test things thoroughly before that kind of a jump. Check into events, make sure our subtle tampering with time isn't destroying anything in the present. That will take some research. It won't be quick."

"OK, what's the next step?"

"In a few hours, I'll be ready to start hooking up the equipment. By the way, what direction are we heading?"

"Ha! I wondered when you'd ask. I don't come crawling to the boss for everything."

"So where are we?"

"As of the last time I checked, we were at latitude 40 degrees fifteen minutes 12 seconds north, longitude 60 degrees, 33 seconds west. In layman's terms, that's about 100 miles northeast of Bermuda. Course zero nine five."

"Sounds like you have a destination in mind."

"Absolutely. Remember our discussion back on the riverbank, about what happens to your position as you move in time?"

"Yep."

"Well, your opinion was that you'd stay pretty much in the same place physically. But since you admit you haven't the foggiest what's going to happen, I figured we could use all the sea room we could get. So I've given Hamilton orders to take us to the middle of the North Atlantic, equidistant from Bermuda, Newfoundland, and the Azores. Estimated time of arrival on the coordinates I've picked is in about twenty-four hours. Think you'll be ready by then?"

"I'm afraid so," Kittery said, curiously reluctant.

39

THE INTERCOM LIGHT flashed in the control room.

"Captain here," said Hamilton.

"This is Sandusky."

"Yes, Admiral?"

"Captain, the civilian—Mr. Kitt—has finished looking over the schematics. He's ready to install the equipment and needs to make some adjustments to the reactor. Can you come to our cabin?"

"On my way, sir."

A few moments later, Hamilton was seated on the berth opposite Kittery, looking over the schematics.

"Let me see if I understand this, Mr. Kitt. You need the reactor shut down for about an hour, so you can make some alterations?"

"Yes, sir."

"And what, exactly, are you going to be doing to the reactor?"

"Removing one of the control rods, sir."

"Excuse me?"

"I need to remove one of the boron control rods."

"One of the control rods, as in, one of the control rods that absorb the neutrons, thereby keeping the fission reaction contained, and keeping the reactor from going super-critical and melting a hole through the ship and sending us all to the bottom? One of *those* rods?"

"Yes, sir."

"Are you going to put it back?"

"Not exactly."

Hamilton glanced at the admiral but was met with only a steely glare.

"Mr. Kitt, I am operating under orders from ComSubLant and, via that office, Admiral Sandusky. He seems to repose a great deal of confidence in your abilities. But let me ask just one question. Do you know what the hell you're doing?"

"Yes, Captain, I do. I hold a Masters Degree in nuclear engineering from M.I.T. and a doctorate in particle physics from Yale University. Sir, meaning no disrespect to your engineering staff, I probably know far more about this reactor than does anyone on board. I can state unequivocally that my experiments will not pose a danger to the operation of the ship."

"Fair enough, but I'm not going to take that on faith. Why don't you start at the beginning and tell me exactly what you intend to do with the control rods and the rest of the reactor? Until I'm comfortable with the project, it's not happening. I say that with respect, sir," Hamilton added hastily, glancing at the admiral for reassurance.

"Perfectly understandable, Captain," agreed Milo. "You'd be negligent otherwise."

"Thank you, sir."

"On the other hand, the confidentiality of this technology is a factor too. I'm sure Kitt would like to explain more fully, but I'm under orders to see he explains as little as possible. And since I'm a history major myself, I don't even know what the hell the two of you are talking about. Kitt, what can you share with the captain to give him the comfort factor he needs?"

"Sir, it's like this," Kitt began. "As you know, every reactor built in the United States now conforms to the one-control-rod rule."

"Yes, you mean the ability to shut down the reactor, even with only one control rod inserted?"

"Exactly. And the reactor here has six control rods. I'm removing one of them, so in the absolute worst-case scenario, you still have a five-to-one redundancy factor. Do you concur?"

"Yes, that's true. But why are you removing one of the six?"

"I need to apply a magnetic field to it to perform an operation on the neutrons contained in the rod. There will be no damage to the rod and it can afterward be reinserted in the reactor.

"And you'd rather not get into what you're doing with the neutrons, I suppose."

"I'd rather not, sir. It touches on the key scientific breakthrough itself."

"And the other five control rods stay in place?"

"I won't touch 'em."

Hamilton took a moment to digest it all.

"We've never removed a control rod at sea. You've got to wait for the radiation levels to decay enough to be safe for workers. That can take days."

"I brought on board some lightweight robotic equipment, just for that purpose, sir."

"You're going to remove the control rod with robotics?"

"There's no other way, for the reason you just said. I'll cut the seal on the control rod tube using robotics, and weld it again the same way. The radiation won't be a factor."

"How long do you think the modification will take?"

"Less than three hours."

Hamilton digested this information and finally stood up.

"OK, I can live with all that. We routinely run tests in which the control-rod drivers fail, and we have to control the reactor with only two of the rods. As you say, we can shut the whole thing down if we need to, with just one. And we'll operate submerged. At five knots, we can go 24 hours on battery power. That way the boat will be dry-dock stable. But there's a condition."

"Yes, sir," said Kitt, trying to play the part of the deferential young scientist.

"I'm going in there with you, and I want Lieutenant Hoskins, our engineering officer, in there as well. We can use standard protective clothing. I want to see first hand what you're doing. And if either I or the Lieutenant has a problem, the experiment's going to stop until we're comfortable to proceed."

"That's reasonable, sir. To be honest, you and the engineering officer can probably be more helpful to me than the admiral, whom I'd have to use otherwise." Kitt grinned. "No offense, Admiral."

"None taken. Sounds like a great time for me to take a nap. So, Captain, are we good to go?"

"I believe so, yes, sir."

"Then, gentlemen, please do whatever it is you were talking about doing. Just let me know when you're finished. And, Mr. Kitt?"

"Yes, admiral?"

"Flip the light off as you leave, if you wouldn't mind."

"Enjoy your nap, sir," said Hamilton good-naturedly.

Milo flipped the light back on as soon as they'd left, and began studying the charts again.

40

SIX HOURS LATER Michael Kittery stepped back from his work. The replacement of the control rod had gone smoothly. The remaining time had been spent hooking up the tokamak, which had been set up in a machinist's work-room, directly aft of the reactor.

Captain Hamilton had ordered the room cleared of all ship personnel. Not only was the space ideally furnished for Kitt's purpose—every tool he could need was right there—but the starboard side of the room was, conveniently, the ship's hull itself. Now the tokamak was connected in both directions: to the neutron collector which had replaced the control rod at one end, and at the other end, via electromagnetic channels, to the metal hull of the ship.

Milo had been helping where he could while having no idea what the equipment did.

"So, Boss, remind me again how this is supposed to work."

"It's pretty simple. When the mutrino or anti-mutrino plasma's in sufficient concentration, this mechanical switch will open the electromagnetically-guided path, sending the particles directly into the steel hull, where they should spread out evenly."

"Oh."

"And then, obviously, the backward (or forwards) moving time flux will encapsulate *Chrysalis*, and carry it along with the mutrinos."

"Of course."

"The longer the switch is on, the further back or forward in time we go."

Kitt stared at what they'd built, trying to think of anything he'd overlooked. He glanced at the instruments, pleased to see the tokamak working perfectly, and the mutrino concentration already at acceptable levels.

"I think it's ready," he said, at last.

"Should we break out a bottle of champagne?"

"Maybe later. Right now I think we keep this as low key as possible."

"Will we feel anything?"

"I have no idea. The Hershey bar I sent forward in time, when it appeared again, seemed unharmed. It wasn't like it exploded or anything."

"Well, that's reassuring."

"I don't know if we'll sense anything at all—noise, motion, pain, weird visual effects. I just don't know."

"OK, so Boss, how do we do this? I mean, do we just flip the switch? Do we like, need to be sitting down with seatbelts on or something?"

"Yeah, if we had chairs with seatbelts, that probably wouldn't be a bad idea."

"But we don't."

"No."

Kittery stared at the switch. Weeks of research and planning were about to be tested. The entire civilization of earth was at risk, theoretically. Although it seemed unlikely a 30-amp circuit breaker could do so much damage.

Maybe the scientists at Los Alamos felt this way with the first atomic bomb. Did he, Michael Kittery, have the moral courage to follow in those scientists' footsteps? He'd promised Hamilton that none of this could possibly endanger the ship—and he believed that to be true. But damage to the time-space continuum of the universe? That was a different question.

Milo sensed his uncertainty.

"I think your stalling."

"Yeah, I am stalling. I'm actually scared as hell, right now."

"We're only going a tiny amount back at first, right?"

"Right. You see the three buttons, connected to solenoids? The red one sends us back in time. The blue one sends us forward. The gray one in the middle stops the movement. I'll press the red one, wait one second, then press the gray one."

"And how far back will that take us?"

"Well, if my calculations are correct, and they may not be, somewhere between a few minutes and maybe as much as twenty-four hours."

"That's quite a range."

"True, but the computer will keep track of the exact time the connection is open. Then we'll check the radio with the ship's antenna as we discussed. And once we see how far back we've gone, then for future time jumps I can calibrate more precisely."

"I see."

Neither said a word.

"We're stalling, Boss."

"Yep."

Kitt glanced at Milo and grabbed the workbench with one hand.

Milo grabbed with both hands.

"Ready?" asked Kitt

"Hit the switch."

Kitt reached out and pressed the red button, which glowed softly. Then he pressed the gray button.

Nothing seemed to happen.

"Is that it?" asked Milo. "Did you do it?"

"I think so. Did you feel anything?"

"Not really. My stomach growled, but that's normal. How 'bout you?"

"Yeah, a little nausea, but I think I was just nervous."

"So, did it work?"

"I don't know. Let's check radio broadcasts."

Milo reached Hamilton on the intercom.

"Captain. I have a strange request, such as I warned you about."

"Yes, sir."

"Please send an antenna buoy to the surface. I need BBC channel 17 piped down to engineering."

"Aye aye, sir."

"And, Captain, I want no one else listening in on this or any other channel. Is that clear?"

"Absolutely clear, Admiral."

In a few minutes both Kittery and Milo heard the voice of the British Broadcasting Company echoing through the engineering compartment.

It was the international news hour.

After a moment Milo reached up and switched off the speaker.

"Well, Boss, I guess your calculations need a little work," he said.

Kittery leaned against the bulkhead, his face white.

"You heard it, then?"

"Of course I did. They were talking about the upcoming elections in France—the elections that took place almost a year ago."

"Holy crap. So it works."

"We're time travelers," agreed Milo. "Damn."

They stared at each other, not sure whether to be pleased, terrified or some other emotion.

"But everything seems so normal," said Kitt, glancing around, as if expecting something to be out of place.

"I think—" said Milo.

"What? Think what?"

"I think the next step is to try going forward. You know, to make sure we can get back."

"Oh, right. Yeah. OK, so we can move in time. Wow, I'm just… But it's quicker than I thought. A lot quicker. Or maybe there's an acceleration factor. The longer the mutrinos are flowing, the faster you go. Or maybe—"

"How 'bout a little less theory, and a little more forward gear," prodded Milo.

"Right. This time the computer will close the circuit for exactly the same amount of time, adjusting for the forward-motion speed differential."

Lights blinked off and the deck dropped out from under them. Kitt and Milo were thrown against the bulkhead along with every loose tool or piece of hardware. *Chrysalis* rolled nearly onto her beam ends, and then back the opposite direction. Men and equipment went flying across the room and crashed into the opposite wall. A tool chest tipped over, sending its contents spraying like shrapnel.

"Goddammit!" yelled Milo, as a wrench smashed into his forehead. Kitt was trying to stand up but the deck was too steeply tilted. He lost his balance again and careened off a workbench, sliding down on top of Milo who just had time to raise his arm for protection. A chair slid by and Kittery reached out, hoping for a handhold, but he tripped and fell against the instrument panel that contained the circuit breakers. *Chrysalis* gave a final lurch and then steadied herself. The lights came back on, and the deck leveled.

"What the hell!" Milo exclaimed.

"I didn't know there could be so much turbulence 500 feet underwater!" said Kitt, rubbing a bruised elbow.

"That was a surface wave—a big one!"

"A surface wave? How is that possible? Unless—of course! Time travel moved us some distance through space as we moved through time. The mathematics were always a little unclear about—, geez, what a mess!"

"The ship's built to handle wave action so there's no

danger there. But we'd better get this place straightened up," said Milo, gathering several screwdrivers and looking around for the tool chest. Kitt began helping, and for awhile neither spoke.

"I think," said Kitt, "from now on we'll have to be a little more careful with—"

"Holy *fuck!"* Milo raced across the room to where the red button was glowing brightly. He frantically smashed his hand down on the gray button.

The deck of the submarine again tilted upwards horribly and then dropped like an elevator. Kitt and Milo once more were thrown off their feet, as a shower of small equipment and supplies washed over them. Then, just as quickly, the deck stabilized. Everything was quiet.

Milo looked at Kitt, who was staring at him in horror.

"How long?" said Kitt, finally, the words catching in his dry throat.

"Several minutes, at least."

"Oh Jesus," said Kitt. "Several *minutes!"*

"Where are we, Boss? Where are we?" Milo was white as a sheet.

"I—I don't know." Kittery stared around him in confusion. "But the ship's intact. We didn't destroy the ship!"

"That's right. The ship's intact. So we're still in the ocean. It feels like we're not on the surface anymore either."

They were silent, reaching out with their senses, trying to detect—*anything.*

Milo walked over to the intercom and turned up the radio.

There was only static.

41

BRODY FLANNAGAIN, THE seneschal of Castle Bally, sat in the Great Hall and watched the after-dinner ritual. Baron Tully O'Ruairc, his employer, wiped the coarse fabric of his sleeve across his face, smearing chicken grease into flesh. A pack of dogs in the corner waited expectantly. It was the baron's custom to toss the remains of his food to the dogs.

The largest grew impatient and snarled outright, but the others stayed silent. A few nights earlier one of the animals had leaped for the meat prematurely. A broadsword had sliced off the dog's head.

O'Ruairc raised his own upper lip, portraying more vacant gum than tooth, and snarled.

"Grrrrr," he said, as he dangled the remains of the chicken leg tantalizingly from two fingers, swinging it back and forth.

Flannagain knew the baron was hoping this dog, too, would lose control, so he could enjoy watching another head removed. Dog and baron stared at each other, but the animal finally retreated.

"Baah!" said the baron. "That one's smarter than he looks. Here!"

He tossed the meat into the corner, and the pack exploded. Teeth flashed, claws ripped, and the surrounding area was quickly soaked in blood. The morsel of chicken had disappeared and the dogs were reduced to licking the floor, hoping to find something nourishing amidst the blood. And the blood itself wasn't bad.

The seneschal, a thin man of middle age, with gray hair and a sallow complexion, was typically the baron's only dinner guest. When necessary the table could seat forty, but the baron was not fond of entertaining.

Other than the vast table and wooden benches, the room had no decoration. Three wrought-iron candelabras were suspended by ropes from the ceiling, which succeeded in providing a dim light sufficient for eyes that had adjusted. Even in daytime, only modest natural light gained entrance, and this by way of narrow archers' slits cut in the stone, at the mezzanine level.

No tapestries or works of art hung on the walls. No wool carpets were laid on the floors. And the ventilation was nearly as bad as the lighting. "This is a castle, not a palace," an earlier baron had noted with pride, and correctly.

It had been built nearly a hundred years previously by the second Baron O'Ruairc, after the home of his father had been leveled twice in attacks by outlaws. By using it as a military base, that baron had succeeded not only in pacifying his own fief but in absorbing two others owned by enemies to the west. Each successive O'Ruairc, while weak as administrators, had inherited a talent for war, and their holdings steadily increased. By the time the present baron, Tully, succeeded to the fiefdom it was one of the largest in Ireland.

However, the latest baron proved incompetent not only in administration but also in battle. To date little harm had come, for Tully's only military quests had been lending his sword on two occasions to the Ard Ri, or High King, for help against the Kingdom of Munster.

Baron O'Ruairc proved craven at the very first battle, falling from his horse and feigning injury until the skirmish was over.

Donnchad Ui Neill, the High King at Tara, had not been deceived, and when a similar evasion occurred two years later, he resolved to dispense with the baron's military assistance.

Flannagain—through his connections at Tara—knew the High King was grateful O'Ruairc was a coward. His predecessors had proved so successful in battle, and their holdings increased so rapidly, that the high kingship itself might be their next target. Tully's military incompetence was a blessing to the Ui Neills.

So rather than drive him from his fief as Donnchad could easily have done, the Ard Ri lent O'Ruairc support whenever necessary, thus forestalling any possible challenge from his northern flank.

With a staunch ally in Donnchad and a fief pacified

for over twenty years, the stone walls of Castle Bally had not lately been of use.

Baron O'Ruairc spent his time feasting, sleeping, throwing morsels of meat to savage dogs and (when the mood suited him) enjoying the pleasures of any young woman who caught his eye in Ballycastle village. Everything else he left to his very competent seneschal.

And that was precisely how Flannagain liked it.

"Excuse me, my lord," the seneschal interrupted.

"Yes, Brody, what is it, what is it?" the baron said, impatiently. "You've been trying to get my attention all evening. I guess there's no escape. What report of doom have you for me tonight?"

"Hardly a report of doom, my lord. Quite the contrary."

"Oh? Good news finally? Somewhat out of character, don't you think?"

Flannagain accepted the jibe, having long ago learned that minor verbal victories always improved the baron's mood, making the seneschal's own goals easier to achieve.

And there were many goals. It was Flannagain who determined how much wheat and barley to seize from the peasants. It was Flannagain who bartered the crops to traders from the south for all Castle Bally's material needs. It was Flannagain who hired and fired servants and consulted with the chef on what the week's menu should entail. And it was Flannagain who sent the guards to the proper house to "invite to dinner" any girl unfortunate enough to have pricked the interest of the baron.

"Perhaps out of character, my lord," said the seneschal,

trying to look properly chastised, "but no less welcome, wouldn't you agree?"

"Quite, Brody. Quite. Now you have me curious. What is this news?"

"The sheep yields, my lord. It appears we have something of a bumper crop in new lambs. And with the barley fields expanded by a hundred acres and the seeds already in the ground...well, we won't have to worry about food this year."

"Excellent! I am sick of hearing about famine, famine, famine. One gets the impression that all our peasants do is eat, eat, eat, and that's why there's never any food, so then there's always famine, famine, famine!"

The baron paused. "Hmmm. That was funny, I do say."

"Yes, very well put, your lordship. Perhaps we could have the scribe take that down."

Flannagain raised his voice. "I say, scribe. We have something for you here."

An overweight, balding, monk waddled hastily into the room from the direction of the kitchen, trying to swallow an over-sized mouthful of something difficult to chew.

"A quotation from his lordship," noted Flannagain. "Are you ready, scribe?"

"Of course, sir. 'Er, just a moment if it please you, sir."

The monk was flustered, not knowing what to do with the food. Finally, he took the grisly mess he'd been gnawing and put it in a pocket of his robe. The other contained writing materials.

"At your service, my lord. And yours, Mr. Flannagain," the scribe said at last.

"Very well, then, here it is. With apologies, my lord," he said to the baron, who nodded.

"'There is always famine, famine, famine because all the peasants do is eat, eat, eat.' You have that, scribe? Very well, cast onto parchment, several copies I think. Perhaps one should be sent to the abbot. Give him something to consider."

"At once, sir. Will that be all?"

"Yes, scribe." The bulbous monk shuffled backward out of the room, his head bowed in respect. Just as he disappeared from view, there was apparently a collision, for the sound of metal clanging to the floor echoed through the hall. Flannagain rolled his eyes, but the baron scarcely noticed. Servants and their misfortunes were beneath him.

The seneschal continued. "According to spot checks, we will surpass any prior year in terms of yield."

"How do you account for this, Brody?" asked the baron, not especially interested.

"No single factor, your lordship. The weather has been cooperative. But a variety of administrative measures we took at the beginning of the season are already bearing fruit, if you'll pardon the phrase."

"Well then, do you have an idea for how we could most profitably address the situation?"

"I do have a proposal, my lord. A very simple one."

He knew the types of proposals O'Ruairc preferred.

"All the better. Out with your simple proposal then."

"My lord, I propose that we retain a higher percentage of the yield this year, on both crops and livestock."

"Brody, last year you proposed we retain a higher percentage of the yield because of the crop failure."

"Quite, my lord. In a year of famine, it was essential to increase your percentage because otherwise, the total yield to Castle Bally would have been down, and we could hardly allow that. But it makes just as much sense to increase our percentage again this year. With a bumper crop, the peasants can afford to give more."

"That's hard to refute. I assume you have specific numbers in mind?"

"Yes, my lord, I would propose that—"

The baron suddenly yawned with fatigue and waved his hand in a silencing motion.

"Brody, please, I did not mean for you to explain all your arithmetic. I have confidence in your judgment. Do whatever you think best with respect to the sheep and the—well, the sheep and so forth."

The baron waved his hand dismissively, as if already bored with the conversation. "Now, I have a more important matter to discuss."

"Certainly, my lord." Flannagain knew what was coming.

"There's a girl in the village. I believe we've spoken of her before, but I saw her again, buying yarn at the market—the one who wears the pretty clothes. I must get to know her."

"Do you mean Avelyn, my lord? The wench who serves the monastery?"

"That's it! When could I meet her?"

Flannagain sighed, knowing what the baron meant by

"meet." And it was true—they'd had this discussion before. Flannagain had strongly advised against taking Avelyn. The Church was growing in power—not just in Ballycastle, but in all Ireland. Even the High King had converted to Christianity and was loath to go against the priests' wishes. And the abbot of Ballycastle Monastery considered himself Avelyn's protector, Flannagain had determined. Little good could come of crossing the abbot.

"My lord, I will do whatever you order, as always, but I would urge caution. The abbot takes a great deal of interest in this girl. He would not look kindly to her being taken to the castle—even for one night. The abbot grows steadily in power. It might be best not to offend him."

As soon as he'd spoken the words, Brody realized he'd used the worst possible argument.

"Not *offend* him! Growing in *power*!" The baron rose from his chair in dismay, his face flushed and his hands trembling.

"My dear sir, I own this fief. I own everything in it. I own this chair, I own those dogs, I own *you*. I own that monastery and every monk and abbot within. And I most certainly—do you hear me—most *certainly*, own that girl, Avelyn. I insist she joins me for dinner! Do you understand?"

"Of course, my lord. It shall be as you order."

"Good, now what about the blacksmith's daughter? Is she well yet?"

Deidre had been brought to the castle a week ago, but the girl arrived with a fever. Brody had been worried she would die—inconvenient as that would have been. But she recovered and this morning O'Ruairc's healer pronounced her well enough for the intended activities.

"She is, my lord. I had her brought to your chambers knowing you'd ask for her tonight."

"Excellent. I hope you locked the door. We don't need any more escape attempts like happened last month."

"Quite, my lord."

Brody retired to his own chambers and considered the orders he would issue on the morrow. A proclamation would be made in the morning regarding the increased tax. The peasants would be furious, so he'd need a small company of guards on hand. That could be arranged.

More complicated was seizing Avelyn. He would go himself, with two of the castle's strongest guards. The last thing he wanted was a big scene with yelling and a flight through the streets. Certainly not tomorrow with the grain decrees being posted.

Afterward, he would seek an appointment with the abbot and offer a considerable donation, out of his own pocket. The monastery had never refused a donation before, and a favor deserved a favor. He would ask only for a tempered response in the matter of the girl.

Flannagain was skilled at such diplomacy. By tomorrow evening Avelyn would be locked in the baron's chambers and the new crop levies would guarantee more wealth in the seneschal's own pocket. He was already one of the richest men in Ireland, though he bore little sign of it. Flannagain took a final swallow of the wine he'd poured and, as satisfied as a man can be with his work for the day, retreated to bed.

42

THE YOUNG ACOLYTE walked swiftly through stone hallways. Crossing the small interior courtyard, he passed the newly-completed fountain donated by the local mason and came to a staircase—also cut from stone. At the top, the monk turned left and approached a large oaken door. It was actually two doors, which swung inwards from the gracefully-curved height where they met. A woodcarver had spent considerable time etching Ballycastle's history into those doors. A scene depicting the burning of a priest was near the top.

The acolyte pounded the iron knocker twice. The noise reverberated in the stone halls, becoming deep and important.

A muffled voice from inside made its way dimly through the thick oak.

"Yes, come in, come in."

The acolyte twisted the iron lever downward and pushed against the door. It creaked as it swung slowly into the room.

A small fire burned in one corner of the abbot's chamber which—combined with the rich Byzantine tapestries hanging on each wall and laid generously on the floor—might have provided warmth. But in these latitudes, the monastery had a chill that no peat fire could dispel.

The acolyte stood with his head bowed in front of the great desk.

"Your Grace, it's Avelyn, at the main gate asking to see you. She says you summoned her."

"Avelyn's here? I'll come right away."

Father Conardy set the parchments he'd been studying aside, stood up, and hastened towards the door. He turned to the acolyte.

"Please tell Father Gilceigh that I shall be delayed from vespers, and to proceed on my behalf."

Then he hurried off.

Avelyn awaited the abbot with eyes downcast as she had been taught was appropriate for a woman visiting the Christian sanctuary. Technically it was prohibited for a woman to enter at all, but a small receiving room had been built just outside the gates. Its plain decor reminded visitors of the ascetic life of those who lived within. No Byzantine carpets or gold candlesticks tried to warm this room. And the outward display of poverty suggested to thieves that the monastery was unworthy of plunder.

As he entered, Father Conardy dropped his clerical formality and held out his hands.

"Sum tam libenter ad te, mi puer."

He always spoke to her in Latin. "I am so glad to see you, my child."

Avelyn took the hands in her own, raised her head, and smiled warmly.

"You asked to see me, Father," she replied in the same language. "A note was left under my door."

"Yes. It might have been better if you'd been home to receive the message."

"But I did receive it, because you so cleverly thought to write it and leave it under the door."

"Oh, Avelyn, remove that innocent expression from your face. You forget that I've known you since you were a small child. My point, which you understood perfectly, is that you were not home when any woman in the village might be expected to be at home. And this is the third time this week I've sent for you, and all three times you have been found absent."

"Which is precisely why the note was such a good idea, Father. If you'd thought of it earlier, I'd have come all the sooner."

"Well, the thought was not so obvious. You are the only woman in the village who could even read such a note."

"For which I have you to thank, and for which I shall be eternally grateful."

"You're welcome." Father Conardy accepted the compliment, but then a look of consternation passed over him. "You've done it again!"

"Done what, Father?"

"Succeeded in keeping this conversation on every

subject but the one I wished to pursue. And you've done it deliberately."

Avelyn stared at the floor.

"My child, let us not be adversaries. It is only your welfare that I seek. You are seventeen years old, eighteen next month. You have no family. You—"

"Father, that's not true! *You* are my family. You really are a father to me, a real father."

The abbot's face softened, and he laid his hand on the girl's shoulder.

"Avelyn, your words are music to an old man. You are a daughter to me as well. But you must be settled more permanently, as God intended. Avelyn, you must marry, you cannot go on as you are."

"Well, Father, I can't just click my fingers and be married. These things take time, you know."

"For many, it would take time. But you could walk down the main street of Ballycastle and look at a dozen young men with those eyes of yours and by the time you reached the end, you'd have a dozen proposals of marriage."

"My apologies, Father, but you speak nonsense. First, I wouldn't even see a dozen young men. Most would be at the inn drinking poteen and boasting how many achars of land they will farm when they leave home. But they'll never leave home—they don't have the ambition. Second, I'd make a terrible wife."

"Lassie, you mustn't talk so. God has put you in Ballycastle, and it is in Ballycastle that you must live. Now it's true that some of the lads are not quite so ambitious, but I can find it in my heart to forgive them. If they stay at home they share in their fathers' fields with the prospect of one day owning them outright. On their own, it is much harder. After all, what are their prospects?"

"They could leave Ballycastle! The world doesn't begin and end with the borders of Baron O'Ruairc's lands."

"Leave Ballycastle? But where would they go? The Doon fief to the south is hardly different, and would not be likely to welcome strangers."

"I'm not talking about the Doon fief. I'm talking about leaving this whole area. Father, when I was young you took me once to your room in the monastery. I must have been only seven or eight. You had the most beautiful carpets and tapestries. They did not come from Ballycastle, and they did not come from the Doon fief. Where did they come from, Father?"

The abbot shifted uncomfortably. "They were a present from the Archbishop in Armagh, but I don't see what—"

"But they weren't made in Armagh, father, were they? Where were they made?"

"Well, as I recall, the archbishop mentioned he'd purchased them from a Byzantine trader who'd sailed all the way to Ardmore. An Arab, I believe he called him. The carpets are likely from Byzantium."

"*Byzantium!* What a word, father! That's just what I'm talking about. No young man in the village has even *heard* of such a word. Why couldn't Seamus Larkin set sail in a curragh for Byzantium, and never come back?"

"Sail a—? Avelyn, you speak of things you know nothing about! The Byzantine Empire is no place for the likes of Ballycastle's youth. I hardly think a curragh could reach Byzantium. And learning to sail one is very difficult."

"You see? You see, Father? 'No place for the likes of Ballycastle's youth,' and yet you want me to marry one of Ballycastle's youth and live in this hopeless village forever!"

"Avelyn!"

"And you're wrong about learning to sail a curragh. It's not as hard as you think, and I expect a well-built curragh with a good navigator could go to this Byzantium place. Or anywhere beyond. All that's lacking is the will, and that's what's wrong with this whole village, Father, the will! There *isn't* any! I'm not even sure if God's will exists here anymore!"

The abbot rose in fury. "You blaspheme!" he cried out and slapped her face.

She stared at him, shocked. He'd never done such a thing. He was staring back—stunned by his own action.

Avelyn dropped to the floor and began to cry.

The abbot kneeled immediately.

"Forgive me, child. That was a wicked thing I did. I am so sorry."

Avelyn allowed herself to be helped to her feet, wiped the tears, and bowed her head submissively.

"No, it is I who should ask forgiveness. I know I must marry soon. But the thought is like a pair of hands around my throat, choking out my life."

"It need not be so, child. For centuries the maidens of Ireland have married the young men of Ireland. Life has not been choked out of them. Rather their unions have given birth to new life and made them whole. It is the role God intended for you, and it would be wrong to deny Him."

"I do not seek to deny the Lord. But if it is His will that I should marry, why did He create me as I am?"

"Perhaps it is our fault—what has happened. By taking you in and providing shelter and work, we have shown you another path and given you a chance to be independent and forsake your natural role. We had thought to be doing God's will, but now I am not so sure. Perhaps the kinder way would have been to let you seek shelter in the village, for if you had, you would be a wife and mother by now. Surely that is best."

"Is there no other way, Father? Is that really my only choice?"

"Well, I could send you to the nunnery in Armagh. But you'd make a terrible nun, and we both know it."

Avelyn smiled.

"Look, there is someone I want you to meet. He's a very satisfactory young man, Conar Malki's boy, and the Malki family is one of the more prosperous in the village. Lendl is their eldest son and stands to inherit the right to farm that portion of the baron's land. He's approaching the age where he needs to take a wife. Now I've promised nothing, but I've asked Conar to bring his son to your hut tomorrow at noon, for you to be formally introduced, and I really think—"

Avelyn looked at him with horror. "You must be joking, Father!"

"Avelyn, don't fight this! I just want to introduce you

to the young man. Is that so wrong? All you have to do is be polite."

"Father, I know Lendl Malki. He's a drunken, stupid oaf! I'll not let him near me, I'll—"

"Avelyn! Stop it! It's already arranged. Conar and Lendl will be paying you a visit tomorrow at high sun. I suggest you leave now and give thought to what kind of meal you can prepare. I know that vegetables have been scarce this season but here we have our own gardens and if you need anything—"

"You said at high sun?"

"Yes, I'm glad you're being sensible. They're taking a special leave from the fields just for the occasion. I'll be there too, of course, to make the introductions. Then, I'll make some excuse about duties here at the monastery and leave you all alone. That's what everyone expects."

"Yes, Father, that is what everyone *expects*."

The abbot looked at her, puzzled, but then continued.

"Avelyn, I truly think this will be for the best. Tomorrow may be the beginning of a new life."

"Yes, Father. I'm sure it will be."

Avelyn started for the door but stopped abruptly, turned, and faced him.

"Where is Byzantium, Father?"

"Byzantium?"

"Yes, where is it?"

"The Byzantine empire, my child, is far to the south-east of Ireland, hundreds of leagues. Perhaps a thousand."

"How did the Arab trader reach Ireland, if it is so far?"

"By boat, the miles are easily conquered. He would

have passed through the Pillars of Hercules, far to the south, and then come north along the Aquitaine coast, no doubt stopping in the land of the Angles before reaching our fair isle. I suspect the journey would have made quite an epic. But Avelyn, what's all this interest in—"

"Thank you, Father," Avelyn quickly interjected, changing the course of the conversation. "I'll be leaving now."

"Go with God, Avelyn."

43

AVELYN'S PLAN FOR leaving Ballycastle had developed as her skill with the curragh improved. The boat made all the difference. No single woman could hope to travel anywhere in Ireland without facing a host of misfortunes. Avelyn had no illusions regarding the lawless state of the Irish countryside.

But in a curragh, she could avoid all that. By keeping to the coast she could navigate around the entirety of Ireland if needed. Stopping at small villages along the way, she could buy provisions with reasonable safety. The townsfolk might find her situation preposterous, but as she would be a stranger and quickly gone they would not interfere.

Navigating around Ireland, however, was not what Avelyn intended. There was another land out there across the sea. It was one of the worlds beyond—the land of the Angles. Angland, as Father Conardy called it. The metal coins (which she received from the monastery) came from this place, and all spoke of it with respect. And there was the great city Londinium, founded by the Romans. It was said that travelers from all over the world journeyed there and that the city contained more sights than could be experienced in a lifetime.

In many ways, Avelyn was competent to make such a journey. Her relationship with the monastery had provided an education not usually associated with anyone outside the Church. She spoke Latin fluently and was certain she could find Londinium. She even spoke Anglish reasonably well, though she considered it barbarous. The Church was a great repository of knowledge and some of the best maps in Ireland were held by the monasteries. Avelyn had studied them with fascination.

Shelby had taught her coastwise navigation and how to steer a straight course at night by reference to the North Star. And Avelyn had money. Wherever she went, she would not be a pauper.

It was not absurd for Avelyn to believe she could flee Ballycastle and travel by herself to another land. Her only real foolishness, perhaps, was in believing that in another land the imperatives of society would be any different.

Nonetheless, until her talk with Father Conardy, the idea had been largely a fantasy. Her hideout on Rathlin Island had become a staging depot. She had already ferried out food, clothing, and other supplies and stored them near the rough lean-to that she'd constructed with Shelby's help. Shelby had long ago ceased questioning her plans. The old Druid at times seemed guided by his own design, but it seemed to coincide with her own.

Lying on the straw pallet in her cottage, for what she

knew would be the last time, Avelyn was almost glad the decision had been forced. If the abbot hadn't arranged the meeting with Lendl Malki—an almost-certain prelude to marriage—she might never have acted. But now she had no choice. Whatever dangers might be found in sailing a curragh alone to Angland, they could hardly compare to the certain danger of staying in Ballycastle.

If it weren't Lendl, it would be another. Her independent status in the village was viable only through her ties to the monastery. If Father Conardy was now pushing for marriage, there would be no way to avoid it.

Yet the thought of leaving home was awful. Tears welled up as she lay on her straw pallet and tried to preserve the important memories. Whatever might happen in the *worlds beyond*, she would never come back.

So she called forth the kind and caring face of the abbot and held it there, seeking to memorize the wrinkles on his brow, the deep wisdom in his eyes, and the tenderness with which he treated her. She would never see him again. She did the same with others she wished not to forget, and then, with places and events dear to her.

Avelyn was not sleepy, despite having worked feverishly from the moment she'd returned from the monastery—tidying up her cottage, placing in a small bundle everything she would need not already stored on the island, and most importantly, finishing her washing and sewing for the monks. She neatly folded and stacked the completed pile on the table, with a note in Latin that would ultimately find its way into the hands of the abbot. She owed him more than a note, but it was all she could give. She read it one last time.

Father, I love you with all my heart. You took me in as a child and turned me into a woman. I speak not of the advance of years, which would have turned me into a woman regardless. I speak of what I hold in my mind because of you—my greatest teacher. But dearer than all you have taught is my simple memory of you, my greatest friend. My true father. It is a treasure that will never be lost.

I have left Ballycastle forever. My fear is that you will fret unnecessarily for my safety. All I can say is that you know what you have taught me, and you also know that I would not do anything foolish.

I do not claim the path I have chosen is without danger. But, as you can best understand, I believe it has been chosen for me by God. I truly believe it is God's will that I leave Ballycastle.

I can hear your stern voice now questioning my certainty, and you would be right to do so. But the time for questioning has passed. Ultimately, one must act as one believes correct. Not acting at such a time is a greater sin than merely being wrong. I may be wrong Father—you did teach me humility—but at least I am doing what I believe is right.

Thank you. Thank you. Thank you. I am forever your loving daughter—

Avelyn

44

FATHER CONARDY SET the note aside with trembling hands and lowered himself into the hut's lone chair.

"Well what is it, Your Grace?" asked Conar Malki. "She's off on some errand I take it. How long must we wait? I should be in the fields, not running around like an old woman finding a wife for my son here."

Lendl Malki, who was wearing a stupid grin, blushed and kicked at the dirt floor.

"Well, Your Grace, speak up!" Malki insisted. "I say, are you quite well, Your Grace?"

Father Conardy sat with his head in his hands, elbows on the table, moaning softly.

Conar Malki crossed the room and laid a hand on the priest's shoulder, shaking it slightly.

"Your Grace, I think we deserve an explanation here, I think my son deserves a—"

He did not finish the sentence. The door to the cottage burst open and two of the baron's guards rushed in, followed by Brody Flannagain.

"Good day, Your Grace," said Flannagain, surprised to find two peasants and the abbot, where he'd expected to find Avelyn, alone. "Where is the girl?"

The older of the peasants answered quickly.

"If you mean the girl, Avelyn, kind sirs, we were just wondering ourselves. If you please, we had an appointment to meet her and quite obviously she is not here."

Flannagain turned to the abbot.

"Your Grace, where has Avelyn gone, and when will she return?"

Conardy glanced up from his chair and Flannagain noticed his face bore the look of a man completely at peace, odd though that seemed in the circumstance.

"May I ask, Brody, why you wish to know?"

"We have been sent by the baron to invite Avelyn to the castle for dinner."

"Sir, Your Grace—" It was Conar Malki who spoke, addressing both of them.

"What is it?" snapped Flannagain.

"I spoke the truth, we had planned to meet the lass. But if the baron wishes to see her—. Well, if it please you, may my son and I be excused from this affair. My fields lie waiting."

"But Father, does this mean I'll not be marrying Avelyn?" wailed Lendl.

"Quiet, fool. We are too late for that, and best we are!"

"You have sense, peasant," said Flannagain. "And you," he nodded towards Lendl, "best listen to your sire. Both of you, begone!"

He turned to the guards. "Search the village. When you find her, bring her to the castle. I'll meet you there."

The guard captain saluted, and soon Flannagain was alone with the abbot.

"Brody, everyone knows what an invitation to dine at the castle means, and this vile deed is being done despite Avelyn being under my protection. Apparently, my power in Ballycastle is waning."

"Let us speak openly, Your Grace. Your power has never been stronger and we both know it."

"And the baron?"

"He doesn't care."

"You know, Brody, what will happen if you seize Avelyn?"

"I had hoped you and I might come to an accommodation."

"Hardly. If you seize Avelyn, I will send word to my superior, the Archbishop of Armagh, informing him that O'Ruairc wantonly insulted the Church and that I had him excommunicated."

"Your Grace—"

"I'm not finished. The Archbishop will immediately notify the High King, and make it clear that an excommunicated baron was an affront to God. The Ard Ri will probably just send word to Lord Fakis, whom we know lusts after the Antrim fief, and inform him that the High King no longer acknowledged O'Ruairc's claim to this land."

"Your Grace, you must not—"

"I'm still not finished. We both know Donnchad's support is the only thing keeping O'Ruairc in that castle.

The moment it's withdrawn, Fakis will attack. And he'll kill the baron—to ensure the Ard Ri doesn't change his mind again."

Brody was worried. He hadn't thought about an excommunication, let alone what would flow from it. The danger was very real.

"Your Grace, these matters are above my station. Surely there is some way all this trouble can be avoided. Perhaps it might be possible to convince the baron to rethink the harvest tax increase, for example."

Father Conardy shook his head and laughed softly. "None of it matters, now, Brody."

"How so, Your Grace?"

"She's gone."

"I see she is gone. But to where?"

"As God is my judge, I have not the slightest idea."

"Then we will find her. And when we do, we can resume this conversation. I'm certain we can resolve any—"

"I don't mean she is gone from this cottage. I mean she is gone from Ballycastle. Forever."

"She fled Ballycastle? She knew of our coming?"

"She did not know of your coming."

"Then why did she go?" Flannagain was already worried about how he'd explain this to the baron.

"Because she is the most intelligent, capable human being this town has ever produced and, being so, she knew she had to leave."

"You paint riddles, Your Grace. If she has fled, the guards will pursue her."

"They will not catch her."

"Of course they will. How far could she have gone?"

"The odds would seem to favor you, but I say again, you will not find her."

"And I say 'Why not?'"

"For years Avelyn has been under my protection, as you know. Now she is under God's protection. It is obvious, seeing the events unfold over the last few days. It was *I* who precipitated a situation that forced her to flee. And I now realize my actions only just saved her from your baron—a fate which would have surely killed her.

"Since God has taken a direct interest in the matter, it might be well to recall another time God assisted with an escape. It was the Hebrews fleeing Egypt and, if memory serves, the army sent in pursuit fared poorly. You will never find Avelyn."

"We will find her, Your Grace. And then I will be back to negotiate. Please give thought to your price."

Flannagain left the hut before the abbot could respond. It would be a tough negotiation, but the opening moves had been established. Surely he would not make good on his ex-communication threat. And even if he did, nothing would happen on a political level quickly enough to keep Avelyn from the baron. If worst came to worst, Flannagain told himself, he could simply turn traitor and work for Fakis.

Capable seneschals were always in demand.

45

ON THE FIFTEENTH day, Kren made landfall off Verkie, the southern tip of the Shetland Islands. He steered the flotilla westward for nearly one hundred leagues, turned south, and instituted a new policy: ships would heave-to during the night.

The high latitudes combined with the proximity of the solstice meant very short nights. Nonetheless, Torsten found the delay intolerable.

"We have maps of these waters, Kren. What is your concern? Are we off course? Have you lost your way? If so I could understand, but I have never known you to be off course."

"It is not our course that concerns me, Uncle. I have the utmost confidence in our position. But I have little confidence in our maps."

"Our map makers are among the best in the world. You've said so yourself."

"They cannot record what has not been told, and they cannot be told what has not been seen."

"Do you think there is that much land around here that has not been seen?"

"Yes. We are skirting a group of islands called the Hebrides. I have spoken to those who have been among them. No two agree on their location, nor their arrangement. The mapmakers draw them from speculation—they admit it freely. And let me tell you this: nowhere is navigation so treacherous. Small islets and rocks appear and disappear with the state of the tide. One seems to be in open water, far from land, only to see a jagged tooth rising stationary from the waves, waiting to rip the soul out of a longboat."

"But the delay—"

"Uncle, a few days matter not, compared to the possible loss of half the ships. Or even one of them. I do not know what gods rule these waters but they are not friendly to us. We are children of Thor and Odin and that is sufficient to see us to victory, but the local gods are not to be trifled with. By heaving-to at night, we not only exercise prudent seamanship; our action will be considered a mark of respect by the deities."

"And how long will your orders on this stand?"

"Indefinitely. All we know is that Ireland is about three days south of the southernmost tip of the Hebrides—an island called Mingulay, which we may miss altogether."

Kren was fortunate. The next afternoon, after nine hours of sailing, he spotted Mingulay. It was recognizable by its curious shape, which resembled a fat walrus lying on its back, tusks pointing skyward. The tusks were needles of rock and the fat stomach a broad hillside.

Kren gave it wide berth and altered course two points to port. Ireland itself was only an island and it was conceivable, if they sailed too far westward, that they might miss it entirely. What lay beyond was uncertain.

Kren's plan meant they might sail too close to the land of the Scotti, but that seemed a lesser danger. If they came ashore in Caledonia, they could set a new course from there. But if they missed Ireland altogether, they could be lost in the Western Sea.

After three days without sighting land Kren altered course again—five points to port.

The fourth morning after leaving Mingulay, as the sun was nearing its zenith, the lookout on the lead ship hailed down from his perch atop the mast.

"Land!" he shouted. "Land, dead ahead."

Kren smiled with satisfaction. His orders of the previous night had proven correct. The course change had produced Ireland for them and, had they continued during the night, they most likely would have wrecked their ships on the approaching coastline.

"Heave to!" Kren ordered.

"Lookout!" he yelled. "Describe what you see." Kren would have preferred to climb the mast himself, but his bad arm kept him bound to the deck.

"Sir, it may be only an island, but the mainland appears to be south of it. I'm seeing a thin line of haze that may be the loam of the land."

Kren nodded. That would make sense. Like Caledonia, Ireland might have a coastline of many islands, and it was only natural their first glimpse of her would be one. The haze to the south, as the lookout said, most probably was the mainland.

Torsten stood against the rail and gazed south. But from the deck, there was nothing to see. The long Atlantic rollers produced a gentle, easy motion to the ship. The other vessels in the flotilla had formed up with Kren's, heaving-to almost within arm's reach of one another. Most of the men not directly engaged in handling the ship were lined along the port rail with Torsten. All were curious. Kren joined them.

"Uncle, I give you Ireland!" Kren said, smiling.

Jumping onto the railing, holding a mast shroud for support, Torsten hailed the crew in a voice strong enough to carry to the other vessels.

"Followers of Thor, it is a great thing we have done! In these small ships, we have fought wind and wave, navigated among the most treacherous islands on earth, and sailed uncharted seas. Others have spoken of this land's existence, but we shall be the first to bend it to our will. Thor is proud of our deeds. And He is especially proud of Kren, our valiant sailing master, before whom the oceans of the world bow in submission. Hail Kren!"

And from all seven ships roared an echo: *"Hail Kren!"*

"Tomorrow the great Odin himself will be at our side, joining us in battle. We will test ax against ax, and shield against shield. When we are finished, Ireland will lie like a woman before us, ready to be taken. And we shall have her! Who shall follow Odin and me into battle?"

And from all seven boats came a single, throaty cry *"I!"*

And who shall join me in taking Ireland?"

"I!"

"Warriors, show me your weapons!"

And from the seven boats, hundreds of men drew their axes, spears, and swords, holding their choice of weapon high, catching the glint of the cold northern sun.

"Hail Thor!" cried Torsten.

"Hail Thor!" echoed the warriors.

"On to Ireland!" And with that final war cry, Torsten sheathed his sword and leaped down from the rail.

Kren had been watching this performance with amusement and knew the melodramatics would be spoiled if sail weren't immediately set and a course chosen.

"Helmsman, fall off two points! Velksen! Alar! Trim the sail!"

Kren's ship seized the wind, heeled over with determination, and began cutting purposefully through the waves. The six other longboats followed.

46

"THAT WAS QUITE a speech," said Kren to his uncle when they were alone. "I felt it called for getting underway at once. Unfortunately, we have no course to steer, nor do we know where we wish to go."

"We know exactly where we wish to go—to the first Irish settlement we can find. And we know our course, for that is the course that will take us most quickly to the Irish mainland."

Kren gave the matter some thought. He considered the location of the island and the relative bearing of the Irish coast, took a final glance at the location of the sun, and then issued further orders to the helmsman.

In four hours, with the sun still high, the lookout called again to the deck.

"Sailing Master, I can now see the land to the south clearly. I do not think it is an island."

Kren started to ask a question but then had a better idea.

"Gunnar! Harald! Lend me a hand here."

"Yes, sir!"

"I must reach the top of that mast. I cannot direct the flotilla without seeing this land myself."

"Yes, sir," said Harald again, looking puzzled.

"I want a second halyard rove around one of the masthead blocks. The end of that halyard can then be secured around my shoulders, and in that way, I can be hauled up."

"Hauled up, sir?"

"Yes, Thor's breath. I know it won't look dignified, but that can't be helped. Now organize that halyard."

Soon Kren was standing on the lookout step himself, with one arm around the mast for support and the other shading his eyes. He stared a long time towards the land, and then signaled the men to lower him back to the deck. Untangling himself, he reported to Torsten.

"Uncle, I believe we have found our settlement."

"What did you see?"

"Thanks to the angle of the sun the Irish mainland is well shadowed. I could make out what appears to be the opening of a fjord. They would call it a firth, perhaps, if they speak the Angle's tongue. Now, an inlet such as this in our land would shelter a settlement, would it not?"

"In our land, yes. But who can predict the customs of foreigners?"

"In matters of the sea, there are no foreigners. Any village on any coast must interact with the water as part of its daily commerce, else why be on the water? And that means they will locate in a good harbor. Or, put another way, where one finds a good harbor, one will almost always find a village."

"Perhaps, but I am reluctant to trap ourselves down a fjord unnecessarily. How can we confirm the existence of a settlement?"

"I have already done so. I could see the opening from the masthead. While I watched I saw no less than three sailing vessels enter. Quite likely, they are fishermen, returning with their day's catch. And they would hardly return to a spot which had no village."

"Very well. We will attack tonight—just before dawn."

"I would caution against that, Uncle. The fjord is unknown to us, in length or shape or obstacles. Come daylight, I can far more easily navigate."

"Are you saying entering the fjord at night is impossible?"

Kren considered the question. There would be moonlight. The weather was fair.

"Not impossible."

Torsten laid an arm on Kren's shoulder.

"Nephew, no man is your equal in navigating ships. But you know little of battle. Were we to sail down that fjord in daylight we would be spotted right at the entrance, and the entire village would await our coming, not with open arms, I think. More likely with cross-bows, axes, and whatever weapons these Irish possess. No, it must be at night. There is no other way."

"You have bowed to my wishes in our journey so far, Uncle. I will bow to yours in this matter."

"Kren, you are truly my brother's son. Now, we have much to attend to."

Torsten called for Knut, one of his officers.

"I want all weapons checked, and sharpened as needed. You can almost hear them rusting on these sea voyages. I want the men fed before they take their sleep, and I want them asleep early."

"It shall be done, sir. And I've some thoughts on how the ships might be best deployed when we reach the village. If you'd care to hear them—"

"With pleasure." The two plunged into a discussion of tactics.

The ships led by the laughing Valkyrie plunged onwards through the cold Atlantic swells. Spray flew from the bulwarks and the sails were taut against their rigging as they closed upon the Irish coast.

47

AVELYN SAT COMFORTABLY among the boulders and watched as a goat searched for grass nearby. Suddenly it spotted her and stared, not certain if greater safety could be found in flight or immobility. Reaching a decision, it leaped away and disappeared into the woods.

I fled just like that, she thought.

It was her second day on Rathlin Island. The morning she'd left Ballycastle began with a visit to Shelby's hut down near the water before even the fishermen were awake.

"Shelby! Wake up! It's me."

"Me who?" said a groggy, sleepy voice from inside.

"Me, *Avelyn*. I'm in trouble."

The door swung open.

"Come in, lass, come in. A mite early for one of your jaunts to the island isn't it?" He noticed the heavy bundle she was carrying.

"Here, let's get this pack off you."

Avelyn set it down gratefully, arching her shoulders back and forth to restore circulation.

"What sort of trouble?"

"Marriage trouble." Avelyn was too tired to say more until she'd caught her breath.

"So, I reckon the monks finally realized what an unsettling influence you were on the young men around town, eh?"

"Something like that. Oh, Shelby, it was awful. Father Conardy has even figured out who I'm to marry. That yokel, Lendl Malki. I've an appointment to meet with him and his father at noon today."

"That's it? You're just to meet with him? Is that why you're running away?"

Avelyn looked at the old man's perceptive eyes and then at the pack on the floor.

"I guess it's obvious I'm running away."

"Aye, lass."

"Well, you know this village. If I'm to 'meet' a young man today I'll be engaged to him by tomorrow, at least in the eyes of the townspeople, and I'll be married to him in a week—a fortnight at most. If Father Conardy himself wants it to happen I'll have absolutely no say in the matter. Am I wrong?"

Shelby walked over to his bench and found a length of rope needing a splice. Returning to the hearth, his deft hands began the process of braiding the two ends together. Avelyn watched quietly, finding the practiced movements comforting. She wished her own life could be fixed as easily as Shelby could repair a parted shroud.

"No, you're not wrong," he said. "'Cept you forgot a few things. Beggin' your pardon, but in a month you'd be pregnant, and in nine more you'd have a wee one, and then your days of roaming the hills and sailing the curragh would be over. At least until you were so old that walking would be a pain, and the wet sea air would inflame your joints. Then, you'd only be fit to stay home by the fire and reflect on your memories—except by that point you'd have lost the chance to have any.

"You're right to flee this place. I've known it was your destiny from the first day down at the water when we spoke of the curragh."

Avelyn smiled. "You're the only one who understands. I could never live that life. Never!"

The old man's tone grew urgent. "I'm not talking about what life *you* want, child!"

"What do you mean?" She asked slowly. "Then what *are* you talking about?"

"Avelyn, I built your curragh and I taught you to sail it, and I even helped you fix up a hideaway on Rathlin Island. But I did none of that to help you avoid marriage."

"Then—why did you do those things?" she asked in a whisper, scarcely breathing.

"Because it was the will of the Earth and the Sea, that's why! You carry a power, Avelyn. I saw it that first day. The Earth and the Sea have an interest in you and they made it known. They had a task for me, and I hope I've performed it well."

"What task, Shelby?" Avelyn was still whispering. For some reason, an icy terror had come over her.

"The task of providing you an escape from Ballycastle. The curragh was the only way. You wouldn't last three hours on the roads. And the island, that was part of it. Every seafarer needs a land base, and yours is Rathlin. But there's something you should know about that island."

"What should I know?" The hair on her neck was prickling.

"You're a Druid, Avelyn! You pretend to be a Christian because you don't wish to offend the abbot. But in your heart, you're a Druid. You respect and practice the old religion. You understand that the spiritual world is all around us, residing in every tree, rock, and wave. You're attuned to the Earth and the Sea, not to Jesus. Can you deny it?"

Avelyn went white. It was blasphemy to suggest such a thing! How did he know what was in her heart? She'd never spoken it.

Shelby gripped her tightly by the shoulders.

"Can you deny it? Answer me!"

"I don't know!" she cried in frustration. "Can't I be both?"

But she wasn't both, even though she tried to be.

Shelby released her and walked back to the hearth.

"I don't know if you can be both," he said. "But that's not important now. Here's what you need to know. Rathlin was the meeting place for Druidic priests of old. My grandfather took me there. It was a place of rituals…of magic. The cave I showed you on Rathlin, with the statues—that's where the ceremonies were performed and the fires were lit. You will be close to the Earth and the Sea there. It's an island of power. You will feel that power and *it will work its way into you.*"

"Shelby, I—"

"I've kept the curragh ready, not knowing when the time would come. Now it is time and you must flee."

"Shelby, you're scaring me. Why do I need to flee? If not to avoid marriage, then why?"

"Something evil is coming, Avelyn. It will consume the village. The Earth and Sea have spoken. And they want you out before it arrives."

Avelyn regarded the old man. She'd known he was a Druid—a real one. He practiced the ancient ways; performed the rituals. That meant he spoke to the Earth, to the rocks, to the trees; or at least thought he did. Druids believed they could see into the future. But she'd never known one to develop a premonition; to be given a warning from the Earth, and a task to perform. But if the spirits were to entrust anyone in Ballycastle with a special task, it would certainly be Shelby.

"What evil? What is coming? When?"

"I do not know, lass. I have not been given that knowledge. But I've known for weeks that there would come a time when you would wish to flee, for your own reasons, and that I must help you. Now, let us be done with this talk. You must be on your way."

"Shelby, I didn't come here to say goodbye!"

The old man paused, suddenly uncertain. His look of confusion made Avelyn laugh, a disarming and refreshing sound among this talk of doom—much like a ray of sunshine during a storm.

"I want you to come with me, Shelby," Avelyn proposed. "Together, we can sail that curragh anywhere on earth! What is there here that's not worth leaving? And if what you say is true, and some dread is about to descend on Ballycastle, that's all the more reason to get out. Come with me, my friend, and we'll see the world together."

Shelby stared at the fire, and Avelyn respected that a lifetime of wisdom was being brought to bear. Finally, he shook his head sadly.

"Thank you, lass. But it is not the plan. It is not what the Earth wishes for either of us. But your offer lightens my heart. Whatever I have done—has been repaid. Now let us speak no more of this and see you on your way."

Avelyn opened her mouth to protest but changed her mind. He wanted to go, but a power to which he'd devoted his life wished otherwise and nothing she could say would avail. She walked over and kissed the old man lightly on the cheek.

"I understand. But I'll miss you dreadfully."

Shelby gave her a hug, then pushed her away gently, and turned to the task at hand. Like they'd done so many times, she slipped between the gunwales of the curragh and he eased the craft along its log rollers into the water.

A brisk sea breeze was blowing across the harbor. Avelyn raised the halyard while Shelby held the craft against the pilings.

The two stared at each other for a few moments and then Shelby pushed the craft out into the bay.

"Off with you, lass! Make haste, and never return!"

"Goodbye, Shelby," Avelyn said with a wave, wanting to cry, but too excited to do so.

She seized the tiller with one hand and grasped the mainsheet with the other. A gentle south wind was blowing.

Avelyn eased the mainsheet and the curragh picked up speed. She had only to steer, which was easy for the stars were bright—perhaps brighter than she'd ever seen them. Was there something to the old man's belief after all? Did the Earth wish her to escape Ballycastle? And if so, was he correct about a great evil coming?

Avelyn pondered these questions but soon was lulled by the gentleness of the waves, the glory of the stars, and the steadiness of the wind. Her little curragh danced lightly across the sea, and Avelyn felt one with the elements. She had left everything, yet strangely felt like she had everything she needed, here in the moment. Despite being completely alone, she felt a presence around her—both comforting and friendly.

Avelyn arrived at her island's sheltered bay shortly after the sun broke above the eastern horizon. After pulling the curragh onto the beach, Avelyn walked a hundred yards inland to her lean-to hut, protected on three sides and provisioned with wool sheepskins, some food, and a bucket of water. She slept until noon.

That had been yesterday. Now her plans were vague. She needed more provisions, so she'd gone fishing earlier. Her net brought in over a dozen salmon from the mouth of the stream which flowed into the bay. The fish were now drying on racks.

She'd need three times that many before she could leave for Angland. But she was in no hurry and growing languid. It was as if the Druidic spirits, satisfied in her flight from Ballycastle, wanted to keep her on the island.

The pack contained her entire hoard of silver

coins—which would keep her from starving in any land. But in the meantime they were cumbersome and—on impulse—she'd buried them in a cache near the campsite.

For now, Avelyn lay against the rocks, soaking up the warmth of the sun, observing the goats, the sea birds, and occasionally a fish that would break the surface of the bay. She was waiting for something but had no idea what.

As Avelyn closed her eyes in contentment, a cloud moved in front of the sun, and a cold shadow passed over her. A frigid gust of wind blew in from the west. Avelyn opened her eyes in surprise. The sun broke through and the breeze died.

She tried to relax but could not. She felt the Earth had spoken to her, as clearly as it had spoken to Shelby. And the shadow which crossed the sun had been a warning. But what it was a warning of, she could not see. Nor was her own role clear. She reached out with her senses, seeking answers, but none would come. In frustration, she headed back to her shelter. Another dozen fish could be caught and salted before sunset.

But the premonition stayed with her. She would never eat the fish.

48

THEY ATTACKED BEFORE dawn, the ships borne by the flood tide and a sea breeze. Each man carried a round wooden shield and wore a metal helmet and nose plate. Chain mail was not popular with the Norsemen, who preferred heavy leather jerkins and skirts for protection. Their weapons were varied and reflected personal preference. Axes, spears, and crossbows were common. Swords and fighting irons, less so, except among the experienced fighters. Most also carried a knife.

Vikings attacking an unknown coast could not estimate what resistance they would meet. And sea warriors far from home must win their first battle, to gain a land base. So the Norsemen needed to be merciless. But that was their nature.

The ships approached the village's small wharf in single file, each drawing up just long enough to unload the men. A small crew piloted the craft onwards to an anchorage.

At first, it seemed the Vikings would be able to form up and attack in unison before an alarm was sounded.

Unfortunately, a pack of dogs came on the scene and begin howling, as the last of the Norsemen disembarked.

Crossbows silenced them quickly, but by then a few townspeople had risen to see what the dogs were up to. The sight of foreign ships anchored in the bay, and a pagan army milling about with shields, axes, and torches was incomprehensible, and most did not recognize their peril. One who did, ran to the market square and rang the large bell which existed to signal danger or calamity. The harsh metal clang cut through the pre-dawn darkness.

Hearing the bell, and knowing the advantage of surprise was about to be lost, the Norse warriors let out a collective battle cry and swept over the village.

Ballycastle's ability to offer resistance to a well-trained army of warriors arriving in the middle of the night was nil.

&

Two Vikings crashed into the door of the first hut they encountered, which broke from its hinges and flew inward. Three elderly fishermen lived inside. Two of them managed to rise before a Viking ax removed the head of the first, and a sword plunged completely through the stomach of the second. The third fisherman, wide-eyed with terror and seeking to draw his wool blankets around him, was dispatched with a knife to the throat. The Vikings left the hut with their weapons dripping blood. One tossed a burning torch into a straw bed, and in seconds the cottage was a blazing pyre.

A Norse party of four swept through a row of huts just west of the harbor. A puzzled, elderly woman stepped out wearing a wool wrap, but the Viking outside had already started his downward stroke the moment the door opened and it was unstoppable. The woman's head was cleaved like a melon by the ax. Her two grown sons were rising from their beds when another Viking rushed in and killed them both with quick knife thrusts.

A third band of Norsemen broke into a cottage near the market. It was the home of a barley farmer, his wife, and three daughters. The first Viking burst in and killed the farmer immediately, then noticed the others were women. Calling to his companions, he reached for the nearest girl and flung aside her nightclothes. He forced her off balance and she fell back onto the bed screaming.

The destruction of Ballycastle proceeded methodically. Torsten's orders were to kill all men and boys. Any women who would make useful slaves for trading with the Danes, or for the Norsemen's own use, were to be captured. Other females, too old or too young, were to be killed along with the men.

Despite these orders, in the madness and fury, such distinctions were often missed. Young pregnant women were often mistaken for portly men in the darkness and slain in their beds or as they tried to rise. One party, finding itself confronted by a large man who stood in the doorway of his hut with a pitchfork, refusing to die and wounding Norsemen as fast as they came at him, was overcome by tossing one of the torches through the open window and setting the room ablaze. The high pitched screams revealed women and children sharing his fate, but it could not be helped.

ꕥ

Kren left *Freya's Song* under the command of a seaman and followed Torsten into the village. Despite Kren not being a warrior, his uncle liked him nearby for advice.

Their arrival had gone smoothly. Kren had steered the first longboat up to the small wharf, which was far more convenient than having to beach the vessels, although he'd been prepared to order that if necessary. The warriors could jump into shallow water and wade to land if needed. The wind made it easy to approach the village silently, under sail, but if they'd been repulsed the longboats would have had to claw off a lee shore. Navigational worries were now behind him, the men landed, and the boats anchored.

His uncle walked swiftly up the main road, with twenty elite troops. This special unit ignored the civilian population, for its job was to seek out military outposts and engage them before a counter-attack could be launched. So far, they had found nothing.

As the massacre of civilians continued, Kren was surprised no armed force had appeared. Was it possible Ireland was soft and could be invaded with ease? On his raids into Aquitaine, after the collapse of Charlemagne's dynasty, Kren had seen villages where there simply was no armed opposition.

Torsten's band rounded a corner and in front of them, at the edge of the forest, stood a large stone building of two floors and a tile roof. It was surrounded by a stone fence and an impressive iron gate.

"Halt!" Torsten shouted, and the others formed up

behind him. "Odger!" he called, and an older man with specks of gray in his beard came to his side. Odger was the most widely traveled Norsemen in their party, having participated in the raid on Lindisfarne and the attack on Nantes. On expeditions with the Swedes, he had even been in battle at Riga and Novgorod far to the east.

"Old friend," Torsten asked, pausing for breath, "what have we here? A fortress? I find it poorly designed if that be its purpose."

Odger stroked his beard in contemplation and then walked over to the gate and peered through the bars before returning.

"It's a monastery."

"What's that?"

"It's connected with their Christian religion. There was one similar at Lindisfarne."

"You mean it's a shrine?"

"Not a shrine, master, or at least not solely a shrine. Those dedicated to the Christian religion, to the exclusion of everything else, become monks and live in such places. They do little except speak to their god, and seek wisdom."

"Are they armed? Might they attack with religious fervor, as do our Berserks?"

"No, Captain. The Christian religion teaches peace. Monks are passive."

"Then perhaps we should ignore this place."

"There's no threat, Captain, but monasteries are often filled with treasure, for many bring gifts to their god."

"This is no time for looting," admonished Kren.

"We'll worry about treasure later," agreed Torsten.

"When the rest of the town is secure we'll come back and kill the monks. Let's keep going."

Less than an hour after their boats landed, the Norsemen had overcome the entire village and taken more than eighty female prisoners. Most everyone else was dead or mortally wounded. Torsten was assembling a command headquarters back near the harbor. When the first light crested the eastern hills it revealed the remains of the village and the fearful destruction wrought by the invaders.

"Well, Uncle, you've won a great victory here. But it seems your men left alive only women of childbearing age. Did they kill even the children?"

"Conquering new lands is not for the timid, Kren, or for those with scruples. If we weren't so far from home and surrounded by enemies, it might be possible to keep the children as slaves. That's normal. But we can't afford a large body of prisoners. We don't have the resources for—"

"Killing children is despicable."

"I take no pleasure in it, be assured. Even Great Odin looks away. But not all battle is glorious. In truth—"

Kren was not listening. The sailing master was staring at something up on the hillside to the south, something the morning sun had just illuminated. Torsten followed his gaze.

There on the rise, black and menacing despite the shaft of sunlight falling directly on it, was a small castle. A dozen flags waved in the morning breeze and Kren thought he could see men pacing back and forth along the walls in practiced disciplined movements. There was no question of this being a religious structure.

"Perhaps Ireland is not so weak after all," said Kren.

"By Thor, why have they not attacked!" asked Torsten. "With such a fortress, and the garrison it must hold, we should have been obliterated within moments of that damned bell going off. Why have they not attacked?"

49

BRODY FLANNAGAIN STOOD before the fireplace in the dining hall. He was weary, having just returned from overseeing the search for Avelyn, and he'd hoped to enjoy some sleep before daybreak. But the baron left orders to be awakened the moment he returned, so Brody waited resignedly until his master was roused from bed. The expression on the face of the chamberlain who relayed this message, or rather the complete lack of expression, told Flannagain what sort of mood O'Ruairc was in. He prepared for the verbal torrent.

"Brody? Brody are you in there?"

The oafish, bellowing voice echoed down the hall in advance of its owner.

"Yes, my lord," Brody replied with poorly-feigned deference. Fortunately, subtleties of tone were lost on the baron.

O'Ruairc blustered in.

"So, you're finally back. I assume you have good news."

"My lord, I do not. The search continues as we speak."

"Well, damn, Brody. Until now, I've considered you

quite competent. Not to say you can't use guidance now and then, but on the whole, quite satisfactory."

"Thank you, my lord." Flannagain knew this speech, and how to deliver his lines.

"But see here, man, it's been days since I asked you to bring the wench, Avelyn. How long does it take to fetch one of my village girls? If I didn't know your habits, I'd say you're enjoying her yourself, before turning her over to me. There's no excuse for it, simply none!"

"You're quite right, my lord. The situation is intolerable. But the girl's a sly one. From our questioning, it appears she must have fled Ballycastle the very night you asked for her. We've scoured the roads south and east, as you know, and I've even sent horsemen over the lands to the west, though how she could survive in that country, I know not. But we've found no trace of her, nor have we found anyone who has. It's as if she just vanished, my lord."

"Young girls of Ballycastle do not vanish, Brody. Leastways, not unless they vanish into my bedchambers!" The baron paused a moment. "Well now, that was funny!"

"Quite, my lord."

"So where is she, Brody? Where could she have gone?"

"I did have one thought. Perhaps one of the fishermen helped her escape in a curragh. But I've questioned all of them—even that old fool, Shelby. The truth is, none of them were gone from the village, even for a short while during the time Avelyn escaped. And they can all prove it."

"What about the monastery? The priests would hide her if they could."

"We've searched there, of course, my lord. Nearly tore

the place apart, but found nothing. And the abbot himself was surprised at her disappearance. Remember he and two of the villagers were at Avelyn's cabin expecting to meet her at noon.

"I will not call off the hunt, Brody. I do not care if it requires every man at arms in Ballycastle, every castle servant, every peasant from the fields; every hag from the village. The search will continue until I receive what is mine. Do you understand me?"

"I do, my lord. But if you will permit, I have a theory."

"Out with it!"

"I'm quite certain she fled by one of the southbound roads. It was really her only choice. And as you know we have not entirely succeeded in eliminating brigandage from the highways."

"Another of your failings."

"Yes, my lord. But I think it likely young Avelyn was simply robbed and murdered, probably the first night she took to the road. The murderer would wish to hide the evidence, so might be expected to bury her in a shallow grave, or at least cover her with stones. It would take only moments, and would prevent us from ever finding the body, except with sheer luck."

"Hmmm. Murdered, you say? Well, it would not be the worst outcome. Far better for her to die than escape. But how do we know for certain, Brody? We can't simply assume."

"My lord, I find it the only possible explanation. Nothing else explains the facts. If she had fled down the highway unmolested we would have caught up with her long since. She had no horse. But to simply vanish? It's not possible. Unless she vanished into a grave. Because that is the *only* explanation, I submit it is the *correct* one."

A bell began clanging somewhere in the direction of the village.

"What the devil?" asked the baron, turning vaguely towards the noise.

"It's the village bell, my lord," said Flannagain in alarm. "It hasn't rung for a quarter-century!"

"Well, what does it mean, Brody?" A look of concern, almost of fear, crossed the baron's features.

"It must be an emergency, my lord. A fire in the village, or a child drowning in the bay, perhaps. We must go at once!"

"Ah, a fire, you say? Or perhaps a drowning." The baron had regained his look of indifference. "Now see here, Brody. Seems we were in the middle of a conversation. Cannot this matter of the bell wait until morning?"

"As you wish, my lord, but it might be good for you to be seen presiding over the village in a time of crisis. Merely to be there on horseback, observing, would have a settling effect on the rabble, and would earn you respect in their eyes."

For the second time in several days, Flannagain instantly regretted the words.

"*Respect* for me in their eyes! Respect for *me*! You forget yourself, Brody! It is I who condescend to grant them respect—if I will—not the other way around. I find this lapse most distressing, Brody, I…"

A guard burst into the drawing-room.

"My lord!" he exclaimed, dropping to one knee and bowing his head swiftly.

"What is it man, what is it?" The baron was becoming flustered.

"It's an attack, my lord! The village is under attack!"

"Impossible!" said Flannagain. "Who's attacking? Who would dare attack Ballycastle?"

"I do not know, master. But from the walls, we can see large sections of the village ablaze, and there is the sound of fighting. And the screaming, my lord—" The guard could not continue, overcome with concern for his own family.

Typically in an emergency, it would be Flannagain who would take charge, efficiently dealing with whatever civil disturbance had occurred—famine, thievery, even a plague on one occasion. But he'd had no exposure to war. Coward though the Baron might be, he at least had military experience.

"My lord, if we are under attack I can offer no advice. I await your orders."

Flannagain realized the baron had turned a ghastly white and was staring straight ahead, towards the door, whimpering slightly.

"My lord?" Flannagain prompted once more.

The seneschal finally realized there was only one person in the castle who could take command, and it wasn't the baron.

"Bar the gate," he ordered the guard. "Roust out the garrison—all of it. Have the Captain meet me in the courtyard.

"At once, sir."

Flannagain took another look at the baron and noticed a pool of yellow liquid expanding at his feet.

50

AVELYN WOKE TO the smell of burning wood. In Ballycastle, wood smoke was common—especially in the morning as the women prepared food for the day. But Avelyn had grown accustomed to the special scent of her island—the rich salt-laden air, the tingling smell of the pines, and at low tide the slightly decayed aroma of the marshlands. The only time she smelled wood smoke was from her own fire, which she banked securely at night.

While enjoying the final moments before arising, her mind deduced that wood smoke could only mean someone else on the island. Avelyn jumped to her feet. She had thoroughly explored Rathlin and if she needed to hide, she could. On the other hand, if there were an intruder, she would be safer in the curragh.

She ran down to the beach and launched the boat. The wind was southerly, forcing her to tack out of the cove.

It was a good way to start the day, she thought—spray flying in her face, cleansing any remaining sleep from her eyes.

A smile came unaware to Avelyn's face. The pleasant rhythms of life on the island had eased her worries about the future. *In fact, what did it matter if there were an intruder?* In her curragh, she was free to sail anywhere and might leave for Angland anytime. Today, perhaps.

Her desire to find the source of the wood smoke was actually no more than an excuse to go sailing, now that she thought about it. Avelyn looked closely at the shoreline, seeking the telltale rise of a plume of smoke from a solitary campfire. With this wind, the smoke might disperse quickly, and blow away to the north. That would mean she'd need to keep a sharp lookout on the—

Avelyn cried out in alarm. She turned her eyes southwards, seeking the coast of the mainland. She'd been a fool! The smell of wood smoke was still in the air, here at sea, south of the island. And with the wind blowing from the south the smoke could only be coming from the mainland itself. And the mainland was twelve miles away. It must have been caused by a tremendous fire. But what was burning? A forest fire would produce that kind of smoke, but the forests around Ballycastle were soaked from the springtime rains. It could only be the village. Ballycastle was in flames!

Avelyn pushed the tiller hard over and the little craft's bow spun across the wind, the sail whipping to starboard. She hauled it tight and began tacking towards the mainland. She must return. There would be wounded to attend; homeless to feed. And her closest friends, Shelby and Father Conardy, might be injured. Or worse. Despite her impatience, there was little she could do to make the curragh go faster. With the wind dead south, it would be difficult to sail into the harbor. She would take the boat ashore on the western headland. A path led from the point back to the village, and she would be able to run the two miles faster than sail them.

Shelby had known. This was the evil he had foreseen. But was a fire evil? In any case, Avelyn was glad she'd tarried on the island. A fine thing if she were happily on her way to Angland in complete ignorance of the disaster, and the fate of her village.

"Please Lord Jesus, let them come to no harm," she muttered softly while looking at the waves. And there were some ancient sayings—some talismans—that she spoke as a Druid. But these were addressed to the waves themselves, not to the Lord Jesus.

Plumes of smoke became visible as she steered south, and while they brought dread to her heart, they made navigation much easier. By the time the sun was halfway to its zenith, she had fetched the bay's western headland. She grounded the curragh and pulled it as far out of the water as could be managed. The tide was rising and she knew the craft was in danger of floating away if left to itself. She retrieved a length of braided twine from the forepeak and secured one end to the boat's stem. Sloshing through the wet sand she climbed up to higher ground and fastened the other end to a tree.

Avelyn paused for breath and looked back out to sea. Ominous darkness was building on the horizon which made it almost certain a storm was coming. Within a few hours, the wind would veer westerly, as it always did with these summer storms. Combined with the high tide, the little curragh would be pushed none-too-gently against the beach. It could not be helped.

Avelyn raced up the rocky hillside thick with underbrush. Thistles tore at her legs but she ignored them. Soon the ground leveled off and she found the path leading to the village. Setting a pace she could maintain indefinitely, Avelyn began running.

The tall oaks and pines had been soaking up spring rains for over two months, and now they exuded a heavy scent. Overlaying this was the growing smell of burning wood, and another smell, hideous and nauseating.

The first outpost of the village which Avelyn passed was the hut belonging to Arker, the shepherd. It had burned to the ground. Only the stone chimney remained, futilely pointing to the sky. Ironically, it was the only object in the ruins not smoking. Avelyn approached cautiously. Something was puzzling her. With reluctance, she looked into the charred remains but could not spot anything that might once have been Arker.

She had expected to find such scenes and had braced for them. But this made no sense. If a fire had broken out in the village, why had Arker's hut burned? It was a quarter-mile away from the walled portion of Ballycastle, and no spark or flying ember could have blown this far, to single out this one hut. And it was equally impossible this was the only hut to have burned. One cottage could not have caused the plumes of smoke she'd seen from the water.

Finding no answer, Avelyn continued running down

the path, wider now and smoother. But she ran less quickly, fearing something she could not name.

The walls of Ballycastle appeared. Ten feet high, the stone construction had been smoothed over by masons and afforded no foothold. These walls had been built during the reign of the first O'Ruairc and were intended as protection against raiders from Doon. Oddly, because the village had been built first, the walls communicated only with themselves and did not tie into the castle nearly a half-mile away. The village had been built around the harbor—to serve the needs of the fishermen. The castle had been built on a hill. One of the things Celts knew how to do was build forts on top of hills. So now the two entities existed independently: the walled village by the sea and the castle above it.

There were two gates into the village: the South Gate which faced the castle, and the West Gate, which faced Ballintoy—the nearest village up the coast. The path Avelyn was following ran parallel to the wall and up to the west gate. Normally she would have gone that way, but a growing apprehension held her back. Although it was not a conscious thought, she wanted to see the village before it saw her.

She inspected the walls more closely. Since they'd been built, the forest had grown closer. One massive oak soared upwards, extending its tentacled branches in a canopy, and a large branch now extended over the wall. O'Ruairc's predecessors would have cut it down, but the current baron was not interested in trees.

Grasping its lower branches, Avelyn swung herself up

to the first limb and kept climbing. Soon she was in a position to see over the wall and into Ballycastle itself.

It was a scene of horror.

Much of the town had burned. Flames still rose from a few huts, contributing to the two plumes of smoke which she'd seen from the water. Tears formed in Avelyn's eyes and she made no attempt to stop them. This was her home, even though she'd been forced to leave. Now it was destroyed.

She heard the crying of women—a gentle hopeless sobbing that wrenched her heart. Her eyes sought the source, but she could not spot any of the villagers. Climbing higher, she passed the limb which overhung the wall itself and finally she came to the highest branches that could support her weight. Springtime was not so advanced that the leaves presented a barrier to vision. From her perch, she could observe a wide area.

She saw people now, which was reassuring. Then she tensed. They were not villagers. The sun glinted off bright shields and close-fitting hats made of iron. They were carrying weapons of some sort. Axes or spears, mostly. These strange men appeared to be engaged in rounding up anyone left alive.

Who were they? Might they be servants of the High King, sent to help with the disaster? She noticed two of the men grappling with a young woman. It was Kelna, oldest daughter of Liam, the baker. Kelna was trying to break loose. Her dress was torn to shreds and now she was screaming: "Let me go! Let me go!"

One of the men lashed out with the back of his hand,

crashing it into her face, and Kelna fell to the ground either unconscious or physically defeated. Two of the others picked her up roughly by her arms and dragged her away.

Now Avelyn understood. Ballycastle had been invaded by a foreign army. No Irishman would wantonly destroy a village, or brutalize women so publicly. The Irish were a warlike people in many ways, but their violence was directed against other fiefs. Two opposing tribes might fight each other in battle, but afterward, the victors would restore order. They would not harm the women and children, and they would certainly not burn a village.

A burned village had no value. And an opposing Irish army would have attacked the castle, not the village. Avelyn shifted her gaze south, towards the castle itself, high on the hill. From what she could see it had not been damaged. The O'Ruairc flag still stood, and there was no activity around its gates at all.

But there was no doubt the village had been invaded by foreigners—people from the worlds beyond. But which ones? The Angles? Possibly. A tribal chief from over the sea might have set out to conquer new lands. But Father Conardy was well informed on events in Angland and had told Avelyn, that for the first time since the Romans, the country was at peace under the powerful King Offa. Trade was prospering throughout Britannia, and even with Ireland. These could not be Offa's soldiers.

But if not Angles, then whom? Avelyn's knowledge of the world beyond Angland was dim. She'd just learned of Byzantium, but that was a thousand leagues away. Of course, there were other lands; other countries.

After an hour observing from her tree, Avelyn made a decision. Before today, her life had been dedicated to escaping this village. In a sense, she had already done so. But now everything had changed. The Ballycastle from which she had fled no longer existed. Now, all that mattered was to determine if Father Conardy had survived. And Shelby. If wounded, she could heal them. If dead, she could bury them. And if by some miracle they had not been harmed, she could help them escape.

Avelyn waited in the tree until dusk and during that time saw many things that she'd rather not have seen. But the waiting gave her time to plan. She would go to Shelby's hut first. It was closest. If the hut had been destroyed she would make her way to the monastery. She knew a secret entrance to the hidden, underground vaults.

The approaching storm finally arrived and fully extinguished what little light remained. Rain began, and the wind veered. Lightning flashed somewhere, but the thunder was muffled and much delayed. Avelyn climbed out along the oak bough. One of the few cottages left intact abutted the wall and Avelyn was able to jump onto its roof and from there to the ground. Now, she was inside the village.

If she were caught there would be no escape. And she could not help her friends if she were a prisoner herself.

Avelyn held few advantages, but she did hold some. The invaders were unaware of her. They must believe all the villagers had been captured or killed. And Avelyn knew the town. She knew the secret passageways between walls, the alleys that led to dead ends, and which huts had more than one entrance. Her biggest disadvantage was that the burning of the town had changed its look and layout. Frequently, she found herself confused and taking a wrong turn.

Most of the huts in Ballycastle had been constructed of adobe mud with a thatch roof. The fire had destroyed the thatch and anything flammable the huts contained. But the walls still stood, determined and unrelenting, as if making a statement that Ballycastle would one day recover.

In the utter darkness of the night's rainstorm, Avelyn had only to keep close to the walls to fade into them completely. She spied an armed patrol coming towards her, and there was no question of hiding. Instead, she nestled against one wall of a burnt hut, turned her face away from the road, and kept perfectly still. The patrol walked right past.

Despite her success at concealment Avelyn, was getting drenched. Her long hair was matted and even the wind could not do much with it. After climbing the tree, crossing the wall, and hiding among the mud-soaked alleyways her face was a dirty smear, and her woolen brat, a wet rag. Avelyn suspected she could lie down in the street with her head against the ground and no one would notice her.

Moving clandestinely through the village, she finally arrived at the harbor. Her perch in the tree had provided no view of this part of town. Now, she saw the ships which must have carried the invaders to Ireland. She counted seven of them, all anchored in the bay, with their sails furled and only a few men on each (at least judging from the closest one). The rest were little more than shadows.

She had never seen vessels so large, nor shaped so oddly. They resembled giant curraghs, but with stems and sterns that reached into the sky. And their rigging was different. The closest one carried a bow piece in the shape of a head, with blood-red eyes, laughing hideously. Avelyn shuddered.

She crept nearer the water, closer to Shelby's hut, down at the shore. But there was no hut. Huddled against the burnt and smoldering remains of the nearest cottage, Avelyn surveyed the scene. There were three curraghs tied at the water's edge. Two had been smashed, but one had been spared. Perhaps the invaders—realizing the town was theirs—had decided it was foolish to destroy any more property.

But where was Shelby's hut? Then she understood. Shelby was a carpenter. He worked with wood, not mud. His was one of the few cottages made entirely of oak beams and logs—scraps remaining from his boat-building. Now, knowing what to look for, she saw the remains. It had succumbed utterly to the fire.

Avelyn accepted the fact that Shelby was dead. The invaders would have no use for an old man. There were many young women left alive, but she saw not a single adult man. And no elderly women. And—most tragic of all—no children. They must have killed everyone except the young women, who they were no doubt enslaving. Such evil was difficult to grasp, and her hatred for those who had done this was immeasurable.

Yet she had to know about Shelby. Slipping away from the relative safety of the wall she crossed the open grass down to the water, mostly sliding on hands and knees. A hundred yards away a body of men stood against the wharves, guarding the invaders' ships. The men were laughing, and speaking loudly in a tongue unfamiliar to Avelyn. It was not Anglish or even Latin.

Reaching the ruins of Shelby's hut, Avelyn found a few charred planks and logs in a collapsed pile. Not knowing what she hoped to find, Avelyn lifted several of the boards.

There was Shelby. His head was just visible among the debris—eyes closed and his body motionless.

Avelyn dropped to her knees and listened for any sound of breathing. But the wind and the rain made too much noise. She placed her palm against his neck, hoping to find a pulse.

"Shelby!" she pleaded softly. "Shelby, don't be dead! We can still escape!"

There was no pulse. Finally, she withdrew her hand.

Shelby opened his eyes.

Avelyn almost screamed. A corpse had come to life. But then the old fisherman smiled and Avelyn relaxed. It was her friend, not death.

"Lassie, why did you come back?" he managed to say, through forced and pained breaths.

"I came back to rescue you, old bag of stones," Avelyn said, tears flowing.

"Avelyn, the time for my life is over!

"No lassie!" he said, seeing her start to protest. "My legs are crushed and when I breathe I reap more pain than air. I will not live long, nor do I wish to. Do you understand? *Nor do I wish to!*"

Avelyn forced herself to nod, through the tears.

"You should not have come back, lassie. I arranged your escape. Have all my efforts been for naught?"

"I did escape, Shelby. But when I saw the village burning I had to come back."

"Aye, you are not one to abandon a village, even when it abandons you. But it's too late."

"I must do something, Shelby! I can't just leave!"

"You *can* leave, Avelyn. This village is not important. *You* are important. You are meant to escape—though it's not clear yet, why. But if you stay and are overcome by the evil, then the death of the village will have been in vain and the purpose of the Earth thwarted. You must go at once!"

"Shelby, I can't leave you. And I can't leave Father Conardy. I don't know what's become of him."

"You can leave me, Avelyn, because I will let myself die. And as for the good abbot, use your sense! What would he say if he were here now? You know he would agree with me. And another thing, girl. The abbot is a powerful Christian. If he is wounded, or a prisoner, he will marshal the power of his god to achieve his purpose. What you can do is small, measured against the power of the abbot and his god. And if he is dead, you can do nothing but get yourself captured. Follow his guidance, Avelyn, for you know what it would be. And follow mine, for in this I am in agreement with the Christian."

"But what happened here, Shelby? Who are these people? Why are they burning the village and killing everyone?"

"Does it matter? Obviously, they are conquerors—a

foreign army—from some land we know not. They will be merciless, for that is the way of such foes. Avelyn, you must flee again, and this time do not come back, unless…" A look of puzzlement crossed the dying man's face. "Unless you are meant to come back. Your future is unclear to me. But I know you must leave Ballycastle at once. Go!"

"I *am* going, old friend, and you're coming with me. Now be quiet while I get these boards off you!"

Avelyn stood up and began pulling the timbers from around the old man's body. A loud voice came from the harbor. The words were foreign but the intent was clear. They had seen her. Other voices joined in. Three of the men began running in her direction. Shelby reached up and gripped the girl's shoulder.

"Avelyn, go!"

The old man's body collapsed, lifeless. Avelyn gasped in horror. Shelby had caused his own death by a force of will. There was no longer anything of her friend among these burnt timbers but a skeleton of flesh and a worn and tattered cloak. On impulse she grabbed the cloak and wrapped it around her shoulders, casting aside her own brat.

As she turned to face her attackers, Avelyn felt a strange force enter her. Despite fatigue and utter sorrow, renewing energy raced through her. Weariness and despair fell away like leaves from a tree.

She wiped her face clear of mud and tears and brushed her wet hair aside. She stood proudly, without fear, and turned towards her enemies. A vision came to her and, with outstretched arms, she turned the vision into words.

"You are doomed, men of the worlds beyond!" she cried. "I lay a curse on your souls for what you have done. You will never subdue this land. You will die here and feed the crows with your rotting carcasses."

She used the language of the Angles, hoping some would understand her.

The heart of the storm arrived, and the sky flashed with lightning. Thunder rent the night air.

⁂

The Norsemen halted and dread came upon them. Many understood the Anglish words, but all realized they'd just been cursed. Nowhere had they seen an Irish man or woman stand defiantly before them. This was some kind of omen, a spirit creature rising from the ashes. They hesitated.

⁂

Avelyn knew it was her only chance. Darting from among the burnt timbers, she ran fast towards the shore and the one remaining curragh. Avelyn threw her weight against the craft, pushing it into the sea, slowly at first—then faster. The tide was high and the boat floated quickly. She waded into the harbor, seeking deeper water.

Realizing now it was an escape attempt, the Norsemen resumed their chase, running towards the curragh, determined to head her off.

Avelyn leaped into the boat and—with movements honed by weeks of training—raised the sail instantly and hauled it tight. The wind was now westerly, which meant that she would have to start on a port tack. But a port tack would take her among the shallows near shore where the invaders were trying to intercept her. Already, they'd waded deep into the water and were close to the spot where she would come about. Her escape would be over before it began. Avelyn was filled with unbearable grief: for her village, for Shelby, and now for herself.

But the sky filled once more with lightning. The largest bolt crashed into the mainmast of one of the ships, reducing it to splinters and nearly setting the craft afire. Just as suddenly, the wind backed around to the south, only for a few moments, and a tremendous gust blew over the harbor. Another of the ships, its sail not properly furled, and its hull perpendicular to the wind's new direction, heeled far to starboard. Much of its cargo had earlier been unlashed and barrels now fell against the leeward rail, upsetting the craft further. Water poured in over the gunwales and the longboat capsized—its ballast dragging the vessel swiftly to the bottom of Ballycastle's deep harbor. Even those aboard who could swim were not given the chance, for they were trapped in the wreckage and drowned.

Yet the effect of this wind on Avelyn's curragh was fortunate. Seeing its approach, she steered away from the shore, and jibed. With the sail now perfectly set for a south wind, the curragh flew out of the harbor, past the reach of the Norseman waiting to ambush her in the shallows.

⁂

Kren was back aboard *Freya's Song,* where he'd just witnessed—to his horror—the loss of another ship. Equally important, someone in a fishing boat was trying to escape.

It could not be allowed. That one craft could warn the entire Irish coastline and ruin the element of surprise. Kren gave orders to his crew. The longboat's sail was raised, the anchor line cut with the swipe of an ax, and the vessel turned from a peaceful thing at rest to a wild, charging animal in pursuit of prey.

&

It was all Avelyn could do to steer her curragh between the remaining longboats and their anchor lines, but finally, she was clear and racing for the harbor entrance. The ship chasing her was a quarter-mile astern but Avelyn knew it would close the gap quickly.

She reached the headlands and her boat heeled as it met the waves of the open sea. The storm had turned the surface into a maelstrom.

Both craft were now out of the harbor. The pursuing vessel had the advantage, for its longer keel and greater weight were less slowed by the waves than was the tiny curragh.

Avelyn knew she would not reach her island in time. Despair overcame her and she was tempted to put up her helm and surrender. Why not get it over with?

But the wind changed direction again, and now came from the north. Avelyn watched as the longboat's sail buckled and she knew the ship could not maintain its heading. With a headwind, it was now the curragh and its lateen sail which held the advantage. The longboat was square-rigged and did poorly tacking into the wind. The curragh drew ahead, despite the waves, and it was soon apparent—if this wind held—the smaller vessel would reach the island first.

A quarter-hour later Kren abandoned the chase. Sailing the longboat up to the island in darkness and during a storm would be foolhardy. The curragh, with its shallow draft, could hide easily in bays or coves that the longboat could not enter, and it would be difficult to seek a suitable anchorage from which the crew of the vessel—already at a minimum—could be sent in search of the girl. Far better to run before the wind back to the mainland with its good harbor, wait out the storm, and then return with a full crew when the weather cleared in the morning. Possibly the island was settled, in which case, it would require more than a handful of warriors to subdue it anyway.

Kren gave the orders, the longboat jibed, and the sheets were eased for a downwind tack. Silently, and unseen by the crew, Kren gave a quiet nod of respect to the girl who had so courageously made her escape. She was a true sailor, that one. A pity she had to be his enemy.

The distance between the two craft widened rapidly—the longboat rushing before the wind back to Ballycastle harbor and the little curragh tacking against it towards the island.

Unnoticed by either, a black monolith rose eerily from the waves in the widening space between the two vessels. Like a gigantic whale, it emerged from the depths, hung motionless, rolled partially on its side, and then sank beneath the surface.

51

KITT AND MILO were frozen, staring at the intercom on the wall and hearing only static. Suddenly the captain broke in.

"Admiral, this is Hamilton, are you there?"

Milo picked up the mic.

"Yes, Captain?"

"Admiral, there are some strange as hell things going on with this ship. Are you running any of your experiments right now?"

"Affirmative. I'll meet you in the control room."

"Aye aye, sir. Please hurry."

Milo turned to Kitt. "We've got some 'splaining' to do."

The young physicist was ashen, and trembling slightly. Milo gripped him by the shoulders.

"Look, this is no time to panic. Whatever's happened, the ship's intact so we're safe for the moment. And no matter how scared you and I might be right now, we can't let the rest of the ship know it. And that means calming the captain down first. Once we've done that, we'll figure out what to do next."

Kitt nodded dumbly.

"Don't worry about what to tell Hamilton," Milo assured him. "I'm good at this kind of thing. You just support me if I need some scientific mumbo jumbo. Let's go!"

Kittery didn't move.

"Milo, until we knew we could return to our own time, we'd agreed not to go more than a few hours. But if that switch was closed for possibly a minute, I don't even want to guess how far back we've gone. No radio signal—at all? We could be back in the early 1900s. Maybe earlier." His voice was barely audible.

"I understand. But we've got to take it one step at a time. And the first step is calming down the captain. Come on!"

Milo pushed Kittery none too gently towards the door.

"TenShun!" barked the OOD. Officers and enlisted men snapped upright as the admiral entered the control room.

"At ease," Milo responded. He walked over to where the captain stood. Milo's confident bearing was like a tonic. He held the upper hand, and the first step was to keep it.

"Make your report, Captain," he said, authoritatively.

"Aye aye, sir. At approximately 2100 hours," Hamilton checked the ship's digital clock, "that was about twenty minutes ago, sir—we were proceeding under your orders on a course of 0-9-5, thirty knots, and at a depth of five hundred feet."

"And?"

"With no warning, Admiral, even though it appeared the ship was at a depth of 500 feet, we were rolled by a surface wave. You must have noticed it."

"I'm more interested in what *you* noticed," said Milo, deflecting the comment. "Please continue."

"Well, I did the obvious. I blew negative ballast, and ordered full down angle on the diving planes. That got us below the surface. Then the instruments went haywire."

"Haywire?"

"The digital readouts started flickering, as if they weren't getting a consistent reading. I've never seen that happen before, not to all the instruments at once. We knew we were submerged because the wave motion had stopped. But without instruments, we didn't know how deep. So I ordered zero angle on the dive planes. About that moment, the ship tilted violently, as if we were on the surface again, even though we'd been diving for several minutes. Or at least we *thought* we had. I dove again, and suddenly all the instruments were giving clear readings. I leveled off at two hundred feet and ordered all stop. That's where we are now, sir. As you can see the instruments are working fine again."

Milo glanced at the control panel and noticed nothing out of the ordinary. *Chrysalis* was level at two hundred feet.

"Yes, Captain?"

"That's it. I was pretty shook up, but then I remembered Mr. Kitt here was performing his experiments, and maybe there was a connection. I'm hoping one of you can shed some light."

Milo realized Hamilton's attempt at professionalism

was a thin veneer, and the man was both dismayed and bewildered. The rest of the crew was silent.

"I see. Well, you're correct. We were testing some of the equipment. And obviously the experiments were responsible for the effects you noticed. As I understand it, your position readouts were giving faulty indications, or confusing indications. Is that correct?"

"Well, sir, I guess you could put it that way. It could have just been the instruments themselves that were faulty. But dammit, Admiral, after I gave the order to dive, we all felt the ship dive. We had to be at least a couple of hundred feet underwater, and then we're on the surface again. I don't see how faulty instruments could cause that sensation."

"So—we have erroneous instrument indications, and a feeling of disorientation among the crew. Interesting. That's one of the reasons we like to perform these tests. See what happens in real conditions."

Hamilton noticeably relaxed.

"Admiral, you're making me feel better. I guess you're right. Screwy instruments and a little vertigo. For a while there I thought we'd entered the Twilight Zone or something."

"Don't feel bad, Captain. I chose not to warn you because I didn't want you anticipating any symptoms. This way I got your honest reaction. The effects you describe were predicted by Mr. Kitt if that makes you feel any better."

Milo turned to the civilian. "Mr. Kitt, without giving away anything classified, could you explain why your experiments produced an interference with the instrumentation, and a sense of vertigo here on the bridge."

The young scientist had regained his composure.

"Yes, Admiral. You see, Captain, we're testing a device that reverses the magnetic field surrounding the ship—about a thousand times per second. That would affect the instruments. But the human inner ear, which controls your sense of balance, is affected by magnetic disturbances also. When I engaged the synthesizer it sent shock waves through the magnetic field, causing disorientation and instrument anomalies. We'll probably have to add more nano-fiber shielding if we're going to get this thing working properly."

Milo winked at Hamilton. "Clear as mud, Captain?"

Hamilton smiled back. "Sure, Admiral. That's kinda what I figured."

"Very good. Now, I'm going to ask you to stand by for the time being. We know these experiments are causing havoc with the instruments so I'm a little reluctant to keep charging along on our original course. We don't know if the effects of the polarity synthesizer are only temporary or if there's a residual element involved."

"Aye aye, sir."

"Just two requests for the moment. First, I'd like to know what the fathometer reading is right now."

"Sonarman?" Hamilton turned to a seaman first class in front of a row of instruments.

"Holy Jesus Mother of God…" The seaman's voice trailed off in disbelief.

Hamilton walked over to the panel.

"Here's another strange one for you, Admiral. We're showing water depth of only seven hundred feet under the keel. That's pretty shallow for the middle of the Atlantic."

Hamilton punched some buttons. "Both sonars give the same reading, sir. That's very unusual if we're dealing with faulty instrument readouts."

Milo glanced at him sharply, but it was obvious the captain was not overly concerned. With an admiral in the control room, Hamilton was a subordinate following orders.

Milo, on the other hand, was very concerned. Faulty instruments were checked by testing them against each other. If they both gave the same reading then the readings were accurate. And from their last position check, there was no spot in the ocean within hundreds of miles that could produce a water depth reading of only seven hundred feet. Hence, either their last known position was wildly incorrect, the two fathometers were wrong, or the submarine had traveled hundreds of miles in minutes.

None of these were possible.

"Well, Captain," said Milo, "let's not worry about anything the instruments tell us for awhile. It's likely our navigation's been off for a couple of days. Kitt was testing equipment long before he took over the reactor."

That was an open enough statement that when Hamilton's brain realized the impossibility of their position he could grab onto something.

"Now, my second request is this," Milo continued. "Bring the ship to periscope depth and let me check things visually."

"Aye aye, sir." Hamilton nodded to the officer of the deck, who barked the orders.

A seaman activated the periscope controls, and Hamilton nodded to the admiral.

Milo took the control bar firmly in his hand, prepared himself mentally for anything, and looked. There wasn't much to see. Wave height was three to four feet. It was raining. Judging by the wave pattern, Milo estimated the wind at twenty-five knots. Mostly it was just dark. Milo thanked God for that. If it had been nighttime a few minutes ago and now it was broad daylight, he'd have had some real explaining to do.

Milo lowered the periscope.

"Very well, Captain. Take the boat to 200 feet and keep her there. I need to talk to Mr. Kitt about the instrument problem. Expect further orders in roughly an hour. That will be all."

"Aye aye, sir!"

As they left the bridge, everyone jumped to attention. Routine had been established.

52

"THE TWO JUMPS in time accounted for the movements of the ship, that's obvious," said Milo, as soon as they were alone. "We start 500 feet below the surface, and suddenly we're on the surface. The captain gives the command to dive and the ship dives. Then we jump again—this time by accident—and suddenly we're on the surface once more. What I don't understand is why moving in time should bring the ship to the surface."

"If I had to guess I'd say the mutrino-flux somehow provides a gravity-shield," Kitt postulated, running his fingers through his thick and disheveled hair. "Centrifugal force from the Earth's spin tries to fling the submarine outwards. That force is powerful enough to take the ship to the surface but there's still enough gravity to keep it from rising higher. Otherwise, we might be launched into orbit. Instead, we end up precisely at sea level."

"Fine. Whatever," said Milo. "But now what do we do? I got Hamilton calmed down, but I'm still pretty shook up."

"I guess we have two choices," said Kitt. "One is to correct our mistake and try to move forward in time, back to our own period. Then we could start all over again and try to do it right—move an hour or two at a time with a lot of checking for what effect our time travel was causing.

"The other choice is—well—since we're here, we could have a look around. Find out where—and when—we are. And only then try to go forward again."

"Makes sense. Which do you prefer?"

Kitt began pacing.

"The truth is, we can't go forward in time until we know what point we've come to. Otherwise we won't know how far forward to go. And if we overshoot our own time—well, the future's the last thing I want to tamper with. This thing is dangerous enough already. We just have to accept that the experiment went a little haywire."

"Shit happens," agreed Milo.

"And because it did, we have no choice but to learn the date. By asking, I guess."

"So we just mosey into some harbor with a nuclear submarine and ask if someone knows what year it is?"

"Absolutely not! The further back in time we've gone, the more important it is that we don't do anything which could alter the future. We can't let anyone see the submarine."

"And the alternative would be—?"

"Well, couldn't we find somewhere remote, go ashore in a dinghy, and keep the submarine out of sight?"

Milo considered this.

"Our biggest problem is going to be figuring out where

we are. The GPS systems won't work. Hamilton will shit when he finds that out. Our dead reckoning plot might be interesting to look at, but it won't tell us much either. You heard what Hamilton said. The fathometer shows a water depth of only 700 feet."

"What's the significance of that?"

"Your time travel moved the submarine from the middle of the Atlantic to somewhere on the continental shelf. That's the only place we could see a fathometer reading of 700 feet, unless we're near a mid-Atlantic island like Bermuda or Iceland. Which is possible."

"So time travel moves us horizontally on the surface, not just vertically," mused Kitt. "Maybe the mutrino-flux is…"

"Boss, stop with the mutrino-flux for a second. Do you realize if I hadn't positioned *Chrysalis* half way between Europe and North America, we'd probably be a few hundred miles inland right now, and probably dead!"

"Are thanks in order?"

"Don't mention it. But we're still left with the problem of figuring out where we are. Once we have an accurate fix, *Chrysalis* can track our position with inertial navigation, but getting that fix will be a bitch."

"Didn't the ancient mariners navigate by the stars?"

"For latitude, sure. That's what I intend to do. But it wasn't until the eighteenth century that someone figured out how to determine longitude from star sights. And you know how they did it?"

"Fill me in."

"With a clock! If you know precisely what hour of the

day it is, and of course the month and the year, then you can consult tables which tell you where the stars should be, for a particular longitude. You measure the difference, and that tells you where you are."

"I see the problem."

"Ya think! *Chrysalis* has the most accurate timepieces on earth but we don't know what they should be set to. We don't even know for sure what *century* they should be set to."

"So what do we do?"

"First, determine latitude by star sights. Then I'll draw a latitude line on a chart of the Atlantic, from coast to coast. After that we'll figure out where a person could be on that line and get a depth reading of 700 feet. That will narrow it down quite a bit. Then we'll head either due east or west—don't know which yet—and as soon as we sight land, we'll use radar to paint the shape of the coastline. Between our latitude, our depth, and a particular coastline, I'm hoping we'll be able to fix our position."

"And then?"

"Then we do as you say. Find a stretch of land that looks mostly uninhabited, and go ashore in a dinghy. With luck we can find someone, try to figure out a language to communicate in, and ask a very simple question."

Kitt grinned. "Something like, 'Hey mister! You got the time?'"

"Or at least the year," added Milo, smiling.

53

CHRYSALIS HAD SURFACED and was wallowing easily in the swells, as Milo strode resolutely into the control room. The men came to attention instantly.

"At ease."

Milo decided to be grimly serious.

"Captain, I'd like the following orders recorded and adhered to, until further notice. Effective immediately, I want no one on this submarine, other than myself, to a) look in the periscope, b) venture topside, c) monitor radio traffic or d) send a radio message. Absolute secrecy is essential at the moment."

"Aye aye, sir." Hamilton nodded to the officer of the deck. "OOD, kindly record the admiral's order in the log, and see that it's included among the ship's standing orders."

"Aye aye, sir."

"Thank you, Captain. I need to go topside to take a star sight. I suspect that most of our navigational instruments may be faulty. But unless some fundamental change has happened to the universe, the stars should still be where we left them."

That produced a few smiles.

Of course, Milo knew, a fundamental change had just happened to the universe, so it was anyone's guess where the stars would be.

"Do you require assistance, sir?"

"Negative. I'd prefer to go alone. I'd be obliged, however, if your navigation officer could loan me his sextant."

"Kirkpatrick!"

"Aye aye, sir!"

Milo watched as the junior officer turned a combination lock, opened a small metal door, and withdrew an oak box. He retrieved from it a curiously primitive instrument, rarely seen in the control room of a nuclear submarine. Yet Milo knew every navigation officer, on every ship in the world, carried at least one sextant and treated it reverently.

"Thank you, Ensign. I appreciate the loan."

"Keep it as long as you wish, sir. I can see it's in good hands."

Milo nodded, then climbed the ladder to the bridge cockpit atop the sail.

On Milo's World War II-era sub there had been a large, cumbersome wheel which opened the hatch. The modern version of that wretched wheel was a heat-sensitive solenoid. Milo pressed his thumb against it, a light went on, and almost soundlessly the hatch cover slid back. One thing hadn't changed. Residual water from the deck fell onto his face and he tasted salt.

Milo hoisted himself the final distance and then stood

upright, alone, in the open air. As would any seaman, he first checked the wind, which was out of the north. Then he studied the waves. They were larger, more aggressive, than could be explained by the wind-speed. That implied the recent passage of a storm. Wind always calmed down first.

Next he looked for land, not expecting to find any. But there were coastlines both to the north and the south. *Chrysalis* had—with incredible luck—positioned herself in a channel. The clouds were parting and a quarter moon appeared, which cast a pale light over the sea.

It seemed likely the land to the north was only an island. Radar would produce an accurate sketch. That would come later. First he needed a star sight. A few hours earlier, probably no stars were showing, but many were now visible between swiftly-moving clouds. He finally located the North Star, Polaris, the most useful to navigators in the northern hemisphere. That proved they were definitely *in* the northern hemisphere.

A few minutes later, Milo had an accurate fix. He didn't bother to look at the angle, or write it down. By tightening the set screw on the sextant, he would be able to check it below in good light.

Now he indulged himself. Carefully placing the sextant on the deck, he leaned against the coaming and gazed out over the water. Where they might be on twenty-first century maps was of only passing interest. This was probably not the twenty-first century. Milo was staring into history. These waves were from the past. These clouds had long since disappeared in time. The moon was an old moon. The wind blowing on his face had not blown for years.

He was looking—actually looking—at history. No ivory tower historian had ever seen what Milo was seeing. No Ph.D. professor ever had the benefit of really being there, observing first hand.

Of course there wasn't much to observe. An ocean was an ocean. Coastlines seen at night were similar. Was it real?

A wave, larger than the others, crashed against the bow of the ship and the spray drenched Milo's face. He gasped from the shock of cold water.

Real enough, he decided. Milo returned to the control room, carrying the all-important sextant with its locked angle-reading on the North Star.

"Captain, I need a 360 degree radar paint delivered to my quarters as soon as possible," he said. "And I want that done remotely. My orders regarding anyone going topside stand. As soon as that's completed take her back down to two hundred feet and hold this position."

"Aye aye, sir," said Hamilton.

Entering his cabin, Milo went immediately to the desk, examined the instrument, and wrote down a figure on a piece of scratch paper.

Milo chose a book from among the many he'd brought, and found the page he was seeking. He glanced at the figure on the scratch pad, and then back at the page in the book. Finally he took a ruler from the drawer and drew a line on a nautical chart of the Atlantic

"Labrador, the U.K., or Holland," he said, mostly to himself. Then he reached for the intercom.

"Captain, do you have those radar paints yet?"

"Just finishing, Admiral. I'll send a messenger down with them immediately."

Milo was content to stare at the chart while he waited. There was a knock on the door and Kitt took the proffered envelope, handing it to Milo.

After studying the images for several minutes, Milo looked up.

"Ireland."

"Ireland?"

"I know exactly where we are."

"Ireland?" Kittery repeated.

"We're just north of the Irish mainland and south of an island called Rathlin. Due south on the mainland is a long bay or firth which leads to a town called Ballycastle."

Kittery leaned over Milo's chart and studied the position plot.

"Are you sure?"

"Yes. We're at 55 degrees, two minutes, north latitude. Assuming we're still in the Atlantic, that puts us off the coast of Labrador, Ireland, Scotland, or Holland. Of those, only Ireland shows the coastlines our radar painted. And it's a perfect match. That makes it definite."

"So what's our next move?"

"I guess we go ashore in a sparsely populated area and ask someone you-know-what."

"I'm in your hands, Milo. As far as I'm concerned you're giving the orders now."

Milo paused.

"It's dark now. Our clocks say 0300 hours. I don't know

if that agrees with local time or not but I do know it's dark upstairs. Let's get some sleep until, say, 0600. Assuming it's light by then, we'll have *Chrysalis* surface, provide us a dinghy, and we'll head towards shore. The question is, which coastline? Rathlin Island or the mainland?"

"Remember it's important we cause as little interference as possible."

"Let's go for the island then. Assuming it's not uninhabited, the residents aren't likely to be major history makers."

"So we try to sleep for a few hours?"

"Yeah." Milo smiled, both knowing it wouldn't happen.

54

THE CAPTAIN USED a spoon to cut his soft-boiled egg as he sat at the settee table with Kitt and Milo. Since coming on board, the admiral and the civilian always ate their meals alone, in the privacy of their cabin—formerly his cabin. Today, Hamilton had been asked to join them for breakfast. A steward brought in the trays with a generous supply of coffee, and quickly retired. Each man ate in silence.

As became his rank, the admiral spoke first.

"Captain, I realize that events of the last twenty-four hours have put a strain on the officers and crew. I know that you and everyone else are confused by what's going on."

"Yes, sir."

"You may be wondering if there's more to the experiments Kitt and I are carrying out than merely testing concealment technology."

"Admiral, the best concealment technology in the world can't move a submarine from the middle of the

Atlantic to somewhere on the continental shelf in the space of a few minutes."

"Is that what you think happened?"

"What else could have happened?"

"Your instruments could have been faulty all along. Isn't it possible you thought you were in the middle of the Atlantic, but weren't?"

"When all of the ship's instruments agree on where the ship is and when our dead reckoning plot agrees as well, that's not instrument failure. That's where we are."

"What if I told you this technology could also confuse a submarine's navigation systems, not put 'em out of action, just make it appear the boat is somewhere it's not."

"That would call for pretty sophisticated technology, sir."

"And what kind of technology would it take to move a submarine several hundred miles in a few minutes?"

Hamilton fidgeted with his spoon, stirring the remains of the egg in random motions.

"OK, sir, I see your point. No matter what explanation I come up with, it has to be way beyond today's technology. So what's the truth? Have we discovered how to move submarines as fast as rockets, or have we figured out how to take control of a ship's instruments without the officers being aware? Or is it some third explanation?"

"I'm not at liberty to say."

"In that case, Admiral, why am I here?"

"Because, Captain, I need your cooperation. This is the Navy, not a ladies' tea party, and we don't have time for bruised egos. I have my orders, just as you have yours.

I'd prefer to tell you everything and even I don't know everything. Even Mr. Kitt here doesn't know everything.

"But I will tell you this. The United States has got its hands on the biggest scientific breakthrough since we split the atom. It may be bigger than that. It may be more like discovering electricity. I'm not going to tell you what it is. I'm not going to tell you what it can do with this ship. All I'm going to say is that you and the crew are going to observe a lot of strange crap between now and when we get back to Norfolk.

Hamilton took a sip from his coffee, and said nothing.

"You can theorize all you want—I can't order you not to. But don't expect any explanations. The important thing is that this discovery was made by American scientists and it's going to be used for American purposes—at least until the secret gets out to the rest of the world, which it will eventually. In the military, new tech yields only a temporary advantage."

"So what you're saying, sir, is that since we're all on the same team, don't worry about it?"

"Are you willing to play by those rules?"

"Do I have a choice, sir?"

"Sure. Tell me right now you want to be relieved of this duty. I'll send a message to ComSubLant and request a transfer to a different boat. The last thing I need is a captain who isn't 100% behind me. And you needn't worry about the effect on your career. I'll think of some technical reason why this boat isn't best suited for the purpose; something that won't implicate you. I'll be full of praise for your cooperation."

Hamilton took another sip of coffee.

"No, thank you, sir," he said finally, setting down the cup. "I appreciate the offer but I've never been a quitter. If I can best serve my country by closing my eyes and just following orders, that's exactly what I'll do. But I do make one request."

"Go ahead."

"If any of these experiments could endanger the ship, I think I have a right to know."

Milo glanced at Kitt.

"I can assure you, Captain," said Kitt, "that the ship is not in danger, nor will it be."

"Satisfied?" Milo asked, knowing Kitt was lying.

"Yes, sir."

"Since that's settled I'm going to tell you where we are. You can feed our position into your inertial navigation computers and update the plot on an ongoing basis. Your radio equipment probably won't work, except for transmissions originating from this ship to onboard receivers. The same goes for your satellite navigation systems. Forget 'em. Your ship's sensors, on the other hand, should all function normally—that is radar, sonar, infrared, etc. So rely on those to update your position. One thing that for the moment I cannot tell you is the proper time. I believe that all the ship's timepieces, from the simplest mechanical wristwatch to your digital chronometers, have been thrown off. They will operate normally from now on, but don't assume they're accurate in terms of real time. Not until we return to Norfolk. There's a relativity factor involved with these experiments—if you've read Einstein."

"Aye aye, sir. May I see where we are then?"

Milo indicated one of the charts on the desktop and pointed to an "x" he'd penciled in. Hamilton couldn't help raising his eyebrows.

"We're off the north coast of Ireland?"

"Correct."

"And I'm not supposed to worry about how we got here?"

"Correct."

"Very well, sir. And what are my orders?"

"No raised eyebrows when I tell you?"

Hamilton smiled. "I'll try, sir."

"Surface the ship. I want one of your inflatable dinghies prepared with an outboard motor and enough fuel for five or six hours of cruising. And I'll want oars, too, of course. Mr. Kitt and I will be visiting Rathlin Island, just north of our present position. There are some triangulation measurements we need to take."

"Aye aye, sir. Makes as much sense as anything else, and you'll notice I don't even have a puzzled look on my face."

"Thank you, Captain. That's probably worth a citation right there."

"Will you need anything else, sir?"

"Yes. I'd like the mess steward to prepare some food. Something for lunch, and in case we're delayed and have to spend the night, enough extra to keep us going for another few meals. Might throw in a pair of sleeping bags while you're at it if you carry that kind of thing." Hamilton nodded. "Also a fairly complete first aid kit, because I don't like to go anywhere without one. Packs for carrying it all.

Oh, and a couple of VHS radios so we can communicate with each other if separated, and also with the ship.

"While we're on that subject, I'll want *Chrysalis* to dive after we leave, but to come to antenna depth every hour on the hour, to receive any radio signals we may send. Don't expect them, but be there to receive them if necessary. And let's use Marine Band 12. Don't allow anyone to monitor any other channels, on any frequency."

"Aye aye, sir."

"Also, could you outfit us with a couple of small arms, .45 caliber semi-autos if that's what you carry?"

"Do you think that's necessary, Admiral?" asked Kitt.

"I don't think it's necessary. But if I find I'm wrong, I'd hate to be without weapons. This is Northern Ireland. Right, Captain?"

"Yes sir, I agree. Whatever your mission, I'd feel more comfortable knowing you weren't defenseless."

"Then there's only one more thing. In the top drawer of this desk is a manila envelope. If we're not back in 48 hours, and you've had no further word from us—then and only then—open that envelope and read what's inside. It will be your orders on how to proceed."

"Aye aye, sir. If you'll excuse me, I'll go make the arrangements."

Once alone, Kitt turned to Milo. "What are you going to say in those written orders?"

"Well, we don't know what may happen to us on the island. If we're killed Hamilton deserves to know what's going on."

"But what will you say?"

"For once I'll tell him the truth. What he might to do with it is anyone's guess. Perhaps he'll read it and go insane. Or perhaps he'll figure out how to get *Chrysalis* back home. Anyway, what would you tell him? Would you have any advice?"

"I'll add some notes about how to work the mutrino equipment, but...well, we barely know what we're doing ourselves."

55

THE AVON INFLATABLE bounced across the waves, propelled by a 55 horsepower outboard. The morning after the storm, the wind was brisk and the sky clear.

Kittery sat in the bow and held on to the lifelines. As a scientist he was observing the world around him, and had already noticed something unusual—the air. There was a purity and cleanliness to it that made him feel he was breathing air for the first time.

Milo was in the stern, one hand on the outboard's tiller while the other grasped a tie-ring for support.

"Do you notice it?" Kitt yelled, cupping one hand to his mouth to make himself heard above the roar of the engine. "Do you notice the air?"

Milo nodded. "It's the real thing!"

Aside from air, Kitt could detect nothing to indicate they weren't in the twenty-first century. Perhaps on the island that would change. A chill ran through him. There was no way to prepare for an encounter with history.

How far back had they come? Kitt guessed early

20th century or perhaps the latter half of the 19th—the Victorian era. If the switch on the mutrino dispenser had been connected for roughly three minutes, which was the best they could approximate, then they should have traveled back about a hundred years. But it could be twice that. Or half that.

Kitt tried to remember what had been going on in the late 1800's. In North America, that was just after the Civil War. But what was going on in Ireland? He was glad he'd brought along an historian.

There were probably people on the island. But how many? A village? A few shepherds? Kitt's hand brushed against his .45 pistol, hidden in a shoulder holster. The presence of the gun both reassured and worried him.

Milo had brought up a detail that Kitt had overlooked: language. Even in the twenty-first century, language barriers were a problem. The dimension of time would make it worse. People had spoken English for hundreds of years in Ireland, but would it sound like English? Would they be able to make themselves understood? Milo claimed to be as proficient in languages as he was in history, but he'd never faced this kind of challenge.

Kitt turned off his active brain, and concentrated on just breathing the air.

Soon they were near enough to choose a landing spot. The island was moderately hilly, and covered with forest.

They had considered circling the island first in the boat, to find the best place to land, but decided it would be dangerous if someone saw their outboard motor. Instead, over a mile from shore, Milo silenced the engine and set up the oars.

"Nothing rows worse than a damned inflatable," said Milo with disgust.

"I'll spell you when you get tired," said Kitt.

"A young kid like you? No offense, Boss, but rowing's an ancient art. Now you're probably good at video games and such, but not something practical. What would an intellectual like you know about rowing?"

"I was on Yale's rowing team my senior year, and we took second place in our division for single scull."

"Well, why didn't you say so? If I'd known we had real talent on board, I wouldn't have asked for a motor. But I guess I'll pump a few to warm up the muscles and then let you have the fun."

The little craft made its way awkwardly through the waves. The inflatable was indeed cumbersome and it took a long time to cover the final distance. Milo studied the coastline as they drew closer.

"See anything?" asked Kitt, who had taken the oars and was facing backwards.

"Luck's with us. I think we've found the only place on the whole coast with a harbor. Kind of a small cove."

A rock peninsula jutted out from the bank, nearly sealing the entrance, and inside the water was calm.

"Take her in, Kitt, steady as she goes."

Milo spotted a goat observing them from the rocks near shore. It was their first living creature. He looked at it reverently for a moment. The goat stared back.

"Only a damned goat," he said, in frustration.

The goat darted into the forest.

The inflatable rounded the miniature headland of the peninsula and settled into the calm waters of the cove.

"Holy Jesus!" said Milo.

Kitt dropped the oars and spun around.

On the beach was a boat. It was very strange—a sailing craft made of hides. Its mast was only a pine sapling.

"So there are *people* here," said Kitt, avoiding the bigger question of whether they'd actually gone back in time.

"And judging by that sailboat, I don't think they're modern people," said Milo, addressing it.

Kitt said nothing, but kept rowing.

Just as they touched shore, Milo hopped into the water, seized the bow, and dragged the dinghy onto the sand. Kitt stowed the oars and climbed over the gunwale onto solid ground.

Other than the primitive sailboat, there was no sign of civilization. The spruce trees came down nearly to the water's edge. Seagulls floated above them. The goat had returned to its perch among the rocks. The weather continued clear. There was no wind.

"Should I shout 'Anybody home!' asked Kitt.

"I'd rather you didn't. This place is giving me the creeps."

"Why the creeps?"

"I don't know. I've got a feeling we're being watched. Whoever owns that boat is around here somewhere."

Kitt walked over and touched the sailboat, hesitatingly at first. Then he grabbed the mast and pushed it firmly. The vessel rolled ponderously to one side with a protesting creak. He touched a nearby tree, feeling the bark with his fingers. Then he rubbed his hands in the grass. He scooped up some of the sand, sniffed it, and let it fall through his fingers to the ground. On impulse, he picked up a rock and threw it as hard as he could out into the water. It splashed, then sank.

"What the hell are you doing?" asked Milo.

"I don't know. It's just… I don't know. I'm trying to find something that feels different. We've gone back in time. At least, we're pretty sure we have. Things shouldn't feel the same. Everything should seem weird or strange or something, don't you think?"

"Don't ask me! I've never done this before. What kind of *weird* are you talking about?"

"Well—"

"You're not saying you thought everything would be in black and white, or maybe colorized like an old movie, are you?"

"Not exactly. But it all just seems too normal. Look, seagulls are flying around. The waves are splashing on the beach. The air feels humid, and you can smell the salt air. It's just like reality. But it can't be reality. I mean, something has to be different."

"Like what?" asked Milo. "What were you expecting?"

"Oh, I guess I expected we could see the world around us vaguely, but we couldn't be a part of it. Like it would be distorted or something. Seen through a lens. But nothing different at all? You know, Milo, maybe the experiment didn't work. Maybe we haven't gone anywhere."

"Oh, I think it worked. Remember, *Chrysalis* can't pick

up any radio signals. And that little sailboat looks like something out of a museum. But, hey, I always assumed that when we went back in time, we'd be back in time. Wasn't that the plan?"

"Yeah, but I never thought it would work, for Chrissake! Not like this! This is too real. Scary real."

"Don't freak out on me, Boss. I'm still curious how far back we've come. Let's grab our packs and walk up into those trees. I see a path."

They had gone barely fifty yards when they came to a camp. A lean-to made of pine boughs had been built facing away from the water, obviously to protect from the winds off the sea. A circle of stones constituted a fireplace, and overhanging the ashes was an iron pot supported by a tripod made from fresh saplings.

"This is just too bizarre," said Kitt.

"Not at all. Reminds me of when I was a Boy Scout. Had to build tripods like that to earn our campfire merit badge." Milo tested the structure's sturdiness. "This one's rather well built."

Kitt glanced around nervously. "I think I'd be real happy to see a troop of modern-day Boy Scouts pop out from that forest about now."

Milo reached down and touched the ashes.

"Still warm," he said.

They exchanged a glance, and Milo tightened his grip on the .45 caliber pistol. He nodded to Kitt and continued down the path.

A voice spoke to them from the trees.

"Dia dhuit ar maidin."

Kitt jumped back in fright, tripped over a rock and nearly fell. Milo crouched, and drew his weapon.

The voice spoke again. It was soft and pleasant. And very feminine.

"Dia dhuit ar maidin."

It was as if the forest itself had spoken.

The voice grew impatient.

"An bhfuil tú Gaeilge a labhairt?"

"Show yourself!" demanded Milo. He put his weapon back in the holster, but stayed crouched down, ready to fight. Or run.

Kitt had regained his footing, but was staying behind Milo, completely unnerved.

A young woman stepped cautiously from behind a tree and stood silently, looking down at them.

Long auburn hair hung loosely about her shoulders. Her skin was lightly tanned. She wore a long woolen dress, pulled in at the waist with a leather braid. Another strand of leather was attached above the bodice, and secured the garment loosely against her neck.

Bright green eyes stared at the two men with curiosity and a hint of fear. Her lips were parted slightly. And despite the unkempt nature of her hair, and a face darkened by the soot of an open fire, she was lovely.

Kitt's eyes locked with hers and they stared at each other. They were like two species of animal, neither moving, neither wanting to miss any movement by the other.

She's scared, thought Kitt. She's more scared even than we are. But she's curious about us. Then he realized something a woman might have noticed immediately. The girl had been crying. Her cheeks were red and there were traces of tear stains.

Milo stepped towards her cautiously, his hand outstretched in a universal sign of peace. She began backing away. Milo stopped, and lowered his hand.

"We've got to establish communication quickly," whispered Milo to Kitt. "There could be others nearby, who might be more aggressive."

"Do-you-speak-English?" he asked, saying the words slowly and carefully. "Can-you-understand-us?"

"Ní féidir liom a thuiscint," she responded.

A strange look came over Milo. He was quiet for a moment. Then he spoke in a low voice, with conviction.

"An bhfuil Gaeilge agat?"

The girl nodded, and a smile came to her face.

"Labhraím Gaeilge!" she said.

"Mar sin, is féidir liom," responded Milo.

"Milo, what language is that? Do you know it?"

"I used to. My mother taught me. She liked to preserve the ancient tongue. But it's been fifteen years since I heard it spoken. That's why I didn't recognize it at first."

"Well, what is it?"

"It's Irish Gaelic. I should have thought of that, considering where we are. Duh. Philologists say it's one of the world's least changed languages. That's why I can understand her, although the accent is very different from my mom's."

"What does it tell us about the year? When was it last spoken?"

"Oh, it's spoken even today. Some speak it as their primary language. That's why my mother knew it."

"So it doesn't tell us anything."

"I think in modern times, even a native Gaelic speaker would understand English. This girl doesn't. And look at her clothes. I'm guessing nineteenth century. Maybe earlier."

"Cé as tú?" the girl interrupted.

Milo turned to Kitt.

"She wants to know where we're from."

"Don't look at me! You're the one having the conversation!"

Kitt preferred to keep his distance. A live, breathing woman standing here asking questions was unnerving. They hadn't rehearsed this.

Milo and the girl exchanged some more words.

"I told her we're from a distant land. She says she guessed that."

"Ask her what the year is!"

Milo hesitated, nervous about the answer, but finally he asked the question.

"She says we're in the Earth-year fourteen thousand, nine-hundred twenty-three."

"Huh?"

"That's not the Christian calendar. I'll rephrase the question. Again the response came quickly, but this time Milo paled and stepped back. He questioned her once more, but the reply was the same.

Milo turned to Kitt. "She says she's a good Christian, and knows the Christian calendar well." Milo gulped.

"And?"

"She says this is the year of our Lord Jesus Christ the Savior, Son of God, 792."

Kitt's mouth dropped open. His hands twitched nervously, and for a moment he could only stare at his partner.

"Seven…seven hundred—, Milo, that's—" He couldn't finish.

"Right, Boss. The Dark Ages. We've landed in the middle of the Dark Ages."

56

LAUREN REGAINED CONSCIOUSNESS slowly.

The last thing she remembered was trying to hear what her husband and the old man were talking about through the locker door. Then the world turned upside down. She'd fallen against the opposite bulkhead, hit her head, and lost consciousness.

This whole thing had gone far enough. She went to the lavatory and did her best to straighten up. Gary would be horrified to learn she was making these little journeys herself, and with no one to guard the door or check to make sure the corridor was empty. But so what? She could hardly not use the restroom when she needed to. If someone saw her, she'd deal with it.

Lauren had lost her wits back in the barn. Trying to hide had been stupid. But now she realized that if Michael or anyone else discovered her presence on the submarine, they'd probably just laugh about it and find a way to send her ashore. She'd had plenty of time to invent a dozen credible explanations—all of them based on the theme of a neglected wife trying to find her husband. No law against that, certainly. *And who could prove otherwise?*

Of course if she *were* discovered all her efforts might be wasted. At best it would damage any leverage she held Michael. So the question was, what to do now. And again, she came to the same conclusion: more information was needed. And that meant waiting for Gary to show up with his twice-daily food service.

As if on cue, there was a slight knock on the door and in came seaman Keldorf.

Lauren took the salami sandwich and bit into it ravenously. She'd not known how good a meal could taste until she'd become obliged to wait for it. Gary seemed content to sit and watch.

Lauren could feel Gary's eyes on her while she devoured the sandwich, perhaps wishing it were him pressed against those lips. Lauren seductively licked at the corner of her mouth.

"Tell me, Gary," she began, "what do you know about those two men? One old guy and one younger guy? They've been hanging around this storage area. I can hear them talking through the door."

"Oh, they're not terrorists. At least the older one isn't. He's Admiral Sandusky. Came aboard in Virginia. They say he's pretty much running the ship."

"An admiral? Are you sure?"

"Pretty sure. I don't know if its true but Woody says he heard the admiral's from Naval Intelligence." Gary paused a moment, considering.

"Hey, that makes sense! I bet he's chasing the same

terrorists you are. Maybe we should tell him you're here. You could help each other!"

"No," Lauren protested, quickly. "That wouldn't be a good idea." She paused, searching for a reason.

"You see in the spy business we have what are called *cells*. A cell is only a small number of people. No one is ever supposed to talk to someone from another cell. That way, if we're captured and tortured by the enemy, we won't be able to reveal secrets about our fellow spies in the other cells. So I mustn't meet the admiral. He's in a different cell."

"Oh."

"OK, so what do you know about the other man—the younger one?"

"The civilian? I don't know his name, but he's supposed to be a scientist or something. He's testing some new equipment—at least that's the word we got in engineering. That's why they evacuated everyone out of the reactor area. I think the civilian was going to do some experiments with the reactor. Say, I hope he's not the terrorist! I wouldn't want a terrorist fooling around with the reactor."

"It's possible, Gary. And if so, it will be my job (and the admiral's of course) to stop him. But can you tell me anything else about what he does on the ship when he's not down here? Where is he now, for example?"

"Oh, he's not on the ship now, he went ashore with the admiral."

"Wait, you said we were in the middle of the Atlantic."

"Yeah, but we weren't. Woody told me there's some experiment going on, so we weren't where we thought we were or aren't where we think we are now, or something like that. I don't understand it, but I think Woody does."

"So, where's my husb— I mean, where's the civilian?"

"Like I said, he went ashore with the admiral. I wouldn't have known about it 'cept I was on duty at the engineering station in the control room. We surfaced and the admiral and the civilian left together in one of the inflatables. Had some supplies with them too. Food or something."

"So, are we back at Norfolk?"

"I don't know where we are. I don't even know where we were. But we're not back at Norfolk."

"Well, when we surfaced, did you see land anywhere. Or other boats? Or anything to give you a clue?"

Gary smiled. "I guess you don't know too much about a submarine."

"I don't know anything about a submarine," admitted Lauren, honestly. "This is my first time on one. But I know about terrorists," she added, needing to keep his awe intact.

"Well, when we go on a cruise, we don't usually get topside—I mean go out on deck where we can look around—until the cruise is over. Once we stayed under the polar ice pack for two months and— "

"So what you're saying," Lauren interrupted, fearing tales of the ice pack, "is that you have no idea where we are, how close to land we are, or what anything looks like on deck?"

"Well, I know what things look like on deck. It's under water. We went right back down to 200 feet after they left."

"Oh, so we're submerged again? That's amazing. You don't feel a thing."

"When you don't feel a thing, that's when you know you're underwater. On the surface, the boat rocks back and forth like a canoe. We took a real wallop last night. You probably slept through it, but we heeled right over. You'd almost have thought *Chrysalis* was out of the water, falling back in. Must have been a big surface wave."

Lauren was silent, digesting this. Obviously, she wasn't going to learn anything on board. Kitt and this admiral were using a submarine because the invention must have military potential. The admiral—no doubt—was overseeing the project for the Navy. It was all beginning to make sense.

"Gary, here's what we have to do. We must figure out a way for me to leave this ship—either before they get back, or next time they leave. You said they took one of the inflatables. There must be others. We have to figure out a way I can get off this submarine."

"I don't think that's possible," said Keldorf. "Last time we only surfaced for a few minutes, just long enough to get them out the hatch. You'd have to use another hatch. 'Course there's one right here, just above the reactor storage area. I don't know. Someone would probably see us unless it was at night. I don't think I'd want to do something like that. I could get in a mess of trouble if the chief found out."

Lauren chose a strategy.

"How old are you Gary?"

"Uh, I'm eighteen."

"And where'd you grow up?"

"Borger, Texas."

"Well I don't know Borger, Texas, but I'll bet it's a pretty nice place."

"Ah, it's not much. Just a lot of oil fields, and cattle." He bowed his head, dispiritedly.

"Did you have a girlfriend back there, Gary?"

Keldorf blushed. "Oh, you know, sorta."

"What's 'sorta' mean?"

"Well, I guess I liked her more than she liked me."

Lauren stayed quiet, letting his insecurities build.

"I can't imagine a girl not liking you, Gary. I like you a lot."

"Huh?"

"I think you're very handsome. That girl in Borger must have been pretty stupid."

"Emily? She wasn't stupid, she was—"

"She was a fool, Gary. To have someone like you interested in her, and to let him get away. I wouldn't make a mistake like that!"

Gary blushed again.

"Ah, I don't know. I guess you're just saying that, huh?"

Lauren moved closer to him.

"Mind if I sit here, it's a little cold on that side of the locker."

"Uh, sure, go ahead."

"I don't know what's come over me," said Lauren. "I just feel so—warm—when you're near."

Lauren closed her eyes, put her head back, and breathed deeply. Her left hand began stroking Keldorf's right leg, coming higher and higher up his thigh.

57

AVELYN SAT BY her fire and served the leaf-scented hot water she prepared each morning. Serving something to eat or drink was a time-honored act of hospitality. And it gave her time to think.

After returning from the mainland the prior night and escaping the invaders' ship, She'd collapsed asleep. It was the strange sound coming over the water that had awakened her. Terrified of what new danger might be approaching she'd left the lean-to and rushed up the slight rise into the forest. From there, she could see the small boat approaching, but what she saw was unbelievable. It flew through the waves as fast as a seagull skimming the water. And the noise it made was like distant thunder that never ceased.

Finally the little boat slowed, and the noise ended. She saw oars and watched as they covered the remaining distance in a normal way. Perhaps this was some detachment of the invaders. Maybe they'd given up the chase last night only because they knew they could return the next morning. But even so, it was odd they should send a tiny craft instead of the powerful sailing vessel which had chased her before.

Out of curiosity, instead of fleeing inland where she could never be found, Avelyn stayed near the water and observed the boat as it reached shore and two men got out. The craft was very odd. Its leather skins were so well wrapped it was impossible to see where they were sewn together. And the bright orange and white contraption which hung off the stern was incomprehensible. Perhaps it was some kind of fishing gear.

Yet the boat was not nearly so odd as the men themselves. Most striking was their height. Avelyn was considered tall herself. But these were giants in comparison.

And they wore clothes made from strange fabric. As a seamstress, she was intrigued.

Her interest growing, Avelyn hid in the forest and watched them advance up the path. She finally concluded they were not invaders. Or at least not *the* invaders. They were something altogether different. Perhaps Angles. Or even—it was possible—Arabs from Byzantium!

She decided to show herself, and so far no harm had come of it. They seemed as curious about her as she was of them. The older one even spoke a few words of Irish (although with a hideous accent). The younger one, who was closer to her age, spoke none at all.

And they were Christians. They'd asked her the year in the Christian calendar, obviously to determine if she was a Christian herself. And Christians were unlikely to harm her. But how odd they should arrive here, on this island, right after the massacre in Ballycastle. Had their god, or rather God, sent them for just that reason? But why here? One would think they'd have their hands full on the mainland, caring for the wounded and trying to convert the invaders who were very obviously not Christians.

It was lucky they both spoke Latin.

ණ

"We're lucky she speaks Latin," Kitt whispered to Milo as they watched the girl prepare something that looked similar to tea.

"Yeah, I'm glad I tried that when she couldn't understand my Gaelic. But I'm surprised. In this century, Latin in Ireland would only have been spoken by the clergy, or certain high-ranking officials, maybe. She must be unusually well-educated, or somehow connected to the Church, despite living on this island."

Avelyn handed them cups—simple containers carved from wood.

"Quod nomen est tibi?" asked Kitt. What is your name?

She paused, as if considering whether she should answer truthfully.

"Avelyn est nomen meum," she said at last.

"My name is Milo," said Milo in Latin, tapping one hand against his breast. "His name is Kitt," he said, nodding towards Kitt.

"Milo. Kitt," she said, pointing to each in turn. "Are you from Angland?"

"No, we are not from England," said Kitt, amazed he could converse in Latin. He'd never thought it would have application outside a botany lab. He was even more amazed the girl seemed real. But was she? Were they actually over a thousand years in the past? Could this...*person*...actually be alive, talking to them like this? He resisted the urge to reach out a hand and touch her, half suspecting the hand would pass through her body and the illusion of the girl, and her clothes, and everything on the island would vanish in some kind of inter-dimensional, collapsing time-vortex.

But he didn't want her to vanish. She was fascinating. And very pretty.

"We're from America," he continued, trying to hold up his end of the conversation while his brain worked to make sense of it all. "It's far from here. Across the sea." He pointed westward, and watched as her green eyes darted curiously in that direction.

"Near Galway?"

"We're not from Ireland at all," said Milo. "We came from across the ocean, many days in a boat," he added.

"You jest with me!" she said, a touch of anger on her face. "Everyone knows you cannot cross the Western Sea! It goes on forever—to the end of the world."

"No, actually it doesn't," said Kitt, trying to get the girl's attention back on him. "There *is* something on the other side."

The girl stared at him, astonished.

"Kitt!" said Milo abruptly, in English. "We're crazy! We shouldn't be talking about this!"

"You started it!"

"I think we should leave," said Milo. "Right now. Immediately."

"But—"

He didn't finish. Avelyn jumped to her feet and gasped. Kitt followed her gaze out to sea. There, not more than a mile offshore—and rapidly approaching—was a sailing ship. The vessel was close enough for them to see waves breaking upon its stem, spray flying back against the sail.

Milo grabbed his binoculars and studied the craft. Then he looked at Kitt. "We may have overstayed our welcome, Boss. I think we're about to be attacked by a Norse longboat."

"A what?"

"A Norse longboat. Not the boat itself. It's what it carries that's the problem."

"What's it carrying?"

"Vikings. Some of the most bloodthirsty warriors who ever lived."

58

"QUICK, INTO THE forest!" cried Avelyn.

"Do you know that ship?" asked Milo, not moving.

"Invaders! They destroyed Ballycastle. I escaped. Now they've come for me. We must hide!"

"If we leave immediately, we can probably outrun them," said Kitt.

"Yeah, but I don't like the idea of Vikings seeing a 55-horsepower motorboat. And more important, now we can't let the girl get captured. We told her what's on the other side of the ocean. Eventually she'd remember, and tell them. They hear there's land on the other side of the Atlantic, you know what will happen."

"It's not supposed to happen yet, is it?"

"It's not supposed to happen for another two hundred years. This girl gets captured and you really *are* talking about tampering with history. You could throw off everything."

"I can't believe we were so stupid!"

"Yeah, me neither. But she's right. We'd better get out of here."

"Well we can't just leave the dinghy. They'll see it."

Milo nodded. The tide had risen and the inflatable was now floating a dozen yards off the beach. Milo drew his .45 caliber pistol and fired six shots into the rubber fabric.

Avelyn screamed.

Deprived of flotation, the weight of the outboard pulled the dinghy under the waves instantly.

"C'mon!" yelled Kitt. He grabbed Avelyn's hand without thinking and they ran into the forest, together.

59

KREN WAS AT the tiller of *Freya's Song* for the short trip to the island. On board were two dozen warriors, plus Sigurd Ingvar, a battle chief.

He called to Ingvar to join him at the tiller.

"I can get you to the island, but how will you find her?"

"She's only a girl. How hard could it be? Look, I'm sure your uncle knows his mind, but I don't understand why we're even bothering."

"She has a boat. She could warn other villages."

"We'll put an end to those plans."

Kren smiled. "She escaped easily last night. Now, I hear the men are calling her a spirit girl who can command lightning and control the wind."

"Stories told among the men are not worth seagull droppings. She yelled some kind of curse, and got them all spooked. But it's nonsense. If the girl were a spirit, why did she need to escape in a fishing boat? Why not just flutter away on the breeze?"

"That wind was uncanny," observed Kren. "I was in

the harbor when it backed violently and cost us another longboat. Then it changed again and helped her escape. Maybe we *should* fear her."

"Don't be ridiculous. Winds change direction all the time in a storm. A village wench escaped, and now everyone's trying to make excuses."

They were nearing the island now. It was not small, and Kren guessed it would take hours to sail around it. There would be many hiding places. Pine forests covered the hillsides, further complicating a search. Kren did not see how they could find the girl if she didn't wish to be found. But that was Ingvar's problem. With luck, they could be back in the harbor by nightfall.

Suddenly, several sharp cracks, like the blows of a hammer on metal, sounded from the direction of the bay.

"I think she's trying to frighten us off," said Kren, smiling.

"It will take more than loud noises," scoffed Ingvar.

"There's her boat, in the cove. You can just see its mast."

"Can we land in there?" asked Ingvar

Kren examined the surrounding terrain and was able to estimate the depth of the water.

"Looks ideal. If there's a sand beach, we won't even need to anchor."

Kren ordered the sail furled and they coasted into the small bay. Oars were extended, but stayed motionless, above the water. The longboat slowed. Timing the moment carefully, Kren raised his hand high, and then dropped it sharply. The oars dipped into the water, made a single backstroke, and *Freya's Song* came to a stop just as the keel touched the shoaling sand. It was a very protected cove, without wind or waves. Kren gave orders and lines were run from the bow of the longboat, and mid-ships, up past the beach.

"Now we'll see how our Spirit Girl does against real Norseman," said Ingvar. "It shouldn't take long."

60

"THIS WAY!" CRIED Avelyn to the strangers, who finally decided to quit talking and follow her.

But follow her where? There were dozens of hiding places—a grotto behind a waterfall, tall trees where upper branches could conceal anything—but it wasn't that simple. She now understood who the strangers were. They weren't Christians at all. They were sorcerers. Necromancers. Conjurors! She'd seen the one raise his hand and from it a noise louder than thunder had come. The strange boat obeyed his command and vanished beneath the waves. So where was one to hide sorcerers? Could they *be* hidden? Did they *need* to be hidden? Might they not render themselves invisible—or better yet, blast the invaders with lightning?

Then it came to her. The perfect place.

"Follow me, sorcerers!" she cried, and led them deep into the forest.

61

THE NORSEMEN STOOD among the ashes of a recent campfire and Kren kicked a still-smoldering log. This had been the girl's base. The lean-to, store of provisions, and campfire all spoke of someone who had not merely fled here the previous night, but who was inhabiting the island. The single bed of pine boughs made it likely she lived alone. But why would anyone—let alone this Spirit Girl—live on a remote island off the coast of Ireland? And if she lived here, then what had she been doing in the village, the evening after the attack?

As the men formed up, Ingvar and two of his *hersirs* (senior warriors) went ahead to plan the search effort. The air should have been warming, but high clouds floated in from the west and the sun was blocked. The calm of a summer day had given way to something stiffer and Kren suspected another storm might be in the offing. If they didn't find the girl quickly, they might have to spend the night—a thought Kren found unsettling. The island hated them; he could feel it. Kren wished he were back on the banks of the Sognefjord in Norway, enjoying a meal at Torsten's hut, his uncle's wife baking haddock in the rock oven. The hut would smell of salt air and pine logs and it would be safe. Kren hadn't felt safe from the moment they'd arrived in Ireland.

Yes, they'd won a great victory. They had obliterated a village and captured or killed all its inhabitants. But there was something here that hadn't been conquered. Something…elemental. And it was even *more* present on this island.

Ingvar began issuing orders to the search parties.

62

KITT RACED THROUGH the trees, doing his best to keep up with Milo and the girl. He couldn't believe this was happening.

Their only goal in coming ashore was to learn the date. But they'd foolishly revealed the existence of a new continent—probably the most dangerous fact that could be divulged in this time period.

And somehow they'd stumbled onto a Viking invasion and were—themselves—now in danger.

Avelyn was leading them up a steeply-climbing, rocky path, that paralleled the west side of the island. Reaching a high clearing, they stopped and cautiously looked back towards the bay, keeping themselves hidden.

"They've beached the longboat," observed Milo, in English. "Now they're sending out search parties."

"We can't let her be captured, can we?"

"Boss, you might want to start thinking about your own hide right now. We don't want to be captured either."

"Come *on!*" Avelyn insisted, using hand signals to underscore her urgency.

Kitt tried to turn off the thinking part of his brain, so he could pay closer attention to the trail they were jogging along. It was less steep but still climbing, as it meandered up through forests of pine, ash, and juniper. He guessed from the height of the sun it was nearing mid-day. The air bore the smell of the sea, and the wind was brisk. The path itself was overgrown with roots, and cluttered with rocks strewn across it. Moss was everywhere.

"Avelyn," Kitt called out to her, and she paused, turning back briefly. "Where are you taking us?"

"To a place where we'll never be found. Please hurry."

Kitt was directly behind her, on the trail, and he studied the girl closely. She looked back frequently, as she urged them onwards.

Sweat dampened her forehead, and long hair was matted against it. Her chest heaved as she climbed swiftly, and she gasped occasionally from the exertion. Kitt was breathing hard as well. With all his laboratory work, the scientist knew he was not as fit as he'd been at the height of Yale's rowing season. Looking behind him, the only person who seemed undaunted by their grueling pace was Milo himself.

Kitt turned his attention back to Avelyn.

They could not allow her to be captured by Vikings. No other people could put the knowledge to such instant and dangerous use. So what options were left? They could help her avoid capture, but that would be temporary. The sensible choice was probably to kill her. It was the only possible way of undoing the damage they'd done. With the girl dead they could summon *Chrysalis* and escape.

But killing the girl would be a terrible thing to do. An evil thing. It would be murder. Or would it? After all, she'd been dead over a thousand years already. Technically, this young woman running beside him was a decayed corpse—less than that even, merely dust—as far as Kitt's world was concerned.

A root caught his foot and he stumbled. Avelyn grabbed his arm to steady him, and smiled reassuringly.

He smiled back.

Dammit. The girl was no more a corpse than he was. She was not dead, nor would she be for a long time, perhaps.

But of course she was dead. She had died a thousand years ago.

But she wasn't dead now.

Kitt's head was spinning. He knew it was foolish to be thinking about any of this at the moment—during his own escape attempt.

But she wasn't dead now.

It was an important concept. Kitt suspected the key to their whole experiment might lie in that one thought. He needed time to think it through, but there was no time.

Avelyn was now leading them on a trail high above the ocean. Bushes of thorns and thistles scraped their legs. A gnarled and twisted pine barred the way. Avelyn maneuvered around it and kept going. With difficulty, Kitt and Milo made it past the tree as well. But Avelyn had vanished. They could see the path continuing along the cliff. Yet the girl wasn't on it.

Long Atlantic swells crashed against white limestone at the base of the cliff. A blast of wind came from the sea and Kitt grabbed an overhanging branch for support. To be blown off this narrow trail and into the ocean would not be difficult. Had she fallen?

Then they heard laughter behind them. Avelyn was standing there, her long hair blowing horizontally and a smile of devilment across her face.

"You may be sorcerers," she said. "But your powers are limited! You walked right past me!"

"We were trying to follow, and you vanished," said Kitt, defensively.

"Yes," said Avelyn, "I did. Look!"

She pulled aside a bush and revealed a crevice between two boulders. More than a crevice—an opening. Grinning mischievously, Avelyn sat down and entered it, feet first.

"I'll be damned, it's a cave!" said Milo, and followed.

Kitt hesitated only a moment before easing through the opening himself. It was damp and he slid the last few feet. Only a thin beam of sunlight came through the cleft in the rock.

When his eyes adjusted he saw two figures standing against a wall, a dozen feet away.

"Hey, someone help me up!" he called, but the figures did not move. A hand reached out from a different angle and grasped his arm. Kitt cried out instinctively and pulled away.

"It's me, Kitt, relax," said Milo.

"I'm over here," said Avelyn.

"Who the heck are those two?" he said, gesturing towards the far wall.

"They are the Earth and the Sea," she said. "The one on the left is the Earth. The other is the Sea."

Kitt, his eyes adapting, realized he was looking at two statues carved from the rock.

"You mean they're gods? You worship them?"

"They are not *gods*," Avelyn said firmly. "They represent the spirits of the Earth and the Sea. Touch them. The Earth is cold. The Sea is wet."

Kitt realized he was in small cavern with a high ceiling. He stood up and walked over to the statues. They rose barely four feet off the floor, and maintained empty, bland, expressions. He touched the one Avelyn called the Sea.

"Hey, it is wet!" he said, and then looked up. There was a slight drip coming from the overhanging limestone. Then he touched the Earth. It was cold—somewhat colder than might be expected. But they *were* in a cave.

"This place gives me the willies," said Milo in English.

"You sorcerers are odd," Avelyn remarked. "I thought you'd understand, and feel at home, in such a place."

"We're not sorcerers," said Kitt. "Why do you keep calling us that?"

"Because you control magic, of course. One of you spoke words of power, and cast a spell on the boat, commanding it to sink. And it did. That is powerful sorcery, is it not?"

Kitt remembered Milo shooting the dinghy.

"We're not sorcerers, Avelyn. We're—"

"Careful," Milo interrupted in English. "Remember we've given away too much already."

Kitt sighed. "Or not enough. We need to think this through very carefully. In fact—"

Avelyn interrupted. "Excuse me," she said in Latin. "You will be safe here. I need to go outside and look around. I will bring food for us."

"Is it safe out there?" asked Kitt. "Shouldn't one of us go with you?"

"We're a long way from the cove. The invaders will not find this place, or even come this far inland. And I'm at home, here. I can move around quietly—hide if needed—far better if I'm by myself. I'll return before nightfall. Will you wait for me here?"

"Of course," answered Kitt.

"You may rest if you want—even sleep. It's very safe here. And if you're thirsty, you can even drink from the Sea."

Avelyn positioned her mouth to collect the water dripping onto the "Sea" statue, to show them how it was done.

Kitt smiled, enjoying her playfulness. He was a little sad when she disappeared back up through the cave's entrance.

Avelyn hurried swiftly along the path. She wanted to give the strangers all the privacy they needed.

She knew what they were discussing. They were trying to decide whether to tell her the truth about who they were, and why they were here. Avelyn was desperately eager to know about them. They were like nothing in her world, and they had incredible magic. How powerful was it? Would they be willing to use their magic to help her? An idea began forming, but she pushed it away quickly. It was too soon for such thoughts.

Instead, she let herself think about the one called Kitt. She remembered the touch of his hand on hers. And how he'd looked at her with that quizzical expression while they were running in the forest. His eyes were so—inquisitive. She wondered what he saw when he looked at her like that. Unconsciously, Avelyn's fingers slipped through her hair in a gentle, caressing motion, but she was not aware of it.

Then she remembered the invaders and what they'd done. Her hands clenched into fists, and a small furrow appeared in her brow. The wind picked up.

Milo grinned. "Hell of a cute girl," he said.

"Yeah, I wonder how old she is."

"She's over twelve hundred years old. I hope you're not forgetting that fact."

Kitt was silent.

"Which brings us to the question of our next move," continued Milo "There's a submarine out there standing by for radio contact. You've got several dozen Viking warriors swarming over the island looking for that girl. And we've told her too much to let her be captured, because that could change history.

"Anyway, you're still the boss and it's your call. All I'm asking for are marching orders. Do we stick with the original plan and try to get back to the ship, or do you have something else in mind?"

"We have to rescue her, Milo, but not because it could change history. We don't control history. We don't even control the future. Or at least not much of it."

"What *do* we control?"

"The present. And you can only occupy one present at a time. We're here now, and anything we do or don't do should be based on this reality, not on what might happen in the future. That's not our job."

Milo looked at Kitt in horror.

"The future? Well Jesus H. Christ! Where do you think we're *from!*"

"Where we're from doesn't matter. It's where we are *now* that counts. And right now, we're here. We have no right to influence future events."

"Have you lost your mind! That's what we're trying to avoid, 'influencing future events.'"

"Then forget about the future. Look at today. Right now. This is where we are. The future will take care of itself."

"Kitt, how can you say that? Did you forget what the whole point of this experiment was? We're trying to determine if time travel can change the past. And if it does, will that change the future? We're right now at a very pivotal moment in time—and what happens to Avelyn could change history. We've taken a terrible risk by going into the past."

"We're not in the past."

"Of course we're in the past! You heard what she said. This is the year 792!"

"Right now, the year 792 is the present."

"Boss, I say this with all due respect. What the *holy fuck* are you talking about? Did your brain turn to mush or something?"

"I think I figured it out as we were racing up the hill. I was trying to avoid not stumbling, but sometimes my brain works like that. It solves tricky problems at weird times."

"Well, clue me in!"

"Milo, remember down at the beach, I kept touching things, trying to figure out why everything was so normal?"

"Yep, and everything *was* normal."

"Exactly. And take Avelyn. You just said she's 1,200 years old. As far as the 21st century is concerned, she's been dead a thousand years. She's merely dust."

"Point being?"

"Well, I was thinking—given what we've told her—we can't let her be captured by Vikings."

"Right."

"And then I realized: the only way to truly ensure she'd never divulge the information we gave her, would be to kill her."

"Now, hold on a sec…"

"But killing Avelyn would be a terrible thing to do. Unless you think she's already dead. Do you?"

"Well, not exactly."

"And that's when it hit me."

"I'm listening."

"We're thinking about this all wrong. Those pebbles back on the beach are real pebbles. The bark on that tree is real bark. Avelyn is a real person. She is no less real than you and I are real. She's no less dead than you and I are dead. We haven't resurrected ancient corpses, and we're not peering through some sort of chronological looking-glass. We're in *the present!*"

"But we're not from *this* present, Boss."

"No, we're from an abstract place called the future. It's that distant future that's ephemeral. This is reality—an active, vital, dangerous reality. The future consists only of possibilities, infinite possibilities.

"What are you saying, exactly?"

"I'm saying we absolutely have the power to change history. At least, history as we know it. So what? Have not a thousand other men, a million other men, in fact *has not every person who ever lived*, held that power?"

"Well, I suppose so, if you put it that way."

"That's the way it is, and it makes it obvious what our next moves should be."

Kitt was thinking so hard he was pacing back in forth in the dark cave—not even aware he was doing so.

"Milo, no one can do anything more than make the best decisions possible in their own time. We're in *this* time. How we got here doesn't matter. We've been handed a set of challenges and we're trying to sort them out based on how we think they'll affect the future—over a thousand years from now."

"Well, yeah—"

"But that's insane. When we were in our own time—let's call it our original time—did we worry about how our decisions were going to influence events a thousand years in the future?"

"Of course not."

"So why are we doing so now?"

Milo could only stare at him.

"Up until this moment, I've been constrained by the thought that any action, or inaction, might change history. But implicit in that fear is a belief that history—or rather, the future—should not, must not, be changed. What incredible conceit, to believe that one's own history, one particular version of the future, was the best possible, or even the only possible!

"Look, a billion future lives might never come into being if we affect events now. But a billion other lives might be generated instead."

"So how do you choose between them?" asked Milo.

"You *don't*. You *can't!* That's up to God if you will, or at least someone with a higher pay grade than mere mortals. Certainly *we* can't make such choices. But we don't need to. That's not what we're charged with."

"What are we charged with, then?"

"Back there near the water, we realized we couldn't let Avelyn be captured by the Vikings, because it could change events a thousand years in the future."

"And now you don't care."

"It's not that I don't care. It's that we can't plan out the next thousand years. The proper decision is to rescue Avelyn because it's *the decent thing to do*. And that's how every decision should be made. In any time. In any present. In any future. It's called morality."

"So you're saying…"

"I'm saying let's quit pretending we're gods. And start being human."

"Which means rescue Avelyn, for her own sake. Not because of what she might tell the Vikings."

"Precisely. All we have to do—if we want to do the right thing—is to do the right thing *now.*"

"Which means find a way to keep Avelyn safe from the Vikings. OK. That's a start. But we can't rescue her without exposing more of our technology. And if we start down that road we might as well tell her everything about us, which of course she won't believe. Or do we make up something about being Moors from Spain, with mystical powers or whatever and then figure out a way to get her off this island?"

"No. I don't want to start our first trans-chronological communication with a lie."

"You want to tell her who we are—where's we're from? Seriously?"

"I'm thinking about it."

"Here's what I'm thinking about. You're not an eighth-century person, and this isn't our home. We're trespassers, if you will, on someone's else's property: Dark Ages, Ireland. And you've got a U.S. Navy submarine out there cruising around in thousand-year-old waters, with no one on board realizing it.

"Now that we know the year, don't you think we should get back to the ship and make sure that taco-maker works in forward gear, as well as reverse? And if it does, and we're able to return home, then I'd say the next move is to open a case of champagne and get outrageously drunk. The next morning we can put a pot of coffee on the stove and figure out what the hell it all means. But not now!"

"Sure, Milo, that's the sensible thing to do based on our earlier plans, but things are different here. Can't you feel it? The air, the rocks, the—everything! I feel like I'm alive, in a way I've never experienced. There's a vibrancy here, a purity that doesn't exist in our world. And Avelyn, she's—, well, just being with her, just talking to her, looking at her, it's, it's—"

"Love?" volunteered Milo.

"Give me a break." Kitt rolled his eyes in exasperation. "What I was trying to say was that this is probably—no, this is definitely—the most exciting scientific experiment that's ever been performed. We haven't brought back to life a human being from the past, and her whole world with it. We've actually moved across time and entered that world ourselves. It's now the present! This is reality! In fact—just think—there must be other worlds out there right now as well. Other realities. This is fabulous. It's unbelievable!"

"You're right, Kitt. But it's so fabulous and unbelievable that we've got to keep our wits. I don't know why we thought we could just come ashore, meet someone, and not get emotionally freaked out. But the question stands: what's our next step? Do you really want to get more caught up in events here than you already are?"

"Yes, I think I do. Or at least I'm not ready to go back to the ship yet. I want to keep the experiment going a little longer. We're here and it's happening. We've turned the eighth century into the present. Maybe we'll never be able to do it again. And we're collecting data—incredible data—every second. So let's broaden the experiment and tell Avelyn the truth about who we are. It's exciting! We should be sharing it. Not trying to hide it!"

"Maybe. But it's a heck of a shift in strategy. Are you sure you know what you're doing?"

"No, but it feels right. And if we don't tell her the truth, then we have to be dishonest. You already said we're trespassers in this place and time. Do we also want to be liars?"

"It would only be a white lie. But look, I was just trying to be the voice of reason, which is out of character. If you want to jump on this time-machine, roller-coaster and not even hold onto the hand rails, I'm not going to stop you. We've hijacked a U.S. Navy submarine and taken it a thousand years into the past. Who knows what the rules are? You want to tell the girl? Sure, why not. Tell her everything. I ain't going to stop you! Holy crap, if we get out of here ourselves without going crazy it'll be a miracle."

Kitt grinned. "You're probably right about that."

&

Avelyn returned at dusk carrying a small bundle of food.

"What did you bring?" asked Kitt.

"Cheese and some dried fish. I have supplies stored in several spots on the island.

They ate in silence. Kitt was going to offer Avelyn a drink from his Nalgene water bottle, but before he could do so she performed her trick again, and drank from the God of the Sea, letting water drip into her mouth. It was an inexact process, and when she pulled away with her face wet, Kitt noticed her eyes shining with exhilaration.

He watched her closely: a lovely girl, so alive and vibrant, playfully drinking from a natural fountain. He wanted to touch her again, feel her hand in his, play with her wet hair. She looked up, and he knew he'd been caught staring. But she only smiled, and lowered her eyes.

"Please come over here, Avelyn," said Milo. "My partner has something to say."

She walked back from the Sea statue and sat down near Kitt.

"Have you decided to tell me who you are, and where you're from?" she asked.

"How did you know that's what we were talking about?" asked Kitt, suddenly nervous that what he was about to divulge would paint them as lunatics and send Avelyn fleeing the cave.

"What else *is* there to talk about?" she asked, suddenly quite serious.

"Go ahead, Boss," said Milo, in English. "I'll just listen. This oughta be good."

Kitt breathed deeply, then began forming the Latin phrases carefully and slowly.

"Avelyn, you sailed your boat here from the mainland, right?"

"Yes."

"Can you ever remember a time when your people had no boats?"

"We've always had boats."

"But sometime, somewhere, someone must have been the first person to make a boat—to create a boat."

"I suppose so."

"Before that first boat was created, it would have seemed impossible that a person could travel across the water."

"Before there were boats, it would have been impossible."

"But only because they didn't know about boats. In other words, something may seem impossible, but it may not be impossible at all."

Avelyn looked at him quizzically.

"Better just take the plunge, Boss," said Milo. "I'm starting to get confused myself."

Kitt sighed.

"Avelyn, what I'm going to tell you will seem impossible. But it's the truth. Do you understand?"

"Yes."

"Remember the first thing we asked when we met? We asked you what year it was. Why do you think we asked that?"

"Because you are Christians—Christian sorcerers, I guess. Although I didn't know there were such things. You wanted to test me to see if I knew the Christian calendar."

"That was not the reason. We asked you the year because we did not know the year.

"How could you not know the *year?*"

"If you sailed your little boat to a distant land, when you got there the first thing you would do is ask the people where you were, because you wouldn't know. Correct?"

"Yes."

Avelyn, we didn't ask you *where* we were. We asked you *when*. We asked you the year. We did not know what the year was."

"Your journey involved *years?* Did you come from Byzantium?"

"No, no. Our journey required only minutes. And we know *where* we are. We are on an island just north of Ireland. But we didn't know the year."

"I'm sorry. I'm trying to understand. But I don't."

"Avelyn, think about it again. If you travel a long distance, when you get there you don't know the place, so you ask *where* you are. We did not ask where. We asked *when*. Do you understand what kind of journey we have made? Why would we have asked *when*?"

The girl shook her head. "Kitt, I don't understand."

"We traveled across *time*, Avelyn. Our boat doesn't travel across distance, it travels across the years themselves."

Avelyn's face turned white.

"You're mad!" she cried, scrambling to her feet and backing away.

Kitt waited.

The girl paced back and forth in the narrow confines of the cave, glancing at them occasionally. She finally walked back to Kitt and sat down next to him. But she would not look at his eyes. She pulled her legs up to her chest, clasped them in her arms, and a shiver ran through her.

For a while no one spoke.

Finally Avelyn looked up.

"You are saying you can travel across years? You can travel across time? Not even sorcerers can do that. I don't believe even the gods can do that!"

"Think about our boat," Kitt said, trying to make the case, logically. "Did you see how it crossed the water, before we began using oars? Did you see how fast it went, without sails? Without anything? Think about what Milo did. He used a device that made a loud noise, and the boat sank."

"I already know you're sorcerers! That's what I've been saying."

Milo sighed and turned to Kitt, who looked helpless.

"She's got a point, Boss," he said in English. "If this were the nineteenth century or later, any gadgets we had would represent advanced civilization—evidence of being from the future, maybe. But here in the eighth century, they'd equate gadgets with magic."

But Kitt wasn't listening. He put his hand gently on Avelyn's cheek and raised up her head so she was forced to look directly at him. She gave a pleading glance, and looked down again. Kitt understood. This was too much for her. She was scared, confused, and exhausted. What must she have been through? An attack by Vikings? Hiding on a deserted island? All alone? Kitt's heart went out to her. It was dreadfully unfair to expect her to understand anything he was saying. But he couldn't stop now. It was too late.

"It's true, Avelyn," he said, almost in a whisper. "You must believe me. I need you to believe me."

She turned her head away further and began to cry.

He pulled her to him and she did not resist.

Kitt did not know how long he held her while she cried. Finally, when the tears stopped and her breathing was quiet, he kissed the top of her head and laid her gently on the floor of the cave. Then he covered her with his jacket.

63

THE GATES OF the castle had been closed for two days. During that time, by order of the seneschal, no one was permitted to enter or leave. A stable hand, overcome with worry for his family in the village, had tried to escape by climbing the wall.

Flannagain would have ignored it—one less mouth to feed—but unfortunately, the baron was there and ordered him shot with an arrow. No further escape attempts had been made.

The fortress was now an island under siege, and as with any siege, the problem was food.

Flannagain timed his approach to the baron immediately after the evening feast when his lord was more likely in good humor.

The mongrel dogs were absent. On Flannagain's order, they were caged in the supply room, to provide stew meat. Tonight's dinner was the first using canine ingredients, but no one had told the baron.

As Flannagain approached, O'Ruairc smiled.

"My dear Brody," said the baron, "Despite the problems outside our gates, my chef surpassed himself with the evening meal. Don't know where the damn dogs have gone. We'd have quite a fight over tonight's fare."

"Yes, my lord. Unfortunately, it is the castle's food supply that we must discuss."

"Brody, you're such a storm crow! Here I am in pleasant humor and you bring me some new problem. Am I to suffer no pleasure in this life? Am I being tested like that Christian fellow, Job? I could not abide boils."

Flannagain understood that the baron, once over his initial terror and finding himself invincible inside the castle, had reverted to his status of pampered nobility. The invaders had become a mere nuisance; something to be dealt with by his capable seneschal.

"My lord, as you know, the castle is in a state of siege. We can send no one out and likewise can receive no one in. Our supplies run low."

"Don't be ridiculous, Brody. We sent that messenger, Blunar, last night. Probably halfway to Tara by now. When the Ard Ri hears of this outrage, he'll have all Ireland in arms. His army will arrive any day."

"My lord, Blunar's head arrived this morning, affixed to the tip of a crossbow arrow. I think our chances of sending word to Tara are few."

"His head? How ghastly! Why was I not told at once?"

"You were sleeping at the time, my lord. I judged it would serve no purpose to awaken you regarding a mere servant's head."

"Very sensible. Should we send another servant?"

"We could try, my lord. But even if one were to get through, it would not help our immediate problem. We have food only for a few more days. Water is not an issue, because of the well. But you'll recall we were awaiting new supplies when the invaders attacked. Otherwise, our situation would not be so dire."

"Well, what do you intend to do about it? It is your job to see to the castle's needs. Your job!" he emphasized again.

"My lord, I would welcome suggestions, but our best option might be to negotiate a truce. We could send out a messenger under flag of parley. I can't believe the invaders wish to devote the resources necessary to keep Castle Bally under a state of siege indefinitely. They must assume we could hold out for months. I'd be surprised if we could not find grounds for an accord."

"Well, see to it, see to it! You know this matter of replenishing our supplies is quite serious. What with this Avelyn affair, and now these invaders, it's been far too long since I've had a new girl from the village."

"Yes, my lord. I'll send out a parley flag at noon tomorrow."

Brody retreated with all the deference he could muster.

64

IT WAS DARK as only a cave can be at night. Kitt and Milo were sleeping. Avelyn slipped quietly through the small crevice in the rock. The moon was out, and the wind had died. So close to midsummer, the night was not cold and the air was refreshing.

She followed the path farther inland, through a forest of spruce trees and aspen. Moonlight danced eerily among the boughs. She was not frightened by the shadows, for she was a shadow herself, blending with the forest.

She came to a small lake and sat down by its edge. This, she believed was the spiritual heart of the island.

Crickets were chirping. A doe and two fawns stepped cautiously down to the lake and drank eagerly. This far inland, and protected by the trees, the water was calm.

Avelyn shivered and pulled her knees up close, grasping them in her arms. A breeze came from nowhere and rushed across the water, disturbing its surface and startling the deer.

I did that, Avelyn thought. I shivered, and so did the lake.

The deer were becoming anxious. The doe raised its head, sniffing the air. Avelyn let her mind relax and the deer did as well, stepping back into the water.

What was happening to her? It had started when Shelby died in her arms. She felt something had passed out of him and into her, some spiritual force.

And the wind helped her escape. Lightning destroyed the mast on an invader ship, and a violent gust had overturned and sunk another one.

Or was it all just coincidence?

Here on the island, the spiritual forces seemed even stronger.

She stood up and walked away from the water. The deer looked up, startled, but Avelyn relaxed her thoughts and the deer continued drinking. Another coincidence? A star appeared, almost directly overhead.

On impulse, she began turning, keeping her eyes on the star. Her hands fell away from Shelby's cloak and as she turned faster her arms stretched outwards. She felt the Earth reaching up through her, seeking expression.

She stopped, stumbling slightly from dizziness.

"You are right, Shelby!" she said aloud. "I could feel it!"

"Once you've felt the power of the Earth, it will never leave you," he'd said. "It will always be there, ready to help you."

She recalled similar words from the abbot.

"God never ceases watching over us. He hears our prayers. And answers them."

Were they talking about the same thing? Was it the same power? Was she now sensing it, on the island?

Could she *control* it?

She pushed the thought aside, and in its place came, unbidden, the image of Kitt. She recalled how he held her while she cried, and how he laid her gently on the floor of the cave, believing she was asleep. He placed his coat over her and she had been warm. Now, with the benefit of rest, she could consider everything they'd said.

Either the sorcerers were mad—utterly so—or they had powers a god would envy. To travel in time? Kitt said they possessed something like a boat—a device—that allowed them to move across time as Avelyn could move across water. And that it had been "invented," much as boats must have been.

Yet why were they *here*? Why had they chosen the year 792, and this particular island?

Maybe, thought Avelyn, it had been chosen *for* them.

Of course! The sorcerers had been sent for a purpose, and it was obvious what that purpose was. But somehow they didn't realize it. That wasn't surprising. The sorcerers might not even be real.

No, Kitt was real. She discarded that theory. In any case, they would have to be convinced, somehow, to do what God—or rather, the Earth—wanted.

But which was it? God? The Earth? Were they the same? It was all so confusing! How could they be the same, when Christians and Druids hated each other? But what if it were the same power—manifested differently, understood differently? And what if she could use that power?

The abbot would say: "You don't use God. He uses you."

And Shelby had said: "Yes, we Druids have power. But only so long as we obey the wishes of the Earth and the Sea."

Yes! It's the same thing. And as a Druid trained as a Christian, I understand both sides. I can use this power against the invaders. And of course, it's what the Earth wants. And God, too. Everyone hates them!

Her mind seethed with ideas. It was all making sense now. She understood why the sorcerers had arrived, what her role would be, and what she had to do.

It was several hours before dawn and a weariness enveloped her. But she was not ready to return to the cave. Gathering some pine boughs, she lay down and used Shelby's cloak as a blanket.

Comfortable, but too excited to sleep, her mind leaped between thoughts of Vikings, Druids, Earth spirits, and Christians. Then she thought of Kitt, how he'd held her hand while they ran through the forest, and how he'd kissed the top of her head so softly. She was going to take advantage of his feelings for her, but she pushed away the guilt.

It was the only plan that would work.

65

KREN WATCHED FROM shore as *Freya's Song*, under command of his first mate, cleared the bay and headed for the mainland. The vessel caught the morning's sea breeze perfectly, heeled to port, and gathered speed.

Sending the vessel away had been his idea. Ingvar's men had spent all of yesterday seeking the Spirit Girl, but—other than her campfire and the boat—had found nothing.

Searching a wilderness island for a single female was far different than snatching women from their beds in a nighttime raid. But, the solution was obvious: give the Spirit Girl a reason to come out of hiding, by making her think they'd left.

So the Norsemen—half the original complement—were now lying prone in a semi-circle a hundred yards from the campsite, concealed by the tall grass. *Freya's Song* would return later that day, at which time Kren expected their quarry would be captured. He lay down in the grass to wait.

Hidden behind a tree, just inside the forest, a pair of eyes watched their every move.

66

"WHERE DO YOU think she went?" asked Kitt.

After waking up and finding Alysen missing, they'd climbed out of the cave and were now sitting on the path, with their backs to the rock ledge, looking out over the ocean. The wind was mild, and the sun was already warming the moist air.

"I have no idea, but I'm sure she'll return. She left us yesterday, and then came back."

"Yes," said Kitt, despondently.

Milo looked sharply at his partner. "Miss her?"

"Yeah, OK, I do miss her. It's been a while since I've been this attracted to someone."

"High-stress situations often fuel romance. I guess being chased by Vikings together is sort of an aphrodisiac, huh?"

"Very funny. But I'm not kidding."

"What is it, the sexy Latin accent?"

"Hardly. I think she's one of the most intelligent

women I've ever met. You can look into her eyes and see it. She's always thinking."

"Just like you."

"Maybe more than me. And look at how she handled herself yesterday. We were more flustered than she was. She took command of the situation, knew what to do, and got us to safety. She's very resourceful."

Milo stood up, walked to the edge of the cliff, looked over the sea, and then sat back down.

"I'm impressed she escaped the Vikings and sailed her own boat here from the mainland. It's rough water in that channel. She must be quite the sailor."

"It's not to my credit," continued Kitt, reflectively, "but I think most of the women I've been attracted to up until now—well—there really wasn't much there."

"Skin-deep beauty, like you said about Lauren?"

"Yeah. Gorgeous to a fault, but Lauren uses her looks as a weapon. It's why I've kind of turned off on women lately. It never works out. But now…"

"OK, Boss, someone's gotta bring this up. I hope you're not forgetting the age difference, with Avelyn."

"Age difference? What the fuck, Milo. I'm only twenty-five. And she's at least seventeen. That's not exactly scandalous."

"Oh, she's at least seventeen alright. I'd say about one thousand, two hundred seventeen."

"Well, she doesn't look it."

"You're right about that," agreed Milo.

"Not that it could go anywhere, of course. I'm still married."

"Oh, c'mon Boss. If anything happened between you and Avelyn, I'm pretty sure that counts as a *prior relationship*. It's over a thousand years before you get hitched. I don't think, technically, it would be cheating."

"I doubt the divorce lawyers would see it that way."

"Who won't be born for another…"

"Thousand years. Yeah, I know."

Avelyn appeared, coming up the path carrying blueberries in a fold of her dress.

Both men hurried to stand up, but she urged them to stay put—choosing to sit directly opposite them, cross-legged, with her back to the sea.

"Like blueberries?" she asked, smiling. "There's a wonderful patch just below this cliff. Here!"

She popped one in each of their mouths and then ate several herself.

"Well, you seem cheerful this morning," said Milo, noticing her face bore no trace of tears. "How long were you gone?"

"Quite a while, actually. I had much to do."

"Don't you think that was dangerous? I'm sure the Vikings are still looking for you."

"I needed to do some thinking, and needed to speak to the Earth and the Sea."

"Well, why leave the cave? I'll bet, to you, those statues aren't just stone. Right?"

"What do you mean, *just* stone?"

Milo grinned.

"I thought so. You're a Druid!"

"What's a Druid?" asked Kitt.

Milo ignored him.

"In fact, I think you're a Druid, who was pretending to be a Christian."

"I *am* a Christian!"

"Hmmm. And what do you think it means to be a Christian?"

"I know that God sent the Lord Jesus Christ to save us, and if the Earth and Sea are willing, we shall be saved."

"I rest my case."

"Rest your mouth, Milo," said Kitt. "It's too nice a day to argue religion."

He passed around a bottle of water and handed out biscuits. "Too bad we shot the dinghy. I'd be up for some water-skiing."

Avelyn looked at him doubtfully. "What is *'water skiing?'* I don't think that's a Latin word. Is it something they do in the future?"

"Oh, you believe us now, do you?" said Milo, but noticed Avelyn was looking only at his partner.

"How do you know we're from the future?" asked Kitt. "We might just as easily be from the past."

"No. Sorcerers would need more powerful magic than they have today, to create a boat for traveling in time. You could only have come from the future."

Kitt smiled. "Very perceptive. But we're not sorcerers."

"So *when* are you from?"

"Want to guess?" asked Kitt, with a grin.

Avelyn's eyes flashed. "It's not a game!"

Kitt was chagrined. "You're right. I apologize. We are from the year two thousand twenty."

"Only a little more than a thousand years?" she pondered. "Well, there must have been more progress in the next thousand than there was in the preceding."

"You're right about that!" Milo interjected, playing historian. "Here in the eighth century, not much has changed for several thousand years. Everyone still uses sails to propel their boats. They use horses and oxen to do their work. And everything those animals can't do, the people do themselves.

"But around 1750 things start changing. Civilization develops all kinds of tools, and things we call machines. They now do most of our work for us."

"So everyone has these time boats, or whatever you call them?" asked Avelyn. "Everyone moves across years? It must be very confusing."

Kitt looked at the ground.

"Well, actually," said Milo, "Kitt, here, invented the thing and this was the first time we used it. We came to this year, and this place, on our first try—by accident."

"I see," she said. "And I'm honored. Even if it was an accident." Avelyn was looking at Kitt again. "On the other hand, maybe it wasn't."

"Oh, yeah," said Milo. "We were talking religion, weren't we? Hey Kitt, I think our pretty young lass is a Druid!"

"What *is* a Druid?" asked Kitt, again.

"Druids believe in the spirits of the Earth. Every rock and tree is a god. Every wave in the ocean is a being of supreme power."

"Don't be silly!" said Avelyn. "Every wave is part of

the sea. Every rock is part of the earth. It is the Sea and the Earth, together, which have the power."

"So what are those statues?" asked Kitt.

"Druids used to come here to perform ceremonies. They built the statues."

"But what are they for?" asked Kitt

"Druids talk to the spirits," explained Avelyn. "The Earth spirit and the Sea spirit are the most important ones. The statues are links to the spirits themselves. When a Druid priest builds a statue, the statue is the spirit."

"What she's saying, Kitt, is that the statues are idols. She worships them."

"No! You don't worship the Earth and the Sea. You worship God! The Earth and the Sea are for power and knowledge. God is there for love. You worship God. But the Earth and the Sea give you the power and knowledge to do so. At least, that's what I believe..." Her voice trailed off.

"So you're a Christian *and* a Druid?" asked Milo. "Don't you find that a little difficult?"

Avelyn stood up. "No! It's not difficult," she said angrily. "Why should it be difficult? Why does everyone have to think they're so different?"

She turned abruptly and looked out at the ocean. The sky that had earlier been clear, began to fill with dark clouds, one of which chose that moment to blot out the sun. A gust of wind followed it.

Kitt rushed over and put his arm around Avelyn's shoulders.

"Hey, it's OK. My partner likes to get argumentative,

sometimes. But he'll shut up for the moment. Hear that, Milo? You will shut up for the moment."

"Sure, Boss! Sure! If she can handle both, I've got no problem with that."

"Milo, make yourself useful. Maybe get some food out of the pack, or something."

Milo disappeared down the cave entrance, knowing when three's a crowd.

Avelyn let her fingers touch the arm that was around her. She studied it, noticing the light brown hair, the smooth, unblemished skin. It was a strong arm, but it had never worked in the fields. It had never cast a fishing net. This man's strength lay elsewhere.

"He's right," she said softly. "That's why I got angry. Because he's right. It's very difficult to be a Christian *and* a Druid. It shouldn't be, but it is."

Kitt did not respond. Instead, he pulled her more tightly to him, and Avelyn felt his lips gently touch the top of her head again. She liked the sensation and wondered how it would feel to be kissed on the lips.

Her plan was going to work. It was already working. But her guilt increased. It would be so nice to just stay here in his arms. She closed her eyes, letting herself enjoy the moment—and gathering the strength she'd need to destroy it.

Milo returned with jerky and a bottle of water. Kitt and Avelyn were standing together with their backs against the cliff, looking out over the sea, his arm around her. The weather had cleared again.

Milo sat on a nearby rock and began chewing the jerky.

"Care to share some of that," Kitt asked, after a few minutes, turning towards him.

"Who? Me? Oh, sorry. Thought you'd forgotten about me. Yeah, I think I've got some more in here." Milo reached into his pack, pulled out two more sticks and handed them over.

"Problem with jerky," he said casually, "is that you've got to drink a lot of water with it. Stuff's so dry it will suck the moisture right out of your body if you don't drink water. Here—" He handed the water bottle to Avelyn, who drank deeply before passing it to Kitt. The young scientist smiled at her, and Milo saw her squeeze his hand.

"Well, I can't speak for the rest of you," he said, "but I've always hated eating breakfast in silence. I don't suppose we have anything to talk about.

"No, I don't suppose we've got much to talk about, seeing as how we've escaped capture by a Viking war party, seeing as how we claim to be visitors from 1200 years in the future, seeing as how we don't know anything about each other but our names. No, can't think of a single thing to discuss. Good jerky, though. Damn good jerky." He took another bite and began chewing. His sarcasm did not go unnoticed.

Finally, Avelyn replied.

"The Vikings, as you call them, aren't a problem. They've left."

"Are you sure?" said Milo, surprised.

"I went down to the cove this morning and hid behind a tree. They loaded their supplies onto the ship, which pulled up its anchor and headed south, back towards the mainland."

"Then they've given up trying to capture you?" said Kitt.

"Yes. They were foolish to think they could capture me."

"I'm not sure you should be so confident," said Milo.

"Why not? And we have other things to talk about anyway."

"Yes, that was my point," said Milo. "There's lots to discuss. Care to go first?"

"Well, here we are, two men from the future and a young Irish girl sitting on the side of a hill, looking out at the sea, and eating this terrible meat that must be from the future—though I would have guessed it was from the time of Christ. The question is, what do we do now?"

Milo and Kitt glanced at each other.

"You probably need to leave, don't you?" she prompted.

"Well, there's no hurry—," Kitt began.

"Yes," interrupted Milo, "If the Vikings have left and you're in no danger, we do need to leave. You see, Avelyn, we don't belong here—not on this island and not in this time."

"It's very reasonable that you want to return home,"

Avelyn agreed. "So I think I should probably go away. I assume it's something you must do in private."

"Avelyn, wait a minute!"

"Why wait, Kitt? You know you must leave."

"You think I want to leave? I don't. I don't want to leave *you*. Avelyn, I—"

"What he's trying to say," interjected Milo, "is that he's sorry he has to leave."

"Yes. So best we get on with it, don't you think?"

"No!" said Kitt, "I don't understand why—"

"Goodbye," She said, smiling at each of them, and then she leaned over and pecked Kitt on the cheek. "Goodbye," she said again. "I will never forget you."

"Avelyn!"

"And I hope you never forget me. Please, do *not* forget me." She stared into his eyes meaningfully and then turned away.

Before anyone could respond, Avelyn ran down the path and did not look back. The pine forest enveloped her and she vanished—almost as if *she* were the sorcerer.

"Hey!" cried Kitt, staring after her. Then he turned to face his partner. "Goddammit, Milo!"

"What?"

"You ran her off!"

"I didn't run her off! I simply agreed that we have to return to our own time. Don't blame me just because your sweetheart hit the road."

"My sweetheart!"

"Boss, I understand the attraction. No one blames you for crushing on her big time. But face it. The feelings weren't mutual. And that's probably a good thing because it wasn't meant to be. Do I need to insult your intelligence by spelling out the reasons?"

Kitt stared down the path, but Avelyn was gone.

67

SEAMAN GABLER USED a soup spoon to ladle mayonnaise onto his pastrami sandwich.

"I think I'm going to be sick," said Woodruff.

"You think that's gross?" added a petty officer. "I used to work in a meatpacking plant. Wanna know how they actually make that pastrami?"

"Not really."

"So these hanging beef carcasses move along an assembly line, know what I mean? The first guy takes a knife and…"

ONK! ONK! ONK! The intercom over their heads sounded the three low-pitched notes that signaled the submarine was about to surface.

"Prepare to surface. All hands, prepare to surface."

"That pisses me off," said Gabler. "They should either get rid of those three notes or the announcement because everyone knows the three notes are always followed by the same announcement. Kinda insults the intelligence.

Like we're not smart enough to figure out the notes by themselves."

"Yeah, that's good thinking Gabler," retorted the chief. "I think someone oughta make you an admiral, 'cause you're so goddamned 'telligent. Think of all the 'lectricity you could save the Navy by getting rid of those notes!"

"Or getting rid of the message, Chief. Either one's OK with me."

"Either one's OK with Seaman First Class Gabler. I'll sure as hell relay your cooperative attitude to the goddamned Pentagon. Now get your goddamned cooperative butt to your station, and spare me the horseshit!"

A submarine on the surface was not quite a fish out of water. It still possessed deadly potential and could fire most of its weapons. But it gave up its primary defense: invisibility. In the history of submarine warfare, more submarines had been destroyed immediately upon surfacing than had ever been destroyed by depth charges while they hid under the waves.

Gabler and others now raced through the ship, manning the torpedoes, doubling up in engineering, taking their stations in the Control Room, and otherwise, preparing *Chrysalis* to face adversity.

The five-inch cannon and twin anti-aircraft guns emerged automatically out of the deck, controlled by the weapons computer. When she broke through the waves, she would be at 100% fighting efficiency.

The fact that the waves *Chrysalis* was breaking through were 1200 years old, and there was no military power on the planet that could even dent her hull, made no difference.

The men inside the black cylinder went dutifully to their stations, preparing to thwart an attack by fighter aircraft, low-level bombers, enemy ships, or even cruise missiles. And had any appeared, *Chrysalis* would have defended herself superbly.

It was the captain's duty to determine which, if any, of these dangers were present. For that reason, the boat—as usual—paused at periscope depth before surfacing completely. It's radar and surveillance masts were raised.

"Sonar shows no ships within twenty miles, Captain," barked a crewman, bending over his instruments.

"No messages from ComSubLant," Captain, said another. The lack of ComSubLant messages via satellite meant either that the world was not at war (which was the likely meaning) or that some enemy had blasted the Navy's communications satellites out of space, which was unlikely, but still a possibility.

"No aircraft, Captain," noted the third technician.

These reports suggested *Chrysalis* was emerging into a non-hostile environment and the captain should have relaxed. But he didn't.

"Radarman, say again your report," Hamilton queried the technician.

"No aircraft visible on the screen, Captain."

"No aircraft at all? At any altitude?"

"Correct, sir."

"Isn't that a little unusual? There weren't any aircraft the last few times we surfaced either."

"Yes, sir. It's unusual, but I've seen it before. Once,

down in the Southern Ocean, we didn't see any aircraft for two weeks."

Hamilton was about to protest that the Southern Ocean was one of the most isolated spots on Earth. They were now in the North Atlantic, just west of Scotland, below one of the world's most heavily traveled air corridors. But were they? Hadn't the admiral warned him about being too sure of anything, especially instruments and electronic devices? Weren't his orders essentially to ignore everything strange and unusual. In fact to expect it?

"Very well. Up periscope!"

At least Sandusky had given him permission to use the periscope on his own ship, while the admiral was away.

In a minute he saw it: a gray inflatable bouncing off the waves, heading right for them.

"Surface!" said the captain.

Chrysalis eased the final twenty feet out of the waves. Water poured off her conning tower and weather decks. In a few minutes, the wind would dry the steel plating and the sun would turn the black metal into something too hot to be touched by bare skin.

"Deck crew, prepare to retrieve inflatable."

Half a dozen seaman emerged from a large hatch aft of the sail and made ready to bring the motorboat and its crew on board.

The skipper was not sure where on the surface of the globe he actually was. Nor did he understand what mission his ship was on. Or how the current operations supported that mission.

But, by God, he could still send out an inflatable and retrieve it on schedule. That had to count for something.

⁂

Milo filled two glasses with Scotch and handed one of them to Kitt, who stared at it in disgust before draining the whole thing.

"Any more of this around?" asked Kitt.

"Alcohol on Navy ships is prohibited, which is one of the reasons I left the Navy. But I smuggled a private stash on board in one of the crates. Figured we might need some booze on this trip. Have a few bottles of Chianti, too. Picked up a taste for it in the Med."

"No. Right now I'd rather stick to Scotch. I could use a refill, Milo."

"When we get back to Norfolk—and assuming they haven't thrown us in prison—I'll be pleased to buy you a whole case of Johnny Walker Black. But for now, we have work to do."

"I'm not in the mood for work."

"Well by God, you love-sick puppy, you'd better get in the mood!" snapped Milo. "Let me review our situation. We have just been rescued from a previously Viking-infested island. Our good and gullible friend, Captain Hamilton, has not seen fit to question how we came to lose the other inflatable, and why we needed a second one to pick us up on the west side of the island. Now, we're back aboard and Hamilton's waiting for new orders.

"I don't know how long I can keep this up, and may crack before he does. All he has to do is ignore my standing orders on radio communications long enough to request a confirming authorization from ComSubLant regarding my authority over this ship. He'd be in his rights to do that. And once he does, and finds there is no ComSubLant—"

Kitt looked up with a grin. "Yeah, exactly what *does* a submarine captain do when he requests orders from ComSubLant and finds it doesn't exist?"

"Actually, there's a procedure," Milo admitted, matter-of-factly. "The Navy has to assume, in the event of a nuclear exchange, it may be impossible for a ship commander to establish contact. Every skipper carries sealed orders for what to do in that event."

"And what would those orders say?"

"*Chrysalis* is an attack boat, a hunter-killer. Her orders would probably assign her to free-lance, search-and-destroy patrol, with the enemy's missile subs being the prime target. Any enemy vessel a secondary target."

"Assuming, of course, the captain knows who the enemy is, and assuming he can't communicate with higher authority."

"Of course," agreed Milo. "Attempting to contact a superior officer would remain a priority."

"But in this case, the superior officer is on board. And whatever suspicions the captain may have, he can only confirm or disprove by contacting a different superior officer, right?"

Kitt was frustrated and was taking it out by verbally sparring with his partner.

"I get your point," Milo conceded. "But that doesn't mean we have time to sit around and get drunk. We've learned the year. Let's do the calculations necessary and get *Chrysalis* back to the twenty-first century."

"A moment ago, Milo, you called me a love-sick puppy. Maybe I am. You know I miss her already? I can't quit thinking about her."

"Thinking about her's OK, Kitt. But you can't let it debilitate you. We're still in the middle of probably the most dangerous mission in United States history. The best thing we can do—you can do—is get this ship back to the good 'ole US of A. Do that for me, and I'll take you to this club I know on Manhattan's Upper East Side. They've got a guy at the door who won't even let the women in unless they're hoping to get laid. He says he can tell."

Milo walked over and put his arm around Kitt.

"C'mon, Boss, let's find that calculator, and see if we can get home."

68

THE SUN WAS halfway to its zenith, and the Norsemen were getting bored waiting. Kren knew that Ingvar and most of his men now doubted she would ever come. A few were already grumbling, but at least they obeyed orders. Yet, why would the girl not return to her campsite? The lack of breeze was an asset. There would be nothing to mask the sound of her approach and they would hear her well before—

There she was. The Spirit Girl was standing silently in the midst of them. How had she done that?

Kren was fascinated. The auburn hair cascading off her shoulders was radiant, her slender body was relaxed, and she stood utterly still. Her eyes were fixed on a point far out to sea, her lips slightly parted. The effect was so disarming that none of Ingvar's warriors moved or even made a sound.

Then she opened her mouth and spoke softly, in Anglish.

"Arise, warriors," she said. "I am ready to be captured."

Her words were gentle—a loving mother calling her children from their sleep.

Kren stood up quickly, realizing too late it would seem he was following her orders. Well, perhaps he was.

Ingvar also was now standing and began issuing commands.

"Everyone up," he called out. "Seize the girl, bind her! What are you waiting for?"

A dozen warriors rose out of the grass but moved towards her sheepishly. Several brushed grass from their tunics and stretched their stiff muscles—clearly reluctant to approach the Spirit Girl.

Kren watched with amusement.

Smiling and cooperative, she held out her hands, inviting them to bind her wrists.

The Norsemen did so, but without the usual skylarking and lewd jokes that would normally accompany the capture of an attractive woman. In fact, rarely would they have stopped with jokes.

Kren was prepared to order the men not to harm her, but it was unnecessary. The warriors seemed loath even to bind her hands.

"Guard her well!" ordered Ingvar. "Our ship will be back soon and I want off this cursed island. There's no glory to be won here. Just another female slave to round up!"

There was much glory to be won, thought Kren. Somehow, they just weren't the ones winning it.

69

Captain Hamilton sat in the control room and fretted. He'd been told by the admiral to expect further orders within the hour, but he wasn't looking forward to those orders. They'd be as enigmatic as all the rest, and complying with them would yield not a clue as to what purpose they served.

The business with the dinghy was a good example. He'd equipped it with overnight supplies and small arms as requested. Then the following morning they'd made radio contact and requested a second inflatable be sent to pick them up on the west side of the island. What was it all about? If they were testing scientific equipment, why didn't they take any equipment with them?

And when they returned, and the captain might have deserved an explanation of the missing dinghy, the admiral nodded curtly and asked him to dive and remain stationary. That had been an hour ago and here they sat.

Hamilton tried to convince himself he was more upset than he really was. With the admiral running the ship,

Hamilton was acting more like an Executive Officer, and he'd always liked that job. There were fewer ways to screw up.

But something didn't feel right.

Hamilton turned to the officer of the deck.

"Take her up to antenna depth, OOD. I want to establish contact with ComSubLant."

"Aye aye, sir," the officer barked, automatically. "Sir, with respect, the admiral issued a standing order that we weren't to use the radio. I logged it in myself, sir, and it's still operative according to ship's log."

"That's fine, Joe, that's fine. Appreciate you being on the ball. But the admiral's orders don't apply to the commanding officer contacting ComSubLant. That's routine and takes priority."

This wasn't true, but it sounded good.

"Aye aye, sir."

Chrysalis rose to antenna depth, a modest step that did not require the crew going to stations.

"No priority one messages, Captain."

"Small vessel bearing 0-8-5, Captain. Range 4,000 yards. Heading about 1-8-0 degrees, speed seven knots."

"Type of vessel?" asked Hamilton. Perry knew he was violating the admiral's orders by even coming to antenna depth. It was the one disloyalty he was going to indulge in, and only to be able to avoid disloyalty in the future. A request for a confirming authorization of the admiral's status was not out of line. He probably should have made one earlier.

If during that very legitimate process he should find

it necessary for the safety of the ship to take additional actions, that also was his prerogative. In this case, that meant identifying the vessel by whatever means necessary—including the periscope.

Hamilton checked off these legalistic points in his head, already planning for a court-martial.

"Type of vessel?" Hamilton barked again.

"It's just—I can't quite say, Captain," admitted the sonarman. "It's about thirty meters long, but I'm getting a vague return off it. I don't think it's steel. Might be a fiberglass yacht. Sorry I can't do better, Captain."

"That's OK, sonarman. If it's not steel, it's probably not going to blow us out of the water."

The men chuckled. Even if it were steel, it would have a hard time damaging *Chrysalis.*

"I'd better take a look though. Come to periscope depth."

Chrysalis rose upwards slowly until she was floating just slightly beneath the waves.

"Raise periscope."

Hamilton pressed his eye to the lens.

"I'll be damned," he said. "Some crazy millionaire went to the trouble of building a Viking longboat."

"Mind if I borrow the periscope, Captain?"

Hamilton spun around. The admiral had just entered the room, with the young civilian beside him. His lips were tightly compressed in a thin line, and his eyes radiated fury.

"Aye aye, *sir!*" The captain came immediately to attention, mostly out of guilt. "Admiral, we came to antenna depth so as to send a routine communication to

ComSubLant. My sonarman picked up a craft of some sort. We were just in the process of trying to identify it."

"I see. We will discuss this later. For now, if you will please let me have a look, I'd be obliged."

"Aye aye, sir." Hamilton backed away and the admiral took his place. Milo pressed his face against the eye socket and studied the image in silence.

"Very well, Captain," he said, pulling away from the instrument. "Unless you have an objection, I'd like to suggest your *routine communication* to ComSubLant be delayed indefinitely. Please take *Chrysalis* down to 200 feet. As I said earlier, you can expect new orders, shortly."

"Aye aye, sir."

The captain was so shaken at being found out there was nothing he could say but those three words. As for contacting ComSubLant—to hell with it. If anything were amiss, ComSubLant would be trying to reach *him*. And there were no messages, priority or otherwise. Hamilton decided he'd done his duty.

"Please follow me, Mr. Kitt," said Milo brusquely.

Arriving at their cabin,

Milo nearly threw Kitt in and slammed the door behind him.

"What was all that about?" asked Kitt. "I thought you were going to give orders to take *Chrysalis* back out to the Atlantic, so we could get home again."

"Yeah, but then I looked in the periscope."

"And?"

"The Viking longboat. It's back. They were only pretending to give up the search. Obviously, they headed south, then turned around again and came back to the island. The whole thing was a trick. I'd bet a month's wages they left men back there at the cove, knowing Avelyn would show herself the minute she was convinced they'd left. And it worked. That's why the longboat is now returning to Ballycastle. The girl's on board, Kitt. I'm sure of it."

Kitt was silent for a moment.

"You didn't have to tell me that, did you?" he said at last. "You could have ignored the whole thing and taken *Chrysalis* away. Why didn't you?"

"Well—"

"I'll tell you why Milo. It's because you know we have to rescue her. It's just as obvious as when we were on the island. All our lofty theories of time travel, and the danger of changing events in the past, or the future, or whatever the hell it is—it all amounts to nothing when you're presented with a simple case of right and wrong. We're in the eighth century, things are going on, and we've become involved. Like I said before, simple decency is the only law you need to live by. It's the only law you *can* live by. Right now, simple decency means we help Avelyn. Do you agree?"

"A rescue attempt means getting heavily involved in local events. That means possibly even more change to the twenty-first century, in order to do now what we feel is right."

"We don't know anything will actually be changed," noted Kitt. "That's just one of the theories. But, yeah, we might be tampering heavily with the future. Is it worth ripping apart the fabric of space-time, to rescue one girl captured in a Viking raid? You're the historian, but I'd guess there must have been tens of thousands of girls captured in Viking raids. Avelyn is just one of them. Is she worth it? I know my answer, but what's yours?"

"Well, Boss, Avelyn isn't just one of tens of thousands of girls captured by the Vikings. She's our friend. I'm not saying that makes her special. But it changes the situation for *us.* I never had much in the way of fancy morality or ethics or whatever you want to call it. And this time travel stuff is way beyond me. But I like to think I wouldn't walk out on a friend in a bar fight, and if we turned tail right now and headed home, I don't think I'd care to look in the mirror again for a long while.

"And another thing—I don't recall anything about the 21st century that was so goddammed fucking perfect that it couldn't stand to be shaken up a bit. I say let's rescue the girl."

"I agree. But how do we do it, and what do we tell the captain while we're doing it?"

"The answer to the first is dependent on the answer to the second. If we want to keep Hamilton and the crew in the dark, that's going to limit our options."

"You're not suggesting we tell them the truth are you?"

"I think it's time we considered the possibility, yes. It's one thing to land on a relatively deserted island, ascertain the year, and then get back to the ship (although we didn't exactly pull that off cleanly, did we?) It's a whole different matter to oppose an armed force of Norsemen. To be honest, I'm not quite sure how to go about it."

"Milo, we can't tell anyone on this submarine what's really happening. Word would spread and half the crew might go insane. More importantly, you've eliminated any hope of time travel being kept a secret when we get back home. And keeping it secret is crucial. We've been through that before."

"OK, if we can't tell the crew, then we either carry off Avelyn's rescue by ourselves, secretly, or we invent some tale about needing to use a nuclear submarine to rescue a fair damsel in distress, from several hundred people who are dressed like medieval Vikings. I'm a hell of an inventive guy, Kitt, but I wouldn't know where to begin with that one."

"Then we have no choice. We're going to have to rescue Avelyn by ourselves, and in such a way that the crew has no idea what's going on. Can we do it?"

Milo pulled out the Scotch bottle again and refilled their glasses. He swirled his around, watching the rattling ice cubes.

"One thing I've been trying to figure out, Kitt, is why they're expending the resources necessary to go after this one girl, on a remote island."

"Does it matter?"

"Yeah, I think it does. It's relevant to the tactical situation. Let's remember the year, 792. I looked it up in our library. That's a full three years before the history books record any Norse landings in Ireland. We may have stumbled upon the first one. They've got an element of surprise going and want to keep it that way. That would justify the energy they've expended to capture Avelyn. They don't want her warning the rest of the Irish coast."

"Makes sense."

"Which means you're probably looking at a Norse expeditionary force, consisting of a flotilla of longboats, probably what they called the *Busse*-class. Those were best for long-distance voyages—as this would have been. And they'd have brought more than two or three vessels. Probably at least half a dozen or so."

"Point being?"

"I'm just speculating, but you're probably looking at hundreds of Norse warriors now occupying Ballycastle—which we can assume is where they're taking her. This isn't going to be so easy."

"Milo, why don't we just blow that Viking longboat out of the water with a torpedo?"

"Because Avelyn's on it!"

"Oh, right." Kittery looked perplexed. "Maybe I'd better lay off this Scotch for a while."

"Much as I hate to admit it, I think we're going to have to perform this rescue the hard way. We'll wait until the longboat reaches Ballycastle and Avelyn's been taken ashore. Then we go in and fetch her out."

"Fetch her out with what? Those .45 caliber pistols?"

"We'll go in armed to the teeth, obviously."

"You're talking like you're some sort of commando."

"I was, Kitt. I'm an ex-Navy SEAL."

"What!"

"I guess I never told you that part of my naval career.

Special Ops in 'Nam. Learned how to knife people so they don't make a noise while they're dying. Learned how to break a guy's neck with one arm, creeping up on him from behind. Learned how to swim underwater for three minutes without breathing. Best goddamned time I ever had."

"Do you still have those skills?"

"I guess we're going to find out."

"So what's the plan? Swim-up on some Viking underwater, break his neck with one arm, and then knife him so he doesn't make any noise while he's dying?"

"Yeah," said Milo. "Something like that, maybe."

70

ONCE ASHORE, KREN gave orders for the Spirit Girl to be held in one of the huts under guard, and not be harmed. He found Torsten with a group of *hersirs* on the far side of town, facing the castle.

"I'm glad you're back, Kren. We can't understand why the castle's garrison hasn't launched a counter-attack."

"Maybe there aren't enough troops and they're waiting for reinforcements."

"It's possible, but—"

A long note was sounded by a horn atop the castle's ramparts, a creaking was heard as the gate ascended, and there—revealed to all—was a rider on a white horse. A long pole rested on the left stirrup, and atop it fluttered a white flag.

The horn blew again, and the man rode towards them.

"After little ado, the mighty castle spews out a single warrior," scoffed Torsten. "He'll soon be within cross-bow range."

"This looks like a messenger, not a man-at-arms. Let's hear what he has to say."

As the flag of parley approached, Kren noticed the messenger was surprisingly frail, of middle years, and balding. He looked terrified.

The horse stopped ten yards away and the man stood up in his saddle, holding his hand forward in greeting. *"Thiocfaidh mé i síochána!"*

"Oh damn," said Torsten. "A messenger who does not speak our tongue is useful only as arrow bait."

"Perhaps Odger?" suggested Kren.

"Odger!" roared Torsten. "Pass the word for Odger!"

It was only a moment before the old warrior came hurrying up.

"Yes, Captain?"

"We have a messenger who doesn't speak our language." Torsten nodded towards the frightened man on horseback. See if you can find one in common."

Odger tried several before the messenger smiled, and responded.

"He speaks Latin, Captain."

"Do you?"

"Yes. After we sacked that monastery in Aquitaine, I stayed on and—"

"Just see what the fool wants."

Odger spoke to the man at length, before turning back to Torsten.

"His name is *Flangan*—best I understand it. He claims to be the chief administrator of the entire *fief*...whatever a *fief* is. He is second in command to the Baron Oruk, or Rurk or something. Who can pronounce these names?"

"Names don't matter," said Torsten. "But do you believe that about a chief administrator? He's no warrior. How could this man hold such a position?"

"I believe him, Uncle," said Kren. "These people are at peace…or *were*. A lord would not require a strong man at arms as an assistant. Rather, he might choose someone like this, who no doubt is a capable clerk."

"Well, what does he want, Odger?"

"He proposes a truce."

"How can we have a truce? The fighting's barely begun! The castle hasn't even answered our challenge. Who would want a truce?"

"*He* does, Captain. And he says he speaks for his lord."

"Uncle, if you'll permit me?"

Torsten nodded.

"Odger, ask him what the terms of this truce might be."

After further dialogue, Odger turned and spat on the ground.

"I find these Irish contemptible, Captain."

"Just tell us what he said please, Odger," urged Kren.

"He says that—assuming we've come from a distant land—it is probably for land that we come."

"A very clever clerk, indeed," said Kren.

"He says the richest land in all Ireland, able to grow more barley on one achar than can be grown on three achars here, can be found only a half day's sailing to the south. It is a fief—that might be their word for chiefdom—called Doon, which is an enemy to his lord. *Flangan* offers a base from which to launch the attack in return for our leaving this fief, and conquering Doon."

"You're right, Kren. He's very shrewd," said Torsten.

"Do you believe him, Odger?" asked Kren, "Could it be a trick?"

"I'm not acquainted with Ireland, sailing master. But these people are not warriors. Maybe this kind of cowardice is normal."

"I was having trouble understanding why the castle wasn't attacking," said Kren. "But if we've stumbled upon a completely non-warlike nation, then everything makes sense. Those in the castle saw what was happening to the village, and simply barricaded themselves in."

"I don't believe it," said Torsten. "That castle was built by warriors—it's a military fort. Anyone can see that. The only question is, why won't they fight?"

"We know not when it was built, Uncle. It may be hundreds of years old. Times change; traditions change. It would not be the first time a period of war was followed by a long peace—one in which the people grew soft."

"The sailing master speaks truth, Captain," interjected Odger. "In our attack upon Noirmoutier, we found a city totally dependent on the protection of their King, Charlemagne. But he was ill and his sons were feuding. There was no one to defend the town and it fell easily to us, despite stout walls."

"Then do the two of you counsel that I accept the offer of this puny clerk?"

"Uncle, I believe he is offering simple surrender, however he may choose to phrase it. This story about a kingdom to the south may or may not be true, but need hardly concern us. If they're willing to open the gates of the castle, on some vague promise of ours to move south, then what do we have to lose?"

Torsten was silent for a moment, staring at the castle.

"Kren, I think I understand the kind of man this baron is. He hides in his castle and sends out his—clerk—to talk to us. He didn't even come himself. What sort of leader does that? Anyway, I have a plan."

He turned to Odger.

"Tell the messenger we accept the proposal. It is true that we seek only a place to farm, and if the best lands lie to the south, we shall proceed there with haste. Tell him we look forward to meeting the Lord Baron, and bestowing upon him a gift, as token of our friendship."

When this was translated, the man on horseback beamed with pleasure. He spoke more words to Odger and then sat back again, anxiously smiling at all those around him.

"He says, Captain, that if there is to be a treaty of peace between you, he has been authorized to invite you and whomsoever of your chiefs as you wish, to dine in the castle tomorrow at high sun. At that time, details of your travels to the south can be discussed, and a pact of friendship signed between you."

"Tell him we accept the invitation, and say I will bring fifty of my most trusted chiefs, as well as the gift."

The man on horseback appeared daunted when told there would be fifty Vikings arriving for dinner, but he recovered quickly enough.

"He will send a chamberlain to this gate tomorrow, at noon, who will guide us to the castle, and collect the gift."

"Thank him, but tell him it is our custom to deliver gifts directly to the lord."

The man on the horse considered this, nodded to Torsten, and then turned his horse around and galloped back to the castle.

"What's this about a *gift*, Uncle?" asked Kren. "Since when do we bring *gifts* to conquered tribes?"

"When it's necessary, Kren." A thin and foreboding smile crossed Torsten's lips. "When it's necessary."

His uncle would say no more.

71

BRODY FLANNAGAIN SAT at his desk and pulled a cloak about him. The fire in the corner had burned out hours ago and he could not justify a new one. The castle's wood supply was nearly depleted. A pity, he thought, that they had not stockpiled some of that despicable peat moss the villagers used in their fires.

Of course, if they had stockpiled peat they could have stockpiled wood. The baron owned the forests. They hadn't stockpiled anything. Why should they have? No one expected a siege.

The real question was: what to serve the dinner guests who had just laid waste to their host's village and murdered hundreds of its citizens? Not only was it an awkward social situation—they had very little food. Every dog in the castle was eaten, save for the baron's six, pure-bred hounds. O'Ruairc would order the servants themselves into the pot before he'd give up his hounds.

Until a peace treaty was signed—and that was the

whole reason for the meal—there really was no way to *serve* that meal.

Flannagain was distracted by the sound of a mule braying loudly in the courtyard, no doubt protesting its own short rations. Damn animals. Who could get any work done with—

The mules! That was it. They had two mules in the castle and the one horse. There remained a half-bushel each of barley and onions. With sufficient thinning, yes, they might just muddle through. After all, the invaders were coming to sign a treaty. The meal was only a formality. And he would forbid the servants to eat anything for the rest of the day, on pain of death. That way, the final reserve he'd set aside could be thrown in as well.

They could feed fifty guests just enough mule-stew to fill their bellies. With ample drink at hand—they had plenty of ale, thank God—the invaders would be in good humor and eager to sign the treaty. It had taken diligence to prepare it in Latin, but now that matters had been converted from military to diplomatic, the seneschal's confidence returned.

Flannagain called in his staff and began issuing orders.

72

KREN SAT IN the hut they were using as headquarters and watched Torsten file the blade of his sword. *Hersirs* were seated on the floor around him.

"Tomorrow, at the castle, I don't want anyone killed until I've unsheathed my own sword," Torsten said. "Then I want everyone killed. Any questions?"

"Sounds simple enough," said Grimsson, approvingly.

"I find it hard to believe anyone would be stupid enough to invite fifty enemy warriors for dinner," said Knut.

"They didn't," said Kren. "They invited our captain, and 'a few of his chiefs.' It was our captain's idea to bring along more of our 'chiefs' than expected. The messenger was appalled, but had no choice."

"Another thing," added Torsten. "I expect they'll try to feed us lavishly and make us drowsy. Tell your men to eat sparingly. Praise whatever they offer but refuse second helpings."

"What about this 'gift,' Captain?" asked Knut.

"After the meal, when discussion turns to the treaty, I

will suggest that their lord entertain himself with the gift we bring, which of course will be a woman. See if you can find one suitable, Knut."

"Er, yes, Captain. We have plenty. But they've all been captured from this village. It seems odd to make him a present of one of his own women."

"Hmmm. That's true," agreed Torsten. "Kren, what about that female who escaped? The Spirit Girl or whatever they call her? She, at least, had courage so can't be from this village. Is she pretty?"

"Pretty enough," he agreed, not liking this turn in the conversation. "The baron hardly seems worthy of her, though."

"Then all the more certain he'll be distracted," said Torsten. "With our Spirit Girl as bait, I have a hunch this Irish lord's head will be more easily removed from its unworthy shoulders. Kren, bring her here after dinner, so we can have a look."

Torsten turned away and began once more filing his sword blade.

73

LAUREN KITTERY, WITH the increasingly-cooperative help of Gary Keldorf, was making plans for escape.

The seaman had become increasingly malleable. Flirtation was all that was usually necessary—although Gary would balk occasionally at some request or proposal and then Lauren would use a light caress or a head placed wistfully on his shoulder and his trepidations would vanish. The biggest problem was persuading him to open the cargo hatch once they were on the surface.

Apparently, there was some rule against opening hatches without direct authorization of the captain. Even then, if some switch in the control room was not set for "red," none of them would open at all—regardless of authority. It was a safety feature.

Lauren was afraid she might have to have sex with Gary to solve the hatch problem, but it had not been necessary. During one of Keldorf's protests, Lauren wrapped herself around the seaman and kissed him passionately. She apologized immediately, explaining she'd been overcome with appreciation at the way he was helping her catch spies. After that, there were no more protests.

He'd even thought of a solution to the red light problem. If they waited until one of the other hatches was being opened—most likely the main entry port—then they could open the cargo hatch at the same time. The only risk was that Lauren would be seen, but Gary explained that if they kept it open just long enough for her to slip out and if she immediately got in the water and swam away from the hull—and if all of this occurred at night—the chances were no one would notice.

"You mean I'm going to have to get wet!"

"Well, uh, I guess so," Gary replied. "I can't think how else to do it."

"But I can't let my purse get wet. I'm carrying—well, I'm carrying secret data files."

"I'll get a Ziploc from the galley. That'll keep everything waterproof."

Earlier Gary had recommended she wait until they were back in the submarine pen at Norfolk. Otherwise, the captain wouldn't be opening the main entry port of *Chrysalis*, and without that, they couldn't open the cargo hatch. So Lauren had resigned herself to a long wait. In the meantime Gary was keeping her supplied with food, paperback novels, and—Lauren admitted—a degree of companionship. Although Gary was more a faithful puppy.

She was just finishing a chicken sandwich while reading the last chapter of Zane Grey's *Call Of The Canyon* when she heard the light triple tap that was Gary's private signal. Lauren sighed, put the book down, ran a hand through her hair by habit, and opened the door.

Gary was agitated and breathing heavily. A trickle of sweat ran down one side of his face. His eyes darted back and forth, looking up and down the passageway as if he was afraid he'd been followed.

"What is it?" asked Lauren. "Come in. Hurry!"

"Thanks, I, I—"

"Relax, Gary. I'm sure there's nothing to be worried about."

"I'm not worried! It's just that I think you're going to be able to get away tonight!"

"Tonight! Leave the ship? Are we back in Norfolk?"

"No, Woody says we're near Ireland. Anyway, the chief's been told—Chief Budge, I mean—that *Chrysalis* is going to surface tonight about a hundred yards from shore and send off the admiral and the civilian in one of the inflatables."

"You mean like they did before?"

"Yeah, I guess. Only, last time we were several miles from the coast and it was daylight. Now, I hear we're going in after dark, and a whole lot closer to shore. So I guess if you can swim, you could get off the ship tonight."

"That's wonderful, Gary! Yes, I can swim. I have my scuba certification. But how cold is the water?"

"I'll find you a wetsuit and fins, and a waterproof bag for your clothes and stuff."

"Perfect. Then I'll be fine. You say we're near Ireland?"

"That's what Woody says he heard."

"Well, Ireland's as good as anywhere. At least they speak English. And I still have my purse, thank God."

"What will you do when you reach shore?"

"I'll change into my clothes, walk to the nearest road, and then hitchhike—or call an Uber if I can get a cell signal. Otherwise, I'll find a house and ask to use their phone. I'll have to make up a story and explain that—"

"Hey, I don't think you have to make anything up. Just tell 'em about the Arab terrorists. Everybody hates terrorists. Anyone'll help you."

"Of course you're right, Gary. What was I thinking?"

"Good luck, Lauren." Gary seemed despondent.

"Oh, Gary, we'll be together again. I'll use my connections to find out when *Chrysalis* gets back to Norfolk and I'll be there at the dock to welcome you. Maybe we could go out somewhere—see a movie or something."

"Are you kidding? You'd go to a movie? With *me*?"

"Well of course. If you'd care to invite me."

Lauren reached out and ran her hand caressingly down Gary's cheek.

74

THE SONARMAN KEPT his gaze riveted on the display screen—beads of sweat forming on his brow. The captain and the admiral were standing directly behind him, watching closely.

"Come right, two degrees."

Chrysalis, running at periscope depth, changed direction slightly as it eased its way up the Ballycastle firth. The moon had not yet risen, and even the stars were obscured by a low overcast—almost a mist. The firth of Ballycastle was over 300 feet deep at its opening but shoaled to a dangerous sixty feet.

"I'll go farther in if you want me to, Admiral," said the captain. "But I'd prefer to drop you off about here."

It had called for inventiveness to produce a story that explained their present actions—though perhaps less so in the captain's state of resignation. Milo had told Hamilton that the equipment being tested had a variety of applications, many of which could not be explored except in very unorthodox ways. This journey up Ballycastle's firth, and an undercover night landing of himself and the civilian onshore, equipped with heavily-loaded packs, were all part of that testing.

It had been a stroke of luck that Hamilton hadn't even looked over their list of needed equipment. He'd just sent the ship's quartermaster to their cabin with orders to provide anything they asked for—and to keep it confidential.

So Kitt and Milo now had another inflatable, fully-automatic M-16 rifles, handguns, combat knives, grenades, smoke bombs, a miniature flamethrower (might be useful), black facial paint, camouflage fatigues, boots, a pair of marine radios, food, bivouac gear, plenty of ammunition, medical supplies, and backpacks for carrying it all.

The plan called for surfacing only long enough for Milo and Kitt to be loaded into the inflatable. Then *Chrysalis* was to wait just outside the firth, submerged to antenna depth.

"This will probably be fine, Captain," said Milo. "Let me check the periscope."

Milo stared through the lens for several minutes and what he saw was what he hoped to see—a completely deserted, heavily treed shoreline fronted by a rocky beach. Looking down the firth he could not even make out where it ended and could see no sign of the village even though their charts placed it less than a mile ahead. The mist had thickened into an actual fog. Better and better.

"Looks ideal, Captain. Carry on."

Water poured off the ship's conning tower as *Chrysalis* surfaced—only a hundred yards from shore. Seamen carried supplies out the exit port and launched the dinghy.

They cast off immediately.

75

"WHAT IS THIS, Milo, our third inflatable? How many does the ship have?"

"Nice thing about the Navy, Kitt, is that ships hold a lot of cargo. Poor bastards in the Army have to carry stuff, so they go light. But in the Navy, you just pile everything into a big hull, and the hull doesn't care. I'd guess *Chrysalis* has a dozen or more of these little boats. I could shoot this one and several more full of holes and our friend Hamilton wouldn't even miss 'em! And as I learned on the island, shooting inflatables is great sport!"

"Nice to know all those taxes my accountant says I'm paying are going to good use."

"Can't put a price tag on fun, Kitt!"

Milo was steering for a spot several hundred yards up the firth, deeper in than *Chrysalis* could go.

No one noticed as a shadowy form emerged from a small hatch just aft of the submarine's sail, and slipped silently into the water.

❧

In the control room, a red light blinked rapidly on a console.

"Sir, I got an indication that number six cargo hold was opened for a few seconds. It's closed now, sir."

"Are you sure, Heisel?" asked Executive Officer Simpson. "Why would number six open?"

"Beats me, sir. But I saw it. Just for a few seconds. Then it went out. D'ya think this is one of those faulty instrument indications we're supposed to ignore?"

"I don't know, Heisel. I guess I'd better report it."

Simpson spoke to the captain.

"Red light on number six? Is he sure?"

"Says he is, Captain. Heisel's pretty reliable."

"Well, let's play it safe. Send someone to number six and make sure it's closed properly."

"Aye aye, sir."

In a few moments, the hatch condition was confirmed safe.

"Conn, give me low speed turns forward on the starboard screw, back on port. Prepare to dive."

"Aye, sir"

The opposite thrust pivoted *Chrysalis* slowly in the darkness until the hull was pointed towards the mouth of the firth.

"All ahead, slow. Periscope depth."

Chrysalis vanished into the dark waters and soon the only ripple was from the periscope itself.

"Down scope," ordered the captain, knowing they

could determine their position more accurately with sonar. The ship cleared the headlands as the seabed dropped beneath them. Soon *Chrysalis* was hanging motionless, submerged, in deep water.

"Maintain position, XO. You've got the conn. I'm turning in."

"Aye aye, Captain. I've got the conn."

Hamilton walked towards his cabin, shoulders slumped, looking awfully tired. In normal circumstances he would have stayed in the control room, this close to shore. But he was beginning to not give a damn.

76

THE SPIRIT GIRL was chained to a wall in the stone hut Torsten was using as a headquarters. Hemp lashings had been replaced with iron cuffs, on the advice of Ingvar, who insisted the girl could not be trusted and would try to escape.

"So I take it she put up quite a fight, our little Spirit Girl, eh, Ingvar?" chuckled Torsten. "I'm glad to see that, for once, your men obeyed orders and did not use her themselves. She appears untouched."

"She hasn't spoken a word since we left the island," he muttered.

Kren, watching from across the room, didn't bother explaining how the actual capture had occurred. And she hadn't spoken a word because Ingvar had gagged her. Kren removed it after bringing her here, but she remained silent.

Most captured women screamed at them, cried hysterically, or glowered angrily. But the Spirit Girl conveyed neither terror nor resignation. She gazed around curiously, eyes bright with intelligence as if soaking up knowledge for future use.

"What do you make of her, Kren?" Torsten asked, joining him in the corner.

"I don't know if she's a spirit, Uncle, but I find her bewitching. I think it's time we tried to talk to her. She spoke to us in Anglish on the island."

Many of the Vikings could speak and understand Anglish, for it was merely a Saxon dialect.

"Hmph! Go ahead, if you will. Anglish is a disgusting language and I see little to discuss with a captured slave. So long as the baron finds her distracting."

"Then by your leave, Uncle."

Kren walked over and smiled, hoping to relax her, although she looked relaxed already.

"What is your name?" he began. "I'm Kren."

"What does my name matter?" she answered. "You barbarians would not be able to pronounce it. And were you to try, I would find the attempt repulsive."

Torsten sprang to his feet and prepared to strike her, yet Kren held him back.

"Forgive me, Uncle, but the baron won't appreciate damaged goods."

"Maybe I should throw her to Ingvar's men and tell them to enjoy themselves. That'd remove her taunting grin, by Thor!"

"It might also remove her value to the baron. Let's see what she has to say. I find her fascinating."

"I find her disgusting!"

"Uncle, I've seen hundreds of women brought to you, and whether they fall on their knees and beg for mercy, or spit at you and throw curses, you have yet to be moved by any of them. Yet, in her first sentence, our Spirit Girl manages to upset you?"

"Upset? Why should I be upset with a slave girl chained to the wall?"

"Precisely. So may I continue?"

Torsten retreated to his seat near the door and sat down, angrily.

"As you say—your name does not matter. But the men call you a 'Spirit Girl?' Are you a spirit?"

"I don't know what you mean by spirit. I am flesh and blood. So if they mean someone dead and risen from the grave, then they are wrong. But if they mean someone who embodies the wishes of the Earth and the Sea, and who calls upon those powers to lay a curse over all of you such that you will die here and never return home, and your bones will rot, and your flesh serve merely to feed the crows of Ireland, then yes. You might call me *that* kind of spirit."

There was silence in the room as if a staying spell had been cast, as well as a curse. Torsten was first to recover.

"It remains to be seen, Spirit Wench, whether the bodies of my warriors will feed your Irish crows. Though were that to happen, I expect it would be the best meal they'd ever enjoy, judging by what I've seen of this pitiful village. But it is a certainty that tomorrow your body will feed the lusts of that baron in his dark castle. And after he has finished with you, and we with him, then you will be tossed to those same warriors you hope will one day become crow bait, and they will be invited to feast on you as well. When that is done—and that may take a while, for there are many warriors and they are always hungry—then you will either be tied to a rock and dropped into the middle of that fjord out there, or I will personally supervise your dismemberment while you hang from a gallows. Either would give me pleasure. When the time comes, perhaps I'll think of a way to do both."

Avelyn turned to him and spoke calmly.

"Or perhaps neither," she said. "For I see your end clearly—you who would command this rabble. I fear it soon will be leaderless, for the flesh will be burned from your body while you scream in agony and run hither and yon seeking a way to douse the fires. But douse them you will not, for even after they consume your physical being and your life ceases, yet will the flames continue to torment your soul unto time everlasting. Your sins lie heavy upon you, leader, and you will go soon to be cleansed of them by fire. The cleansing may take a while," she added, daring to make direct eye contact with her captor. "For the flames are many and they are always hungry."

"Get her out of here, Kren!" screamed Torsten, *"Before I rip the tongue out of her head and her head off her shoulders!"*

"Yes, Uncle. I agree. I'll have her taken to one of the other barns and make sure her guards don't speak any Saxon at all."

"Do whatever you want. Just arrange it so I don't have to see her ugly face again."

The statement betrayed his uncle's anxiety for it was obvious the girl was not ugly. Remembering her skill and courage at sea, Kren regretted the terrible things they would do to her.

77

KITT AND MILO dragged the inflatable up the rocky shoreline and into the trees. After hiding the dinghy underneath fallen pine boughs, they changed into their gear. Milo had decided they could not leave the ship dressed as commandos. It would make no sense.

"Note to file," observed Kitt, as he pulled on his camo pants while sitting awkwardly on the side of the dinghy. "Next time, change clothes *before* we cover the boat with pine needles. They're sticking in my butt!"

"Bitch, bitch, bitch!" whined Milo. "Didn't your dad ever take you camping? When I was a kid, I used to wait *all year* until I could go off with my dad and get pine needles stuck in my butt."

"Just remember, Milo, this commando thing was your idea. I never pretended to be good at it. Look at me! A knife strapped to my leg, and a couple of pistols strapped to my belt. All I need is a secret decoder ring."

"I can't say you instill confidence, Boss. That second

pistol is a grenade launcher for Chrissake! Be careful with it."

Milo suggested they parallel the shoreline but walk just inside the forest. This would keep them from losing their way, yet shield them from enemy patrols who would either be down at the water or stationed along the roads. Milo's strategy was simple. They would 'take out' every sentry they came upon. Kitt suspected that 'take out' meant *kill.*

"I swear Milo, you've read too many GI Joe comic books. You make this sound like the marines landing on Iwo Jima."

"Military tactics don't change a lot, Kitt. It's two of us against a Viking invasion force, and all this fancy gear will mean nothing if one of them steps out from behind a tree and slices your head off with an ax."

"So that's why I'm going first, huh?"

"You're going first so if you get into trouble I can save your ass. Now shut up and keep walking."

78

AVELYN WAS AGAIN chained to the wall of a building. She recognized this one as old Crancy's horse barn and wondered what had become of the horses. She knew what had become of Crancy.

The one named Kren had left, and Avelyn was sorry to see him go. He was a despicable invader but seemed almost kind by comparison. He'd left two others to guard her and, initially, they ignored her. But as time passed, occasionally one would point to her and say something funny (or perhaps lewd) and they'd laugh.

Avelyn was exerting her will to make them tired, hoping she could lull them into sleep. But the attempt was making her wearier than the guards. It had been a long day.

Only the night before, at the lake, she began sensing what seemed like power growing within her. She could reach out with her mind and touch other minds—even influence her physical surroundings. After all, had she not sent a shiver of wind across the water, merely by force of will? Had she not calmed the deer with her thoughts?

Or—she wondered again—had it just been a coincidence?

The next morning she'd tried to make sense of it all. Were the Earth and the Sea changing her, transforming her into something that served their purpose, giving her the power to perform a mission? What mission? Opposing the invaders?

Obviously, the Vikings—and what they did—must be repugnant to all benign spirits, including God. Especially God. She wanted to be their instrument for defeating the invaders—but even if she had some power, she didn't have *that* much. Perhaps she could calm a deer by relaxing her thoughts. That would be very different from convincing Vikings to walk into the sea and drown themselves.

The thought of having spiritual power—in any amount—was beyond frightening. She remembered the night in Shelby's hut when he'd warned her about the island, and how it would change her. She'd been scared then, but of what she didn't know. Now she knew. If Druidic spirits were using her as a vessel to influence events, it was terrifying. But also a bit exhilarating. More likely it was nothing but her imagination.

Yet it was enough to form a plan. Her role was not to defeat the invaders directly—she had no ability to do that—but to motivate those who did have the power: the sorcerers.

Kitt was falling in love with her. She knew this as a woman, not from any knowledge given her by the Earth and Sea spirits.

If she allowed herself to be captured, Kitt and Milo would realize it because sorcerers see everything. And they would try to rescue her. And that meant they would use their sorcery against the invaders.

Hence she had left Kitt abruptly, walked calmly into the Viking camp, and surrendered. Now, she was waiting for the sorcerers to do their part and obliterate the invaders.

Of course, the plan depended on her ability to avoid physical harm as a captive, and so far she'd done well. On the island, they'd barely touched her. Yet now it seemed her power—if she had any—was slipping from her right when she needed it most.

The guards would soon be unsatisfied with mere jesting.

One of them came over, smiled wickedly, and spoke unintelligibly. But the meaning was obvious.

She focused mentally on turning him away, but it had little effect.

79

THE FOG WAFTED onshore and cloaked Ballycastle in cold dampness. Viking sentries were becoming lost, despite flickering torches whose soot mingled with the clinging mist.

According to rumor, in an ill-considered move, Torsten had captured the Spirit Girl. Those who had been to the island refused to discuss her, which further unsettled the others. Some said she had invoked a curse on the Norsemen that doomed them to die and be eaten by crows. Everyone was eager for morning.

A bird flew overhead—perhaps a crow. It screeched loudly in protest of the mist which frustrated its nightly search for food. One of the sentries heard the sound and paused in fear.

An arm came out of the darkness, wrapped itself around his neck, and pulled in a downward snap. The sentry's body fell to the ground and was dragged quickly into the shadows.

ൾ

Kitt was impressed. "I'll be damned," he said. "You really do know how to break someone's neck with one arm."

"You see, Boss? Who says your tax dollars are wasted? SEAL teams get the best training money can buy."

"But did you have to kill him?"

"Have to? Hell, I wanted to. Vikings killed defenseless civilians for fun. Now I get to have fun."

"Where do we go next?" asked Kitt, glancing around in the fog.

"Well, this isn't going to be easy. We'll need to search the town, which means checking every barn or cottage we come to. A lot of 'em have burned down, so that'll help."

"Should we split up, to cover more territory?"

"With respect, you'd be no match for a Norseman with a weapon. I think we'd better stay together."

Between the fog and their camouflage, they passed through the village like wraiths.

Five more times Milo came upon a Viking and killed silently, using either an arm or a knife.

Kitt motioned Milo aside.

"I understand the need, but isn't all this killing a significant risk to the future? Maybe I'm having second thoughts. We're not just here occupying space, which is bad according to some theories. We're materially influencing events, which is bad according to *any* of the theories. Who knows how the descendants of these Norsemen might have affected the future?"

"Fuck their descendants, and fuck the future," said

Milo, icily. "I thought we settled all that crap back on the ship. We're rescuing Avelyn from these assholes. Got a problem with that?"

Kitt took one look at his partner's eyes and quickly consented. "Nope."

The ex-commando nodded and continued his exploration.

Despite the risk, they eventually decided to take opposite sides of the street, with Milo checking doors on one side and Kitt on the other. They came to a barn saved from the fire by its stone construction. Kitt opened the door.

ɞ

Avelyn's captors had moved her to the floor, hands chained over her head to the wall. She was fighting them off, and the would-be ravishers had made small progress. Her clothing was ripped, but still on. One of her assailants was trying to position himself between her legs, but she kicked him perfectly in the groin. He blasphemed the Norse Gods for a full minute, and then pulled back his arm, ready to punch her.

ɞ

Kitt opened the door.

What he saw was Avelyn chained to the wall, and two men apparently trying to rape her. Not thinking, he reacted on instinct—tapping reserves of strength he'd not used since rowing for Yale—and smashed into both of them, knocking the two lust-filled Vikings off their feet and onto the floor of the barn. Then he started kicking the nearest one in the head as hard as he could.

"You fucking, disgusting piece-of-shit," he screamed at Avelyn's attacker, kicking him over and over again in the face.

If there had only been one, Kitt's battle strategy might have worked. He had the element of surprise and a considerable height advantage.

But while the Norseman under attack tried to protect his face with his hands, the other jumped up, retrieved an ax from against the wall, and maneuvered directly behind Kitt.

The young scientist was too enraged to have noticed, but Avelyn saw the danger.

The Viking—with both hands—raised the weapon high, and was about to begin the downward stroke that would cleave his enemy's skull like a melon.

Avelyn screamed.

A deafening roar filled the barn and the Viking's head exploded. The ax paused in mid-stroke and fell harmlessly to the ground. The corpse collapsed, as blood pumped from severed arteries.

Kitt leaped back in fright, giving the warrior on the ground a chance to jump to his feet. The remaining Viking pulled a long knife from his sheath and was about to thrust it into his opponent's chest cavity. Then his own stomach exploded outwards as another thunderous boom rocked the barn. Kitt and Avelyn were drenched in blood and pieces of flesh. The final Norseman dropped to the ground, and the straw turned red.

"Well, whaddya know?" said Milo in English, standing complacently at the door and looking with wonder at his handgun. "Some damn fool sailor loaded this thing with fragmenting, hollow-point bullets!"

Avelyn was trembling violently.

"Sorry, ma'am," he continued in English. ".45 caliber, hollow-point, 230 grainers leave a mess, and that's just a fact."

Kitt had fallen to his knees, in shock. Milo holstered the weapon and walked over to him. The ex-Navy SEAL spoke softly, strong hands gripping the scientist's shoulders.

"I'd like to say 'relax and take it easy,' Boss. That was a damn close call. But right now, it's the girl who needs comforting, and it'd be better coming from you."

Kitt looked at him uncertainly and then nodded. With an effort, he knelt by Avelyn. She was still chained to the wall. But he put one of his hands on her shoulder and squeezed it.

"I'm sorry it took us so long to find you."

"But you did," she said, looking at him with gratitude. "And you rescued me."

Kitt saw the beginnings of a smile, but then she started to cry.

80

WHEN LAUREN SLIPPED out of number six cargo hatch in her wetsuit, a watertight bag fastened by a cord to her waist, she eyed the dark water splashing against the side of the hull and almost gave up her plan. It looked cold. She thought wistfully of the warm, cozy paint locker with Gary's chicken sandwiches and *Call Of The Canyon* to keep her company.

Then she thought of the divorce and the money, donned her fins, took a deep breath, and dove head-first into the Atlantic Ocean. The current coming out of the firth was strong and she drifted a hundred yards along the shore before her fins touched bottom. Once on the beach, she removed them and began shivering uncontrollably.

Looking back, she noticed the ship had disappeared and found it difficult to believe her time aboard was over. Not that she wasn't ready for it to be.

Stumbling up to a high point above tidal reach, she sat down and opened the bag. Inside were dry clothes, sneakers, her purse, and one luxury: a towel.

In a few minutes, she had dried off, changed into regular clothes, combed out her hair, and slipped on tennis shoes. She discarded the fins, wetsuit, and waterproof bag. All she needed was the USB key, her passport—which she always carried in her purse—several credit cards, and her phone. Everything fit easily into her jean pockets. She tossed the purse as well, knowing she could buy a better one in London—maybe that little Gucci number she'd had her eye on. If she needed cash, she'd find an ATM.

Top priority was a hotel. Anything with a bed, a bath, and a phone would be great; and an Uber the next morning that would get her to an airport—any airport.

Gary had learned there was a town named Ballycastle at the end of the narrow bay. Lauren headed in that direction, staying close to the water so she'd not get lost. Even if there were no hotels, she'd find a bar and "make friends." If the bars were closed she'd go to a private house and invent a story about being stranded. In 48 hours she'd be home or at least getting pampered in a first-class seat on an airliner.

After stumbling over endless rocks, driftwood, and shore debris, Lauren finally came to a sign of civilization. Well, sort of. It was a small seaside cottage, recently burned to the ground. She could smell the burnt wood. And on the other side of the road were several more cottages—all burnt. No bars here, thought Lauren.

This was strange. What could have caused everything to burn? Well, this was the outskirts of somewhere. If she kept going she'd probably get to the town center. Please God, let the bars still be open. She needed a drink.

The swim, plus the long hike, were taking a toll. Maybe

the Irish lad she'd meet in the bar would have to carry her out. She'd let him. She'd let him do more than that if he'd promise to get her to an airport in the morning.

Lauren continued plodding down the street.

This wasn't the best part of town, she decided. There were no electric lights, the streets were dirt, and here were more of these burned-out little huts. A cloying odor hung in the air, which reminded her of Tiki lamps. If someone was throwing a garden party, she'd crash it.

Lauren turned a corner and stopped abruptly. Coming towards her were two of the raunchiest men she'd ever seen. They were short and stocky, both blond in a greasy kind of way. They were probably actors or performers of some sort, for they were dressed like old warriors, with axes and leather tunics. Yosemite Sams, Lauren thought, recollecting the short cartoon character with the long beard, and the angry expression.

They seemed just as surprised to see her, stopping as well. One put a hand on the hilt of his pretend weapon.

Lauren recovered quickly, knowing all about actors and their egos.

"Well, am I glad to see you two warriors!" she smiled teasingly. "A rough part of town, where a girl can get hopelessly lost, and along come two strong men to rescue me! Well, mission accomplished! And if you'd care to lead the way, I simply must show my gratitude by buying you both a drink! Those costumes deserve a reward. But please, someplace that takes credit cards! I've got zero cash. Zero."

The two actors looked briefly at one another. Then,

moving swiftly, they flanked Lauren, each grabbing an arm, and dragged her roughly back the way they'd come.

"Hey, wait a minute guys!" Lauren blurted out. The two men ignored her. "I said *wait a fucking minute! God damn you!*" Lauren tried to struggle free, which was a mistake. The men let go of her arms, and one of them punched his fist into her stomach. Lauren collapsed, striking her head on a stone as she fell. She just had time to feel overwhelming anger, mixed with a growing sense of confusion, before she lost consciousness.

81

TORSTEN AND A dozen *hersirs* were asleep in a cottage containing only two beds.

One had been claimed by Torsten. He lay face-up on the mattress, snoring, with only his boots and sword removed.

The other belonged to Kren, second-in-command, who had declined it.

"It would yield no rest for me, Uncle," he'd explained earlier. "It yearns for the prior owners and is repulsed by my touch."

"Baah! You speak of the bed as if it were a spirit," Torsten mocked. "I know you are close to the gods, Kren, but this bed has no thoughts. And should it have any, I'd ignore them."

"There is much here in Ireland that has thoughts. It's as if the gods were everywhere: under every rock, in every tree, in the stones of the houses. They are not our friends. And this bed abhors me. I will sleep on the floor in that corner."

"As you wish."

So the other bed had been claimed by Grimsson, not necessarily third-in-command, but large and ill-tempered enough to settle the matter.

The others had arrayed themselves best they could and Torsten was not the only one who snored.

In the middle of the night, the door burst open.

Torsten was awake instantly and reached for his weapon.

The sentry identified himself hastily. Viking warriors, roused suddenly from sleep, were prone to sweep their axes across the necks of arriving messengers.

"I bring news, Captain."

"By the gods of war, if you're going to wake me up like this you'd better have news! What is it?"

"Our sentries are missing."

"What do you mean, missing?"

"I assigned ten men to the rounds, sir. They report back regularly. Six of them were overdue. I sent the other four to investigate, but they've found no trace. It's not like my men to leave sentry duty, sir. They know the penalty."

"The penalty is death. Either they've been killed, or I will have to kill them. And I doubt they've been killed. More likely, someone discovered a cache of that yellow liquor these Irish make. It's strong stuff."

"It may be as you say, Captain, although I would vouch for my men. There's another possibility, sir. Some of us were wondering—"

"Wondering what?"

"Well, there was a rumor that the Spirit Girl—"

"The *who?*" interrupted Torsten, irritably. "I know of no girl spirit unless you mean *Freya* herself."

"I know not her name, Captain. But I've heard that a female was captured whom the men call a Spirit Girl."

"Valhalla protect me!" growled Torsten. "*That* Spirit Girl's only a damn slave wench, chained to a wall in that horse barn up the hill. And if it weren't for the fact that I have a use for her, she'd be chained to a rock at the bottom of the fjord, feeding the fish with her carcass!"

There was silence in the room.

"So I take it she is special in some way, Captain? This Spirit Girl?"

"By Odin, will you quit calling her a—oh, go ahead, call her any damn thing you want. What does she have to do with this anyway?"

"Well, sir, some of the men— Well, they're saying they heard she delivered a curse on our heads, vowing we would all die and be eaten by crows."

"Oh, they did, did they?"

"Well, yes, sir. With these sentries disappearing and all—well, the other sentries are worried."

"Worried! My Norse warriors are worried? About crows? About a slave girl chained to a post?"

The door burst open again. This time it was Craynor, one of the men sent to look for the missing sentries. He had been running hard and sweat poured from his brow. His face was pale.

"Calm down, Craynor. Look like you've seen a ghost," said Torsten.

"I, I found 'em, sir! Two of 'em, in that horse barn up the hill."

"And?"

"They was dead, sir! Horrible dead. There was pieces of 'em all over the barn. No weapon I ever saw would do that to a man. It looked like—"

"Like what, Craynor?" asked Kren.

"Like maybe birds got at 'em, sir! Maybe crows, sir! I… I guess you've heard the rumor, about the curse and all."

There was silence in the room. Kren looked at Torsten, who appeared to be speechless.

"Craynor, we left the Spirit Girl in that barn," said Kren. "With two sentries guarding her. Those must be the dead men. But what about the girl? Was she killed too?"

"No, sir! So that's where the Spirit Girl was? Must have been her that called in the crows."

Torsten seemed to have come out of his shock.

"Dunsen, pass the word to the garrison. Tell them we have missing sentries, and two warriors dead. And tell them the damned spirit wench has escaped again. She's to be captured and brought back here at once."

"Yes, sir!" Dunsen started for the door.

"Grimsson!"

"Yes, Captain!" The war commander stood at attention.

"Roust out the men! Have them join the search. I want the Spirit Girl captured and in chains before the sun comes up."

The burly Viking rushed out the door.

82

"I THOUGHT THE girl's statement about crows was dramatic emphasis, not to be taken literally," said Kren, as he walked with his uncle and two guards up to the barn.

"So did I," acknowledged Torsten.

They opened the door and examined the two corpses—or what was left of them.

"It wasn't crows," said Kren. "Look, in this case, the face was not even touched. Birds always go for the face, especially the eyes."

"What about the other face?"

"There is no other face, only pieces of flesh and bone. Crows might peck the flesh off a skull, but they couldn't destroy the skull itself."

"Then what did?"

"I don't know," admitted Kren finally. "But it was not crows, and I see nothing here to imply an act of the gods. The chains, which held the girl, were opened in a normal manner. Not blasted off by lightning or sorcery. My only guess is that she was rescued by men who somehow overcame the guards."

"Overcame them? They massacred them! I can't even imagine what weapon could do this to a man's body."

"Perhaps a fighting iron?"

"A fighting iron wielded by a giant, maybe. It would have to be three times the normal size to produce what we see here."

"Well, you would know better than I. But it was some kind of weapon, that seems obvious."

"Not crows?"

"Not crows."

"Then," said Torsten, "there is an enemy about, of unknown force. That being the case, I'm all the more anxious to seize the castle."

"Yes, but now we have a new problem."

"What?"

"We were going to use the Spirit Girl as a gift to distract the baron. Now we have no gift."

They had just returned to the cottage when the door opened and Grimsson walked in smiling, an air of boastfulness about him.

"We caught her, Captain! Two of my sentries found her down near the water. From what they say, she put up almost no fight. Graubor hit her in the stomach, and she fell unconscious."

Graubor and his companion entered, dragging an inert form, face down. At a gesture from Kren, the men dropped her onto the straw-covered floor.

Kren rolled the unconscious woman onto her back,

exchanged a meaningful glance with Torsten, and then stepped away.

"You idiots!" snapped the Norse leader. "This isn't the Spirit Girl!"

"It isn't?" asked Grimsson. "Are you sure?"

"Of course I'm sure! The Spirit Girl did not have this yellow hair, like one of our women. Her hair was reddish-brown, like the other Irish. And these clothes. They're not like any we've seen in this village. Most importantly, this isn't her face."

"No, it isn't her face," said Kren. "But seen in another light, cleaned up perhaps, it would be a very beautiful face."

"What in fucking Asgard does that have to do with anything?"

"If I find her attractive, so might the baron."

83

AVELYN WAS BEHIND a tree making sure her torn clothing at least covered the important parts. Kitt and Milo were sitting on the ground—a polite distance away—talking softly.

"We got your sweetheart back, Boss. What's our next move?"

Kitt noticed that Milo's fighting madness had ebbed with the rescue of Avelyn, and the caustic observations had returned.

"Milo, for Chrissake. I like her. She's cute as hell. But she's not exactly my sweetheart."

"Whatever you say. But my question stands. What's our next step?"

"Well— "

"We have the following options. We're just outside the village and probably safe for a few hours, until daylight—maybe. We can head back to the dinghy and return Avelyn to her island. The outboard has enough fuel. Or, we could take her somewhere else within dinghy range—anywhere up and down the coast for ten miles or so. Or we could take her back to *Chrysalis*."

"You mean we could take her on board and deliver her anywhere she wants to go. Away from Ireland even. We'd make up some story and force it down Hamilton's throat. Is that what you mean?"

"No. I mean we could take her back to our own time."

"We can't take her back to our own time!"

"Sure we could. Either that, or you could stay with her in the eighth century. You might even convince me to stay too."

"That's absurd!"

"OK, so I'd go back with *Chrysalis*."

"That's not what I meant!"

"Why *not* take Avelyn back? We're both fond of her. If we can travel into the past, why can't *she* travel into the future?"

"You must be nuts! Talk about tampering with time."

"Consider it part of the experiment. See if it destroys the universe or whatever."

"Milo—"

They quit talking as Avelyn came out from behind the tree and sat down next to them.

"You're probably discussing what to do next," she said. "Isn't it obvious?"

"No, please tell us," said Kitt, curious to learn what was obvious.

"We need to kill the invaders," she said, matter-of-factly. "Somehow, you rescued me while killing only a few, which I didn't think was possible. We need to kill *all* of them."

"Wait a minute, are you saying you planned this?" demanded Kitt, appalled.

Avelyn turned away, unable to meet his accusing stare.

"You *planned* this!"

Avelyn turned back to him, defiantly.

"Of *course* I planned it! How else was I going to destroy the invaders? I needed your sorcery!"

"Why'd you think we'd even know you'd *been* captured?"

"Sorcerers see everything. And obviously, you did know. That's why you're here."

Milo joined the conversation. "We knew you'd been captured not because we had all-seeing powers, but because we had a *periscope.*"

"Yes, some tool of sorcery. That's what I said."

"But why did you think we even *would* rescue you?" asked Kitt.

"Because, Kitt, I think you care for me."

"You used my feelings for you, *to draw us into a battle?"*

"I had no choice."

She moved closer, put her hands on his shoulders, and kissed him lightly on the lips. "Thank you for rescuing me."

Then she walked unsteadily back to the tree, leaned against the trunk, and closed her eyes.

"So *that's* what a kiss feels like," she said, almost to herself.

Kitt glared at Milo. "Shut up!" he said.

"I didn't say a thing!"

"Yeah, but you were thinking it. I hate an 'I told you so.'"

"Don't shoot the messenger! Besides, I think you make a cute couple."

They heard voices coming from the direction of town. Both men froze.

"A Viking patrol!" Milo whispered. "Let's get out of here!"

"This way!" said Avelyn, and ran off through the trees. Kitt and Milo grabbed their packs and followed.

After several minutes of crashing through the forest, Kitt nearly ran into Milo, who had stopped and was standing by Avelyn, staring ahead. Kitt followed their gaze. Ballycastle was a miserable collection of burnt-out mud huts. But here was a significant building, two stories tall, made of brick and timber, with a tile roof. An iron fence surrounded it, and high stone pillars guarded the entrance. It was a palace, or museum, or—

"What is it?" asked Kitt.

"I think it's a monastery," said Milo. "No time for a history lesson, but all during the Dark Ages, it was the monasteries of Ireland that preserved the art and learning of the Roman Empire. This is one of them, I guess."

"It's the perfect place to hide," said Avelyn. "There's a secret entrance by the wall that leads to the lower vaults."

From the direction of the village, they could hear another party of Norsemen approaching; heavy feet thudding against the ground, with helmets and weapons clanking noisily.

Avelyn grabbed Kitt's hand and ran with him out

of the forest and across the lawn, stopping at the iron fence. An array of boulders was surrounded by a tangle of bushes and tall grass. She pulled aside some of the foliage and revealed a large hole in the ground, just big enough for a person. She gestured urgently. Kitt and Milo slid through and found it expanded considerably once past the entrance, much like the cave back on the island. Avelyn followed, replacing the bushes behind her.

It was utterly dark. Kitt could feel Avelyn's warm breath near him and was grateful when she took his arm and squeezed it.

"Do not fear the dark," she said. "It is our friend, and I know the way."

A blinding, overpowering light filled the passage. Avelyn cried out in terror and covered her eyes.

"What the hell!" said Kitt.

"Standard Marine issue," said Milo. "Five thousand candlepower. Wide beam or narrow."

"Jesus! Can you turn that thing down a little?"

"Sure, Boss. Sorry." Milo dropped a filter over the lens of the electric torch and they were bathed in an eerie red glow.

"Well, you can quit pretending you're not sorcerers," said Avelyn. "But don't fear. Druids are not enemies of the *magi,* although Christians might be. Your secret is safe with me."

Avelyn took the lead. The hole in the ground had expanded to a full-size tunnel and they were able to walk nearly upright, single file. The walls were mud, shored up with timbers, and the path sloped downwards. Kitt noticed the floor was paved with cobblestones. A light moss grew between them. Water trickled somewhere nearby.

They came to a wooden door. Avelyn tried unsuccessfully to open it. She stepped back and looked at the door intently. To Kitt it seemed she was reaching out with her mind, probing for what might be within. A smile came to her face and she stepped forward. She knocked three times, then two times, then three times.

Nothing happened. Then, just as Kitt was about to speak, the door opened. An old man stood there, clothed in clerical garb. His jaw gaped in astonishment.

"Hello, Father," said Avelyn. "I'm back."

84

INSIDE WAS HELL. It was a large room with low ceilings. Wooden posts, holding up a lattice-work of timbers, were in such density it was as if a forest had grown here, beneath the Earth. Torchlight flickered off the walls and smoke hung thickly, finding few outlets. The smell of unwashed bodies—and inadequate sanitary facilities—lay over the room, making the air almost unbreathable. The floor was mud.

Far worse were the cries of the wounded. They lay like discarded clothing, limp packages of flesh concealed in grime, dried blood, and rotted bandages. Some of the forms writhed in agony. Others had stopped writhing. Shuffling among them were dark, robed figures—heads down, eyes filled with despair.

Seeing it all, Avelyn's look of joy which had appeared briefly with the opening of the door, turned to horror. The old man looked confused, as if his weary brain could not grasp what he was seeing.

"How can you be here?" he asked, in Latin.

"I came to help," she said sadly. "But I have come too late."

"It's really you? From the old days?"

"Of course it's me, Father. And what are you talking about? It's been only three days since the invaders attacked."

"No, it cannot be." He looked confused. "But it matters not. To see you again—" He held out a trembling hand and touched her lightly as if to confirm it was not merely a vision. "God has granted me this last wish—"

"Quit talking like that! 'Last wish' indeed. You're not that old, Father!"

"Ah, child, now I am. But talk not about me. How is it that you come to be here? A part of me rejoices, yet another part is thrice troubled for I maintained hope that you, at least, escaped. Now those dreams are dashed."

Kitt watched as Avelyn glanced around the room, eyes smoldering. When she spoke, her words pierced the enveloping gloom like a cold blade.

"Escape? I seek not to *escape.* It is the invaders who must escape me. I have been charged with avenging this evil."

"Avelyn!" cried the old man. "Listen to me. A foreign army has conquered us, burned the village, taken our young women as slaves, and killed most everyone else. They would kill all of us here if they knew. And perhaps that would be best. We cannot live like moles in the ground. We had just time to remove our most valuable possessions to these vaults, our art, and books of learning. We have provided refuge to villagers wounded in the raid whom we found stumbling in the forest."

"I see that," said Avelyn, glancing around the room.

"But they are dying now, and perhaps it would have been quicker and less painful to have left them on their own. What can you do, my daughter, against such a catastrophe? You can only succumb to the horror yourself and deprive one who loved you of his last hope."

"I am not here to succumb to the horror, Father. I am here to inflict greater horror on the invaders."

"Avelyn, you're not listening!" said the abbot, his hands held out in exasperation. "We have no power to overcome them. And even if we had, it is not our role. We are born to suffer and die as Christ died before us. Vengeance is not our way. We are Christians—the children of God. Blessed are the meek, and we are meek indeed in this hour. It is the will of God and we shall do His bidding only by dying and finding peace at his side. Can you not see that?"

"I see that you are a Christian, and if God requires it, then perhaps you must die as you say. But I am a Druid, and God speaks to me through the power of the Earth and the Sea. They call to me now. They demand retribution, and I shall be the instrument of that retribution!"

The abbot was visibly shaken and had to steady himself against one of the overhanging pillars.

"You blaspheme!" he whispered, in horror. "A Druid!"

Avelyn smiled and lovingly embraced the old man. Then she stepped back and spoke softly.

"Yes, Father, I do blaspheme. I blaspheme as I've always blasphemed. And you correct me, as always. Will you strike me down, as you did before? Look at me and say if you see evil in my eyes, or in my heart. If you do, then I am ready to be struck down. I insist on it. For my life would have no meaning if that is what you see.

"But look closely, Father, and tell me if you see not a blasphemer, but rather another mortal, trying her best to do what is right. Incorrectly perhaps. Confused, most certainly. But determined to fight the evil in her own way. If that is what you see, then let us not be enemies. Let us confess we are imperfect mortals who can only do what we think correct.

"And let us cast off these words of gloom and death and rise up and fight evil with whatever power is in us. Maybe it is a different power. Maybe it is only a different manifestation of the same power, working in each of us in different ways. But if we unite and have the will, then I say nothing will stop us. But we must have the will, Father. The will!"

Conardy was silent. He looked away from Avelyn and back towards the room of wounded and suffering people. Then he turned and looked into her eyes. Finally, he smiled and held out his hands.

"Child, you may be the spawn of Satan, sent to test my faith. But if so, then Satan has won with his trickery. When I look into your eyes, I know a sense of peace and I feel close to God. Your words seem blasphemous, but God speaks to us in ways other than words and maybe—whom am I to know?—maybe he speaks to you through the totems of your Druidic faith, as you say."

"I believe He does, Father."

"Then I will put your words aside and listen only to your heart. If you say we must rise up and overthrow our oppressors, then how can I say it is not the will of God? Sometimes I feel that—between the two of us—you are closer to the true Christ, though I have worshiped Him all my life while you blaspheme and pray to idols every chance you get. No matter, I will listen to your hopes—foolish though they seem—and let your conscience command me."

"Thank you."

"Yes, even as I speak the words I sense it is the right course. God grants me that. Yet what power are words? It will take more than a noble heart to overcome the invaders. We have no swords, nor shields, nor the strength to use them if we had. I stand ready to be commanded, but I fear your army is a weak one."

"In that case, Father," said Avelyn, "let me introduce you to my friends."

Avelyn motioned them over.

"Father, please meet Kitt and Milo. They speak Latin, though it sounds strange coming from their tongues."

The old man bowed.

"Pleased to meet you, Your Grace," said Kitt, offering his hand, which Conardy looked at with confusion.

"Handshaking isn't used in this time for everyday greeting," whispered Milo. "A simple bow will suffice."

Kitt bowed.

"I'm curious what land you are from," said the abbot. "I am a student of many accents, yet I find yours outside my experience. No matter. As friends of Avelyn, I welcome you here. But I must ask…are you Christians?"

"We are followers of our conscience," said Kitt. "As is

Avelyn. Others may decide, by our actions, what further labels suit us."

"And what does your 'conscience' tell you to do now?"

Kitt looked around the room, at the scene of death and despair. A small child knelt beside one of the bandaged forms, sobbing disconsolately, and Kitt knew its mother would never rise again. Kitt did not have Milo's command of history, but he realized they had stumbled upon one of the world's great horrors—a Viking invasion.

If time travel were to have any meaning at all—if it was to be anything more than a scientific toy, a curiosity to be used by tourists to visit earlier ages as if they were a Disney theme park—then it must be used to confront the horrors of those earlier ages and to mitigate them where possible. If such tampering would destroy the future, did it matter? Was the future—their present—so sacrosanct that it must be bought with the blood and agony of ages past? As he was increasingly realizing, sometimes it was better to turn off your brain and just do the right thing.

"Avelyn believes we should fight the invaders," he said simply. "And I agree. We will fight to the limit of our ability. What swords we have, we lay at your feet."

"But—" the abbot stammered, "Are there only the two of you? Do you even *have* swords?"

"Don't worry, Your Grace," interjected Milo. "If that's Kitt's decision, we've got swords. We've got swords you won't believe."

85

BRODY FLANNAGAIN HAD been up since dawn preparing for what would surely be the most dangerous day of his life. The Vikings were to arrive at noon. They needed to be convinced of the castle's strength. The stone walls would speak for themselves. What was needed was the appearance of a heavily armed garrison, eager and willing to defend their lord. If the Vikings were bringing fifty warriors, then they must be confronted with at least twice as many armed guards.

Yet the population of the castle, including not only the men-at-arms but also the stable hands, cooks, errand boys, and even chambermaids was barely more than sixty.

Sufficient additional uniforms had been sewn during the night to dress everyone as a guard. Even the chambermaids (with their hair pulled back and hidden in a helmet) could be made to appear as guards—albeit short and poorly muscled ones.

So sixty, ostensible guards could be mustered, twenty of whom were real. By moving them around as the visitors passed key locations, their apparent number could be doubled.

No one—save the baron—had eaten for twenty-four hours, so the food supply was just adequate. The castle staff was weak from hunger and prone to lean against walls while rehearsing as guards. But that was unavoidable. Flannagain knew if it came to a real fight, they were doomed.

From the kitchen, an exquisite yet unusual aroma wafted through the halls. The baron had insisted his pure-bred hounds be on hand for entertainment, apparently believing the Vikings would be impressed by their savagery. Flannagain was glad he'd kept them out of the pot and used mule meat instead.

When the sun was precisely overhead—no sooner—the seneschal admitted all was ready. A horn sounded from the ramparts, signaling the arrival of the Norsemen. Flannagain hurried to a better vantage point on the walls. He could see them marching, single file, heavily laden with swords and shields.

Maybe they went everywhere that way.

The plan was simple. Dine them well, create an atmosphere of goodwill—it was just possible the dogs would prove useful—and then produce the peace treaty for signing. It called for permanent friendship between Baron O'Ruairc and the Norse. The Vikings would agree to move south and attack Doon. If the Vikings killed Fakis the whole affair might be to O'Ruairc's benefit. The next few hours would be critical.

"Brody! I say, Brody!"

The annoyed, high-pitched voice of the baron—finally

awake—carried up from the courtyard. Flannagain sighed with exasperation and hurried down the ladder.

"Yes, my lord," he intoned, as he reached the Great Hall. A fire was already burning so that when the Vikings arrived, its coals would be well lit and give off the appearance of a house in which fires always burned with little thought to the consumption of wood. The castle's final supply had been sacrificed for this charade.

"Oh, there you are. Damn, hardly the time to disappear. We are giving a banquet this noon in case you'd forgotten."

"Yes, my lord. I was just making sure nothing had been overlooked."

"Well something *has been* overlooked, Flannagain. My *breakfast!*"

"A dreadful oversight my lord. I will take a cane to the wench responsible. But it is almost noontime. As our guests will arrive shortly might it not serve better to just this once skip breakfast and proceed directly to the banquet? The main course will be an unusual specialty. One might have suggested you avoid breakfast deliberately, to increase your appetite for a meal worthy of its honor."

"Hmm, a specialty? Well, I do smell it, and it's that which revealed my hunger. But can I wait that long?" He stopped to ponder the notion. "When will these *Wikings*, or whatever you call them, arrive? Such a bother."

The horn sounded again, signaling the arrival of the Norsemen at the front gate.

"They are here now, my lord. And you will be pleased

to know the treaty of friendship is prepared, ready for signing."

Flannagain needed the baron to remember about the treaty. O'Ruairc was not one to keep details in his head.

"What would you recommend, Brody? Should I await them here, or go meet them by the gate? Can't expect me to be familiar with all these affairs of state now, can we?"

"They would be honored to be received here in the Great Hall, my lord. If you'll take your seat, I will bring them to you."

After the baron left, Flannagain hastened to the gate. It was as he'd feared. The Vikings looked like an army ready to fight. He went to meet them nonetheless, and spoke in Latin to the Viking leader, via the translator.

"I bid you welcome in friendship and peace. My lord the baron awaits you in his hall."

One of the Norse he'd seen earlier stepped forward, apparently a spokesman.

"My name is Kren. Our captain is honored by your courtesies and comes also in friendship. As a token of peace, he has brought a gift for your baron and would beg you lead us to him so that it might be presented."

Flannagain took another look at the fifty helmeted Norsemen, and their weapons and shields, but there was no turning back. Even a losing hand must be played to the end.

"Certainly. If you will allow me to lead, I will escort you to him."

The Viking nodded and Flannagain turned and walked

quickly back towards the castle. Behind him, fifty pairs of stout legs began to move in a disturbing rhythm.

As they marched—and even Flannagain realized it was a march—he glanced above and was pleased to see his orders had been followed. Thirty or forty helmeted heads were poking up from behind the parapet. Most held spears or other weapons. He was certain the Norsemen saw them as well.

When the Vikings were inside and the gate was closed, Flannagain called a halt.

"I must see that all is in readiness," he said to Kren, who nodded solemnly. Flannagain left the Norsemen and hurried to the Great Hall. The baron was leaning back slovenly in his chair, but perhaps that suggested confidence. The guards from the parapet hurried in and Flannagain arrayed them on the mezzanine. Then he returned to the courtyard.

"Please follow me," he said to Kren. "Perhaps in single file, as the doorways are narrow." When the warriors arrived in the Hall, they formed up in soldierly rows.

Flannagain turned to the baron. "By your leave, my lord, I will now greet them in your name."

The baron was aghast, seeing the armed might in front of him.

"By your leave—" Flannagain prompted, and O'Ruairc recovered sufficiently to nod his head.

"Friends, my lord the Baron O'Ruairc, sovereign of Antrim fief, bids you be at ease in his house."

The spokesman consulted with his captain and framed a reply.

"My captain thanks your lord, and is grateful to be received in such friendship. We do not know the customs in your land, but in our country, it is deemed polite for guests to present a gift to the host. May we present ours now?"

"It would be graciously accepted," said Flannagain, after a whispered exchange with the baron.

At a nod from the Viking leader, a small commotion ensued near the back of their lines. Flannagain was surprised to see the gift was a woman. And she was like no woman he had ever seen. Her hair was golden, like the sun, and she wore strange garments which clung to her figure and outlined it seductively and graciously. But the woman herself was neither seductive nor gracious. Her arms were bound behind her, and a rough cloth had been tied across her mouth. She struggled violently, kicking out at whomever she could reach.

"We apologize she is not yet tamed," explained the spokesman. "She is a captured slave and my master found her beauty so extraordinary that he commanded she be kept unsullied as a gift to your lord."

Flannagain started to answer but was immediately interrupted by the baron who had risen from his chair and walked over to see the woman more closely.

"Brody, is this the gift the savages bring? Quick now, what do they say about her?"

"They apologize she is not yet 'tamed.' That was the term they used. She's a captured slave girl, kept 'unsullied' for your enjoyment."

"Well, I accept this gift, indeed I do."

Flannagain noticed with concern that the baron could not keep his eyes off the girl. He was utterly distracted. Probably that was the Norsemen's goal.

"A most suitable gift indeed, my lord," agreed Flannagain, seeking to diffuse her effect. "I suggest she be taken to your chambers while we attend our guests. Dinner is ready."

"Take her away? Rubbish. But you're right. I could hardly enjoy her now—not in my famished state. No, I want her in the dining hall. Have her tied to the pillar there, near my seat so I may enjoy her while I dine."

Flannagain realized the baron had nearly forgotten the Norsemen. His entire being was consumed with hunger, both for food and for the girl.

After a polite exchange regarding the gift, Flannagain ushered the warriors into their seats. The female slave was tied to the pillar, as the baron ordered.

The vast table was fully occupied for the first time in the seneschal's memory, and he nodded for the servants to begin serving. It was a terrible ordeal for them—having eaten nothing in over a day. But they understood the necessity. It was nearly as great a hardship for the pretend guards on the mezzanine, who were ordered to stand at attention, halberds and swords seemingly at the ready.

There was no talking among the guests while they ate. Flannagain was concerned none was consuming ale in large quantity. Maybe that was their habit, or maybe they were under orders. He suspected the latter.

Flannagain was also surprised that these large, robust men filled up on fairly small portions of stew. An Irishman would have demanded refills, yet none of the Norsemen did. So much for the problem of running out of food. On the other hand, an army intending to fight might have been ordered to eat sparingly.

By contrast, Baron O'Ruairc ate lavishly—all while not taking his eyes from the slave girl lashed to the pillar. It was the growing restlessness of the dogs, still chained in the corner, that brought him back to his role as host.

"Well, Brody," he said, "I have dined as well as predicted. Don't know what that dish was. But, damn, it was delicious! Almost worth the wait."

"I'm deeply gratified to hear it, my lord."

"Well, on to the entertainment, I should say. Please announce we'll now show them something worth seeing."

The seneschal did so, and the Norsemen turned their attention to the baron, who was smiling malevolently.

"Here dogs!" he said, holding out a piece of meat from the stew, its juices dripping. The dogs were instantly attentive, a few struggling against their chains and whimpering in anticipation. One or two growled hesitantly.

"Dinner is served!" yelled the baron, and flung the morsel into their midst. The pack exploded in violence, all the more acute from the hunger they'd experienced.

Flannagain glanced at the Viking leader and noticed the man was scarcely interested in the dogs. Then he looked at the slave girl. She was staring at the savagery with horror and revulsion in her eyes.

When the turmoil died down and the dogs were reduced to licking juices off the floor, Flannagain knew it was time.

He exchanged words with the baron, who merely shrugged. Then the seneschal gave his rehearsed speech.

"My lord hopes you have dined well, honored guests, and been entertained by his hounds. He suggests it is now time to finalize the treaty of friendship between us. By your leave, I have drawn up the proposal and would present it to you."

Kren spoke a few words to his captain who nodded at Flannagain. The seneschal produced the document from a nearby cabinet and handed it to the translator.

"By your leave," he said, "I will review the major points. First, we ask for a declaration of war by your army, against the Doon fief to the south.

"Second—," But Flannagain was interrupted by the Viking leader, who was speaking rapidly to Kren.

"My master says," Kren explained, "that he needs to review this document in detail. Also, he notes that it may require time for us to translate it accurately into his tongue. An hour or more, at least.

"He suggests that your lord use the interval to advantage by enjoying the slave girl. My master feels it unseemly for your lord to have to wait on us."

This was precisely the turn of events Flannagain had feared. Everything else might be explained as coincidence or cultural differences. But suggesting the baron leave the room and closet himself with a slave-girl—particularly one brought by the Vikings themselves—betrayed their intentions.

These warriors had not come to sign a treaty. They'd come to fight. And why not? They'd already subdued the town. It must be obvious that if the castle were properly garrisoned, they'd have been immediately opposed.

Flannagain found himself bitter, again, that the baron had allowed their defenses to atrophy. With a trained army—an army they could easily have afforded—and with the strength of the castle itself, they might have thrown the invaders back into the sea. The baron's grandfather would have done just that. But such regrets were pointless.

To save his own life, he must now flee. He'd made preparations the night before, suspecting treachery. Hidden in one of the tunnels was a small pack, containing a few clothes, some food, a knife, and—most importantly—twenty pounds in gold coin. This was not the limit of Flannagain's wealth, most of which was buried in a cache outside Ballycastle. But it was the most portable. If he could escape with his pack he could start a new life somewhere.

Flannagain turned to Kren. "I agree. My lord will be better able to concentrate after he's indulged himself with the girl. At the moment, he does appear distracted." Flannagain grinned, as if the two shared a common burden in arranging the activities of their lords. Kren nodded and smiled back, innocently enough.

The baron needed little convincing.

"They're suggesting this would be a good time to enjoy the *gift?* Why, yes. It would indeed."

Flannagain gave the orders and the slave girl was untied and taken upstairs. She was struggling and trying to scream again. The baron followed her, grabbing a flagon of wine from the table. Flannagain gave orders to the remaining servants, knowing they would be their last. He spoke in Latin to Kren.

"I have instructed the servants to obey you as they would me, and provide anything you might request by way of food or drink. I will retire to my chambers and return within the hour. I'm certain this whole affair can be speedily resolved."

"You are most kind," said Kren, bowing, and gesturing to his master to do likewise. It was not a maneuver the Viking leader performed well. Hastily, Flannagain left the room.

86

WHEN LAUREN REGAINED consciousness, and found herself tied up on the floor of a hut, she had gone berserk. Struggling wildly against the coarse rope that bound her wrists and ankles, she yelled furious insults, and threats to sue her captors into oblivion. Finally, she gave up. Lauren was intelligent enough to know when a course of action wasn't working, and the only effect produced by her struggles and screams was a wrist that had started to bleed, and a throat that was becoming hoarse.

So, after the initial fury, she considered the situation. She was in a primitive cottage. Her captors were dressed like those absurd actors she'd encountered earlier. Was it some kind of theater troupe? Or was this a fringe element of the Irish Republican Army that was still in business? That was possible. Such people might be absolutely whacko. They'd kill anyone; blow up any building; perhaps don the most insane outfits to mark their rebellion.

Why else would they be dressed up like medieval warriors? And another thing this theory explained: the incomprehensible language. Lauren knew it was difficult for Americans to understand an Irish accent. But these people weren't speaking English at all. This was some earlier, primitive tongue. Maybe Gaelic. Maybe the cult's members worshipped their distant past, which would explain both the outfits and the language.

Probably they'd captured her as a hostage and hoped to exchange her for one of their comrades imprisoned by the British. That might explain why they seemed to be taking so little interest in her. They were across the room examining their weapons and talking among themselves. Occasionally, one would glance at her but only with mild curiosity as if she were some kind of insect. It was the first time Lauren could remember being in a room surrounded by men and not being the center of attention.

But the terrorists-holding-her-for-ransom theory was comfortable.

Having nothing else to do, she considered the likely chain of events. For the moment, these terrorists didn't know they'd captured the wife of an American billionaire. That would be revealed soon enough when someone bothered to check her pockets and found the passport.

Then the British would learn that terrorists were holding Mrs. Michael J. Kittery hostage. The Kitterys were major contributors to the current administration in Washington. She could imagine the British ambassador hurriedly summoned to the White House. *By all means, hang tough in the case of normal hostages, but for God's sake do whatever's necessary to rescue this one!*

One of the terrorists came over and without so much

as a glance cut the ropes holding her to the bedpost. He pulled her roughly to her feet and proceeded to bind her hands in front of her.

"OK, OK!" she said impatiently. "Didn't anyone ever teach you the magic word? I know what's going on here. If you need to move me to another hideout, that's fine. But why all this rough stuff?"

The terrorist paid no attention to her words but held up to her lips a wooden cup filled with water. Lauren was terribly thirsty, and eagerly let the man pour the water into her mouth. She wanted more but her captors were in a hurry.

Removing the cup, one of the men stuffed something filthy into her mouth and bound it behind her head. She tried to protest this treatment with more frenzied squirming and yelling, but her sounds were now muffled, and utterly ignored.

Grabbed brusquely by the arm, she was hustled outside, finally having a chance to look around in daylight. She was in some kind of mocked-up medieval village, with dozens of little mud huts just like the one she'd been kept in—nearly half of which appeared to be demolished. Maybe a movie had been filmed here. Or perhaps there were sections of Ireland much poorer than anyone in America realized.

But no paved streets, no TV antennas, no cars at all? An old movie set seemed a better explanation. And come to think of it, that wouldn't be a bad place to hide out, or even use as a headquarters, if your theme was "medieval warrior."

Lauren could now see other terrorists joining them from the surrounding huts. They were forming up in procession, and she was kept near the back with her "escort." Were they exchanging her already? If so, they'd worked fast.

The whole band started marching and she was forced to walk with them, best she could. Once or twice she stumbled, but nearby guards steadied her. They were certainly muscular young gentlemen. She might have enjoyed meeting them in different circumstances. Too bad there wasn't anyone over five foot two in the whole crowd.

They rounded a corner and she saw their destination: a castle on the hillside. This wasn't the fairy-tale castle of Snow White or Cinderella. Something was foreboding about this one, what with its walls of dark stone and an ugly wooden gate. Lauren shuddered.

When she hesitated one of the guards shoved her roughly, and she exploded all over again, trying to kick him and yell at him and struggle loose. The assault charges were piling up quickly and she hoped this little band of misfits had some good lawyers, for she was going to wipe them out in civil suits even if they managed to avoid prison.

Inside the castle, they entered a large room with a vast table and she was tied-up yet again, this time to a pillar.

Lauren glanced around the room. Well, I'm certainly moving up in the world, she thought. This place at least has chairs. It's a Hyatt compared to those dirt-floored huts.

And what a bunch of chauvinists. This 'tied to a pillar' stuff is unimaginative. If they were nicer about it, they might have convinced me to jump naked out of a cake or something. Bondage is so passé. No wonder the last *Fifty Shades* sequel bombed.

Lauren kept this light-hearted, internal dialogue going in part to offset her fear that things were far more dangerous than she'd thought. The more scared Lauren became, the more she tried to trivialize. But she was chained to a pillar in an ancient castle, and her captors were ruthless. They'd knocked her unconscious, treated her with disdain and—despite the hostage theory—anything could happen next.

Lauren began to panic. It was a new feeling, this raw fear for her physical safety. Nothing in life had prepared her for it, or provided skills to cope. As she watched the foul-smelling, disheveled men consume food like barbarians, her fear grew further, and she began struggling against her restraints without being aware of doing so.

When the dog show began, Lauren tried again to scream and pulled frantically against the metal ring on the wall. The snarling, violent canines who tore at each other over a few pieces of meat seemed to share innate savagery with everyone else in the room. How the owner had brought them to this state she could not imagine. But looking at the fat, disgusting man at the head of the table, it was obvious he'd simply reduced the animals to his level of debauchery. Lauren's fear was making her nauseated.

Finally, as the meal ended, she was taken from the pillar and forced roughly up the stairs. Her guards opened a door, removed the gag, and shoved her inside. She heard a lock click into place as they left. The only thing in here was a crude bed with a straw mattress.

Soon she heard a key in the lock and the door opened again. It was the gross guy who'd been at the head of the table, earlier. Up close, he smelled like rancid pork.

"Look, mister," she said, fighting for self-control. "This is all some kind of joke, isn't it? I don't know what your little band of perverts is after, but if I'm not released instantly—"

Lauren didn't finish, for the fat man pulled out a knife with one hand, and pushed her off balance and onto the bed with the other.

At that point, the intellectual, plotting, manipulative part of Lauren's brain ceased to function. Something primitive took over, and she screamed.

87

AT A SIGNAL from Torsten, the Norsemen erupted in fury—polite dinner guests transforming into berserk savages. The signal was clear enough. As one of the servants approached, Torsten rose up, unsheathed his sword, and sliced off the man's head. All fifty of the warriors sprang into action. First killed were those unlucky enough to be in the room at the time. The Vikings spread out through the castle, mercilessly hacking apart any living thing they found.

The Norsemen slaughtered the pretend-warriors with ease, and the mezzanine was soon awash in blood, severed limbs, and dead bodies. The warriors spread through the castle, seeking the real army. When they reached the castle's ramparts, actual guards were finally encountered. But these guards had never been in combat, had received no training, and had never experienced an adversary more formidable than an angry peasant or a monk with a grievance. They had swords and shields but no idea how to use them. The battle-hardened Vikings massacred these men as if they were straw dummies, used for practice.

Back in the dining hall, where the killing had begun, only Kren and Torsten remained. After initiating the action Torsten returned to his seat, while Kren had never left his.

"They will have no trouble, Uncle," said Kren calmly, finishing off his wine. "Those weren't real warriors at the gate. It was all a show."

"That's what I suspected but I saw no reason to depart from the plan. Better to let them feed us before we killed them."

"I suppose it's time to dispense with the baron," said Kren.

The men had been ordered to leave O'Ruairc alone, their leader wishing to pluck that fruit himself.

"Yes," mused Torsten. "I wish I could think of a fitting end to that fat coward's life. In all my travels I've found no one more deserving of death. He lets his whole village be conquered without lifting a finger. Then, he invites us to dinner and runs off with the female slave we give him for diversion. He was too stupid to realize it was a trick. I've seen *dogs* with more intelligence!"

At the mention of dogs, Kren glanced at the animals still tied up in the corner. They were barking furiously and straining at their cords—fighting madness and blood scent driving them crazy. Torsten followed his gaze.

"Kren, find two of our men and have them bring those dogs."

In a moment, the four Vikings were heading up the stairs toward the baron's chamber, the dogs held barely in check by their leashes. The animals were snarling and yelping and becoming entangled with each other.

When they came to the door, Kren could hear the girl inside, screaming. Torsten kicked it open.

The scene was predictable. The female slave was already half-naked, under threat from a knife, while the baron removed his own clothes.

The girl's hysterical cries were stilled for an instant, as she looked with new horror at the open door.

"Get her out of here!" ordered Torsten.

The baron, with one leg still tangled in his clothing, lost his balance and fell to the floor.

"Wh-a-a— Wh-a-a-t?" he stammered, trying to cover himself and stand up again.

Kren went to the bed and pulled the girl gently to her feet. She was sobbing uncontrollably and offered no resistance. He grabbed a blanket and wrapped it loosely around her, then guided her to the doorway. He paused to watch, not wishing to miss the baron's demise.

Torsten, with sword drawn, advanced on O'Ruairc who released his bowels in fright.

The baron held his hands outward in an instinctive gesture of protection. Torsten swung his weapon and three of O'Ruairc's fingers were sliced off.

Blood oozed from the stumps. The baron shrieked, staring in horror at his mutilated hand.

Torsten picked up one of the severed fingers and carried it—dripping—over to the door where the dogs were held at bay.

"Here dogs!" he said, imitating the gesture the baron

had used earlier. He held out the object, shaking it lightly and flinging blood across the dogs' nostrils. The animals barked and strained furiously against their leashes, biting each other in desperation.

"Here dogs!" Torsten repeated. He nodded to the men holding the animals and flung the severed finger towards the baron, who'd fallen backward into the corner. The dogs burst through the doorway in a delirium of starvation, and savagely attacked the helpless, yet still-alive, meat being offered. They took no notice that it was their former master. Or perhaps they did.

Kren watched as the Irish lord, screaming in agony, was eaten alive. Finally, Torsten left the room and the Norsemen followed. The baron was dead and the dogs would gnaw the carcass for hours.

No one except Kren noticed, or cared, that the female slave with the yellow hair had fainted. With his good arm, he carried her over his shoulder, back down the stairs, a protective feeling for this comely girl already growing within him.

88

"THE HEART OF the question," explained Milo, "is how do you kill a thousand Vikings when you only have two hundred rounds of ammunition?"

"Are there that many?" asked Kitt.

"I don't know precise numbers. But given the longboats I counted in the harbor, it could be. 500 at least. We have to assume on the high side."

It was a council of war. Kitt, Milo, Avelyn, and the abbot sat cross-legged in a corner of the underground sanctuary. They'd had no sleep the night before and had spent most of the day trying to help the wounded still under the abbot's care. Milo's first aid kit was hardly up to the task. What they most needed was antibiotics, which could only come from *Chrysalis*. But they could not start down that road.

The coals from a small fire glowed in the middle of the room; its smoke whisked upwards through hidden chimneys. Kitt, guessing it was near dinner time, opened his pack and passed around slices of summer sausage, followed by a one-liter water bottle. He noticed the abbot staring at the things coming out of the pack, and tried to see them through the old man's eyes.

The sausage was wrapped in invisible paper with strange markings on it. Then there was the knife Kitt used to slice the sausage—the blade folding out from a dark red handle, bearing a white cross. The water bottle might be the most incredible of all, made of a substance that was as transparent as the water itself. And then there was the pack…

Milo was talking mostly to himself.

"We've got the grenades, the flamethrower, two handguns, and even our knives, in addition to the M-16's," he mused. "But a thousand? How do we overcome a thousand warriors?"

"Forget not, Milo, that the Earth and the Sea wish these invaders destroyed," said Avelyn. "With their help, perhaps I can force the Vikings to march into the bay where they will drown."

"With respect, Miss, last night in the barn it looked like you couldn't convince your captors to even stay away from *you*, much less march into the sea."

"I was tired," she said, dismissing the incident.

"Children, is there not to be the hand of God in any of this?" asked the abbot. "Shall we not pray on the matter?"

There was a disturbance in the outer chamber. One of the younger monks arrived, escorting a gaunt, middle-aged man, in well-tailored but soiled clothing. He was near exhaustion and stumbled frequently.

"What's all this?" asked the abbot rising to his feet.

"We found him in the woods, Your Grace. I hope we did right in bringing him here."

The unidentified man was leaning against the mud walls, eyes nearly shut in fatigue, as he painfully summoned breath. The abbot walked over and studied the face under torchlight. He chuckled softly.

"Well, well. Brody Flannagain. How the great have fallen! I take it by your presence, and in this condition, that much is amiss at the castle. Is the baron still seeking young women? Has the harvest fallen short again? Have new taxes been imposed on the abbey? Or might circumstances have changed a bit?"

Brody Flannagain smiled appreciatively, through the pain and exhaustion.

"So you survived, eh, my dear abbot? We are of a kind are we not? We are both survivors."

"We are of a kind in that we both are breathing. Let's not stretch the comparison."

"I won't. Perhaps we shall bandy arguments at a later and happier time. For now, I am at your mercy. I have no one else. Do with me as you will."

"A tempting offer, Flannagain. Most tempting. Much would I have welcomed it the day your soldiers came to seize Avelyn."

"We certainly failed there, Your Grace. Avelyn slipped through our fingers and I'm certain now lies in a shallow grave somewhere on the Doon road. I find no joy in that, I hasten to assure you."

"I would hope *not!*" Avelyn said, walking into the light of the torches. "But if you're the one who seizes the village girls, I'd find considerable joy in seeing you in such a grave. It could be arranged. Easily."

The seneschal looked at her in shock.

"No!" he said, his voice quivering. "You should be dead! A thousand times dead!"

"Brody, she outwitted you, me, and the invaders, but her tale is a long one. You seek friendship? Why should we offer it? You, who have always been our enemy; who have always done O'Ruairc's bidding; who have represented Satan here on Earth—at least until you were displaced by the invaders—why should we offer you anything but the sharp edge of a sword? We have among us those who could wield it."

Flannagain was silent for a moment.

"I don't deny it, Your Grace," he said, finally. "While employed by the baron I prospered by doing his bidding. But the baron is dead. Or at least I imagine he now is. And I am an unemployed and humbled seneschal."

"You are certainly that."

"A normal man would do as you say, and put a sword through my undeserving body. But you are a Christian and a clever man. The Christian part won't kill me because it is against God's law. I predict the clever part will recognize me as someone who could be valuable."

"Valuable to the worms, perhaps," said Avelyn bitterly, "who would enjoy feasting on your carcass as it rotted in that shallow grave."

"Valuable to the worms, no doubt," agreed the abbot. "But possibly valuable to us as well. Are you saying, Brody, that you'd work for me? For our cause?"

"Certainly. That is what I do. I work for others. I do not see great prospects here, buried in mud under our village. But it's better than submitting to the mercy of the Norsemen. I tried to pretend otherwise but had I made good my escape to Doon, I would have been killed on the instant. They know me too well there."

"You need not face the Doonmen," said the abbot. "I've always respected your cunning. Let's see if God can turn it to good use."

⁂

Milo spoke privately with Kitt.

"It's no good. We just don't have enough tactical information."

"Tactical information?"

"Troop deployments, armaments, strongholds, supply lines. How can I figure out how to kill them all, when I don't know where they all are?"

"You're not giving up, I hope."

"Of course not. I can't back down from the first war I've been handed in decades. But we need reconnaissance. We need to scout their positions."

"And then?"

"Then maybe we'll spot a weak point. If this were 'Nam we'd look for one of Charlie's ammunition dumps. We'd blow it up and disappear back in the jungle. Blowing up ammunition dumps is what guerilla warfare's all about."

"I see the problem. How do you fight a guerilla war against an army that hasn't invented ammunition dumps?"

"Or even ammunition. But the first step is reconnaissance."

"Would it be asking too much to suggest it wait until morning?"

Milo grinned and checked his watch.

"Almost twenty-four hours since we left the sub. Been quite a day, hasn't it?"

"You're having the time of your life, aren't you?"

"Yeah, I guess I am. It may not be saying much, but I guess I am."

They all fell asleep quickly. Kitt and Avelyn were together, his arm draped around her, protectively. Flannagain found a space on the opposite side of the room from the abbot. And Milo lay in front of the tunnel's entrance, one hand on his .45 caliber automatic, safety off.

89

"THEY'RE LEAVING," SAID Kitt the next morning, as he watched the Norsemen from a rock outcropping near the monastery, overlooking the harbor.

"At least some of them are," agreed Milo, sharing the binoculars.

"Here, Flannagain, what do you think they're doing?" asked Milo, passing the binoculars to the former seneschal of Ballycastle. Having met with the Vikings he could best interpret their movements.

"I dare not touch the tools of a sorcerer," said Flannagain, holding up his hands in alarm. "It could endanger my soul."

"It isn't magic. Just a glass that reflects light differently. Similar to a rainbow. Go ahead. Look."

Flannagain took them reluctantly and studied the situation.

"They're leaving," said Flannagain.

"Yes," agreed Milo, "but where are they going?"

"They're probably going to attack the Doon fief," said Flannagain. "I discussed that with them yesterday."

"And what is that?"

"Doon is the hereditary enemy of Antrim. It lies southeast along the coast about ten leagues. Baron Fakis is lord and an eviler man the world has never known. If he is allowed to meet with the Viking leaders before they attack, Fakis will likely help them conquer much of Ireland, in return for keeping his own lands."

"But why would the Vikings bother to negotiate?" asked Kitt. "Why not just attack, as they did here?"

"They had no idea what to expect when they attacked Ballycastle," reasoned Flannagain. "And they had to assume they would meet resistance. Having found Ireland weak, they may choose a different tactic in Doon. Why risk the life of a single man, or destroy so much property, if you can win by negotiation?"

"That's exactly how it happened, Boss," said Milo, nodding. 'The Irish lords formed alliances with the Norse. This group will cut some deal with the guy in Doon to use it as a base, and then conquer new lands beyond. I'd say history is right on track here."

There was no response. Kitt was staring through the binoculars, down towards the waterfront.

"What is it, Boss?"

Kitt ignored him. He was gripping the binoculars so hard his knuckles had turned white.

"Boss, what the hell?"

Finally, Kitt looked up at Milo, his face ashen—his mouth speechless.

"C'mon, Kitt, what's the matter. What did you see down there?

"My wife," he said. *"My wife's down there!"*

"Easy now. Maybe this thing with Avelyn is doing something to your conscience. But we're in the eighth century, remember? Your wife's in Connecticut."

"She's here, Milo. My God, she can't be. But she is!"

"Boss, there is no way—"

"Milo, goddammit, listen to me. My wife's down there on the dock!"

Milo grabbed the binoculars.

Several hundred Norse warriors milled about, their short leather tunics and wool jerkins seeming almost comical. Like an old movie. Woven between them was a line of about fifty women. They were prisoners, obviously, for each had her hands tied to a cable snaking its way along the waterfront.

Milo studied them closely. They were mostly short and had long, auburn-brown hair, similar to Avelyn's. Near the back was someone completely different. She was tall, with short-cut platinum blonde hair. She wore tight-fitting jeans and a stylish, low-cut blouse, ripped in several places. Milo adjusted the focus and was nearly certain he could see a Donna Karan label.

"Jesus H. Christ," said Milo. "Your wife's been captured by Vikings."

Kitt was leaning against one of the rocks, his eyes unfocused and his body limp.

"But, this isn't possible. We're in the eighth century, right?"

"Yep," said Kitt, utterly defeated. "And so is she."

"Your wife *can't be here*—unless she somehow got on the

submarine. But there's no way she got on the submarine. It was just you, me, and the crates. Even if she'd been in the area—even if she'd tailed us to the farm somehow—she'd not have been able to board the sub. We had sentries posted!"

"You just said it, Milo. The crates. That's how she did it."

"What?"

"The day we left Three Forks," explained Kitt, "before you arrived in the submarine, I heard a noise in the barn. I went out, but couldn't find anything. I thought it was Waldorf."

"What's the cat got to do with this?"

"It wasn't the cat. Maybe it was Lauren. It must have been. She trailed us to Virginia. I don't know how. But it's just the kind of thing she'd do. She was hiding in the barn. When I walked in she must have hidden in one of the crates. It's possible. She was taken on board. She's back here with us, Milo, in the eighth century. And now she's been captured by Vikings. Of all the—"

Milo turned to Flannagain.

"What do you know about the tall woman?" he asked, handing the binoculars to Flannagain. "Have you seen her before?"

"Yes. She was the female slave presented as a gift to the baron yesterday. I assumed she was one of them. Most have that same yellow hair. They used her as a diversion. The baron took her to his chambers and that's when I escaped."

"Shit!" Milo said in English. Kitt began to recover.

"Milo—" he began.

"Let me guess. Along with killing all the Vikings, you want me to rescue your wife, right?"

"We can't leave her here! I'd have nightmares for the rest of my life. So would you!"

Milo uttered several more obscenities and picked up the binoculars again. The line of captured women was being led onto the third longboat. Lauren herself was nearly on board. As Milo watched, the woman with the Donna Karan jeans stumbled and was gripped by two strong pairs of Viking arms. She was dumped clumsily into the Norse vessel and disappeared from sight.

For the second time, Milo leaned back against the rock and stared vacantly at the sky. But it was only for a moment.

"Get back to the Monastery," he said to Flannagain. "Tell Avelyn and the abbot to bring our packs and the three of you get back here as soon as possible."

Flannagain nodded and disappeared down the path.

Milo reached into his belt pack and extracted the marine-band radio.

"*Chrysalis*, calling *Chrysalis*. Admiral Sandusky calling *Chrysalis*."

"C'mon, Hamilton. Get your butt on here."

He tried again. "Admiral Sandusky calling *Chrysalis*. Come in please."

The speaker crackled in reply.

"*Chrysalis* here, Admiral. This is Hamilton. Standing by for orders."

Milo paused.

"'Standing by for orders,' he says. "I sure as hell hope so."

Milo pressed transmit and began speaking rapidly.

90

THEY WERE AT a clearing in the forest, not far from the rock outcropping. The abbot dropped the pack he'd been carrying and crossed himself quickly as if hoping to mitigate any satanic forces.

"Everyone listen closely," said Milo. "We've told Avelyn who we are, and where we're from. But I don't think she believes us. She thinks we're sorcerers."

"There's nothing wrong with being sorcerers," Avelyn retorted. "Sorry, Father. I know you don't agree."

The abbot opened his mouth to protest, but Milo held up his hand. "Let's not get into that. For what it's worth, we don't consider ourselves sorcerers. But pretty soon you're going to see things you won't be able to understand. If it helps to think of us as magicians, go right ahead. However, I don't want anyone to go into shock, or faint, or be terrified. Let's get all that out of our system, now. Anyone feel like fainting?"

No one did.

"Here's our situation. The ships are leaving, we think

to attack elsewhere on the coast. They're not a problem for us. But they'll likely leave a garrison of warriors behind. Maybe fifty or so. That's the group we'll have to fight."

"Sorcerers or not, how can you overcome a garrison of warriors?" asked the abbot. "You don't even carry swords."

"We don't need swords, Your Grace. We have more powerful weapons."

"You will use some form of magic, then?"

"Yes. But it won't be black magic. It will be good magic."

"C'mon, Milo," said Kitt in English. "What do you think this is? The land of Oz? You sound like you're talking to Munchkins."

"Hey, Boss, I'm trying to put this on their level. Cut me some slack."

"What will you need from us?" interrupted Flannagain, sensibly.

"Despite our magic, Kitt and I are only two people. If one of us gets hurt, we may need help. You could pull us to safety or whatever. Plus, you know the town. In the meantime, use us like shields. Stay behind, and don't get too close."

"You treat us like children," protested Avelyn. "I can wield a sword."

"You don't even *have* a sword," noted Milo, dismissively.

"I have a knife. Plus, I can invoke the powers of the Earth and the Sea. Will it not take all our efforts to defeat the invaders?"

"No, Avelyn," said Kitt. "I'm pretty sure Milo can wipe out the Vikings all by himself."

"Thanks, Kitt! Now, as I was saying—"

A Norse patrol emerged from the forest and looked at them in astonishment.

Milo drew his pistol and racked the slide. The Vikings moved quickly, surrounding the group and preventing escape.

Milo fired a single round into each of the five closest warriors, killing them instantly.

But the last Norseman ran to the rock outcropping, jumped to the highest ledge, and yelled a warning to the others in the village. A bullet ripped into his skull and he fell forward, plummeting onto rocks a hundred feet below.

Milo jumped onto the ledge and peered over. The warning had been heard. The Vikings were pointing up at the rock and drawing their weapons.

But the ships had left. Thank God the ships had left. It was only the garrison they'd need to fight. He rushed back to the clearing.

"The schedule's moved forward. We go on offense—right now!"

"Will it work, Milo? We've lost the element of surprise."

"No, we haven't. Everything we do will be a surprise."

Milo turned to the others.

"No more discussion! If you want to live, do exactly what I say and do it fast. Flannagain! You carry one of the backpacks. Avelyn, you carry the other."

The abbot began to protest, but Avelyn motioned him to silence and slipped one of the packs on her shoulders. Flannagain was already carrying his.

Milo turned to the abbot.

"Are you willing to bear arms, Your Grace?"

"My son, you may be a creature from the pit. Yet my heart tells me to follow you. I expect it is God's will that I die today, and I accept that fate."

"You won't die, Your Grace. Others will. Now slip this on." Milo helped the abbot into the sling that supported the flamethrower.

"You spoke of Hell, Your Grace. You hold the fires of Hell in your hands. Aim like this, and pull back on the lever. Anyone you're facing will be consumed in flame. Understand?"

The old man nodded.

"OK. Your job is to cover our rear. Stay with us, but keep looking the other way."

Kitt motioned Milo aside.

"The *flamethrower?* Couldn't you just give him one of the pistols?"

"No. You've got to aim a pistol and without training, the recoil would blow the thing out of his hands. The flamethrower's easier—it's more like the power of God."

"And I get one of the M-16's?"

"Yes. Let's review how to shoot it."

Milo covered the basics quickly, including how to change magazines, chamber a round, release the safety, and fire in semi or fully-automatic mode. He noticed Avelyn was watching closely.

"Who do I shoot at?" asked Kitt.

"Every Viking you see. Avelyn and Flannagain!"

"Yes, Milo," answered the girl.

"Carry the packs and stay close behind. If I motion

you over, come instantly and kneel. That way I can grab whatever I need. Got it?"

"I can do more, Milo! I can—"

"Avelyn, I need you to follow orders. Can you do that?"

Avelyn sighed. "Yes."

Milo grabbed the other M-16, plus a spare magazine, and secured a pistol to his hip. He flung a belt of grenades over one shoulder.

Three Vikings appeared. Kitt pulled the trigger on his M-16 and swung the barrel in an arc. The men fell instantly—surprise and pain registering briefly on their faces.

"Nice shooting, Kitt. Let's go!"

As they followed Milo into the village, a half-dozen Norsemen rushed towards them with axes drawn.

Milo shot one, with three bullets to the chest.

"Everyone, down on your knees!" shouted Kitt, with such authority even Milo dropped. Kitt again fired his automatic weapon, killing the other five.

"Nice work again, Boss. Here, take my spare magazine."

Milo led them to the harbor. Peering around the corner of a mud hut, he saw at least thirty warriors drawn up on the wharf and ready for battle—the last of the garrison.

"How do we handle that many?" asked Kitt.

"Like this."

Milo stepped out from his hiding place and began tossing M67 fragmentation grenades at the Norsemen. The waterfront erupted with explosions. A dozen Vikings were killed instantly. Many had their limbs blown off. Several were knocked into the harbor itself where their heavy weapons and clothing pulled them under the waves. Those still alive could see their enemies but had no idea how to fight a god hurling thunderbolts. They rushed to take cover. When the grenades ran out, only eight were alive.

The survivors—perhaps realizing this particular god was all out of thunderbolts—came out of hiding and approached Milo cautiously, weapons drawn.

Milo fired his own M-16. Three more went down before the magazine emptied. He tossed the rifle aside.

An enraged Viking rushed at the Navy SEAL, but Milo pulled out his handgun and shot him in the chest. A spear, flung by another Norseman, grazed Milo in the arm and his pistol dropped to the ground. Milo stumbled backward and fell to his knees. The warriors moved closer—three with axes, one holding another spear. All moved cautiously, protected by their wooden shields—keeping their eyes on their most dangerous adversary, now defenseless on the ground.

Avelyn dropped her pack and—unnoticed—snuck behind the Vikings. She grabbed Milo's discarded M-16 and inserted a new magazine from the supplies she'd been carrying. She pulled back the bolt, chambering a round, and slung the rifle over her shoulder.

A Norse spear was raised and as it was about to be hurled at Milo's unprotected body, Kitt's own handgun erupted, sending a .45 caliber hollow-point bullet into the Viking's forehead and blowing apart the upper half of his skull.

Kitt fired again but his weapon jammed. The nearest two Vikings turned towards him and raised their axes.

Kitt, in frustration, threw the pistol at them and it glanced harmlessly off a Viking shield. The warriors approached menacingly, determined to remove this now-defenseless adversary.

Avelyn stepped forward, and called to them, tauntingly, in Anglish.

"Hey, boys, did you forget the Spirit Girl!"

The Vikings turned towards her in astonishment.

"I curse you again!" she screamed. "I curse you a thousand times! I call forth the anger of the Earth and the Sea and proclaim that you shall be destroyed!"

Almost of their own will, her arms reached towards the heavens in a gesture of command.

A cloud moved in front of the sun, and a shadow was cast over the land.

But to Avelyn's disappointment, the cloud moved on and the sun returned. The Vikings glanced at each other for reassurance, and then rushed the Spirit Girl.

With a sigh of exasperation, Avelyn pulled the M-16 from her shoulder, and emptied the thirty-round magazine at her attackers—the .223 caliber bullets leaving the barrel at 3,215 feet-per-second.

"Time to feed the crows!" she screamed, as wooden shields were ripped apart and splinters exploded. The high-velocity bullets shredded heavy leather tunics, and sparks flew as they ricocheted off ax-heads. Fountains of blood erupted from the Vikings' torsos, as the warriors collapsed to the ground, lifeless.

Avelyn's ammunition ran out.

There was only one Viking left. He faced Milo, who

was now back on his feet and holding a Marine-issue combat knife. The Norseman—ten yards away—raised his ax and prepared to attack.

Milo threw the knife, point-first, at the warrior's face. But the spear-wound affected his aim, and the knife flew harmlessly past the Viking's cheek.

The Norseman rushed forward, ax held high.

From nowhere, a firestorm of napalm engulfed the final warrior, igniting him like a torch. The Viking's clothes, shield, flesh, and even ax handle erupted in flames. The heat was so great that Milo—still half a dozen yards away—had to step back and cover his face.

The blazing Norseman, screaming, took two steps backward and collapsed in a pile of sizzling flesh. The metal ax head, its handle burned away, glowed a dull orange.

Father Conardy stepped forward and stared in astonishment at the weapon in his hands.

"Truly, this is a relic from the Old Testament," he said. "Deuteronomy 4:24, *The Lord your God is a consuming fire.*"

Avelyn, now holding the M-16 rifle at ease, looked over the scene with grim satisfaction.

The Viking garrison had been annihilated.

91

CAPTAIN PERRY HAMILTON sat in his cabin watching a downloaded file of Super Bowl highlights while *Chrysalis* hung motionless at periscope depth. Given the most recent orders from the admiral, his thoughts weren't on football.

Two days ago Sandusky and the civilian had gone off in another inflatable, leaving Hamilton with too much time on his hands. The ship was forbidden all use of radio or television communications other than to monitor the Admiral's shore frequency. He'd been ordered to hold position via sonar just outside the firth. No problem. As long as the admiral was happy, he was happy.

But the latest orders from Sandusky were borderline crazy. Hamilton turned off the video and laid back on the bed, replaying the conversation.

"Captain, this is Sandusky. Please use voiceprint to verify."

Voice-print confirmed the identity of the caller and was mandatory on any order involving the firing of weapons. To date, Sandusky had shown no inclination to use the ship's firepower—a fact which allowed the captain to overlook much of what else had occurred.

"Voice-print confirmed, sir. You may proceed on an identity-established basis."

"Very well, Captain. Are you prepared to follow my orders precisely?"

"Of course, sir." Anything less was mutiny.

"I've been in contact with the CNO himself, via shore facilities, and we've been asked by the Brits for some help. This has nothing to do with the experiments we were sent here to perform. We've been handed this assignment because we're the only U.S. warship on the scene. Do you understand?"

"Yes, sir." The Chief of Naval Operations was two steps below the President, in the chain of command.

"We're on a non-secure channel, so I'll be brief. We're dealing with a terrorist threat that's got to be stopped, and the government's going on offense this time. My feeling is, it's about time."

"Couldn't agree with you more, Admiral. What are your orders?"

"Are you familiar with the old longboats used by the Vikings, their general shape and so forth?"

Hamilton was taken by surprise, but then remembered the craft they'd sighted earlier.

"Yes, sir. We saw one recently. Is that what this is about?"

"Yes. In a few hours, a fleet of vessels built to look like Viking longboats is going to come down the firth. They were part of a cultural exhibit, perfect replicas. Jihadis are using those boats as part of a plan that could bring death to thousands."

"Sir, with respect, I'm sorry, but what you're saying sounds ridiculous. Viking longboats, part of a terrorist plot? Again sir, with respect, what the fuck?"

"Yeah, what the fuck indeed. Craziest damn thing I've ever heard of."

"Can't the authorities just use force and board the vessels, sir?"

"Not in this case. That would generate the kind of publicity the terrorists want. Best if an accident occurred. For example, if the explosives they carry were to be improperly handled they could go off by accident. That would make the terrorists look incompetent. If you know what I'm saying."

"Admiral, are you going to order me to use a U.S. Navy submarine to fire torpedoes into Viking longboat replicas?"

"I am, Captain. But I'm only the messenger here. These orders come from the CNO's office itself. When we get back to Norfolk, I give you full permission and encouragement to take it up with him directly. But in the meantime, my original question stands. Are you willing to follow my orders? Or do we have a problem here?"

"Sir, I can assure you, we have no problem. I can assure you of 100% loyalty, sir. I'm standing by to follow your orders, sir."

Hamilton had gushed out that speech as forcefully as he knew how. Any reluctance to follow a superior officer's orders, especially in what might be considered a combat situation, could land him in Leavenworth military prison for life.

"Glad to hear it, Captain."

"What specific orders do you have for me, sir?"

"There are six vessels. Each has a long bow piece—an extension of the stem. On one of them, the bow piece is almost twice the height of the others. Also, that vessel has a long streak of red paint just below the gunwales."

"And that's the one you want to explode?"

"No. That's the one I don't want to explode."

"I see."

"I want the others destroyed when the flotilla is a hundred yards from the mouth of the firth. Position yourself outside the entrance, and maintain periscope depth so you can keep an eye on them. Their wooden hulls won't show up too well on sonar."

"Aye aye, sir."

"Any questions, Captain?"

"What about the other vessel?"

"Don't interfere with it at all."

"And will you stay in communication with us, sir?"

"I'll try, but it may not be possible. Keep this channel open and monitored. This whole thing's weird as hell and if the CNO changes his mind I want to be able to reach you instantly. If I'm able to maintain radio contact, probably best if I give the firing orders myself, on this frequency. But if not, you know what to do."

"Aye aye, sir. I understand."

But the more Hamilton thought about it, the more he didn't understand. Whoever heard of a nuclear submarine being used to sink Viking longboats? It was beyond crazy.

But the orders were clear enough. In the Navy, if you understood your orders, and obeyed them, you couldn't get in too much trouble.

He glanced at his watch. The ship was at quarters,

although condition yellow was in effect, meaning the men could relax as long as they stayed near their stations. *Chrysalis* was at periscope depth, using propulsion jets to maintain position, and with a perfect angle for firing.

The fish were set to detonate on contact with anything that wasn't water.

Torpedo tubes were flooded and doors opened. Firing could occur with as little as five seconds notice. A continuous periscope watch was being maintained on the entrance to the firth, with orders to notify him as soon as any craft whatsoever were sighted. It was a little odd that nothing at all had been seen, for presumably there were fishermen about. But maybe that had something to do with events onshore.

Hamilton decided to return to the bridge, just as the intercom barked.

"XO, here, Captain. The longboat replicas are heading out of the firth."

"On my way. Battle stations."

92

FOR THE VOYAGE south along the coast, Kren suggested the female slaves be transported in *Freya's Song*, which was the only vessel large enough to accommodate them. If left behind, the garrison would be too distracted. Torsten had approved the plan and transferred to a different boat. His uncle considered the women a bother and wanted to be with warriors, plotting their next attack.

A storm was approaching, and the sailing master suspected it would be violent—quick to arrive, fierce, and soon gone. Already the wind had picked up. Thunder and lightning would be next. Kren hoped they could find a protected harbor of some kind if they needed to on the voyage south.

They were nearly out of the fjord when Kren heard what sounded like waves of thunder rolling off the hills. Was the storm ahead of schedule?

A ghastly, inhuman scream, came from the direction of the wharf. Kren turned with alarm and looked back towards the village. Something was amiss. It looked like, somehow, a man—from their garrison most likely—had been set afire. That would account for the screams. But how could—?

"The garrison is under attack!" he shouted to the helmsman. "Turn the boat around! Drop the sail! Use the oars! Signal to the other vessels. Hurry!"

As sailing master for the expedition, Kren's vessel was leading, and—on the water—he was in command.

The Norse longboats turned as one, the other captains also hearing the screams. Had the army they'd been expecting finally arrived? Was Ireland, at last, going to put up a fight worthy of their prowess? The vessels tore through the water, the captains shouting frantically to the oarsmen, as hundreds of others grabbed their weapons.

❧

Milo's motley band raced through the streets of Ballycastle and back up the trail to the overlook on the hill. It was critical to know whether the Norsemen on the ships had heard or seen the battle, and were returning.

Milo arrived first. It was as he feared. The six longboats had come about into the wind and were now racing back to the harbor, their oars propelling them. The others joined him on the rock and watched their doom approach.

"If those vessels reach shore we'll be obliterated, right?" asked Kitt, stating the obvious.

"Correct. We can wipe out a platoon using modern weapons, but we'll be no match for a battalion—even a battalion armed with spears and axes. We're looking at nearly 500 men, combined."

The sky had darkened with the fast-approaching storm, and the gusty wind was whipping Avelyn's hair across her face.

Lightning flashed, and thunder followed quickly. Another lightning bolt struck near the mouth of the firth.

Father Conardy stepped forward.

"Our fate may be bleak, my children, but we are not alone!"

The old priest went down on his knees, crossing himself fervently and looking upwards. His arms were outstretched towards the heavens, and his head was bowed in humility. There was a great sanctity upon him.

"I invoke the power of God, through our Lord Christ Jesus, and call forth His anger!" the abbot cried majestically.

Lightning struck again, and an adverse gust blew down from the hills onto the Viking fleet. Two of the longboats lost their forward momentum, and the oars faltered, in confusion. But soon both were underway, again, and the fleet surged onwards.

Avelyn glanced apprehensively at the abbot. Then she stepped forward and closed her eyes in concentration.

"I invoke the power of the Earth and the Sea," she shouted, her arms outstretched. "The Viking ships shall be destroyed, and I command it!"

This time a more violent wind tore at the Viking fleet. A mast cracked and plunged into the sea. An electrical storm lit up the fjord, striking nearby hills. The thunder was incessant.

"A curse on the invaders!" cried Avelyn, as a single lightning bolt crashed into one of the longboats. It was the

flagship—containing Torsten and his crew. The wooden vessel was set aflame and all within were consumed—fulfilling Avelyn's prophecy of the warlord's death by fire.

But the remaining vessels—unharmed—bore down on them, their crews seething with outrage and fighting madness.

Unseen by the others, Milo picked up his two-way radio and spoke quietly into the mouthpiece. Then he raised his voice high and spoke commandingly to the heavens, with his own arms raised.

"I invoke the power of the American-made Mark 48 torpedo!" he cried. He held the radio close to his mouth and whispered. "Commence firing."

At first, it seemed nothing had come of Milo's invocation. The wind ignored him and the thunder faded. The electrical storm had moved on.

Then, without warning, the closest ship exploded with a roar that echoed around the hills and a geyser of water erupted, soaring sixty feet in the air. Only the smallest pieces of debris remained to fall back into the sea.

When the smoke cleared, there was nothing left at all.

Then another vessel exploded. And another after that. Then two more ships detonated—including the one on fire—sending twin geysers blasting into the air.

In seconds the entire Norse battle fleet had been reduced to a single longboat.

And then all was quiet.

Avelyn looked at Milo with astonishment.

"Someday," she said, "you must teach me how to do that."

❧

Kren watched, appalled, as his companion ships were destroyed in what could only be an act of the Irish gods. Kren expected *Freya's Song* would be next. He prepared for death, proud in the knowledge he would die at the helm of a Viking war vessel.

After a few moments, Kren was surprised to find himself still alive. He waited a bit longer and then decided the gods' anger must have been appeased—or perhaps their cargo of Irish slaves was being spared.

He had the oars stilled, while he looked over the scene, determined to lend what assistance he could to the survivors. But there were none. The five other vessels—and their crews—had been obliterated. Nothing remained but chips of wood, some still smoldering, floating aimlessly on the water.

93

"THE LAST SHIP won't bother us," Milo declared. "That's the one with the women. It has only a small crew and I expect the fight's been knocked out of them."

"We still don't want them to see us," noted Kitt.

"True. Flannagain, stay here as an observer. Your Grace, please lead us back to the monastery where we can rest and re-supply."

Then he lowered his voice and spoke softly to Flannagain. "Report to us in an hour, and keep your eye out for the female slave with the yellow hair. If she's moved off the ship, we need to know immediately, and know where they've taken her."

"Yes, my lord."

Milo looked at him strangely and then hurried after the others.

&

Flannagain watched as the yellow-haired woman disembarked. She walked barefoot and had to be frequently supported. She looked much as Flannagain expected her to, after being held captive at the hands of the Norsemen. But why they should move her, alone, into the cabin on shore was a mystery—except for the obvious reason of course.

He returned to the monastery and reported the event to the sorcerer-lord, Milo.

"This is the chance we need," said Kitt urgently. "We can rescue her."

"Rescue her? You suggest we walk into town and knock on the door and when they answer we say 'Oh, pardon me, Mr. Viking, but this particular slave actually belongs to my friend Kitt, here, so if you've no objection, we'll just take her with us."

"Well, aren't you the commando? What happened to the guy who could sneak up on people underwater and break their neck with one arm tied behind his back?"

"I never said with one arm tied behind my back!"

"Something like that."

"OK, OK. I'm not saying we shouldn't do it. I'm just trying to figure out the best plan. A rescue operation is tricky. If you go in with guns blazing you might kill the hostage. Or, equally likely, if they realize you're trying to rescue her they may just slit her throat."

"One thing I've learned, Milo, is when you tell me all the reasons my plan won't work, it means you're thinking of something that will."

"Actually, this is a textbook situation. Commando 101. You rescue a hostage by separating her from the terrorists."

"Terrorists?"

"Don't break my train of thought. The point is you've got to separate them. And you do that with a diversion."

"Wait, let me guess. One of us creates a diversion—like we start a fire or something—and then the other rushes in, cuts the ropes, and rescues Lauren."

"Exactly. Only we won't do anything as mundane as starting a fire. I've still got a few surprises in my pack."

"No doubt. When you create the diversion, I'll grab Lauren. Can you guarantee you'll be able to pull all the Norsemen away for a few minutes?"

"A few minutes, yes. But that may not be enough to get her out. I think we'd better have Flannagain up on the rock with a noisemaker. One of those compressed-air horns will do. When he sees them starting to return to the hut, he can blow the horn and then get out of there fast. When you hear it, you do the same."

They waited until dusk. Kitt and Milo had chosen not to explain to the others what they were doing, except that it involved more reconnaissance. For one thing, Kitt was reluctant to explain to Avelyn who this mystery blonde woman was. And there was no guarantee they'd rescue Lauren on their first try, anyway. Until they did, why bring up unpleasant subjects? They asked only Flannagain to join them.

94

KREN WAS ACCOMPANYING two Viking *hersirs* as they patrolled the streets.

"It's one thing to lose a battle on land," said Knut with disgust. "But to lose a sea battle? To lose our ships? It's enough to make me puke on Odin's statue."

"Easy now," said Grimsson. "That kind of talk won't help."

"Talk never helps," said Knut. "Slicing off a few heads is what it'll take to put me in good humor. Trouble is, there aren't any. The enemy isn't human."

"You're not going to start in with that Spirit Girl crap are you?"

"Of course not. The Spirit Girl was only a small part. That's obvious. This whole cursed land is inhabited by spirits. Or gods. Or demons. By Thor, I don't know what to call 'em. You saw what they did to our ships. If that was not the work of the gods, nothing was."

"Well, whaddya think we ought to do about it?"

"Do about it? We can't do anything about it. You can't

fight gods. And look at the men. They're scared. We might as well be commanding Aquitainians. You say 'boo!' and they jump."

A bright light flashed from the direction of the village square, and Kren saw both men jump. The ground shuddered and a sound like thunder reverberated around the hills.

Grimsson and Knut took one look at each other and began running in the direction of the explosion, with Kren right behind them. They reached the square and saw one of the mud huts pouring forth a dense yellow and green smoke—like something wicked in the Earth vomiting a horrible pestilence.

Another sentry arrived, and soon most of the ship's crew had left their stations and were staring at the incomprehensible scene.

It was too much for the already-spooked Vikings. They had rushed to defend against a new attack. Finding instead this dreadful apparition, many fell to their knees in terror. The more experienced warriors stood waiting for commands from their superiors, not knowing if they should fight the demon with swords or bow down and worship it as a deity.

Kren stared at it with as much confusion as the others.

95

KITT RAN TO the hut containing Lauren and found the door was ajar. He paused at the opening.

What kind of reception could he expect? And how would she have explained all this to herself? She must be totally bewildered, as well as furious. Would that make her more or less cooperative?

Kitt opened the door and stepped inside.

A fire burned in a hearth but the ventilation was poor and Kitt's eyes began to water. In the diffused light, he saw her. She was sitting on a wooden bench with her back against the wall and her head slouched forward, asleep. There was something unnatural about her position and Kitt realized her hands must be tied behind her—perhaps to the wall.

Her hair was gnarled and matted. Her clothing was wrinkled, filthy, and ripped beyond salvage. She had no shoes and Kitt noticed signs of dried blood on her feet—probably from walking barefoot. Her face was almost unrecognizable. Any trace of makeup had disappeared.

Her lips were cracked. Smears of mud had dried on her forehead and across one side of her face. Her left eye was black and swollen.

It was a strange experience—seeing this woman in a way she never would have allowed either before or after their marriage.

But in her exhausted, battered face, he now saw vulnerability. He would have liked to pick her up, still sleeping, and carry her off to their home in Connecticut. He would run hot water and set her in the tub, wiping her face clean and soothing her pain. And she would be grateful and love him unconditionally. He could return that kind of love; had always expected to, and had tried to. Kitt leaned over and kissed his wife on the forehead, hoping it would be a different Lauren who awoke.

The eyes opened instantly and looked up in terror as if bracing for some new torment.

Kitt smiled. "Hi, Lauren," he said. "It's me."

The parched lips tried to form a smile and the eyes softened, fear being replaced by relief. "Oh, Michael, thank God…"

But it was only for a moment.

Then he watched, horrified, as the old Lauren returned, and her expression changed to a wall of hate.

"You bastard!" she hissed. "You'll pay for this!"

Lauren tried to stand up fully but fell back, her hands fastened to the wall,

"Let's not argue now," implored Kitt. "We need to get you out of here."

"Yeah, ya think? Out of here and into a divorce court.

But just so you know, I've got the plans for your invention. I've got the leverage I need, and it's going to cost you some serious money now!"

"Lauren, we don't have time for this. Listen to me—"

"No, you listen. You won't believe the hell I've been through. I was almost raped, by the most disgusting, horrible…"

"Lauren, I—"

"But don't worry about him. He was eaten by dogs. I had to watch, so now we're talking psychic damages, on top of—

"And who the *hell* are these damned actors or terrorists or crazy people or whatever they are? I want them arrested! All of them! Thrown into jail and I don't care how much it costs you, but anything left over comes to me! Understand? That's the deal. Because I can't believe what you've put me through, and when this is over— It doesn't matter. I have the plans so I'll get the money anyway. And…and…"

Lauren was becoming hysterical. The momentary glimpse of the loving woman who might have been was gone. This experience had pushed her over the edge, not brought her back from it. He'd long ago realized his wife had married for money, but it hurt to have the undeniable proof. Not only had she never loved him; apparently, she despised him.

They had only moments before the Vikings returned. But how could he rescue his wife without getting clawed in the process? Did he even *want* to rescue her?

"Lauren, we've got to get out of here," he said, forcing

down his emotions. "I've brought a knife, I'll cut the ropes. But let's declare a truce until we're away from here."

"A knife! You brought a knife! You idiot! Look!"

Lauren turned aside and showed her hands, best she could. Chains held her to a large ring-bolt in the wall, her wrists locked in iron manacles requiring a key, just as Avelyn's had been. But this time the key wasn't here. Kitt stepped back in frustration. What he needed was a hacksaw. Did they have one in their packs? Kitt didn't think so. In any case, he could do nothing for Lauren now. He would have to come back. Milo would have to come up with another plan. Another diversion.

The loud horn blast startled them both.

ൾ

The sickening yellow and green smoke finally stopped, and Kren ordered everyone back to their stations. The sooner they could leave this spirit-shrouded land, the better.

Suddenly a ghastly howl sounded from somewhere up in the hills. Kren saw several of the Vikings drop to their knees and cover their ears at this new terror. But just as suddenly, it stopped. Kren understood. The Irish gods were tormenting the Norsemen; wanting them gone. Kren wanted to be gone too.

ൾ

Kitt was in a panic.

"Lauren," he said urgently, "that horn is a warning. They're coming back. I've got to leave. I'll have to find a hacksaw, and—"

"A hacksaw! Just call the goddamned, fucking cops! Bring in the Marines, if that's what it takes! Get me out of here. I want out of here, *now!*"

"Lauren, shut up a minute!"

He'd never told her to shut up, and it surprised her into silence.

"You mentioned my invention but you don't know what it is. Look, it's—well, I invented time travel. We've gone back in time. There aren't any policemen here. This is the year 792 and those people you call terrorists are Vikings! *Real Vikings!* This is the eighth century, for Chrissake!"

Then he raced for the door, taking a final glance behind—though later he would regret it. At first, he saw a look of complete incomprehension. Then, just before he slipped out, her expression changed to utter horror. As Kitt raced through the streets he heard a chilling scream.

"Michael! Don't leave me! Michael—"

Then her voice cut off and he knew her captors had returned.

96

THAT NIGHT, THE Norse survivors were favored by a south wind, which carried their fallen comrades out to sea on a floating pyre. Normally, this was a proud moment, when the victors said farewell and wished them honor on the road to Valhalla. But the gesture seemed hollow, given their catastrophic defeat.

Kren walked silently back to the stone hut which the garrison used as headquarters. There were twenty-two warriors remaining from an original raiding force of more than 700. Ironically, there were plenty of female slaves. Nearly sixty young women were chained in the longboat. And his uncle Torsten—almost a father to him—was gone.

Kren was now the leader of the expedition.

Entering the hut he went to the large peat fire which burned reluctantly, and held his hands to its meager warmth, staring into the coals.

"Do you seek guidance from the coals, sailing master?" asked Odger.

"Perhaps, though I find little. These Irish fires burn with a cold flame, and neither my spirit nor body is comforted. Do you have guidance for me?"

"Even less than has the fire. We've been victims of sorcery; that much is certain. Sorcery more powerful than I've ever known."

"Sorcery? I assumed it was an act of the gods. But if it was sorcery, I suppose it might be traced to the Spirit Girl. We never recaptured her. And sorcery is as good an explanation as any for what killed those two guards in the barn. Or for that matter, the garrison. The Spirit Girl did not escape with the help of crows."

"Baah! Spirit Girl. I never understood that name. A spirit is not a girl. It's possible that a spirit took the shape of a girl for a brief period. But looking for that girl, in particular, would be futile. I doubt she exists now—at least in that form. Perhaps she is at present a bat or a tree or even that peat fire."

Kren considered this. "One thing that puzzled me, Odger, was the fact that almost immediately after she escaped from the barn, another female appeared."

"You mean the slave with the yellow hair? You think there's a connection?"

"You said yourself the Spirit Girl could most likely change at will. If she could become a tree, she could certainly become another girl."

"But they were not alike. The one spoke Anglish and taunted us with curses. The other spoke no language at all…at least none that could be understood. And she finally collapsed in hysteria, as is common."

"Yet there is something different about her," said Kren. "Something foreign. I doubt she's Irish. It's possible she knows something of what happened today."

"You think the sorcery involved her in some way or worked through her?"

"We know little of sorcery. Perhaps the one commanding it must be nearby. And how better than to be a captured slave, sitting among us?"

"Is that what you believe?"

"No, I suppose not. But my thoughts are drawn to her."

"I can at least provide this guidance. You are now commander. If your thoughts are drawn to a woman, have her brought to you."

"I already ordered her separated from the others, and kept ashore. I don't want her abused by the men. But she can wait. There's something more important to discuss."

"I know."

"We are too few to raid other settlements. Our remaining ship is fully provisioned, but the men are dispirited. And I'm not a war leader—merely a sailing master."

"And the cleverest on the sea," noted Odger. "The men will follow your commands—have no worry there. What does your instinct tell you to do?"

"Leave at once. Ireland is not weak and defenseless. It is enchanted and watched over by spirits or gods or sorcerers. But return home defeated? We would all be disgraced. Has a raiding party ever returned in such condition?"

"Not in my memory," agreed Odger. "But I see no alternative."

They were silent for a while and stared into the coals of the peat fire.

"There may yet be an alternative," said Kren, but he would say no more that night.

97

THE FOLLOWING MORNING Brody Flannagain reported to Kitt and Milo that the last Viking ship was gone, apparently having departed at first light. The village was deserted.

"What time is it now?" asked Milo, struggling to come awake.

"The sun is nearing its zenith," said Flannagain. "Avelyn insisted I not wake you earlier, because your magic powers could only be restored by sleep, she said."

"Our magic powers can only be restored by sleep?" said Milo. "That's ridic…"

"Why do you think they left, Flannagain," Avelyn broke in.

"After what they've been through, after what happened to the garrison and the other ships—not to mention that smoking deviltry from yesterday—they must be completely unnerved. Of course they left."

"And where did they go?" asked Father Conardy, also coming awake with difficulty.

"To wherever they came from. They sought to conquer this land. But it has conquered them. They will not venture south to Doon for they have no strength."

"We've got to stop them, Milo!" said Kitt urgently. "We'll have to use *Chrysalis* to stop them! You know the reason!"

Milo was leaning against the wall, wishing he had some coffee and surprised they'd slept nearly till noon. Maybe they'd been worn out from all the fighting yesterday.

He glanced over at Avelyn. The girl was sitting cross-legged and comfortable on one of the sheep-skins. She was alert, watching the others. *How much of what Kitt's talking about does she already understand*, he wondered. *And why does Avelyn look so pleased with herself this morning?*

He shrugged off these thoughts and stood up slowly, limbs protesting. *At least the old abbot is having more trouble with his joints than I am*, he noticed with satisfaction. He walked over to Kitt and put his arm around his shoulders.

"Boss, whaddya say we take a little walk outside?" Milo glanced at Avelyn and winked, not quite knowing why.

The day was warm and the breeze was pleasant, blowing strong from the south. Kitt followed Milo up the trail to the rock outcropping. Milo stretched.

"God that feels good. Try it, Kitt. Nothing like a good honest stretch with a warm summer wind blowing on you."

Kitt joined him on the rock and looked down at the bay.

"Flannagain's right. They're gone. And Lauren's with them."

"Unfortunately, there's not a damn thing we can do about it."

"Do about it? We can go after them. We have to go after them! *Chrysalis* is faster than a Viking longboat I assume!"

"Well, sure. Those square-rigged vessels are only about a hundred feet of waterline length. Even before a strong wind, I doubt they'd go faster than nine or ten knots. *Chrysalis* can cruise at forty."

"Then what are we waiting for?"

"We're too late. Didn't you hear? They left at dawn. At this latitude and season, that's about 4 a.m., which means they've got eight hours head start on us, minimum. With this south wind that longboat could be anywhere in an eighty nautical-mile radius. They might have headed north, as Flannagain believes. But they might just as easily have headed west along the coast. Or tacked south to Doon. Or east to Scotland. Or any heading in between. How do we find 'em? A wooden hull won't show up on radar, especially against the choppy waters of the North Sea.

"And even if we started immediately, and guessed the right heading, *Chrysalis* would need two or three hours to catch up. But we can't start immediately. It would take another couple of hours to hike back to the dinghy, return to the sub, and explain to Hamilton why we have to chase a Viking longboat all over the North Atlantic. Now we're talking a 130-mile radius. Even if we had a scout plane the odds would be against us. And we *don't* have a scout plane. *Chrysalis* would be on a wild goose chase, and the goose would win."

Kitt looked at him with astonishment.

"Good God, Milo! You can't be suggesting we *leave*

her here. A Viking slave in the eighth century! Can you imagine what they'll do to her?"

"I don't mean to be insensitive, but based on what you told me last night, it sounds like they've done a lot of it already. I guess 'more of the same' would be what we're talking about."

"But Milo, what kind of a life are you condemning her to? A Viking slave! She can't handle something like that!"

"Sure, it'll be hard. But I have to admit from what you've told me I haven't formed too favorable an impression of your ex-wife."

"*Ex*-wife?"

"You're not getting her back, Boss. And, no offense, but she sounds like a spoiled, manipulative bitch."

"That's exactly what she is. But a Viking slave? Are you saying she deserves that?"

"I'm saying we don't have a lot of choice, here. OK, her new life won't be a bed of roses. In the beginning, she'll be just a slave girl, as you said. Maybe handed around among the men every night. But with her looks, things won't be that bad forever. In fact, I'll bet in a few months, maybe less—when she realizes things aren't going to change—she'll use her cunning and her beauty to rise right to the top."

"The top of what?"

"I bet she'll end up as number one concubine of their commander, with all the privileges that might entail. Then she'll be right back where she was before—in a manner of speaking. Head bitch."

Kitt's eyes smoldered and Milo wondered if he'd gone too far.

"Who knows?" he added quickly. "Maybe she'll even come to like it!"

Kitt couldn't help smiling, and then Milo smiled. And then they were both laughing. Kitt laughed so hard he had to sit down on the rock.

"God, Milo! You are without a doubt the most sadistic, unfeeling bastard I've ever had the misfortune to know!"

"But with a heart of gold, Kitt, a heart of gold. And speaking of which, waiting for you back at the monastery is a young girl you probably don't deserve. So let's get off this rock and join her for breakfast!"

98

THEY HAD RETURNED to the sea and for Kren, standing at the taffrail, it was a re-birth. The wind was blowing hard, over twelve knots, but he refused to reef. It was too exhilarating. Waves crashed into the wooden vessel as it heeled to starboard and the square sail was tight against the rigging. The female slaves, still chained together in the hold, moaned collectively and more than a few were sick.

Odger had been named first mate of *Freya's Song*, and as soon as he was certain the shields were secure he joined the sailing master.

"We already passed the Hebrides' Tooth, Commander, early this morning. But you did not turn northeast. We are bearing far west of north. Is there some navigational peril I'm unfamiliar with?"

"There are always perils we're unfamiliar with. But those of the sea are perhaps less dangerous than those on land. After our defeat, are we to return home, to scorn and pity?"

"It's a fate we're all dreading, sailing master. I would

have preferred death in battle—a thousand times death in battle—yet what choice is there?"

"Those who have ventured far to the West, past the Faroe Islands, have reported seeing birds. Those birds could only have come from land even farther west. I believe it is our destiny to find that land, claim it, and forge a new nation."

Odger considered this. "So that's why you ordered our rock ballast replaced with hammers, lead anvils, and metal tools from the village."

"Yes."

"We have enough women to build a population, certainly, but we're short on seed-grain, and other basic supplies."

"After we find this new land, and assuming it's habitable, your orders will be to take *Freya's Song* back to Norway, with the smallest crew possible. You'll have two jobs. First, let them know of the new country we are building. That news will more than offset the shame of our defeat in Ireland. Find volunteers to join us. Have them return in *Freya's Song*, along with supplies. I suggest you stay behind to encourage more ships as well, with more settlers."

"Yes, Sailing Master."

"Second, spread the word that Ireland is not weak. Let our people know it's defended by angry gods and magical powers and the Norse kingdoms should leave it alone."

"I shall provide witness that what you say is true."

"Good. Now I'd be obliged if you'd bring the slave with the yellow hair to me."

Odger returned in a moment, dragging the girl behind him. Her legs were stiff from confinement, and she screamed from the pain of the iron manacles. Odger dumped her against the coaming. When the girl looked out at the endless ocean, she moaned. Kren leaned against the rail and studied her.

"Odger," he said, "as you noted these women will bear our children. Each of us will need to pick three. As commander, it is my right to choose first, and I claim this one." Kren placed his hand caressingly on the woman's cheek and was not surprised when she turned away in revulsion.

"I know not what tongue you speak," he said soothingly. "And I know you are frightened. But each day you will be less so. There will come a time when your past life will seem a dream—something that never happened. I have heard captured slaves talk of this.

"There will be much work ahead. We will build huts from scratch and food may be difficult to find, though I've never known a land where fish could not be pulled from the sea. We will find animals and tame them and use their hides. We will gather wood for fires. We will found a new nation and those who come after will speak of our deeds in wonder."

Kren looked deep into her eyes, expecting to see fear and hatred, and knowing he could overcome them in time.

But the eyes staring back were bottomless pits, like windows into hell. And they were filled with only one emotion: deep, unfathomable horror.

He stepped back, shocked by the vision, and a cold shiver passed through him.

"Ignore it," said Odger, witnessing the exchange. "Captured slave girls are always terrified. But they survive, somehow."

It was true, thought Kren. They survive.

The sun was warm, the wind steady, and soon the sailing master's smile returned. *Freya's Song* rode the waves easily, as the Valkyrie on her bow stared northwest, seeking an undiscovered land.

99

THE WIND PRESSED against Avelyn's face and blew her hair into disarray as they stared east over the Irish Sea.

Kitt had earlier explained about Lauren, his marriage, and the fact that they had no way to rescue his…ex-wife. She'd been non-committal but accepting. At Avelyn's request, the two of them had taken a walk—up a trail outside of the village, to a cliff overlooking the sea.

"Kitt, I wanted you to see this place. I used to come here alone and gaze over the water, wondering about the worlds beyond. I was waiting for something—but I didn't know what. I did not belong here and knew the villagers would never accept me. So I dreamed of far places across the ocean."

"Avelyn, please look at me." She turned away from the sea and looked into Kitt's eyes.

"Do you know how I feel about you?"

She took his hand in both of hers. "Yes, Kitt, I do know."

"I don't know how to ask this. I mean, I don't know the right words. I don't know your feelings. But I just know—"

"What do you know?"

"I don't want to lose you."

"I'm glad you feel that way."

"*Are* you glad?"

"Kitt, I need to apologize."

"For what?"

"We talked about it before. I used your feelings for me in the most selfish way. I used your feelings to manipulate you into performing a rescue—thinking to do so you'd have to use your powers to defeat the Vikings."

"Well, I guess you were successful."

"Yes, but I have such guilt. That was a terrible thing for me to do. You were so kind to me on the island, and I paid you back—so wretchedly."

She dropped his hand and turned back facing the water. Kitt touched her shoulder and she turned to him again.

"It's OK. I forgive you."

"Kitt, I need you to understand. You're not the only one with feelings. I just— I just had to suppress mine. There were too many things going on."

"I understand. You were fighting off the Vikings, and it wasn't the right moment for romance."

She hugged him briefly, and then pulled back.

"Exactly. Thank you for understanding."

"Hey, I just noticed something."

"What?"

"The Vikings are gone."

She smiled. "Yes, I noticed that too."

He drew her to him, and she came, eagerly. This time her kiss was not brief.

When they finally broke off, Kitt said: "I guess we have some decisions to make."

"I guess we do."

"Will you come back with me. Back to my world?"

Avelyn thought about what she'd be leaving behind. Her premonition that she'd never eat the dried fish was coming true. Her silver coins were buried on the island, and the deceased yarn-merchant, Mrs. Mulcody, no longer thirsted for them. Perhaps someone more deserving would find the cache. The curragh Shelby had built would never take her to Angland, but the Earth and Sea would deem its purpose fulfilled.

"I was so hoping you'd ask me," she said, staring into his eyes meaningfully. "Of course I will if you want me to."

"It will be frightening. You'll see so many things you won't understand."

"I know your world will be filled with magic."

"It's not magic. It's what we call science."

"When I bring forth the power of the Earth—as you have seen me do—what do you call that?"

"I saw you raise your arms and scream a curse at the invaders. Then a bolt of lightning hit one of the longboats. But it was in the middle of a lightning storm. Do you really think *you* did it?"

"It's very confusing. Sometimes I feel like I'm a conduit, for the powers of the Earth and Sea. When I set the ship afire I could feel the spirits using me, controlling me. But then, other times, I wonder if it's all in my imagination.

When I was in the horse-barn—chained to the wall—I had no powers whatsoever. So, I don't really understand."

"You're not alone. I can tell you that a thousand years from now, people are still trying to grasp their relationship with the divine—with the spiritual realm. No one's figured it out yet."

"Then it sounds like your world may not be all that different from mine."

"Well, I suppose in the most important things, it isn't."

"And in things like this..." said Avelyn, and she kissed him again.

100

"RIGHT STANDARD RUDDER."

"Right standard rudder, aye."

"All back one third."

"All back one third, aye."

"All stop."

"All stop, aye."

Hamilton could never get used to the echo-like manner in which his orders were acknowledged. But the routine was therapeutic—especially useful on this cruise from Hell.

So far, he hadn't screwed up, even with an admiral on board. There weren't any ComSubLant messages ordering his ass back to Norfolk to prepare for a court-martial. If that business with the Viking longboats hadn't been sanctioned by Washington—there damn sure would have been. Best of all, according to the last radio contact, they could pick up the shore party tonight and head home. The experiments were over.

But the weird requests weren't. The admiral had asked for a crate of M-16 ammunition—10,000 rounds—to be left on the beach for later pickup. Something about the local constabulary running short as they flushed out the remaining terrorists. Fine. Whatever.

There was only one piece of bad news: a female civilian passenger. Civilians on board were always a pain in the rear. But a female meant special quarters. And the admiral said this one had to be invisible: no logs made and no acknowledgment of her presence. Apparently, she was some kind of British secret agent connected with the anti-terrorist operation. Now she was being ferried to Washington, probably to meet with the CIA. However, it was essential she be brought into the country off-grid.

With *Chrysalis* on scene and already involved, it had seemed a good solution. Or at least it seemed a good solution to someone at CIA who must have been owed a favor by the chief of naval operations.

They'd have to put her in the exec's cabin, presently occupied by the captain himself. So Hamilton would spend the remainder of the voyage bunking with one of the officers—well worth it, to get this voyage over.

"Up periscope."

Hamilton made a three-sixty degree scan. The night was black and he could see little, not even the shoreline a quarter-mile away. Radar and sonar scans had been negative. It was odd that the only ships they'd seen had been the longboat museum pieces. And they'd had to destroy most of those.

"Surface!"

The dark bulk of the submarine rose silently out of the cold waters of the firth.

"Stand easy. Remain at quarters," said Hamilton over the ship's intercom. "Cargo detail, stand by to retrieve inflatable."

101

MILO SAT AT the back of the dinghy, with one hand on the outboard. The night was black, and he was following a course by reference to a handheld compass. Kitt and Avelyn were together on the thwart-seat.

Earlier, Avelyn had taken a long walk with the abbot but had said nothing of their conversation, not bothering to hide the tears on her cheeks.

Now, with the spray blowing off the bow, and the dinghy bouncing over the waves, her eyes were alight with excitement and curiosity. She rubbed her hand over the strange unnatural fabric of the dinghy.

"I think you should know, Kitt, the Sea finds this slimy thing repulsive," she said, teasingly.

"Avelyn, it's important to remember what I told you."

"Like what?"

"Like, I don't want you talking to anyone, even if they do speak Latin. If anyone says anything, just nod and turn away."

"That would be rude!"

"I don't care. And don't ask questions or remark on anything, until we're alone again. "

"But won't people on this time-boat be curious about me?"

"Of course they will. That's the problem."

"I'm happy to introduce myself."

Kitt grabbed her shoulders gently.

"Avelyn, the men on this ship don't know they've gone back in time! They don't even know such a thing is possible. No one does—except the three of us."

Avelyn's mouth dropped open. "You mean they don't know where they are? They don't know what's been happening?"

"Exactly! I don't know what would happen if they found out. And there's one more thing."

"What?"

"Everything you see is going to terrify you. So prepare yourself. Don't scream, no matter what."

Avelyn smiled. "I'll be good, Kitt."

A wall of blackness appeared unexpectedly, out of the night, and Avelyn stifled a scream. The dinghy slowed and bumped softly against the submarine. Milo jumped onto the deck, turned and helped Avelyn. Kitt followed. The dinghy was pulled from the water, deflated, and passed down one of the hatches. No salutes were exchanged as Milo was not in uniform. Kitt took Avelyn's arm and guided her to the sail.

Hamilton was there to meet them. Kitt appreciated the man's predicament, having to both ignore the female passenger, and suppress astonishment at her outfit. While there had been time to stitch up the torn bodice, her dress was a filthy rag.

"I'll escort you to your quarters, Admiral, and show you the, 'er, additional quarters as well."

"Thank you, Captain. And I'd be obliged if you'd take *Chrysalis* back to the holding position at the mouth of the firth—periscope depth."

"Aye aye, sir."

Hamilton reached for an intercom on the wall and relayed the orders. The dive horn sounded and Avelyn would have screamed again if Kitt had not covered her mouth. She had been prepared for a very unusual boat, but not for 21st-century technology. Kitt realized there was nothing in this passageway she would understand. There was no wood, no cloth, no rope—no material or fabric. And there could be no apparent purpose to any of the strange shapes surrounding her. It would be like touring an alien spacecraft.

They arrived at Kitt and Milo's cabin.

"And the other one?" asked Milo.

"Just across the passageway there, sir. Would you like me to show it to you?"

"We'll manage. I'll come to the control room shortly, with new orders."

"Aye aye, sir."

"Well, Avelyn, how do you like our little ship?" asked Milo, as soon as they'd closed the door.

She was trembling, and tears streamed down her face.

"It's OK, Milo," said Kitt, holding her. "She'll be OK. It's just a little overwhelming."

"Sure. Of course it is. Look, I'd like to stay and help out, but I've got to meet with Hamilton. I'm going to order *Chrysalis* back to the middle of the Atlantic."

He looked at Avelyn. "Think she'll be OK?"

"Sure. I'm going to take her to her own room now. She probably needs sleep more than anything."

"She needs *you* more than anything. Stay with her. And if it were me, I'd be hoping someone would hand me a stiff drink. We finished off the scotch, but the Chianti's in the bureau drawer, there. Help yourself."

Kitt nodded. He held Avelyn until her shaking came under control. She seemed content to just stay there, face pressed against his chest, shutting out the world. Kitt knew she wasn't asleep. Finally, he pulled away gently.

"Avelyn, let's get you across the hall, to your own room."

When they walked in, Kitt expected she'd want to lie down immediately but Avelyn remained standing, drying her eyes, and looking around curiously.

"This is mine?"

"Yes. It's your room. Nothing can harm you here."

"It's so—clean," she said.

"Oh, it's clean! There's probably no dirt on this whole ship."

"How do they *do* that?" she asked. "And how can there be light in here when it's dark outside? There are no fires, no candles. Do you control the sun?"

"Look, I'll explain later. Let's not ask questions now. You should try to get some rest."

"I do need to ask one question," she said. "Where does one, well, I mean, where—" Avelyn blushed.

"Oh!" said Kitt. "Well, it's a little complicated." He showed her the head, trying not to be self-conscious as he explained how a marine toilet worked. Then he excused himself and let Avelyn experiment with everything. Several minutes passed before she opened the door and stepped out.

"Interesting magic," she said, smiling. "By the way, what's the little closet behind the curtain?"

"That's a *shower*. Warm water comes out a hole near the top and you stand under it and get clean."

Kitt pulled back the curtain and demonstrated how to control the water, how a soap dispenser worked, and where the towels were.

"How wonderful! Could I try it now, please? It would be heaven to be clean again!"

Kitt sat on the bunk, listening to the water splashing, and wondered what it would be like to take one's first hot shower, ever. Then he remembered the Chianti and retrieved it, along with two glasses. He poured one for himself, deciding there was no reason to wait.

He was about to pour a refill when the door to the head opened. Avelyn was wrapped in a towel, her hair still wet. A puddle was beginning to form.

She stared at Kitt, who stood up, awkwardly. "Avelyn…"

She said nothing, but kept her eyes on his.

He reached out for her and she rushed into his arms, letting the towel fall to the very clean floor.

102

BRODY FLANNAGAIN AND the abbot toured the remains of their village. Half the dwellings were destroyed. Most had suffered damage.

It was not the destruction of Ballycastle that worried Flannagain, but the killing of the people. Ballycastle was a ghost town. And without a population, what could they accomplish?

They ended their tour back at the gates of the monastery, but the abbot was not ready to go inside. He led Flannagain to a nearby glade where a stream ran between rocks, and a small table with wooden benches had been built. They sat down to rest.

It took the abbot a few moments to find his voice, which—when he spoke—was laced with sadness.

"I built this retreat myself, Brody—many years ago when I first came to Ballycastle. The monastery was overwhelming and there were times I needed to escape its sanctity. I often found God here, and was always closer to Him in this place than in that dark stone building."

"Do you find Him here now, Your Grace?"

"No. I believe God has forsaken Ballycastle because it was consumed by evil. Not just the Norsemen, but the villagers as well. Baron O'Ruairc figured prominently in that evil. As did you, Brody. But none of us were without sin.

"Now all that is gone. The baron is dead. Nearly everyone has been murdered or abducted. I find it baffling that He chose to leave you alive, and can only believe there's a larger plan."

"Will God return?"

"If we show ourselves worthy of His mercy, I believe He will."

"And how is this to be done, Your Grace?"

"I have only an idea, a dream if you will. I envision a wholly different society, Brody. One founded on virtue and compassion. A society in which there is no baron who glowers from his castle and preys on young girls and raises the taxes of those working in the fields. A society in which the weak are protected from the strong by just laws and the might to enforce them."

"A noble dream, Your Grace."

"Perhaps it can be more than a dream."

"We cannot have a society of any kind, without people."

The abbot chuckled softly. "I never gave you a complete tour of the sanctuary, did I, Brody? There are rooms down there you haven't seen. The wounded who will not recover are already dead. The rest are mending."

"How many, Your Grace?"

"All told, maybe two hundred. Perhaps a fourth are women in their child-bearing years."

"The crops are doing well," said Flannagain, his administrative mind churning. "In a few months, we'll have a harvest far greater than what's needed to feed two hundred mouths. We'll be able to store large quantities of food for the winter and have surplus to barter for trade goods. With ample food, the population—small as it is—should flourish. Yet how do we make it to harvest time, Your Grace? There are no food stores in the castle. I can vouch for that at least."

"Yours was not the only storage, Brody. The monastery has underground vaults you never imagined. We have always hoarded grain there, and doled it out in times of famine."

"Indeed? That was most clever of you. We never suspected—"

"Flannagain, there's one thing we must resolve. If we are to rebuild, I will need your help. If we work together and combine our abilities we have a chance at success. At least, if it's God's will.

"But I must be convinced of your sincerity. I must know you have cast off evil and are willing to work for the good of the people. I realize 'good' isn't a concept you've had much acquaintance with, but it can be taught. My question is: are you willing to become a new kind of seneschal—one who is employed by, and serves, an entire village, not merely its noble house? The Franks have a word for it, 'maire' or 'mayor' I believe is the term. A mayor is someone who presides over a village not because he is a lord, but because he is the most capable man for the job; the ablest administrator. And he does so not for his own gratification, but for the good of those around him. I can handle the spiritual side of the community, and I can at least contribute my dream. But I cannot be a political leader—a mayor. Can I trust you, to be that person?"

Flannagain considered the question.

"Your Grace, I don't mean to excuse the deeds. But I am a man of clay. Mold me into a creature of evil and I will be a very competent one. But I can mold just as easily into something else. You ask, 'can you trust me?' Trust can only be built over time. But if you will have it, I give you my word that I will work for your dream and will seek to earn your trust."

He took from his pack a small leather bag, setting it on the table.

"This is filled with gold, Your Grace. It is all I was able to bring when I escaped the castle. Yet I can tell you where more is buried. Much more. I give it all to you, as a down payment on my trust. I hope it can help accomplish your dream."

Father Conardy took the bag and emptied it onto the table. Gold coins poured out, glistening in the sunlight. It was a fortune.

"Very kind of you, Brody. No doubt your gold will be useful. But I just realized I've been a fool. We cannot hope to survive for long here, with a mere two hundred villagers. Word of what's happened will spread to Doon, and Lord Fakis will send an army which we'll have no hope of opposing. Why did I imagine otherwise? It's a cruel God who allows a man to dream, and then shatters that dream with reality."

The seneschal smiled.

"Perhaps we now know why your God was merciful to me."

"Don't jest, Flannagain. I'm in no mood for it."

"I jest not, Your Grace. But as the vaults under your monastery are greater than I imagined, perhaps my talents are broader than you expected. I knew that Ballycastle would be vulnerable, and I discussed this privately with the sorcerer-lord Milo before he left."

"What are you saying, Brody?"

The seneschal reached into his pack.

"He gave me this, Your Grace. It's one of his weapons of magic. He taught me its power. But it must be used sparingly for the sorcerer-lord said that its magic will eventually be depleted. Yet I am quite certain that when Fakis sends his army against us, we can defeat that army at least one time—with this thing of magic. And when word of our sorcery spreads, no one will venture against us for many years."

"I am reluctant to see sorcery brought into our midst, Brody, but it does seem part of God's plan. Does the thing have a name?"

"Yes, Your Grace. It's called an M-16 automatic rifle. We were also given a great deal of something called ammunition, which provides its power. You hold the rifle like this." He demonstrated.

The abbot handled the strange metallic shape with curiosity.

"If this will keep the armies of Doon at bay then we

must use it, of course," he said. "But let us take steps to sanctify its sorcery in the eyes of God."

The old Christian reached into his pack and retrieved a small vial containing a clear liquid. He sprinkled the holy water liberally across the weapon, crossed himself, and mumbled some words in Latin. Then he put the stock of the rifle against his shoulder and sighted down the barrel.

"God works in mysterious ways, Brody," he said at last. "Let us pray."

103

“IT WON’T HAPPEN again,” explained Kitt. “The mutrino dispenser can now be activated only by a computer-controlled solenoid. The software won’t open without a password, and once opened, it will execute only a single time jump. The problem is that my new projections of time-travel speed are only theoretical. We never got a chance to take measurements last time.”

“So how do we avoid overshooting?”

“We’ll do it in stages, taking measurements as we go, and using the computer’s internal clock. I’ll aim us at, say, 1950. If we’re off a bit it won’t matter, and we’ll be able to receive radio broadcasts. Based on what we learn, I’ll calibrate more accurately. Then we’ll try to hit maybe 1995. By the time we finish half a dozen jumps, I’ll have enough data to land us within a couple of minutes of our targeted return time.”

“Which brings up another question,” said Milo. “When should we return?”

“Yeah, let’s talk about that. We can’t return to our

own time-line before our first time jump, because then we'd have two *Chrysalises* inhabiting that time-universe simultaneously. Something might give."

"What?"

"I'm not sure. Maybe the two *Chrysalises* would somehow merge. This whole ship, and everyone in it (except Avelyn, who's unique to this *Chrysalis),* would have a twin. Or maybe the two submarines couldn't exist simultaneously and one of them would instantly vaporize. Or maybe—"

"OK! OK! I see the problem. But here's another problem. In fact, two. If we return let's say a few hours after our original jump, and allowing for steaming time back to Norfolk, then *Chrysalis* will have "gone missing" from the Naval Base for about three days—as far as those onshore are concerned. That's problem #1.

"But as far as those on the sub are concerned, we'll have been at sea for roughly *eight* days. Hamilton, let alone the crew, let alone the ship's logs, won't be able to reconcile the difference, and that's problem #2. The last thing we want is a major Navy Board investigation. With Hamilton's testimony, they'd have our facial composites on every wire service in the country and we'd be thrown in jail forever.

"Do you have a solution?"

Maybe. Let's start with the first problem: *Chrysalis* going missing for three days. Absent orders to the contrary, a commanding officer can do most anything he wants with his ship, including taking it out of the harbor and running practice drills and so forth."

"Even for three days?"

"That's pushing it. But chances are *Chrysalis* was

scheduled to sit there at dockside for several weeks anyway. Hamilton had already met with his superior officer and given his report, which is a break for us.

"Other than crew leave and some minor refitting, there probably was nothing on the agenda anyway. If that's true, the captain could claim he'd held a surprise drill, taking the boat back out to sea for maneuvers. He could say the crew was a little too sure of their leave. We could doctor the logs to reflect all that, and the crew has no idea what's been going on anyway. I'll make sure Hamilton understands the importance of a cover story."

"What if orders to *Chrysalis* were sent during that period?"

"It's a risk. Ship's logs will show no messages were received, despite checking frequently. That suggests a technical problem which they'll eventually give up trying to solve. But it's probably 90-10 the surprise drill story will be all that's needed. In fact, it's probably 90-10 the surprise drill story won't even have to be used."

"OK," said Kitt, "How about problem #2, the non-reconcilable calendar dates?"

"Try this on. We know the equipment we brought on board screwed up all the instruments, and caused disorientation, right? At least that's what we told Hamilton."

"Yes."

"Maybe I tell him the disruption was even greater than that. The equipment we were testing also disrupts time perception and they've been gone only three days, not eight. All kinds of defense applications for that, obviously."

"He'll never buy it."

"Sure he will. You think he's going to suspect we took his submarine back to the eighth century for a week?"

"Good point."

"I'll impress upon him how secretive this whole thing is, and make him understand that if he, or any member of the crew, so much as remember anything that's happened on this cruise—which by the way never occurred—the Navy will not only court-martial him, they'll deny everything."

"What about the torpedoes we fired, the supplies we consumed?"

"Good points, but we're talking details. I'll invent some explanations, have the logs doctored, etc.

"Will he agree to all this tampering with the logs? Isn't that against the rules?"

"Sure it is unless an admiral orders you to do it. Then you have no choice. And I'll put those orders in writing. Hamilton won't object if he's covered by written orders signed by an admiral."

"OK, then that's our plan."

"One more thing, Kitt."

"What?"

"Lauren. Once we return home, she won't be there."

"It makes the divorce easier."

"It makes the divorce messy as hell. Your wife mysteriously disappears. And you show up with a cute young girlfriend?"

"Good point. What do we do?"

"Play ignorant. Phone your wife a few times. Leave messages, kind of snotty ones like you're pissed she's not returning your calls. At some point call the police. In other words, be proactive."

"Do you think the cops might trace her to Three Forks?"

"Maybe, but you can play ignorant, and say it's just the kind of thing she'd do. Say she suspected you had a girlfriend."

"But when they can't find Lauren anywhere…"

"They *won't* find her anywhere. No dead body. No sign of foul play. Nothing to implicate you other than motive."

"And Lauren's lifestyle wasn't that of a nun," added Kitt. "She's been doing the party thing. Jetting around. Nothing too flagrant, but maybe she met the wrong guy one night…"

"Yeah, that's how it'll look to the police. But what about your in-laws?"

"What about them?"

"With Lauren's disappearance, maybe they'll feel they have some claim against you. Neglect of spouse, leading to wrongful death or something. You know trial lawyers."

"I could have my attorney talk to them directly, no animosity, saying I feel as bad as they do, and certainly don't want there to be any financial issues between us. They'll take the bait. I heard they're having money problems these days."

"And, Kitt, on some level, it's kind of the least you can do."

Kitt nodded, chagrinned. "Any more loose ends we haven't thought of?"

"You'll need an identity for Avelyn."

"I think she's an undocumented refugee from Eastern

Europe. Belarus, maybe. Met her in a bar. The Kitterys are owed a zillion favors in Washington. We'll fast-track a green card."

"Then I think it's time to head home, Boss. I could use a 21st-century shower, a stiff drink, and at least a full day without having to lie my head off to a naval officer."

104

"KITT, ARE TRANSFORMERS real?"

Avelyn sat cross-legged on the floor in front of a wide-screen TV. Forty-eight hours earlier, they had returned successfully, and she had spent many of those hours staring at the television.

Kitt sat at the dining room table, chatting with Milo, but frequently glancing at Avelyn. He'd taken her into Richmond yesterday, introducing her to cars and skyscrapers and Big Macs. It had not been as overwhelming as he'd feared. After *Chrysalis,* she had lost all ability to be shocked.

Also, it was obvious this intelligent young woman had never belonged in the eighth century, anyway. At least, that was one of Kitt's rationalizations for having brought her back with them. Another was that with Lauren stuck in the Dark Ages, there might be some temporal balancing needed on a quantum level. He had lots of other rationalizations, equally weak.

Kitt had bought her a full make-over at an expensive salon, followed by a shopping spree at Neiman-Marcus. It was difficult to believe this was the same woman who had stepped out from behind a tree only days ago. It seemed like a thousand years.

Avelyn's hair was now cut in soft layers, with bangs. She wore a form-fitting slacks ensemble by Ralph Lauren, and small gold earrings were just visible as they caught the light from the television. On her left wrist was an elegant Fendi watch. And an expensive perfume wafted through the farmhouse. But all that had been Kitt's idea. The only things Avelyn had requested were a tiny gold cross, hung on a delicate chain around her neck and a Celtic bracelet replica, now adorning her right wrist.

"He was the only father I really knew," she explained. "He said that as long as I wore the sign of the cross, we'd be together."

"And the bracelet?"

"The writing is Irish."

"You mean Gaelic?"

"Yes, Gaelic. It praises the spirits of the Earth and the Sea."

"So it's a Druidic talisman?"

"Yes."

She was picking up English—modern English—rapidly. Her knowledge of the language's earliest foundations obviously helped.

But despite the overloading of her senses, Avelyn couldn't get enough television.

"Transformers aren't real," Kitt said gently. "They're imaginary."

"Oh, that's right," she said. "And the talking people behind the glass are imaginary too?"

"No, the people are real! But what you're seeing are just images. The people themselves aren't inside the television."

"Oh."

"Look, television's complicated. Can we save that for tomorrow?"

Avelyn blew him a kiss and turned back to the TV. She switched channels, finding an old rerun of *Nova*, in which a man in a funny orange coat was talking about billions and billions of galaxies.

&

"OK, Boss, now as I was saying—"

Kitt was still staring at Avelyn.

"Yoo-hoo! Remember me? I realize she's better looking!"

Kitt reluctantly turned around.

"Sorry, Milo. I guess I'm a little distracted."

"A little? You've not heard a damn thing I've said!"

"You said Avelyn was better looking than you."

Milo rolled his eyes. "The issue is the effect of our time travel."

"Look, why travel around in time anyway? Everything we need's right here."

"Yeah, but the whole point of what we did was to determine the effects of time travel on the present. Now, I've been doing some checking around and I've got something to report."

Kitt walked over to the refrigerator and returned with

two beers. He popped the top off his own and leaned back, legs on the table.

"Let's keep it short. It's getting late and I'm going to hit the sack pretty soon."

"It's seven-thirty, you sex-crazed ninny! Take a cold shower, but I need your attention."

Kitt grinned. "I'm all ears!"

"Would that you were. OK, as far as I can tell we didn't destroy the present. I mean, we're here, obviously. The farmhouse is as we left it. I can't see a thing that's changed. I called up a few old shipmates. They knew me, I knew them, and we had the same memories of the past.

"I even called my ex-employer and asked politely for my job back. He said 'Screw you, Milo! After that fiasco in Istanbul, you'll be lucky if you're hired as mess boy on a garbage scow!'"

"What happened in Istanbul?"

"I never told you about the dead chickens?"

"Dead *chickens*?"

"Point is, as far as my life's concerned, nothing's changed. You'd probably find the same."

"Yeah. I guess I haven't been focused on this much."

"It's OK. I've got some ideas."

"Shoot."

"I think the three of us should fly over to Ireland. We could poke around modern Ballycastle, you know, kind of check things out. Maybe we could find some trace of what we did. I'm almost convinced the whole thing never happened."

"That's a great idea! We'd have a blast. Let's find a travel agent."

Kitt pulled up a browser on his phone.

"We're in luck. Atlantic World Travel in Norfolk's open 24/7."

Milo crossed the room and over Avelyn's protest, muted the volume on the TV.

Kitt switched on the speaker and dialed the number.

"Atlantic World, may I help you," said the female voice.

"There's a party of three of us, heading to Northern Ireland," explained Kitt. "So I guess we need to fly into Belfast, the capital. That'll mean changing planes in London, right?"

There was a pause.

"I'm not sure what you mean by 'Northern Ireland,' sir. And I've never heard of Belfast. The capital of the Irish Commonwealth is Ballycastle."

Milo leaned over.

"Excuse me, ma'am. What did you just say? Irish Commonwealth?"

"Yes, you know, Ireland and the surrounding island groups, the Hebrides, Shetlands and so forth."

"That's all one big country, now?"

"It always has been, sir." The travel agent sounded a bit condescending, like she was dealing with morons.

"And the capital is a little village called Ballycastle?"

"I think Ballycastle's population is over two million."

Kitt and Milo exchanged glances.

"So how do we get there?" asked Kitt.

"From Dulles, there are three non-stops daily into *Conardy.*"

"Into *what*!" exclaimed Kitt.

"*Conardy Airport.* The formal name is *Father Conardy International Airfield,* but everyone just calls it *Conardy.*"

"I see," said Kitt. Milo had gone white as a ghost. "And could you book us into a hotel there?"

"Easily, sir. Could I make some suggestions?"

"Please do."

"Well, the city's organized around a large central park, which stretches down to the water. That's *Good Mayor Flanagan Park.* Just about everything over there seems to be named after Good Mayor Flanagan or Father Conardy. They're the two Irish heroes, you know. Anyway, you'll find a number of hotels along the north side of the park, near the water."

"Could you recommend one?"

"Well, I don't know your budget, but the most famous is the '*Avelyn,*' it's—"

"The *what!*" demanded Kitt, again.

"The *Avelyn Hotel.* It's named after the legendary Irish goddess who rose up out of the sea and drove off the Vikings. Oh, and there are some great two-day package tours I could arrange to Reykjavik."

"Why would we want to go to Iceland?" asked Kitt, puzzled.

"Well, as I'm sure you know, it's the world's fashion capital. It's where all the designers are headquartered. Maybe guys aren't into that stuff, but if you're going with your wife or girlfriend, the shopping's unreal! It's only a two-hour flight from Conardy, and they've got the largest indoor shopping mall on Earth, the *Lorendottir Center.*"

There was a long pause.

"I'm sorry. What did you say the name of that mall was?" asked Kitt, confused.

"*Lorendottir Center.*"

"Spelled like—like, Lauren, the girl's name?"

"It's L-O-R-E-N."

"But sounds the same, don't you think?"

"I suppose so."

In a daze, Kitt took her name, mumbled an apology, and said he'd call back later to finish the bookings.

Kitt and Milo stared at each other.

"Wow," said Kitt, shaken.

"So we did change the past," said Milo. "Ballycastle's the capital of Ireland now and Avelyn's revered as a goddess…"

"Fashion center?" said Kitt, disbelievingly. "Iceland is a *fashion* center? You don't suppose…"

"Sure," said Milo. "The last longboat, the one carrying Lauren, might have headed northwest after leaving Ballycastle. They probably had no desire to return home, after their defeat. Let me guess: your wife was into fashion, right?"

"She was obsessed with it, the top brands, all that stuff." He paused, realizing they were talking about her in the past tense. "Milo, I guess you're right. She must have become an important person, wife of the ruler maybe, and kind of left her mark. Is that possible?"

"The Vikings were the first settlers of Iceland. Whatever

culture finally evolved, it might have been started by the people in that one longboat. Assuming Lauren held a position of importance—which is likely—the seeds could easily have been sown for a society that placed a high value on adornment, physical appearance, colorful clothing, that kind of thing. What we'd now call fashion."

"Any idea what that 'dottir' suffix means?"

"It's an old Norse word meaning 'daughter.' Obviously, it got blended into English somewhere. The Scandinavians usually named children after their parents. Like 'Ericson' means 'son of Eric.' 'Petersen' means 'son of Peter.' So Lorendottir would mean—"

Kitt grinned. "I think it means Lauren had a child. I'll be damned. After we got married, she said she wasn't really into kids, and hoped I wasn't either."

"Family planning wasn't practiced a whole lot among Vikings, Kitt. I doubt she had much say in the matter. Anyway, given the name of the mall, maybe it was the daughter who became the big cheese—some kind of queen or first lady or something. Who knows? Maybe the father was the captain of the longboat and claimed Lauren as his wife. Actually, of course he would have. A nice mix of genes. Gorgeous 21st-century woman as mom. Fearless Viking sea captain as dad. No wonder their kid has a mall named after her. We'll have to Google that and learn more about Icelandic history—the new version. Wow, this is amazing."

"So I take it everything is satisfactory in Ireland, here in your time," said Avelyn, coming over and smiling.

"Satisfactory!" exclaimed Kitt, taking her hands. "It's vastly improved."

"The country never recovered from those Viking invasions," added Milo. "That's the common wisdom among historians. But hell, I guess we fixed that. *Father Conardy Airport? Good Mayor Flannagain Park?* My God, they pulled it off! I guess the 10,000 rounds of ammo I left were enough."

"We can still go over there," said Kitt, smiling. "But it may be redundant. I think it's pretty obvious what happened."

"Of course we want to go!" said Milo. "I want to see what caliber of hotel has been named in honor of our fair goddess here. If it's not five stars, I'll complain to the management!" He took another swallow of beer and slammed it on the table with a laugh.

"Hell!" joined in Kitt. "If it's not five stars, we'll buy it and make it five stars!"

"OK, this looks good," said Milo, thinking deeply. "We didn't destroy the known universe like we thought we might. But we did change history. For the better—obviously."

"Well, not necessarily," cautioned Kitt.

"Don't you think we made things better?"

"Perhaps. But you said we didn't destroy the known universe. I think maybe we did."

"Huh?"

"It might be semantics. But we've returned to a universe in which Reykjavik's the fashion capital of the world. You gotta admit—that's not the same universe we left.

This one's different. Not greatly different, but different, nonetheless."

"So I don't understand. How can it be a different universe, yet almost everything's the same? This farm's here. My pickup truck's right where I parked it, with the same amount of gas. Before we left we forgot to take out the garbage, and it stunk to high heaven, just like you'd expect. How can it be a different universe?"

"Damned if I know! We've been back two days and I can't believe this is the first time I've really focused on the results of the experiment. Where was my head?"

"Right where it should have been. Love's eternal, Kitt. That's what you really proved. The greatest scientist in the world completes the greatest experiment ever, and it all counts for nothing compared to the power of *l'amour.* The philosophers and poets could have a heyday with this one."

Kitt grinned. "So, we arrived at an historically-critical juncture in time. We took actions that made a strategic difference. And a lot of things happened differently as a result."

"First thing tomorrow, I'm going to start re-checking everything I thought I knew about history—globally. We need to find out how much we changed."

"Good idea. But most everything around here, at least, stayed the same. And apparently the farther we get from the 'scene of the crime,' the less ultimate influence we had. The fact that your pickup is still parked in the same place is proof of how durable the fabric of time must be. It's not like a pool table at all. We made a rift, an alteration, and yet time cauterized itself. That one change wasn't allowed to spread out in too wide a circle. Of course around Ballycastle, around Ireland, there must be a near infinity of changes. Around Iceland too. But the farther away one gets, either geographically or perhaps through causal connections of some kind, the less influence our tampering had. And your pickup truck had nothing to do with Ballycastle or Reykjavik, so it's not affected at all."

"Maybe it's like an ocean, Kitt. You drop a large rock in the water and it's going to make a big splash right there, but it won't affect a damn thing 1,000 miles away. The ocean will absorb that rock."

"That's gotta be it, Milo. And there's almost nothing you could do that will affect the entire ocean. The fabric of time can absorb quite a bit, and still retain its basic shape and structure. The effects dissipate, just like the kinetic energy of waves dissipates."

Kitt took another beer and drank deeply.

"But I still don't understand how it works, exactly. Did we replace one universe with another that's slightly different? Did we bring into existence a new "branch" of time, like the branch of a tree, the moment we interfered in Ireland? That gets into multiverse theory, which is really bizarre. That's the idea that every combination of time and space already exists, in infinite parallel universes. But in science, we'd call that an 'inelegant theory.' Actually, none of these options make any sense."

"Maybe," said Milo, "they don't make any sense to us, because we just don't have the vocabulary, the concepts, to explain it. It's too far outside our field of reference."

"Yeah, that's likely," agreed Kitt. "I once heard a

science philosopher give a speech on limits of understanding. He used a mouse as an example. The mouse can navigate through a maze, perform tricks that deliver cheese, and so forth. But the mouse will never be able to understand algebra."

"I get it, Boss. We need to grasp the concept of how time works, but we're not smart enough. Geez. Where's Timothy Leary when you need him? If ever there was a time to drop acid and get beyond our normal plane of reference, this is it. But what the heck. Let's see what another beer will do."

Milo popped open a can, and the spray hit Kitt in the face.

"It's going to take more than drugs to really understand this thing. I think we just have to keep playing around with it until the light bulb goes off. We've got to do more experiments. Test some theories. Gain experience."

"Now you're talking!" said Milo. "OK, let's get back to reality for a moment. We go check out Ballycastle, take a stroll in *Good Mayor Flannagain Park*, and fly to Reykjavik for some shopping at the Mall. But where do we go next? If we've proven time-travel works, and can be used constructively, let's go somewhere else that could make a difference. There's no shortage of places in history that could stand some improvement. Let's choose one and make it our next project. We'll have to get Hamilton and his submarine back. Christ, he'll die if he sees us walk up the gangplank again."

"He would, Milo, there's no doubt." Both men laughed at the visualization.

"What we really need is our own submarine," suggested Milo.

"Is that possible?" asked Kitt

"Yeah, it doesn't have to be the latest military wonder. Just something with a reactor in it, right?"

"Well, a crew would be nice."

"You can hire a crew. Believe me, you can hire a crew."

"And where do we get a previously-owned nuclear submarine?"

"It wouldn't be that hard. Obsolete subs are sold for scrap. The first one, Nautilus, they turned into a museum in Connecticut. But the others, they just sell for the value of the metal. We could buy one, but then not scrap it. You're probably talking less than five hundred grand. Have to put some serious bucks into it, to get it running again. But it's do-able. The reactor's the problem. They dismantle those completely when the boats are scrapped. That's why I didn't suggest it in the first place."

"Actually, the reactor's no problem," Kitt explained. "Power companies build reactors. The parts are available. You can buy most everything you need on the open market, and I know enough about nuclear engineering to install one from scratch—at least if I had access to a good machine shop and a couple of machinists. Of course, getting hold of the fissionable material—the enriched uranium—is the problem. Maybe I could smuggle some out of Brookhaven, but we'll cross that bridge when we get to it. You could really get the sub itself running?"

"Sure, as long as you're willing to pay the hired help something more than minimum wage. And then we wouldn't have to keep making up stories about Viking longboat replicas and CIA agents. On that last trip, I damned near wore myself out lying."

They laughed, and each took another swallow of beer.

"OK, this sounds good," said Kitt, getting excited. "We buy an old nuclear submarine for scrap. We restore it, no expense spared. We hire the best crew we can find and tell 'em the pay's good but you can't ask questions. We hook up the mutrino dispenser and away we go!"

"I'm ready, Boss. I think we've got a good thing going here. Screw the patents and the royalties and the Nobel Prize. Let's keep this one to ourselves!"

"But where *should* we go next?"

"How 'bout to Russia just before the revolution. We say that thanks to what they're about to do, their grand-children will have to stand in line to buy toilet paper! Or how 'bout to Pompeii, in 79 AD? We'll go around with sandwich boards saying 'the sky is falling, the sky is falling.'"

"That's sick, Milo."

"Oh, here's one. Talk about something that will make a difference. Let's visit the Ford Motor Company executive offices in 1956. We'll talk 'em out of designing the Edsel!"

"Milo, why go backward? We know what happened in the past. Aren't you curious about the future? You know that mutrino dispenser works just as well in forward gear. That's how we got home."

"OK, let's see. We could go forward fifty years, and see if the Cubs ever win another World Series." Milo paused, reflectively. "Better make that a hundred years. We're talking the Cubs."

"Fifty? A hundred? I was thinking a thousand. That's how far back we went, after all. Wouldn't you like to see what this place looks like in a thousand years?"

"No way! What with air pollution and over-population, I don't think it'll be anywhere I want to visit. No, what we should do is head to Tahiti back around 1600. The Europeans hadn't discovered it yet, and the women were still into free love. In fact, once we get there, we could just kiss the time machine good-bye! We wouldn't need it anymore!"

"Oh, wait. Here's another idea—"

EPILOGUE

NEITHER OF THEM noticed when Avelyn slipped quietly out the side door. She walked barefoot down to the river and observed, with a seafarer's instinct, that the estuary was at high tide. A light fog covered the landscape and the night air was cool.

Avelyn stepped into the river and walked slowly away from the bank until the water was above her knees. The current pressed the light cotton dress against her legs, but her toes gripped the mud, and she stood firm. Moonlight danced and sparkled on the waves. In the distance, she heard the cawing of a crow.

She knelt slightly and dipped her hands into the water. She held them still, enjoying the flow of the river.

"So you're still here," she said aloud, a smile touching her lips. And so is your power. As I expected, a thousand years is nothing to you."

She withdrew her hands, but waited, enjoying the moment, reaching out with her senses, touching all of it.

"I wanted to say thank you," she said at last. "For everything."

Avelyn turned to shore and emerged out of the water. She walked quietly back to the house where the sound of Kitt and Milo's laughter was becoming more pronounced. It was a dark night and the young Druidess was a shadow as she walked alone through the mist, an ancient wool cloak keeping her warm.

ACKNOWLEDGEMENTS

Family

My parents, Koert and Connie Voorhees – Koert says he's *Chrysalis'* #1 fan, and certainly spent way too many selfless hours editing it, not to mention helping me think through some of the important time-travel concepts. He pointed out non-helpful scenes that should be cut, and important ones that needed expansion. He's my spiritual "editor-in-chief." Whatever improvement in writing skill I gained from Chrysalis, much can be blamed on his endless—and excellent—wordsmithing suggestions.

My sisters Beth Walter and Casi Biebl – Beth was the first person to read even the first chapter, which she did in my presence. The fact that she begin laughing only a few minutes into it, I found vastly encouraging. Both Beth and Casi helped me think through some important plot elements, and both had a problem with the romance angle in early drafts, which wasn't working for them. This brings us to:

My daughter Kristen Voorhees – When she told me how much she loved the humor in Chrysalis, I couldn't recall there was any—until she showed it to me. Kristen also helped me with some of the physics (she minored in the subject and served as an undergraduate physics teaching assistant at Middlebury College). Perhaps more importantly, Kristen straightened out the romance angle so it was more believable, and explained why in earlier drafts it wasn't ringing true. "Dad, Avelyn has just had her entire village destroyed, her closest friend murdered, and is being chased by Vikings. Trust me, she's not looking for a *date* right now!" Finally, Kristen suggested the ending would be more powerful if Avelyn actually walked into the river to reach out to the Druidic spirits. Good call.

My older son Erik Voorhees, and his wife Michelle – Erik refused to read *Chrysalis* until I got it published, thus providing a needed kick in the butt. Michelle, a professional graphic artist, helped oversee that important detail of obtaining the best possible "Author's Photograph." (Obviously a high priority.) The two of them took the cover art very seriously, and insisted on some important changes so *Chrysalis* would not be seen as a Romance or Fantasy genre.

My younger son Alex Voorhees – Alex took on the job of getting Chrysalis published from a business standpoint, including all the professional details of interacting with publisher Rex Imperator, finding the best cover artist, organizing e-versions, creating social media and website pages, and other details. As a video game dilettante, Alex took the battle scenes in *Chrysalis* very seriously, and pointed out important technical flaws in some of them. For example, when the last member of the Viking garrison is set afire with the flame thrower, I'd had that figure in such close proximity to Milo that both would have been incinerated. Thank you, Alex—and Milo thanks you as well.

Bruce Hallock, second cousin – Bruce is a professional writer, who gave me both early encouragement and technical suggestions. A first draft had Avelyn serving tea, but Bruce noted tea was not known in Dark Ages, Ireland. I thereafter took all such details far more seriously.

My wife Derry – Among many other reasons, I love her for putting up with me all those nights when I pounded on the keyboard until after midnight. But her first time through *Chrysalis* she pronounced it "A damn fine read!" and I felt both forgiven, and that I'd received the highest praise. Derry also provided help with women's clothing, how it should look and fit, the materials, and the vocabulary to use when describing such things. It was a standing joke between us that as a guy, I needed little assistance with the ship battles, assault rifle scenes, flame-throwers, and such. But with women's wear, I was adrift. Derry came to the rescue.

Technical

Michael Lauterbach – My debate team partner in high school, Mike earned a Ph.D. in particle physics from Yale, worked as a researcher at Brookhaven National Laboratory, and first explained to me about the mathematics of anti-matter particles becoming simpler if you thought of them as moving backwards in time. When I heard that I thought: "Well, maybe they really *are* moving backwards in time." This tells you both where the genesis for *Chrysalis* came from, and also who inspired the character of Michael Kittery. I hasten to add that Mike's wife Margaret is delightful, and nothing like the evil Lauren. Mike was also my primary consultant in making sure I had the physics correct in the novel. He was a stickler for anything even slightly wrong, scientifically. At the final draft he grudgingly admitted: "Well, it's still science fiction, but now it's at least plausible." High praise, from Mike!

Stephen W. Wakefield – He served as Lieutenant and Engineering Officer/Reactor Control Officer, on the nuclear missile submarine *Stonewall Jackson*, SSBN 634. Many of the design ideas in *Chrysalis*, for the engineering of the tokamak, and how to modify the submarine's reactor to accommodate it, came from Steve. His wife, Linda, is already pushing me for a *Chrysalis* sequel.

Robert R. Thompson – Robert is a nuclear physicist, connected with Westinghouse Electric Corp (Bettis Atomic Power Laboratory), and involved with technical aspects of nuclear power plants on U.S. Navy submarines and surface ships. Between Steve Wakefield and Bob Thompson, I had real hands-on, nuclear-reactor expertise at my disposal, for which I'm extremely grateful.

Writing/Editing/Publishing

S. Lynn Diamond – Lynn at the time was Editor-in-Chief of National Jeweler magazine. After reading the manuscript she told me I should quit my day job and become a full time novelist. Thank you, Lynn, for both the encouragement, and the constant pushing of me to get this thing published. And perhaps most importantly for introducing me to the eventual publisher, Joseph Dobrian of Rex Imperator.

Joseph Dobrian, Publisher, Rex Imperator – He took a stab at a quick edit of the first three chapters, and it was done so skillfully I used it as a guide to edit the rest of the manuscript from 163,000 words down to 123,000. Professionalism makes a difference.

McClain Warren, Editor – She reminded me that people have to *do* things in scenes, not just have dialogue; and also that I have a real problem with commas. Thanks, McClain, for these and other constructive criticisms and tweaks. You always said you were determined to make *Chrysalis* all it can be, and you did.

Ellen Moore – A University of Denver creative writing instructor, Ellen convinced me to use language more carefully, avoid 21st century phraseology as much as possible, and inject era-appropriate words and concepts liberally.

To illustrate, she loaned me Jane Smiley's novel *The Greenlanders,* about a Norse settlement. Someday I must return it to her.

Helen Hart – A former employee, Helen both introduced me to Ellen Moore, and also convinced me to become (I first learned the term from her) a "blogger." She said it would be a good outlet for all my writing, and help hone my craft. It's also made me something of a terror with political diatribes on Facebook, but that's another story.

Julieanne Gilchrist and Britt Nemeth – These photographers each (separately) braved winter conditions at the top of Keystone Mountain in search of the perfect author's photo. Note to file: next time, let's do this in July!

OTHER ACKNOWLEDGEMENTS

John Blair Wood – As a next door neighbor growing up—John and his brothers built a miniature version of Camelot and the Joyous Guard Castle in their yard, and we passed many hours play-acting as Knights of the Round Table, with helmets and wooden swords. The seeds of my interest in the British Isles, as they existed during the Dark Ages period from which the Camelot legends sprang, were sown back then, as a very young child. I hope the Wood brothers will enjoy *Chrysalis* even more, knowing those memories were resurrected as I wrote it.

Morgan Llywelyn – I've never met this author, but I'd want her to know that her novel *Lion of Ireland* inspired my interest in the Viking era. Reading her recreation of history made me despise the Norsemen, and what they did in their raids. I'd find myself fantasizing about how to crush them, and that's where the idea of doing so with a nuclear submarine arose. *Chrysalis* allowed me to act out this fantasy.

David Salkin – As a former retail jeweler, customer of my company Polygon, and now a published author working on his fifteenth book, I thank Dave not only for his encouragement, but also for proving you really *can* evolve from a career in the diamond industry, to being a novelist. Who knew?

Sherril Soliman – A friend and business acquaintance from Belfast, who—after reading an early draft of the manuscript—actually took a day off and drove me to Ballycastle, for my first visit, in her BMW Z3 convertible. It was my first tour of Northern Ireland and I remember the two of us in her roadster with the top down, on a hill overlooking modern-day Ballycastle. "OK, so I'm not exactly seeing a firth," she said. "Climate change," I replied. Which brings me to the most important group:

Readers – I hope you'll forgive the artistic license I took with the topography of Ballycastle and Rathlin. I confess to terraforming both the firth (there isn't one, the town sits facing a broad bay) and also Rathlin Island, which is actually not hilly—but which is as large as portrayed.

Some readers have asked if Avelyn did have special Druidic powers. We don't know—nor did she, for certain. But Avelyn was closely attuned to the Earth and the Sea, and any spiritual forces that might emanate from them would have found a ready pathway through the young Druidess. It was a long time ago, and the full measure of the Druids' interaction with the spiritual realm will never be known. Avelyn either did have special Druidic powers, or merely thought she did. Readers are invited to decide for themselves.

Finally, thank you for enjoying *Chrysalis.* I wrote it to be an entertaining story and hope I succeeded.

If you'd like further entertainment, please consider the trilogy *Angel of Death.* Its protagonist, modern-day Sophie Martine, shares much in common with young Avelyn—not least an indomitable spirit and a similar age. You can meet Sophie in the first book of the *Angel of Death* trilogy, *The Forest Creature*, available at www.jacquesvoorhees.com.

ABOUT THE AUTHOR

Jacques Voorhees spent his career disrupting the diamond market through the introduction of online comparison shopping—an innovation for which JCK Magazine ranked him one of the jewelry industry's most influential people.

As part of this work, he's visited eighty-two countries, and written travel books about many of them. Perhaps his most consequential adventure was touring Brookhaven National Laboratories in New York, and learning that the mathematics of anti-matter suggest it moves backward in time. From that revelation came the idea for the time-travel novel *Chrysalis*.

Jacques has lived with his wife Derry in Keystone, Colorado for over thirty-five years, and is now an avid blogger, travel writer, and novelist. In addition to Chrysalis, he has published an action/adventure trilogy *Angel of Death*. www.jacquesvoorhees.com